Twelve Degrees North

A Novel

By

Catherine Lovely

Order this book online at www.trafford.com
or email orders@trafford.com

Most Trafford titles are also available at major online book retailers.

Printed in Victoria, BC, Canada.

ISBN: 978-1-4269-1495-9 (sc)
ISBN: 978-1-4269-1496-6 (dj)

Library of Congress Control Number: 2009934772

*Our mission is to efficiently provide the world's finest, most comprehensive book publishing
service, enabling every author to experience success. To find out how to publish your book,
your way, and have it available worldwide, visit us online at www.trafford.com*

Trafford rev. 10/26/2009

 www.trafford.com

North America & international
toll-free: 1 888 232 4444 (USA & Canada)
phone: 250 383 6864 ♦ fax: 812 355 4082

Author's Note

There is no Victoria Island in the Caribbean Sea. This is a tale of imaginary people in imaginary circumstances. Fictional freedoms are taken with calendar dates, political events, the islands in general and the Intervention in particular.

The book contains no intended portraits of or references to actual individuals living or dead. Any such resemblance that may be discerned is a coincidence and without intent on the author's part. Where public personages are mentioned, no historic accuracy concerning them is intended

Dedication

To my husband, Jerry, with all my
love and appreciation for everything.

Cast of Characters

Pete McKenzie—Tourist on his honeymoon
Janet McKenzie—Tourist on her honeymoon
Sir Jonathan Ward—Prime Minister, Cecil Ward's son
Hamilton Ward—Jonathan Ward's son, Cecil Ward's grandson
Hillary Warren—Jonathan Ward's fiancé
Todd Murdock—Charter Service Manager
Lester Griffon—Congenial proprietor of Red Crab Restaurant
Sir Cecil Ward—Former Prime Minister, Jonathan Ward's Father
Adam—Hillary Warren's former fiancé
Clarence Charles—Jonathan's boyhood friend, treacherous adult foe
Osgood Redfern— Hillary's stepfather, Owner of Redfern Estate, A Tobacco Merchant
Esmee Ward— Hamilton's mother, Jonathan's estranged wife
Dr. Rutherford—Head of the Medical School
Tiff—Gardener/Houseman at Seaside Manor

Carrie—Housekeeper at Seaside Manor
Bobbie Fisher—Student
Rick Benson—Student
Jean Trumbull—Real Estate Broker
Willard—Island taxi driver
Francis Tanner—delivery man
Beatrice Murdock—Todd's wife

Prologue

VICTORIA ISLAND WAS named for the Queen of England. Its capital, Georgetown, was named for the King.

Sighted by Christopher Columbus in 1498, the island's original inhabitants were Amerindians, Arowaks and Carib Indians. Originally colonized in 1650 by the French, the island was subsequently taken under British control in 1771 and so it remained until it proclaimed its independence in 1983.

Less than 100 square miles in size, the island is volcanic in origin. Evolving over hundreds of years, the island has become a fertile oasis with many varieties of trees and plant life with an ever-increasing bird and wildlife population. Verdant and lush with forested mountains, flowing rivers and green valleys, Victoria symbolizes all that is good. It is a palm-treed sanctuary floating in a turquoise sea beckoning to weary travelers. And with hopes of peace and rejuvenating their tired spirits tourists come. They come by air and they come by sea.

These visitors to Victoria are mostly like you and I. They come seeking respite from the winter cold, the pressures of work, and just to have a good time. They like music and they like to dance. They will on occasion even try to limbo. Some will go boating to test their fishing ability in hopes of catching a sport fish. Many snorkel and Scuba dive. Mostly, they take a swim and are content to just read on the beach with a cool drink at hand. For entertainment they frequent local restaurants and pubs and strike up conversations with total strangers.

Sometimes these holiday seekers might drink a little too much and even get a bit rowdy, but it's all in good fun. Mostly they are peaceable, just enjoying their vacations. The island people understand that the visitor's fun time is short and that they want to experience everything they read about and see on television that the fancy advertisements say they should. With calypso music spurring them on, they dance, laugh and enjoy.

Local islanders, having seen it all before, have a gentle and tolerant attitude. They watch, wait, smile, and say…. "Doan pay 'em no mind, jus take der money wile dey here, dey be gone soon. Jus' let 'em enjoy der Calypso Holiday."

Chapter 1
January 1983

T HE CARIBBEAN WATERS glistened under the moonlit sky as the lone cargo ship silently made its way through the familiar waters towards Georgetown Harbor. Francis Tanner sat waiting on the pier in his old, dilapidated truck to receive the scheduled shipment. He scanned the sea expectantly before looking at the clock over the Geest Steamship Company's loading platform. It was a little after three in the morning and the waterfront was deserted.

"Here she comes, right on time," Tanner called out to Cuthbert and Thaddeus, two local black youths he hired on as helpers. Tanner climbed out of the driver's seat leaving the door hanging open behind him. He walked to the back of the truck. Finding the pair asleep he decided not to awaken them until they were actually needed. Besides, he didn't want the bother of listening to them jawing and disturbing the quiet of the early morning; he was enjoying the solitude. Tanner walked to the edge of the deep-water Careenage and leaned against the fender of the truck to wait.

At first he could barely discern the twinkling lights sliding towards him across the pale silver water, but smoothly, steadily, the lights grew brighter until a recognizable form took shape accompanied by a faint hum in the distance.

With the whine of its motors preceding it, the old vessel churned up the water as it reversed its engines and pulled up along side of the pier. Instinctively glancing at the clock, Tanner noted it was exactly three twenty-seven. Lapsing into island patois, the speech common amongst locals, Tanner verbally prodded his workers into action.

While the Captain of the South American ship and Tanner exchanged papers, Cuthbert and Thaddeus offloaded their cargo.

The road leading to the Georgetown School of Medicine was treacherously narrow and winding but empty of pedestrians and traffic and they made good time. Thaddeus rode in front with Tanner while Cuthbert continued to doze in the back propped up against a canvas sack. The hospital-like odor emanating from the contents was overbearing and if it hadn't been for the openness of the truck and the fresh air that flowed around them, the smell of formaldehyde would have sickened them.

For Cuthbert, though, the odor had become so intense that he signaled wildly for Tanner to let him out of the truck. Looking back, Tanner was about to stop so that Cuthbert could climb in front when he realized that he had already arrived on medical school property. Francis gestured toward the entrance sign and Cuthbert understood as he glumly bided his time until the moment of his escape into fresh air. As the truck backed up to the receiving entrance Cuthbert was out of it before Tanner had switched off the engine key.

"Mon, dat smells BAD back der, Woo EEEEeee!" Cuthbert complained vehemently.

"Dat'll teach ya not ta sleep on de job," Tanner admonished good-naturedly.

"What's causin' dat smell anyway?" scowled Thaddeus pacing nervously.

"Chemicals an' supplies fo' de school," responded Tanner. Quickly changing the subject he turned towards Cuthbert and recoiled in mock terror. "Cuthbert, yer color's gone off. Mon, you are absolutely greeeeeen! Walk 'roun in de air fo' a while, regain yourself. Doan wanna lose you befo we finish de job." Tanner momentarily disappeared, chuckling to himself.

Francis Tanner made a point of never talking shop with his men. As far as he was concerned, the less speculation about work that there was, the better it was. Consequently, his men knew very little about the nature of their work other than the fact that they made deliveries in the middle of the night. And, Francis Tanner preferred it exactly that way. It simplified his job a lot. A superstitious, gossipy work force made for unrest and unreliability. And, ever the business man, he knew all too well that dependable help was not only hard to find but hard to keep.

While the men unloaded the truck Tanner gained entrance to the building and opened the receiving door from within.

"All right now, take 'em downstairs an' stack 'em by the wall."

"Like las time, Mista Tanner?" asked Cuthbert.

"Yea, jus like de las time, Cuthbert."

The men carried their cargo down a flight of stone steps to the cellar where it was cool and damp. Looking around the dimly lit storage room they saw it was empty except for a long, bare, glass-front supply cabinet which stood against one wall.

A pile of sealed cartons were stacked on the floor in another corner with three long work tables on wheels which were apparently used to transport incoming supplies to other parts of the building. As usual, the place was deserted. The youths began stacking their cargo against the wall as instructed.

Each wooden crate contained canvas-wrapped goods, sealed and identified with accompanying paperwork taped to it. The crates were heavy and awkward to maneuver down the slippery stone steps but the men completed the task. Finally, after setting the last box down, Thaddeus curiously fingered a tag while observing a Government seal printed in a foreign language. When Thaddeus indicated his discovery to Cuthbert, his companion, still green with nausea, shrugged indifferently. Poor Cuthbert, barely able to keep from heaving, only wanted to go home.

"Come along, come along," Tanner urged impatiently as he herded his men towards the door. The youths retreated up the stairs. Tanner then moved one of the rolling tables over to the shipment they had just brought downstairs and put the documents in his possession conspicuously on the table top.

On the line marked with an "X", Tanner had signed his name. Conscientiously he reaffirmed what was charged to his care by adding a numerical six next to his name. Had he been able to read the Bill of Lading that was in Spanish, old Francis would have known that this had not been necessary as the information was already listed. Nevertheless, Francis Tanner needed to satisfy himself that he had fulfilled his job efficiently. Then and only then did he leave the building, carefully locking the door behind him.

Later that morning at nine o'clock a lab worker verified the shipment's accuracy and entered the information in the record book, Six cadavers, South American origin.

Chapter 2

PETE AND JANET McKenzie put on their Scuba gear and tumbled from their boat into the pleasantly cool turquoise water. Bobbing to the surface surrounded by air bubbles from their entry they instinctively looked around as they made adjustments to their equipment and prepared to make their descent. The reef was directly below them and clearly visible in the early morning sunshine. Swimming to the bow of the boat they followed the anchor line to the sandy bottom gradually equalizing the pressure in their ears as they descended. Looking up Janet could see the hull of the boat floating on the water's surface twenty feet above her.

The reef was alive with vitality— a kaleidoscope of moving patterns and color variations. Parrotfish, angelfish, rock beauties, and squirrelfish flashed purple, red, green and orange amid a stand of giant lavender sea fans swaying gently in the current. Hovering near the surface a school of striped wrasse were floating beautifully suspended like clouds in the sky. A set of four-eye butterfly fish with their false eyes watched them with curiosity.

An avenue of sand led them deeper as the reef rose up around them resembling a city of skyscrapers peopled with exotic tenants costumed in wonderfully fanciful finery.

At thirty feet, as the McKenzies swam effortlessly weightless, a jet-propelled creature glided near them—an octopus. It surged forward in a rapid succession of spurts as it hurriedly disappeared down its hole after discharging an inky black poof.

As Pete and Janet happily examined their undersea environment the current steadily drew them down along the reef. From where they were at the edge of a coral shelf at about sixty feet, the ocean floor dropped away to a black void. Taking one last look before moving on, Pete sighted something move out of the corner of his eye. Turning his head to more clearly identify what it was, he glimpsed a big fish observing him. Grey-black, long and sleek, the animal watched him from a respectful distance away. They eyed one another with curiosity. As the large, dark mass glided by it looked Pete in the face with interest and moved away from the reef disappearing into the indigo depths below.

From the fixed, penetrating stare of Janet's eyes Pete knew she had seen the fish too. Ignoring his hand signal to stay below, Janet started to bolt to the surface. Pete held her back. Slowly they ascended together. Getting to the boat she clung to the ladder and flipped off her mask.

"That was a shark, wasn't it?" she gasped, breathless. Dropping his weight belt into the boat and wriggling free of his tank, Pete gave a kick and heaved himself into the boat.

"It was a barracuda."

"My god, I didn't know they could get that big."

"It really wasn't as large as it seemed," Pete said, shaking his head patiently. "Remember, everything refracted in the water seems about twenty-five percent larger than it really is."

Janet shrugged off her harness, tank and weight belt and handed them up to Pete who was already in the boat. Experiencing a complete loss of confidence she clamored up the ladder to the safety of the boat. "Whatever it was, that fish was huge."

"It was pretty big." Pete grinned.

"It was a shark then, wasn't it?"

"I've already told you, it was a barracuda."

She scowled! "A barracuda. Well they're dangerous, aren't they? Do they ever attack?"

"Normally it wouldn't."

"Not normally," she repeated in a monotone voice as though talking to herself and considering Pete's intent. "And what exactly do you mean by that?"

"Well, if the fish thought you were another fish, because you were wearing shiny jewelry or were wearing something shiny like a belt buckle and the fish mistook the glitter for fish scales, or if you went after it with a spear gun, that would be cause for concern. It might go for you then." Pete smiled indulgently. He dug a towel out of a duffle bag and handed it to Janet. "Look, if you're going to dive and feel comfortable about doing it, you've got to learn to relax and take things you see in stride. The fun of diving is seeing a lot of different fish and sea creatures. That's the reason people dive. The worst thing you can do is to panic every time you see a big fish." He paused to allow his words to sink in. "Hysterical behavior like screaming, splashing, or breaking for the boat attracts just what you are trying to avoid, the bigger fish like shark and barracuda."

"Shark and barracuda," Janet repeated dully.

"Jan, chances are you'll never even see a shark," Pete said reassuringly. "Not in these waters anyway. Sharks generally go where there are opportunities to feed. That's not here. There's nothing here. I wish you'd put your fears into perspective."

"I wish I could," said Janet twisting her hair nervously. "But, they do seem less scary when you explain about them.

"Sharks are like most other fish only larger. They're scavengers. But, because they're scavengers they will attack anything behaving weak or erratic. That's their function. They're built to detect vibration, odor, blood and sound at great distances with a sort of built-in sonar. As a diver, to avoid giving the wrong signal, the trick is to remain calm, to act and not react. Most fish, even barracuda, regardless of their size, are merely curious, not aggressive."

"What should I do if I see a big fish and he knows I am afraid?"

"On deeper dives and in wrecks it's best to stay below if you feel threatened. Seek shelter in the reef itself. Better to play the waiting game than to make a run for it leaving yourself defenseless, dangling from the surface like bait on a line. You obviously weren't thinking when you tried to surface so rapidly. If you had surfaced that fast on a decompression dive you would have been in serious trouble and not because of danger from a shark."

"The bends?"

"Yea, the bends."

Janet's expression was one of defeat. "I don't know if I can do it, Pete. When I saw the size of that fish I got so scared I forgot everything I learned. I just wanted to run away. It appeared out of nowhere. It all happened so fast."

"Don't worry, you'll get used to it," Pete soothed. "You'll probably never see anything that big ever again. I'll be with you anyway. Come on now, let's get some lunch." Trying to lighten the mood, Pete smiled and gave Janet a reassuring hug and playfully ruffled up her hair.

Chapter 3

GUIDING THE BOSTON Whaler through the open sea to the narrow inlet leading into the cove, Pete beached the boat on Hog Island. Taking a picnic basket from under the seat along with some raffia mats and a cooler of rum punch they went ashore. The small island was deserted. Folklore perpetuated the rumor that wild boar still roamed in the interior.

It was high noon and nothing stirred in the torrid heat. Stretched out in the shade the pair viewed the green land mass opposite them.

"See that tract of land over there?" Pete pointed at the uninhabited peninsula opposite them.

Janet nodded.

"Did you know that Jim Jones planned to settle his religious community on that stretch of land?"

"I think I read about that," said Janet.

"Yep, the very Jim Jones who was responsible for the mass murders in Guyana."

"God, that was awful."

"Local gossip has it that the former Prime Minister, Eric Knight, supposedly negotiated a deal with Jones to sell him the land."

"Good grief. That means the massacre would have happened here."

"Amazing isn't it?"

"Incredible! This island is such a paradise it's hard to imagine anything terrible ever happening here," said Janet shaking her head as she considered what might have been.

Chapter 4

LEAVING THE HUSTLE and bustle of New York City and their jobs behind them, the McKenzies looked forward to their first real vacation together. Unable to get away for a proper honeymoon after they were married, they regarded this trip as particularly significant. What they were anticipating was privacy and time to be together without the worry and pressures of their usual schedules.

A pilot with the U. S. Army for five years before becoming a pilot with American Airlines, Pete supplemented his income by writing travel articles. Those extra jobs were in fact paying for this holiday. Janet also worked for American Airlines, having recently been promoted to a staff position recruiting flight attendants.

Janet and Pete met by accident when Janet, who was a flight attendant at the time, was filling in on Pete's flight as a favor to another flight attendant. They struck up a casual conversation at the side of the hotel pool on a layover in Barbados. Janet had been reading a travel magazine and not realizing it was an article Pete had written had made some flattering comments about the piece. Impressed with her intelligence, Pete invited her to lunch without mentioning his magazine article left forgotten by the side of the pool. It was not for quite some time after that that Janet was to learn that the article about Bonaire and Scuba diving had been Pete's article. But, by that time they were already a pair, buddies for more than their common interest, diving.

Swept up into a whirlwind courtship after that, they became practically inseparable. They were married within six months of meeting one another. Now, two years later they were enjoying the belated honeymoon they had been promising themselves all along.

As they explored the interior of Hog Island, the McKenzies began to doubt whether they really wanted to see a wild boar after all. The all too vivid image of a five hundred pound porker savaging them was beginning to make them feel uneasy. Relieved to find nothing of interest, they welcomed the excuse of returning to the beach to sunbathe and snorkel the shallow waters of the warm inlet.

Pete lay on his back on the moist sand near the water's edge.

Janet, in the water, called out to him, "Pete, come see what I've found."

"I'd be amazed at anything here," he called back without moving. "The snorkeling is absolutely terrible."

"Well, I didn't mean for you to get too excited," she giggled "but really, come see."

Devoid of a drop of perspiration and thoroughly baked, Pete picked up his mask and snorkel and plunged into the surf with a yowl, a responsive reaction to the shocking change in water temperature against his burning skin.

"Are you sure this is not just a trick to get me out there to ravish your body?"

"Maybe," cooed Janet coquettishly.

Pete waded out to her, his facemask cocked on his forehead. "Okay, show me what you've found," he grinned.

After a flurry of dives Janet surfaced sputtering, "I've lost it. Just a minute." Finally, obviously pleased with herself, she surfaced and pointed through cloudy churned up water. "Here! Here! It's here."

"What is it?"

"I don't know. That's why I called you."

Pete plunged towards the area where she was pointing. The water was stirred up and he couldn't see anything. To complicate matters, the tide was coming in and the wash of incoming wave action caused a riptide effect as the water rushed back out to sea swirling sand into cloudy puffs around the mysterious object. To minimize the amount of sand being stirred up Pete floated free of the bottom, scrutinizing the area as he waited for the sand to settle. Finally he saw it too.

Resting on a sandy bed of scattered sea grass two boxes the size of orange crates came into view. The boxes were unmarked except for the number one stenciled on each of them. Pete took hold of a box in an attempt to move it closer to shore. Although he tried persistently, it wouldn't budge. The nuisance of the waves combined with the dead weight of the box itself made moving it impossible. The pair surfaced.

"Damned things are heavy," gasped Pete from exertion. "We need help."

"Do you suppose they're from a wreck?" asked Janet.

"No, those boxes are new. From the looks of it, they may even be watertight." Snorkeling around in a bigger circle they combed the area finding a total of three boxes.

"What do you make of it, Pete?"

"I don't know. What immediately comes to mind is some kind of contraband in a sealed container. Must have washed up. We don't want to go opening anything like that."

Chapter 5

THE McKENZIES CAME ashore leaving the mystery of the boxes to the sea. They returned to the happy pastimes of their childhood, nibbling wild fruit and collecting seashells. Finally they stretched out for lunch, a feast of fried chicken, homemade bread, and tropical fruit. Relaxed and lazy they fell asleep under the protective branches of a huge sea grape tree. As rays from the afternoon sun gradually crept over them, intruding into their shade, the sleeping pair grew warm and uncomfortable. Finally, they stirred, awakened sufficiently to stumble into the cool water to revive. Rested and bored they were ripe for frolic.

"Pete, I've been wondering, do men prefer to see a woman evenly tanned where her swimsuit ought to have been, meaning she tanned "au natural" or does it excite them to see traces of white skin beneath her suit?"

Impersonating an aged man with no teeth Pete made Janet double up with laughter. "Well, I'll have to think about that one. I'm not at all sure. Do you have traces of white, young woman?" He leered at her.

"This is a serious question," she replied with a haughty air, "and please, do not get personal."

He put his thumb and forefinger together indicating just the tiniest bit. "Give me perhaps just a wee illustration?" He raised his eyebrows into giant question marks as he licked his lips.

In the interest of scientific evaluation Janet condescended to lower the hip of her suit to reveal a patch of virgin flesh.

As though Count Dracula suddenly blinded by daylight, Pete shielded his eyes with his forearm melodramatically. "Ach…dreadful, dreadful," he drooled. "I never realized what was going on all these years. The government shouldn't allow it. Women should not be allowed to spoil nature's beauty with stripes. Let me think. What can be done? Ah, yes. It's coming to me. There is but one remedy."

"Oh, oh" exclaimed Janet, getting to her feet. Sensing she was about to fall victim to a fiendish consequence, she began to drift away but she was too late. Pete, alias Count Dracula, closed in behind her.

As she ran along the beach he swooped after her shouting at the top of his lungs in a cavalry charge, "Even the tan!" As he caught up with her, he pulled her toward him and together they veered toward the water plunging into the sea in a mock struggle. In the underwater thrashing at precisely the same moment that he made a grab for her bikini bottom, Janet sprung away from him and in so doing she slipped right through and out of her swimsuit leaving Pete clutching a tiny Spandex memento as an irrepressibly evil-minded expression bloomed on his face.

"Don't you lose them," Janet shrieked. "That's my favorite suit."

Having her at a definite disadvantage, Pete continued to clown, putting her bikini bottom on his head like a turban. "Madame would like her palm read?"

Janet went through the motions of trying to snatch her swimsuit away from him but she was no match for his solid six foot three frame outreaching and outweighing her. Breathless and realizing she was struggling in vain, she stopped.

Gleefully Pete untied the top of her string bikini. Pure white breasts poured forth shockingly naked against her uniformly golden tan. But when he realized that Janet no longer seemed to be enjoying the game, Pete backed off. Reading her expression, he looked at her and whispered:

"Jan? Baby? I'm sorry. I guess I got carried away. Forgive me?" He leaned forward to kiss her. Her lips were wet and salty. Standing knee deep in the tropical azure pool he put his arms around her. She was naked against him as he kissed her again. Unexpected passion stirred within him and he murmured thickly, "Oh God, you taste so good. Delicious. Jan, let me make love to you."

"Here?"

"Uh huh, right here."

"Now?"

"Uh huh," he breathed as he ran his hands over her. Feeling her soft, silky firmness he kissed her again, even more passionately. Feeling him masculine and solid against her, she responded to his gentleness, to the touch she knew so well, to the familiar sweetness of his kisses.

Suddenly Pete was laughing hysterically. Jostled from the loving mood Janet couldn't comprehend what was happening. Reading the confusion in her expression Pete tried to control the wave of silliness that had come over him. Unsuccessful, he dropped onto the wet sand weak with laughter.

"I'm sorry, Jan," he offered between snorts of laughter.

"What is it?" she demanded with the hint of a smile on her lips.

"It's you," he said mirthfully, a gleam of mischief coming unbidden into his eyes. "I knew you couldn't stay mad."

"Wretch!" she hissed with feigned anger.

Catching him off guard she pushed him over and as he sprawled laughing into the water she wrestled off his swimsuit. With lightening speed she put on his trunks and ran out of the water. For a moment she thought he was going to try to squeeze into her bikini and she winced. As they ran along the beach they were a comical sight. Janet made a spirited attempt at escape but Pete caught up with her and as he did, he pulled her against him. Her (his) droopy drawers fell to the sand.

"Don't you know you'll never get away from me?" Putting his arms around her, he pulled her back into the water.

Their lovemaking was as uninhibited as their wild surroundings. Confident of total seclusion they were passionate, wanton. They made love with total abandon and when spent, they nestled on the moist sand awash with its regular intervals of small waves lapping the shoreline.

They were so at peace with one another that they were completely unaware that a high-powered telescopic lens had been trained on the cove, and them.

Chapter 6

I T WAS FRIDAY night and the Red Crab was filled to capacity. Pete and Janet were seated at the bar watching the locals have a go at darts while over in the corner a group of yachting types were whooping it up ringed around the piano as one of them banged out his familiar repertoire of oldies. A familiar voice called out to them from across the room.

"Well look who's here. It's taken you long enough to find our venerable watering hole."

"It's Lester Griffon from the Liat Flight," whispered Janet, reminding Pete who it was. Griffon ambled over to them carrying a drink in his hand.

"I'll bet you haven't met this big lonesome fellow on your right. Janet, Pete, Todd Murdock," said Griffon planting a hand on Todd's shoulder. "Todd runs the boatyard up the road. He's a good man to know for yacht and equipment rentals, charters, that sort of thing. He knows the waters around here like the back of his hand."

Todd stood and offered his hand. He was tall and lanky with an affable smile and shy manner.

"If I can be of any help, come by any time," he smiled, revealing a crooked front tooth. "Fixing to do some sailing?"

"Some," said Pete, hoisting his drink to his lips. "But we're particularly interested in diving, maybe some spear fishing."

Todd took out a cigarette, hesitated, looked at it and put it behind his ear. "Been trying to quit and it's been murder." He frowned. "Let me know when you're ready. I'll set something up for you."

"Great! By the way, what about that wreck listed in the brochures? I think it's called the Bianca C."

Murdock laughed. "The Bianca C is long gone."

"Salvaged?"

"Buried. Bulldozers leveled the bluff into the sea and over her."

"Too dangerous?" asked Janet.

"A casualty of the new airport. The runway was extended out into the sea. The Bianca just happened to be in the way of progress."

"From the look of conditions at Pearl's Airport, I would say a new airport will be most welcome, in spite of poor Bianca," Janet offered.

An American student, unmistakable in cut-off jeans, a wrinkled t-shirt and worn-out sneakers, recognized Todd and joined the group.

"What's the latest?" he asked inquisitively.

"Fresh crop from the mainland, Bobbie," said Griffon. "Meet Janet and Pete McKenzie. Bob Fisher is a resident student here."

"Oh," acknowledged Pete. "What are you studying? Don't tell me, let me guess, marine biology? Oceanography?"

"No," laughed Bob, "but a good try. Quite sensible, in fact. Actually, I'm in Med School here."

"Medical school?" Janet's eyebrows raised in surprise as she smiled.

"Really? Wow. That is surprising," said Pete. "I have to hear this."

"It's not much of a story really." Fisher seemed embarrassed.

"Well, tell us anyway. We'd like to hear," persuaded Pete.

"Well, when I wasn't accepted into Med school in the States, I applied here. There's an American run medical school on the island. Competition has gotten real stiff back home. When I learned they had a program here, I applied and here I am."

"Wouldn't they love to interview him on the Jay Leno show?" Griffon ribbed good naturedly, shaking his head. "The interviewer's dream—short answers."

"Yea, a man of few words," grinned Murdock, gulping his beer.

"Leave him alone you two. I think it takes a lot of courage and a pioneering spirit to pursue your dream particularly in a foreign country." Janet groped for a cherry at the bottom of her piña colada.

"I have to admit it does," Pete added warmly. "How many students are there?"

"About 800 in all."

"Whoa, that's a lot of people for this place."

"Sure is," laughed Bobbie. "We've practically taken over."

"Overrun is more like it," kidded Griffon.

Preoccupied with the clock behind the bar, Bob checked his own watch.

"Man, look at the time. I've got to get going. I didn't mean to shoot the breeze this long. Nice talking to you though," he said to the McKenzies. Turning toward Todd he added, "Can I see you for a minute?"

"Duty calls," apologized Todd as the pair started to walk away together.

Stretch, the waiter, came to take the McKenzies' dinner order.

"What's good, Lester?" Janet called after Griffon.

"Why everything, my dear," Griffon said, smiling with an affected hotel air.

"He owns the place, what did you expect him to say?" grumbled Pete as Griffon winked at Janet conspiratorially.

"There's dolphin tonight, sir," the waiter suggested.

"Dolphin!" Janet recoiled.

"It's not dolphin as in Flipper, the mammal," said Pete laughing. "But it is a great tasting fish."

"It's excellent," recommended Stretch.

"Oh," murmured Janet in relief, feeling rather foolish.

They both ordered fish and chips set up on the terrace outside.

"What's the story on the school?" Pete asked Lester, who had just returned.

"It's relatively new and has been doing very well. The students have been ranking above the Stateside average. The school takes in a more mature student. This seems to foster a more intense study atmosphere. From here they go on to St. Vincent for another two semesters. After that they go on to England, Ireland, or to the States, whatever they choose to do."

"Interesting," said Janet. "It would make a good story, don't you think?" She regarded Pete quizzically.

"Are you a reporter?" Griffon asked in astonishment.

"Actually I'm a pilot, but I've been doing free-lance writing on the side. Mainly travel articles."

"Well then, let me introduce you to Doc Rutherford at the school. Maybe he'd okay an article. I would imagine a good report would be helpful to you both."

"I'd really appreciate that Lester. Would you look into it for me?"

"Will do," said Lester. Abruptly he excused himself. The barman was beckoning him, presumably with a problem.

Chapter 7

PETE AND JANET were seated at an outdoor table on the terrace. An ancient flamboyant tree dominated the space spreading its branches majestically. Delicate leaves fluttered in the balmy night air fragrant with the scent of night-blooming jasmine and fresh sea air. Omnipresent tree frogs chorused in the background.

The McKenzies luxuriated in the magical glow of flickering candlelight and soft lighting from hanging lanterns. Janet's hair, curly and sun-streaked, glistened gold. A pretty young woman with wholesome, natural appeal, Janet seemed to radiate a natural glow of her own.

"You look particularly lovely this evening, Mrs. McKenzie."

"Thank you, kind sir." She smiled. Her brown eyes sparkled in the lamplight. "Do you think he'll do it?" she whispered, unable to suppress her curiosity.

"You mean Lester?" asked Pete. Janet nodded.

"Why not?" Pete signaled the waiter for more butter. "See, the fish is great, isn't it?" Pete enthused.

"I've never liked fish very much before. Probably because it was never this fresh." Janet paused and seemed hesitant. "Perhaps I shouldn't have brought up the business of the article?" she said uncertainly.

"No, that was okay. In fact, it might even be interesting."

"I just hope that if you do write it, you won't get so wrapped up in it that it'll cut into our vacation."

"It sounds pretty cut and dried to me, but if you don't want me to do it, tell me before I get involved while I can still back away from it."

She was perplexed. "I just don't want anything to spoil our time here. It is supposed to be our honeymoon and it's our first real vacation. God knows when we'll be able to afford another."

"Consider this." He leaned forward and spoke confidentially. "If I'm working, we can afford to stay longer." He winked slyly. "Besides, wasn't the article your idea in the first place, young lady?"

"Don't remind me. I guess I sort of jumped in before I could help myself." She sat quietly for a few moments regarding her husband. "My husband, the journalist. It's just that I realize how much a big break would mean to you." She put her hand over his. "I just want my man to be happy."

"Wouldn't it be great? When I do get a significant assignment, you can travel with me whenever you want to."

She sighed dreamily. "I sometimes wish I could hide in your pocket so I could be with you wherever you go, safely tucked away close to your heart."

"You're always close to my heart," Pete whispered taking Janet's hand and squeezing it.

Impulsively Janet stood up and walked around to Pete's side of the table. She put her arms around his neck and gave him a quick kiss on the lips. All misty eyed and sentimental she whispered, "I love you," before she headed for the powder room.

Chapter 8

WHEN JANET RETURNED to the table she found Pete and Lester deep in serious conversation. The table had been cleared and drinks had arrived compliments of Lester.

"There isn't another international airport being built that I know of," Pete was saying. "To see one actually being carved out of the wilderness has to be exiting."

"It is," said Lester enthusiastically. "They're dynamiting, bulldozing, flattening mountains and heaven knows what else. Too bad you weren't here when they built up the salt flats. Accomplished that by water-displacement—an interesting process. And, up on the hill there's a sand and gravel pit supplying the asphalt plant. It's in constant operation. People and machinery are working three shifts around the clock."

"What are we doing now?" Janet asked as she returned to her place at the table.

"We're building an airport." Pete checked Janet's expression to see if she was all right. She seemed happy again.

"Who?" she asked.

"The Cubans," said Lester.

"Cubans?" Janet couldn't conceal her bewilderment. "Why are Cubans building the airport?" She looked at Pete uncertainly.

"Come on, Jan. You must know. It's been a really hot issue in the States."

"Listen," said Griffon. "Cubans are good workers. Wait till you see how much they've accomplished already. It's a vast project taking years. It's being finished off now, electricity, radar, electronic equipment, final layer to the strip, that sort of thing."

"Are any planes taking off and landing?" asked Pete. This question, asked innocently, prompted a reply from Griffon that would plague Pete for nights to come.

"No, we're still using that godforsaken strip at Pearl's on the other side of the island."

"Sounds like quite a project, all right," agreed Janet as she made friends with a pathetically scrawny stray cat hovering around her feet.

"It's costing a bloody fortune!" Griffon moved in closer, "US $75Million."

Pete whistled. "Where in hell is Victoria Island getting that kind of money?"

"From many sources actually. Cuba is supplying technical advice and labor. More recently Britain has come into the picture."

"No Lester."

Lester frowned. "Well, we sure as hell know where the money *isn't* coming from, the United States."

"Where is the money coming from?" Pete pressed.

"There's no single place. It's a joint effort."

"Well then, let's just say, who's been the most helpful?"

"I would have to say Cuba," admitted Griffon.

"Lester, that stinks to high heaven and you know it!" Pete's outburst was totally unexpected. It was as though he had thrown a glass of ice water in Griffon's face. A few of the restaurant patrons sitting nearby looked over.

"Ssh," Janet hissed as she squeezed Pete's hand under the table in warning. The people who had looked up settled down and resumed their own conversations.

"Cuba hasn't got a dime of its own to give to anybody." Pete leaned forward toward Griffon and asked very quickly, very deliberately. "We're not talking about Cuba are we?" Janet nudged Pete from under the table. He pushed her hand away.

Griffon shrugged, shifting uneasily in his seat.

"The big one?" jabbed Pete, driving home his point. Griffon shrugged again. "Russia is indirectly subsidizing the airport project," continued Pete as if thinking aloud. "Russia and Cuba," he mused, toying with his drink, delicately balancing his glass on the edge of the table. "That's quite a tight-rope to be on. From what I'm hearing, you're leaning Red, my friend."

Tentatively Pete removed his hand from the glass. As it began to waiver he readjusted it so that it was perfectly balanced. The glass resting precariously on the rim of the heavily varnished mahogany table had become a dramatic focal point. They watched in mesmerized fascination and mounting apprehension as the tumbler adhered to the table edge.

"Quite a tightrope," Pete repeated with the flair of a showman. Suddenly, with a lurch, the glass toppled over the edge sending its liquid contents, a half finished rum punch and melting ice cubes, spewing forth as the glass crashed to the stone floor of the terrace shattering into hundreds of particles flying irretrievably in every direction.

Lester was rattled. "Where Cuba gets its money is immaterial." A waiter came running to attend to the spill and broken glass.

"As far as you care, you mean?" challenged Pete.

"You must understand, we need that new airport," said Griffon emphatically as he crumpled a match cover and tossed it into an ashtray. "We weren't able to get the money anywhere else. Generations would have come and gone without achieving the airport if we didn't have help." He spoke earnestly with great passion and feeling.

"But hasn't anyone considered the ultimate price?" asked Pete, not unkindly.

"Price?" scoffed Griffon. "Offer a beggar on the street a free meal and see if he quibbles about the morality of not being able to return the favor."

"That isn't the same thing."

"The hell it isn't. Look Pete, our country is poor, financially bankrupt with no chance of improving its circumstances for at least the next one hundred years. Suddenly we're given an opportunity for a radical giant step forward. It's an answer to our prayers. Here we are with next to nothing and dreaming of a future for our families, our kids, when an opportunity presents itself offering to make our dream a reality. Is there a choice? Are you telling me we shouldn't "go for it" as you Americans say?"

"What about principle?"

"Principle?" Griffon scoffed. "Maybe we can't afford principle."

"Holy Christ man, can't you see you're being used?"

"Maybe we're using too, and knowing it but at the same time terrified the dream will disappear. No one wants to say or do anything lest the spell evaporates."

Unexpectedly emerging from out of the darkness, Todd ambled over to them. "Hey you two, sorry I had to leave so suddenly earlier, but you wanted me to set up a dive, didn't you?"

"Sure," said Pete. "Wednesday at nine?"

"Fine. Let me jot that down right now before I forget." Todd hastily scribbled a note to himself in a little notepad and stuffed it into his shirt pocket. "Got it. See you Wednesday." He waved and hurried off absent-mindedly.

Lester smiled. "He'll take care of you. Todd's a good man."

"You're a good man too," ribbed Pete. "A bit misguided but sincere." The three of them laughed erasing the tension between them. "Lester, I can't believe that you're so close to the situation here that you don't see what we see. You've just come back from the States. You've read the papers. You must know public opinion abroad. World press speculates that the Reds are building the airport to gain a military foothold in the Western hemisphere. Are you telling us that isn't true?"

"I certainly hope it's not true because if it were, Victoria Island as a free country would be finished before she even has a chance to begin. Man, we're fighting for our very existence."

"Then tell me, why are these communist countries pouring their money into Victoria Island?"

"Purely Internationalist's Principles. Helping the underdog."

"That's bull, Lester."

"Are you saying genuine charity isn't a valid reason? Can't the Good Samaritan offer a gift of food to a beggar without having an ulterior motive?

"Ah yes, but does he take him to the most expensive restaurant in town?" Pete grinned.

The nightly bell pealed. As was the custom at closing time, a costumed crier circulated among the lingering patrons to officially remind them it was time to leave. For no reason at all that he could think of, when Pete heard the bell toll, he had a distinct premonition of doom.

Chapter 9

J ANET AND PETE walked back to their cottage in silence,
the hour was late and the road empty. The day's events
had caught up with them and they were tired. The night
sounds of tree frogs and crickets clashed in noisy competition
with the steady chugging of the gravel and asphalt plant in the
distance.

As a dog mournfully bayed at the moon, they heard
movement up ahead—a chain, crackling brush. Suddenly
a shadowy hulk loomed large across their path. Terrified,
Janet screamed sending the hulk into a frenzy of bellowing
as it lurched about wildly. A cow, having slipped its tether,
stampeded nervously into the brush at the side of the road.

"A thrill a minute!" Pete groaned in exasperation. All at once
a rooster crowed. It wasn't yet midnight. "It's a madhouse here,
even the goddamn bird is a nonconformist."

They reached the screened porch of their cottage and were
grateful to be back. Strains of reggae music could be heard as
it wafted its way up along the beach from a nearby hotel. The

island music was soothing and romantic. Getting comfortably settled in their cottage, Pete went to the refrigerator, took out an already opened bottle of wine and filled their glasses. Happily relaxed they enjoyed the simplicity of the music and ocean background as they sipped their wine. All thoughts of New York slipped from consciousness as they succumbed to pure relaxation allowing the island sounds and scents to envelop them.

"Come on," Pete whispered as he pulled Janet to her feet. "Let's go to bed."

They made love and afterwards, glistening in the moonlight from the mist of perspiration covering their naked bodies they sprawled out in contentment, deliciously caressed by the cooling balmy breezes that floated across them from the open window facing the sea.

The familiar sound of tree frogs musically underscored by the rhythmic cadence of the waves lapping against the shore mesmerized them while the harsh annoyance of barking dogs punctuated the stillness. As sleep overtook them they couldn't help but smile when they heard the unexpected sound of the idiotic resident rooster crowing.

The last image Pete remembered before he fell asleep was of a menacing shadow dancing across the ceiling and walls suggested by a palm frond clacking in the breeze outside. Almost unnoticed by either of them was the improbable sound of an airplane hovering nearby as though ready to come in for a landing.

Chapter 10

HILLARY WARREN STEPPED from the 48-passenger inter-island plane onto the runway of Pearl's Airport in the state of shock, relieved to be safely on the ground. Apart from having seen, mid-air, what she presumed to be airport attendants hurriedly chasing a herd of goats off the landing strip, and barely succeeding, she was horrified anew at being directed to a woefully ramshackle terminal building which resembled the shabby tobacco drying sheds of Connecticut. Inside, the decrepit old structure had deteriorated altogether.

Blessedly rescued from the steamy congestion of immigration and customs' queues she was ushered with the ceremony of a death march into a private waiting room where she was eyed with suspicion as she made a formal customs declaration. Hastily spirited out of the building and into a waiting taxi obscenely decorated with gaudy neon and fluorescent strip signs and a soft-sculpture of a penis in full erection which dangled flagrantly from the rear-view mirror,

Hillary collapsed into the back seat unsteadily marveling that she had never, NEVER, in the whole world seen such a vehicle before in her life.

Finding temporary comfort in the "Jesus Loves You" sticker emblazoned on the dashboard amid the smut, she settled back and tried to get a grip on herself. Almost immediately her driver, Willard, a burly black man, presumably a Rastafarian with unkempt corkscrew curls and a raffish beard, leaped into the car greeting her with, "Hi Baby!" as he leered at her licentiously.

Not wishing to tangle with him she smiled wanly and said, "Hi," mildly reassured that his familiarity had no lecherous overtones owing to the message he advertised across the back of his filthy t-shirt, "God Loves Gays."

On the last leg of her prodigious journey, paralyzed with exhaustion, she was driven in total darkness to her destination. The taxi, irreverently christened "The Pleasure Wagon," careened up and down steep mountain roads and along the edges of narrow cliffside precipices as it negotiated its death-defying sprint with accustomed tenacity. To pass the time, Willard, radio blaring to shatter the sensibilities of any normal mortal, "jumped up" in time to the crooning calypso beat of "The Mighty Sparrow" which flowed out of the loud-speaker while Hillary, anesthetized by fear, sat quietly slumped in the back seat. Finally, an interminable hour later, the taxi rolled to a stop. Pale green with a glazed look to her eyes, Hillary cautiously peered out the window.

"Are we here?" she moaned.

"We sure are, l'il Mama," crooned Willard opening the door for her.

"Thank God," she sighed, almost swooning. "Please, my bags, they're in the back."

"BAGS? You ain't got no bags! They never got off de plane from Barbados."

"What!" Hillary shrieked. Unsteadily she planted her feet to the solid ground. Groaning she faltered and sank back down into the seat.

"What's de matta, you sick or somethin'?"

"A little," she admitted weakly.

"Doan worry, baby, just gimme de key."

"Key? I don't have a key. There should be someone inside."

"Uh oh," Willard muttered under his breath while looking around to see if any lights had been left on. "Baby, dis house is locked up tighter 'n an asshole. Ooooo," he winced at his rough language. "Sorry about dat," he quickly apologized. "But you IS locked out L'il Mama." He paused, obviously thinking. "What's de name o' dis place anyway?"

"Well, it certainly isn't Shangri-La," Hillary mumbled almost inaudibly.

"No, l'il Mama, it ain't Shangra," Willard admitted sadly shaking his head as he pointed to a brass nameplate. He brightened. "Are you sure you got de right place? Look at de name right here." He lit a match over the sign....SEASIDE MANOR.

Chapter 11

C OMPLETELY EXHAUSTED AFTER her epic pilgrimage, Hillary slept like a stone awakening twelve hours later rested, soothed and lucid. Peacefully stretched out in bed she lay wondering whether she had been hasty in coming to Victoria Island. In London her decision had seemed like a good idea. She had thought a holiday with rest and seclusion would help purge her of her depression while at the same time, she reasoned logically, she could inspect Seaside Manor, the property she had inherited from her late stepfather, Osgood Redfern.

After the events of yesterday, however, she was not at all sure. Having traveled two days and over 4,000 miles to have landed in this jungle hell-hole twelve degrees north of the equator…. words failed her for the mixed emotions she felt.

And as for Osgood, he must have been crazy. She couldn't for the life of her understand why he would have done such a thing. How could Daddy have built a home here? And, more to the point, why? As she thought things over, there was no doubt in her mind now. She would wire her solicitors in London advising them of her decision to sell Seaside Manor.

So much had happened to Hillary in the past few days that she had been too worn out to even think about Adam, but now, quietly drifting back in time she could feel the pangs of hurt and rejection stabbing at her anew.

At first she had blamed herself for their confrontation because she had precipitated the whole ugly scene. But, she reasoned, even if she hadn't, the outcome would have been inevitable sooner or later. In retrospect she was furious with herself that she had allowed Adam to make a fool of her. She had been so totally head-over-heels in love with him she would have done almost anything he would have asked. Hadn't she waited for him all through his divorce, supported him while he was out of a job (which was often), and loved him beyond all reason? And then, when by accident she discovered he had been two-timing her, there had been a terrible argument. She was furious with herself because she herself had started it. But what other choice did she have? When he had admitted to her that he wanted to marry her and keep his new girlfriend, Hillary had become hysterical.

Tearfully she had pleaded with him to reconsider and when, demanding fidelity she pressed him for a choice and he acquiesced, she was placated. But the victory was short-lived. In a nightmare all brides-to-be dread, on the morning of their wedding day at Christ Church, the bridegroom simply never arrived. He had jilted her.

In her mortification and disgrace she ran away, far away, from everyone and everything she knew. Disillusioned, she had fled the scene of her pain and humiliation.

In a way she was relieved that Osgood and Mother weren't alive to know about Adam and her shame. Yet, at the same time, she wished she had them to turn to. With pangs of guilt she felt genuine regret that she had always been "too busy" when they had invited her to come to Seaside Manor for a holiday. And, although she hadn't noticed the crushing impact of it before, for the first time in her life she felt totally alone and it was frightening. Had she become that pitiable person depicted in plays and novels as lonely and desperate?

Chapter 12

HILLARY WAS TWENTY-FIVE years old with not one person in the whole world who cared about what happened to her. She was completely on her own and in one scrape after another or so it seemed. In thinking about it, perhaps what happened with Adam was really for the best. Wasn't it better to have found him out before rather than after they were married—and had children? If men were all like him, wasn't it better to know it in advance and protect herself from future hurts by never allowing herself to be so vulnerable ever again? With the calculated determination of one who has been badly burned and has learned a painful lesson in life, she promised herself she would never again allow herself to fall so completely in love.

In considering her approach to life she began to doubt her judgment in other areas as well. Having made what she considered a perfectly rational and logical decision to inspect her property in Victoria Island, here she was in a seemingly sex-crazed country isolated from civilization and helplessly dependent upon total strangers.

Service was nonexistent. Communication by phone was poor at best as the wires were either busy or down altogether. The electricity always seemed to be out and attempting the simplest undertaking was met with instant frustration.

Rejected and depressed Hillary had lost confidence in herself. Disillusioned by her decision to come to Victoria Island she chided herself for her emotionalism, deciding that being honest and open was a stupidity she could no longer afford. Her genuine attributes always seemed to be used against her and people took advantage of her. Yet, that was her personality and she doubted she could change even if she tried. She wasn't even sure she wanted to change. Her spontaneity and her joyful nature was the essence of her spirit, of her. Why should she become a cranky, cynical crone to accommodate the world at large? Besides, in her heart she knew she couldn't change even if she wanted to. It was hopeless. Face it Hillary, you are doomed to failure.

Hillary got up, brushed her teeth and took her swimming costume out of her travel bag. It was still damp from her swim in Barbados. She hung it up in the bathroom. Thank heaven she had at least a few toiletries with her. She washed her pantyhose. She wouldn't be wearing them any time soon, too hot and humid. Looking for a place to dry them she pushed open the louvered door leading to the balcony.

My God, she couldn't believe it! The view was the most spectacular she had ever seen in her life. A pale turquoise bay with the surface glittering like a bed of diamonds spread out before her. Palm trees, pink hibiscus and colorful bougainvillea dappled with early morning sunlight surrounded her as she felt the caressing warmth of a gentle ocean breeze against her skin. The scent of flowers and salt air was intoxicating. Completely forgetting her laundry, Hillary stepped out onto the balcony in time to see a sailboat under full sail glide into the bay. It passed right before her and in the stillness she could hear the sails luffing in the wind as the crew prepared to put down anchor. Closer in toward shore a dozen luxury yachts strained at their moorings. What a refreshing contrast to cold, damp, bleak London.

Brimming with girlish curiosity she ran through the rest of the house, her house now, passing from room to room with an exhilarating sense of discovery. Five bedrooms, six, all with fabulous bathrooms, a huge salon that opened to the terrace, a beautiful terrace with palm trees and lush greenery encompassing the whole ocean panorama. Giant, ancient clay pots overflowing with colorful pink flowers were everywhere. She recognized the dramatic flair of her mother's influence as she flitted from chair to chair testing the furniture on the veranda. Gorgeous natural wicker and bamboo with deep inviting plump white cushions were arranged to take full advantage of the exquisite view.

The setting abounded with good taste, her mother's taste, and for the first time in her life, Hillary felt heartfelt pangs of regret wondering why she had not found the time to visit Victoria while her mother and stepfather were alive.

Continuing on her inspection tour, she charged down the steps like a child at Christmas, rushing past the bathhouse and swimming pool, the tennis court, boat house and motorboats, the beach and a fleet of small sailboats. Hiking her nightdress above her knees she paused to look into the warm, clear water and delighted at the sight of a school of tiny transparent fish skirting the water's edge. With heady exhilaration she continued her quest as she ran along the beach towards the private jetty.

Once on the pier, she danced her way to the very end, her skirts fluttering as she ran, her arms outstretched overhead. Joyously she called heavenward, "Osgood, you sly old fox. Do you hear me? Oh Daddy, I am so sorry. Forgive me Daddy, you weren't crazy." Prancing madcap across the greenheart planking she dashed towards the gazebo at the very end. "You were ...." she hit the water with a splash..... "BRILLIANT!"

Chapter 13

S EASIDE MANOR WAS a magnificent Mediterranean villa situated high on a bluff with a commanding view of Horse Shoe Bay. Seeing it for the first time Hillary was enchanted. The safe protective haven the property afforded was a pleasant surprise and in her aloneness she seemed to feel the villa was an extension of Osgood and her mother comforting her, still looking after her, nourishing her.

Her room was fit for a princess. Tastefully furnished in blue and white, it was spacious and airy with a blade fan softly revolving overhead. The antique four-poster mahogany bed reflected in the mirrored wall of closets was regal against the patterned Wedgwood blue sisal floor covering her mother had designed and ordered from Haiti.

An adjunct to the master bedroom suite was an open-air lava bath and viewing station. When she had first seen it Hillary wasn't terribly impressed but after having bathed there, she was charmed. Languishing in the huge open-air lava tub Hillary contemplated her morning schedule of things to do. Idly surveying the natural volcanic rock formation from the hilltop "Thinking Garden" as the viewing station was identified; she reveled in its peace and solitude. Secluded and tranquil, the garden's only access was from the master suite. Strolling through the garden amid the statuary and benches and a giant sundial, Hillary had discovered a revolving telescope in the shelter of shade vines. The powerful lens provided a commanding view of the entire island and its waters. She remembered that Osgood who had loved astronomy had had a hand in personally designing it.

Wrapped in a towel Hillary padded barefoot to her room and discovering the radio was on, she smiled. Electric power had been restored. Dutifully she went around turning off the lights. She had almost forgotten that the electricity had been off. As she passed the bench at the foot of her bed she noticed with a squeal of delight that someone had delivered her luggage. It had apparently been sent on to Victoria Island from Barbados on the first morning flight.

Quietly standing in the doorway, Carrie, the maid who had admitted Hillary into the darkened villa the previous night, politely awaited instructions as she inquired, "Mistress Hillary, what would you like for breakfast?"

Chapter 14

THE MORNING WAS a whirl of activity as Hillary simultaneously unpacked, made inquiries and appointments on the telephone, and readied to go into Georgetown. Not daring to drive until she knew her way around, she went with Timothy, better known as Tiff, her gardener and houseman.

Speeding along the potted, spine-jarring roads Hillary bombarded Tiff with questions as he intermittently braked and zigzagged around the endless maze of pedestrians who popped up everywhere. There were women balancing baskets atop their heads, mothers with babies, wool-capped gadabouts, cutlass-toting plantation workers, stray goats, truant chickens and as they lurched crazily to avoid it, a cow standing smack in the middle of the road oblivious to the stalled cars on either side of it.

Bypassing the cow, they resumed their drive. Dodging neatly uniformed children with cricket bats darting in and out of his way Tiff whizzed past a row of hillside shanties straining as if on tiptoe to reach a mercifully cooling breeze. Swerving around a hairpin turn in the road they passed a row of rusty, tin-roofed wooden huts incongruously set against a majestic sweep of palm-fringed beaches. At a clearing Tiff pointed out Grand Anse Beach. Continuing on they rounded the bend next to the cricket field where they heard inspiration at work in the competent hands of the steel band practicing inside its headquarters. A little further up the street they paused at the crest of the hill. Spread out before them in a magnificent panorama Hillary could see the city of Georgetown nestled around the Careenage.

The scene was as delightful as the most charming French impressionist painting. Fragile sherbet hues representing cliffside houses intermingled with splashes of white dotted with the rusty clay of Mediterranean rooftops were daubed into a background of the rich green mountain ranges enlivened with the sparkling sheen of palm fronds set into a vibrant shimmer of movement by the off-shore breezes. Pale pink and buff historic buildings with their ancient tile rooftops lined the opposite shore reflecting soft colors into the smooth emerald green and teal waters of the sheltered harbor.

The Careenage was bustling with the excitement of an exotic port of call. Cruise ship tourists in gaily-painted water taxis were being ferried through the still waters past the Gliding Star, an inter-island schooner loading for a trip to Trinidad. Sinewy black natives hoisted perishable goods from the jumble of confusion spread out on the pier below them onto the ship. The cargo coming aboard was comprised of wooden crates of sour sop, tamarinds, sapodillas, lemons and limes, baskets of coconuts, a small herd of goats, crates of squawking chickens and figs, stalks and stalks of green figs, also known as bananas. Alongside the pier, set out in a wondrous array, was a pile of harvested lambie while nearby a discarded pile of shucked conch shells awaited burial at sea. The hub of all the commerce and activity was the Careenage of Georgetown Harbor, indeed the loveliest, most picturesque harbor in the world.

With her Barclay travelers' checks in her handbag and a shopping list in her hand, Hillary visited the bank and then crossed the street to the market square where a pandemonium of people and wares were spread out in a giant central market square. Gripped by immediate confusion Hillary was guided by Tiff through the open air shopping stalls as she selected from among the heaps of oranges, limes and lemons.

Inviting Hillary to notice them and their produce the saleswomen called out, "Dearie, come see the figs," and "Do you need paw paw, darlin?" or "Madame, how about some callaloo?" Smiling uncertainly in the crush of humanity she made her purchases while allowing Tiff to negotiate prices and tote the basket while she paid in her newly acquired EC dollars.

At noon she left Tiff with the groceries and the Land Rover and hurried off up Young Street, a narrow, crooked street edged with open drainage trenches. She was on her way to meet Jean Trumbull of Baird and Trumbull Properties for lunch.

The Nutmeg Restaurant overlooked the Careenage of Georgetown Harbor. "These seats have the best view in town," said Jean, "except for the prison," she added as an afterthought as she pointed across the way to the long white Mediterranean styled building with the green roof which was high on the hilltop opposite them.

"I can hardly believe it's a prison. It looks like an Italian monastery," Hillary remarked regarding the splendid architecture of the structure.

"The local youths irreverently call it, Night School," bellowed Jean, laughing at her own joke. "The former Prime Minister's name was Eric Knight."

Jean and Hillary were on their second drink when during a brief pause in their own conversation they couldn't help overhearing the tour guide at the next table.

"The harbor was created after an eruption when part of a volcanic wall collapsed," the woman holding a red balloon was saying. "The whole island is volcanic in origin. As to the architecture, the historic buildings were constructed from the discarded ballast of the old mercantile sailing vessels. Gives a European flavor, don't you think?"

Hillary and Jean looked at one another and smiled indulgently. "Go on dear," encouraged Jean, "finish your story."

"Well," continued Hillary, "can't you just picture us driving up in total darkness with the electricity out and Willard saying, "We'll get in, Baby, doan you worry?"

"You took your life in your hands, you know," said Jean gravely.

"What do you mean?" asked Hillary, fear creeping into her eyes.

"Willard!" Jean roared. "Why everyone knows Willard," she screamed with the confidentiality of a bullhorn. "He's the horniest stud on the island."

Hillary's mouth flapped open. "But, he's, his t-shirt," she stammered. "You know, the one that says, God Loves Gays?"

"Oh that," said Jean dismissively as she reveled in the gossip while shaking her head sadly. "Poor Willard. He's so broke he'll wear just about anything. Besides," she added with a sly wink, "I don't think Willard can read. He probably doesn't even know what it says." Tipsy, the women giggled uproariously.

Suddenly Jean was staring intently out of the window. Smiling, she discreetly called Hillary's attention to the sidewalk below them. As Hillary looked out of the window she caught sight of a familiar figure on the pavement below. It was Willard and pretty girls surrounded him. They weren't local girls either, maybe they knew better. They were foreign girls. Hillary laughed out loud in spite of herself.

"Well, at least we can guess why he never learned to read," snickered Hillary. "He probably couldn't spare the time." The two of them caught a fit of laughing and couldn't stop.

Although Jean was bawdy she was also outrageously funny. With her infectious humor she was just the tonic that Hillary needed. The sad, wistful, far-away look Jean had detected in Hillary's eyes was no longer there. Hillary seemed to be having a good time and Jean was glad.

As for Hillary, if Jean Trumbull was an indication of what people were like in Victoria, maybe she hadn't made such a terrible blunder after all. Hillary smiled and relaxed. For the first time, she seemed to notice the spectacular scenery coming at her from every direction.

Chapter 15

ALTHOUGH HILLARY HAD been advised to sell Seaside Manor she had decided before she left London that any action concerning the property would be made after she had personally seen it and had conferred with Jonathan Ward, the barrister who had for years attended to her stepfather's affairs on the island. She had arranged a meeting with him to do just that.

Shortly after one o'clock Jonathan Ward appeared at the main entrance of Seaside Manor. Looking immaculate in tropical white he seemed more like a well-bred country club elegant than a West Indian attorney. European in education and appearance, he was an aristocrat by birth and had been educated since the age of seven at Britain's finest boarding schools.

Jonathan Ward was ushered through the courtyard and main reception area to the west veranda, which overlooked the bay. He was directed towards the swimming pool where he found Hillary languishing in the water on a comfortable looking floating mattress. Dismayed to see that she was fast asleep he hesitated before making his presence known hoping she would awaken on her own.

Suspended over the shimmering, transparent cerulean water she reposed jewel-like in a bikini gliding serenely across the surface of the water transported on a lovely white shell-shaped conveyance. Patiently noting it was after the scheduled appointment time, Ward decided he had to awaken her.

"Miss Warren. Excuse me, Miss Warren!"

Hillary's eyes fluttered open as she heard her name. As soon as she saw him she instantly remembered their appointment and gasped with obvious embarrassment.

"Mr. Ward! Oh, please forgive me. I do apologize. I had meant to greet you properly." She made her way out of the pool and over to him. She was soaking wet, completely natural, and more beautiful than anyone he had ever seen.

"My apologies for interrupting such a peaceful moment." He took her hand. On contact it felt cool and soft.

"Jet lag," she offered, dabbing the ends of her blonde hair. "I don't usually sleep during the day." Her green eyes sparkled reflecting the sea behind her. "Come, let's sit on the terrace where we'll be comfortable."

Following her up the stone steps Jonathan couldn't help noticing her long, straight legs. Beaded with moisture, they were lean and firm. She continued up a flower-bordered path. She was tall, but pleasantly so, he observed. Reaching the veranda Hillary wrapped a length of fabric around her.

"Let's sit here." She gestured towards the chairs at a massive round mahogany table. While he was setting up his briefcase Hillary excused herself.

Left alone temporarily, Jonathan glanced about the interior so familiar to him—white stucco walls, high graceful arches, vaulted, heavily timbered ceilings and Mexican floor tiles. The rear of the villa had an unobstructed view of the sea as well as the anchorage below where yachts from Hong Kong to Switzerland seemed to pay homage to the manor house. The west veranda, sheltered from the sun's intensity by a bower of thunbergia vines with cascading white orchid-like blossoms offered comfortable seating and a good breeze—imperative in the tropics.

Hillary returned carrying a manila folder. Disappointingly she had changed out of her swimsuit and into daytime attire. Delicately scented but without a trace of make-up, she wore a colorful caftan that gave no clue as to her figure lamentably concealed beneath it.

Carrie, a bit older but still familiar to Ward, came onto the balcony carrying a tray with a pitcher of iced tea and a plate of coconut jellies. She served them with that intangible invisibility all well-trained servants seem to practice. Discreetly she left the room.

"Magnificent property," said Ward with a trace of nostalgia in his voice. "Being here brings back many memories."

"My memories are yet to be," smiled Hillary. "This is my first visit. It is lovely though, isn't it?" She scanned the veranda and the view of the bay. "Now I appreciate why Osgood and mother loved it here."

"This estate was Osgood's pride and joy," said Jonathan as he reached for his iced tea.

"You've known my stepfather a long time, haven't you?"

He smiled warmly. "A very long time."

"And you've handled his legal affairs here and in London for many years?"

He smiled again. "Many, many years," he readily acknowledged.

"Osgood came to rely on you a great deal. He told me once that in spite of your youth you are a shrewd tactician brilliant beyond your years and experience. He spoke of you in very glowing terms." Hillary smiled disarmingly.

"Unfortunately, Miss Warren youth is fleeting. The ravages of time have a way of creeping over us. When I first met Osgood I was still in law school. I am thirty-nine now. But you flatter me. It was I who held your stepfather in high regard. I shall miss him and his counsel greatly."

"The way he spoke of you, I think he loved you in a way. He never had a son, you know." She sighed sadly as a long forgotten memory rekindled warm in her eyes. "I know very little about Daddy's business affairs. His death was so unexpected, so premature." Suddenly misty-eyed, Hillary fought back tears. Her mouth quivered ever so slightly. She paused to regain her composure. When she continued her voice was hoarse and unnatural. She cleared her throat and paused. "You heard about the plane crash, of course?"

"Yes," he sighed. "Terrible shock, terrible." He too fell silent.

"Well," her voice, once more steady and under control, projected strongly, "I too will have to rely on you as Osgood did, to bring me up to date regarding finances here as well as in London."

Jonathan looked suddenly perplexed and embarrassed. He coughed and shook his head. "You should have been informed, Miss Warren. Osgood knew. I don't have a private practice any longer." He hesitated, groping for the correct words. "While I will not be able to personally advise you," he paused, "I can put you in touch with someone......"

Chapter 16

THE AIR JUST seemed to rush out of her. Her face flushed as her resolve seemed to collapse. She looked hurt, confused and embarrassed as she stammered, "Oh, I'd just assumed... I thought it would be as it always had been. I'm sorry." Catching a deep steadying breath she pulled herself together. "I apologize for having brought you here for no purpose," she said evenly. "I do hope I haven't inconvenienced you too much." She rose to her feet. "At least I am glad that we've had an opportunity to meet," she said kindly to indicate that there were no hard feelings.

Her distress made Ward uncomfortable. Whether out of personal loyalty and respect for Osgood Redfern or out of compassion for the vulnerable young heiress, Jonathan Ward couldn't seem to bring himself to refuse her appeal for his counsel. His only hesitation had been his own lack of time. Already overburdened with work, he wasn't quite sure how he would manage. In any event, he knew he couldn't turn his back on his old friend from the grave.

"Miss Warren, over the years Osgood and I were more than business associates, we were friends. At a time in my life and in my career when I was very young and desperately in need of a friend Osgood was a wonderful friend to me. Out of respect for him and for you, I'll be happy to do whatever I can for you. It will be my pleasure to advise you personally in whatever way I can."

"Are you quite sure?" she asked uncertainly.

"I insist," he said emphatically.

Relief flooded her face. "I appreciated your kindness more than I can say, Mr. Ward, truly."

"Jonathan, please. Now, let's go over any questions you may have."

As they discussed business, Hillary noticed Ward's appearance with more than passing curiosity. Tall and manly yet sensitively vulnerable, his ruggedly chiseled features seemed to be mellowed by the boyish innocence of his smile and the appealing susceptibility smoldering in his eyes as he looked at her. Why did he have to be so disturbingly good-looking?

Completing their business, they moved to a settee on the west veranda where the lovely orchid-like flowers hanging from the thunbergia vines dipped and swayed in the constant equatorial breeze. They spent the remainder of the afternoon chatting, losing all track of time until Carrie arrived carrying a giant silver tray with four o'clock tea and her special rum cakes.

"As I sit here with you in this peaceful setting, I feel as if I've known you for years," said Hillary looking at Jonathan over the rim of her teacup.

"I feel that way too," he admitted as he looked into Hillary's smiling green eyes. "We seem to get along quite well. In fact,

I'd like to know you better. May I see more of you while you're here? Would that be possible?"

"Of course," she said lightly, "I'd like that too."

As he prepared to leave, he took her hand and looking at it as if he were measuring it, he placed his own on top of it.

"Yes," he said, "I would say we fit together quite nicely."

Suddenly self-conscious, she drew her hand away and rose to her feet.

"Gracious, look at the time," she said glancing at her wristwatch. "I've taken up your whole afternoon." She smiled disarmingly.

"To let you know how much I've enjoyed being with you today I'd like you to join me for dinner this evening. Please say you'll accept."

"How lovely."

"Shall we say seven o'clock?"

She smiled giving him a little nod of agreement as she extended her hand. With almost courtly formality he raised her hand to his lips and looking at her he added softly, "until this evening."

She walked with him to the courtyard where his driver in military uniform, hurried to open the car door for him. Without hesitation or any sign of further acknowledgement, Jonathan Ward entered his black, air-conditioned Mercedes-Benz and within moments had sped away down the winding palm-lined driveway. Hillary couldn't help but to have noticed the license plate of his sleek limousine.....VIP 1.

Chapter 17

PETE AWOKE TO the aroma of frying bacon and brewing coffee. Janet had been awake for some time and was reading. She put down her book and smiled at him. "Hi honey."

He yawned and scratched his head, "Hi, who's out in the kitchen?"

"The maid's preparing breakfast."

"Mmm," mumbled Pete, stretching and giving Janet a big bear hug. "Smells wonderful."

She rumpled his dark, curly hair and nuzzled him affectionately.

"You're wonderful."

"What time is it?" he asked.

"About eight o'clock. You slept late this morning. Do you want to take a walk along the beach before breakfast to help you wake up?"

"Yea, that's a good idea." He made a quick trip to the bathroom and pulled on his swim trunks. "Let's go."

The McKenzie's cottage was on the beach directly opposite the mouth of the bay. Picturesquely surrounded by palm trees, bougainvillea, ixora and hibiscus, the seaside bungalow with its gay Mexican architecture was situated dead center on Prickly Bay, a horseshoe shaped crescent of land safely sheltering the yachts moored within it.

On the eastern peninsula, facing west, the customhouse, carved securely into the cliff facing the bay, nestled alongside the boatyard, chandlery, and finger piers of the marina which dotted the coastline. On the western peninsula at the opposite side of the beach from the customhouse, the Calabash Hotel and its beach bar sprawled discretely over twelve acres as a cottage colony.

The McKenzies headed towards the beach and turning right, walked towards the Calabash. Although it was early morning and the beach was empty, activity had commenced on board the yachts. Fresh laundry was being hung out to dry, nude zesty types from a French sloop plunged in to take their first swim of the day, and those ferrying shipboard guard dogs to shore for their morning walk set off in rubber dinghies. Those left behind seemed to busy themselves in the galley because the stimulating smell of food cooking was heavily fragrant in the air.

Making an about-face they proceeded toward the opposite end of the beach. The marina, farther out on the peninsula, seemed full and from where the McKenzies were on the beach they could see a yacht up in dry-dock for repair. Workers had already begun chipping and scraping as they inspected the hull for dry rot.

At the end of the beach they came upon some small fishing boats that had just been launched. Every morning, weather permitting, the same local fishermen set out in the same dilapidated boats in anticipation of harvesting a few meager edibles— grunts, red snapper, squid an occasional sea egg or even a lobster. They headed out beyond the safety of the bay in their heavy lap strake boats equipped with the crudest of handmade snares, spear guns and knives. The rag-tag assembly took to the sea for their objective—anything they could catch, spear, salvage or find.

The men had large families but because the rewards from fishing were inadequate, it was impossible for one family member to supply everyone's needs. Consequently everyone was required to participate, children included. Food was their top priority. Although the island was abundant in tree fruit and no one ever truly starved, the fisherman's lot was a harsh one, perhaps harsher than any other as he was dependent upon the sea for his livelihood.

Their dismal existence etched in their weather-beaten faces and scrawny frames, the men always seemed to have a ready smile and willing spirit. But in their lonely evening hours these same men, dispirited and despairing, looked for escape, often lapsing into combatant drinking bouts as they chug-a-lugged tumblers of one-hundred-forty proof white rum. The next day, comforted by the knowledge they had looked death in the eye and had made it through the night, they returned to their regular work-a-day existence until their next lapse into depression. This attitude of quiet acceptance for one's lot in life seemed to be characteristic of the people in Victoria Island.

"It seems natural to be up early," said Pete, "I suppose everyone tries to get his work done before the heat comes up."

"It sure is bustling," agreed Janet.

"We'd better go back for breakfast," said Pete glancing at his watch. "I told Todd Murdock we'd meet him at the boatyard at nine."

"Wait!" said Janet. "Let me tell the fisherman that if he catches a lobster, we want to buy it—two if he gets any. One boat hasn't left yet. The maid can pick it up from him when he comes back."

"What? You're spending the day out in the briny with me, numero uno lobster fisherman, and you want to buy lobsters from somebody else?"

"Well, I........."

"Listen here, before the day is over I'll have you swimming with lobster!" His ego bruised Pete started off towards the cottage.

Mumbling something about her woman's intuition, Janet put in her bid for two lobsters with the fisherman and ran to catch up with Numero Uno.

Chapter 18

PETE HELPED JANE onto the Rum Runner, a seaworthy old scow reeking of substance and character. The boat shifted away from the pier as Janet stepped onto its deck and Sampson, the mate, held fast for her as she came aboard.

"Take your things below, Mistress?" Sampson asked politely.

"Thank you." She handed Sampson her canvas tote bag.

Janet looked overhead. The sky was bright blue with scattered fair-weather clouds billowing along the ridge of distant mountains. The sea was calm with little wind gusts causing telltale ripples on the water's surface. It promised to be a great day.

Settling into a deck chair in the cockpit she watched the activity ashore with interest while she waited for Pete who was helping with the air tanks. Business was brisk at the icehouse, while the ever vigilant customhouse, she noted with amusement, was typically late in opening. Almost immediately the men finished loading and boarded.

"Everything ready to go?" Murdock called out. Sampson nodded as he let go the spring lines. Todd revved up the engines and slowly they pulled out of the slip, maneuvering the boat away from the marina.

"Look at those houses along the ridge," Janet exclaimed. "Aren't they gorgeous?"

"That one's named, Magnifique." Todd pointed to a dazzling white villa capped in red clay tiles. "Owner is a wine producer, vineyards in the South of France. And that one is the Redfern estate, Seaside Manor. He's an international tobacco merchant. He was just killed in a plane crash. Freak accident. He was coming back here to his own property. The one next to it belongs to Horrez from Venezuela. He's in oil. The area right along here is called The Gold Coast." The Rum Runner rounded a small bend in the coastline.

"That's a private club for gays. Heard some mighty funny stories to do with that place. And that home there, if you can catch a glimpse of it," Todd pointed to a mass of overgrown foliage, "that one's owned by Polansky, the film director. He has homes all over the world. There is funny stuff going on there too." Todd gave Pete a typically male look of confidentiality. "Peter Ustinov is supposed to be renting it this year." Leaving the bay, they headed out to sea.

"What's the history of this place?" Pete asked above the din of the engine. "The locals are either unwilling or frightened to speak about it."

Murdock smiled. "They're very cautious about talking to strangers. And with good reason."

"Don't tell me you're going to give us the same double-talk?"

Todd smiled expansively; his whole face seemed to come to life. "No."

A wave slapped into the side of the boat unexpectedly. At the same moment Pete's visor was lifted off his head by a wind gust and he made a grab for it, catching it. Todd and Janet watched the little drama and smiling at one another, Janet broke into a giggle.

"There's just been a revolution here. A new government has taken power. The locals know it's no time for complaints. The prison is full of dissidents." Todd paused. Pete and Janet watched him, quietly waiting for him to continue.

"So you want a history lesson. Well, let's take it back a few years to the time Victoria Island was a British Crown Colony. Somebody here got the idea Victoria should become independent and along about 1974 Victoria Island did become independent headed by a Prime Minister.

"The new man was ambitious, bright, a real politician. He was once a laborer himself and the people felt he understood them. He represented hope. To be fair, he did achieve some good, but it was short lived. Catapulted into international politics he became power-struck, egotistical, and greedy. Unaccustomed to wealth he suddenly had access to more money than he know what to do with. With a little time and experience, he learned."

Murdock smirked as he removed and reseated his cap on his head. "It wasn't long before his own lavish lifestyle took precedence over what should have been his national objectives. He began to dip into government funds. He was supposed to have bilked the country out of US $75 Million, yet no one dared challenge him for fear of being beaten or killed."

"He had a group of hired cut-throats and ex-convicts, to do his dirty-work. The people called them the Mongoose Gang.

The mongoose on Victoria Island is a flesh-eating creature that snoops out rats and snakes." Todd flipped off the cap of a cold bottle of Carib beer and took a swig.

"Go on," prompted Janet.

"While the Prime Minister was in the United States making a bid for financial aid, his opposition, a few of them former cabinet ministers themselves, discovering they were about to be killed, decided to act."

"Forty-five men, armed with fifteen firearms amongst them, cut the electric power and jammed communications. In the darkness they ambushed the army command post and seized the radio station. With the coup successful and bloodless, the group restored the electricity and telephones and under gunpoint forced the radio station to broadcast a news bulletin over the airwaves notifying the world of their successful overthrow."

"Talk about derring-do," said Janet.

"What about now?" asked Pete. "What's the new man like?"

"He's a different breed entirely," said Todd. "He's cultured, educated and smart as a whip. He's also hell-bent-for-leather on building an international airport and to improve telephone and electrical facilities, roads, and tourism. Everything he was supposed to have been doing, and FAST. He's not only idealistic, he's driven. But don't be fooled, when push comes to shove, he can be deadly. But, from what I've been hearing he's getting himself in over his head with the company he's keeping."

"The Cuba thing?" asked Pete.

Todd nodded. "Touchy situation all right. No one really knows how it is going to turn out. The problem, of course, will be when the project is completed and Victoria Island wants to continue on its own."

"You mean Cuba won't be satisfied with a mere thank you," said Pete with a degree of sarcasm.

"It will be the same old problem of—nothing is for nothing. I hear they're beginning to sound a bit bossy already."

"Do the Cubans have representation at the Cabinet meetings?"

"Supposedly observers."

"It seems like an impossible situation," said Janet, raising her binoculars and scanning the waters. "Is the PM a communist?"

"I don't think so, but both sides are playing it for what it's worth. Right now, they both need each other."

"What do you mean?" asked Janet while trying to keep her fly-away hair under control.

"If the Reds do have ulterior motives for the airfield, like using it for military purposes, they need the PM up front to camouflage their intentions while they work to complete it. On the other hand, the PM keeps them going by regurgitating their own rhetoric, stringing them along until they finish the project. The whole game is a stall."

"In the meantime, what if the PM gets out of hand and won't co-operate?" asked Janet.

"If he doesn't play ball, they'll get rid of him. Believe me; he knows his position very well. He's caught between the proverbial rock and the hard place. He's primed for an over-throw from any quarter and is trying to deal with that situation every day. He's very sensitive to the possibility of a counter coup. In fact, he's obsessed with the notion that the CIA is planning another Bay of Pigs."

"They wouldn't, would they?" Janet looked shocked.

"He thinks they might. Yes, our Prime Minister, Sir Jonathan Ward, has a lot riding on this airport."

Chapter 19

"LOOK! WHAT IS that? Over there." Janet exclaimed pointing as she continued to peer through her binoculars.

Todd cut the engine's speed and looked into the distance. He grinned broadly.

"Well, I'll be damned! Looks to me like you've spotted a whale, girl."

"I don't believe it," she squealed in delight as she searched the area waiting for its reappearance.

"There it is! And look at that giant tail," bellowed Pete.

Todd halted their progress and circled. Spellbound, they watched the whale breach and sound as it continued to move towards them.

"I've never seen a whale up close before," said Janet. Her curly hair was blowing wild in the breeze as she leaned out over the rail.

"Not many people do. At one time whales used to be fairly common around Victoria. They're a rarity now. Glover Island off the mouth of the bay used to be a whaling station. In fact, the giant metal tanks the fishermen used to boil the blubber to make oil are still there. They are the abandoned relics of a forgotten industry."

"You should use it as a tourist attraction," enthused Janet. Todd laughed.

"Don't laugh," said Pete. "Maui in the Hawaiian chain used to be a whaling station and the whole island capitalizes on it as a tourist attraction. It's their biggest draw."

Janet leaned over the railing and looked out to sea as Todd slowly circled the area. "Can you imagine diving and coming face to fact with a whale?" Janet wondered.

"They run in deep water, but you can never tell," Todd winked at Pete. "They get beached sometimes. Most unlikely though," he added not wanting to frighten Janet. "Sometimes they have been known to get off course and come in towards shore but that's never happened here that I've ever heard."

"I think he's gone," said Janet sadly.

"Yep, afraid so." Todd resumed his course and for a spell they continued on in silence until Todd suddenly called out, "Okay, you two, this is the site of the Cassandra. If you're going to dive, get suited up while I put down anchor." With enthusiasm the McKenzies prepared to dive.

The reef below was clearly visible. Sampson dropped the anchor and Janet watched it fall to the bottom leaving a frothy white trail of bubbles as it streaked through the water on its way down.

"Clear as a bell," confirmed Pete as he peered through the twenty foot depth. Overhead, early morning clouds were dissipating under the tropical sun. "It's a perfect day for a dive."

"Take it easy when you first get down," cautioned Todd. "It can get pretty hairy if there is a current running. But, you're lucky, it's clear as a bell."

"Aren't you going with us?" Janet asked in surprise.

"No, I have to stay with the boat. It's a pretty straightforward dive though and Sampson will go along with you to show you the way. Just remember to keep an eye on your air supply."

Pete preceded Janet into the water in a backward roll. Surfacing they swam to the bow of the boat where they gave themselves a final check before descending the anchor line. They got down with no difficulty.

Visibility was clear and there was no discernible current. Sunshine penetrated the water, its shaft of light beaming bright on the sea floor. Heading toward the bottom they followed a sandy avenue that split the reef. Following the crevasse they went deeper as the reef rose up on either side of them forcing them to travel single file until they reached the other side of the reef. The wreck was directly before them.

Ruins always seem to command an awesome respect for the past life they represented. Looming ahead of them as if an apparition from beyond the grave, the shadowy hulk of the ship was dismal and empty, devoid of its former vitality and personality. Nestled motionless in an open clearing of sand and sea grass the decaying eighty foot sailing vessel was enameled with coral and plant life splaying out of its fissures. The ship lay quietly at a depth of 65 feet, its name still legible on the stern—CASSANDRA.

Gliding over the top of the hull to explore the other side where there was apt to be fish unaware of their approach, Pete and Janet came upon a pair of giant gray angelfish and a bottom-dwelling jewfish. At their approach, the angelfish and jewfish slipped from view. Circling the ghost ship they moved toward its bow. The vessel was pointed curiously seaward and lay on the brink of a deep gorge. The scene resembled a bleak graveyard, silent and ominous. The brass fittings had long since been salvaged and what remained was a rotting hulk. Sea growth had begun to cover the wood where the paint had eroded. As Pete began to enter the hull Janet signaled him not to. She directed his attention away from her, behind her. Her eyes were wide open, her expression registering unmistakable fright.

Suspended near to the wreck a large five-foot barracuda watched them. They both knew that barracuda, even a relatively small one could be unpredictable and opportunistic. It was one of the few fish that could attack for no apparent reason and its bite was nasty.

They continued to swim about the wreckage eventually entering the hull that proved only mildly interesting. Pete scraped his leg on a rusty nail as he emerged. It showed a trace of blood. He cursed to himself in irritation.

They kept the barracuda in sight. It remained suspended near to them, continuing to observe them. Pete wondered if it was merely curious or whether the fresh cut on his leg was attracting its attention. He wasn't sure, but when he saw it made no move, he continued on.

They gradually moved away from the wreck. Pete led Janet into more shallow water coming upon the reef probably responsible for the ship's foundering in the first place. And, suddenly, looking around them, they felt relief. Just as quickly as it had appeared, the great barracuda was gone. Nearby, Sampson was patrolling for lobster with a spear gun.

Feeling relaxed again, they swam in and out of the channeled coral enjoying the underwater scenery as they made their way back toward the boat. In passing they saw a snapper, some grunts, and a few colorful parrotfish sweep past them as the fish shyly secreted themselves in the crannies of the reef. They swam through an entire cloud of wrasse and Janet was amazed they didn't come into contact with a single one.

And then it happened. They were swimming tandem, one above the other through a narrow fissure when Janet, while playfully prodding a sea anemone, accidentally dropped her knife. Pete didn't see it come drifting down in front of him until almost the last few seconds. Instinctively making a grab for it he missed, sending it bouncing across the coral into a crevasse. Without a second thought, he plunged his hand into the hole after the knife to retrieve it. Instantly he was impaled.

Seeing clouds of Pete's air bubbles spiraling upward, Janet knew that something terribly wrong was happening as she saw him grappling flat against the reef. She was as his side in moments.

Maneuvering to stand up next to him, she began a tug of war, pulling him, believing he was snagged. When she realized he wasn't snagged but held by something within the crevasse, she quickly alerted Sampson and sent him for another tank of air for Pete. With his rapid consumption of oxygen from exertion from fighting with whatever held him, Pete was almost out of air. Recognizing the danger of the situation, Janet checked her own air supply—600 p.s.i. Even if she left her own tank with Pete, she wasn't certain he wouldn't run out of air before she got him freed.

Calmer than she felt, Janet held up Pete's air gauge and signaled him to breathe more conservatively. Next she let the air out of their buoyancy compensator devices in order to make them heavier, anchoring them more solidly to the ocean floor. Increasing their weight would give them more leverage. They inspected the crevasse and the problem.

Communicating with hand signals, Pete conveyed that he believed an eel had him. Using her snorkel Janet began poking into the opening hoping a foreign intrusion would cause a response from the creature. With his free hand Pete unsheathed his knife and carefully aimed for the area of the pain and for his captor while at the same time trying to avoid stabbing himself. He was working blind. Neither of them could see what was in the hole. Pete hit something. Distracted or perhaps wounded, the moray loosened its grip a split second. Recognizing his opportunity, Pete gave a quick jerk and pulled free.

They remained at the opening of the fissure impatient to examine Pete's hand, which they feared would be badly mangled. Relieved to see his wounds weren't serious thanks to the protection of his gloves, the couple shared a brief expression of thanksgiving.

Quietly mesmerized by the appearance of a dark fluid gradually beginning to ooze out of the hole, they continued to watch as a four-foot length of spotted viper slowly unwound from out of the sanctuary of its reef home. Crumpled and wasted, the lifeless creature was still gripping the finger of the glove Pete had been wearing in its fang-like jaws.

Watching the creature with spellbound fascination, they were startled into a new reality. There, sparkling in the sunlight, Janet's knife was resting on the edge of the crevasse. With embarrassment she quietly retrieved it and as she looked at Pete she breathed a sign of relief at all the trouble she felt she had caused. Her sigh became a strangled gasp as Pete's face reddened. He was out of air.

They surfaced in an emergency ascent buddy breathing from Janet's air supply. Some distance away from the boat they inflated their vests and as they bobbed to the surface Sampson appeared with the extra tank, just in time to help Pete get to the boat.

"Jesus!" groaned Pete. He was pale and obviously shaken. "Did you see the size of that thing? I thought I was a goner." Janet smiled an all-knowing Cheshire cat smile. As if reading her mind, Pete retaliated, splashing her with water. "Go ahead, gloat. I know. You're just so pleased with yourself because you talked me into wearing gloves." Holding up his gloved hand he displayed the missing glove finger, wiggling it. Their troubles behind them, the pair was once again having a good time.

"What happened down there?" Todd called out as the boat pulled along side them.

"Nothing," Pete called out nonchalantly. "Everything is just fine."

Chapter 20

BACK ON BOARD the Rum Runner Janet dried herself with a towel as Pete nursed his bruised hand and scraped leg. Their gooseflesh receded under the warming rays of the sun. Janet tucked a towel around her and moved towards the cockpit. Her hair, whipped by the wind as it was tossed about, was almost dry and resulted in a fluffy mane of tangled, sun-streaked curls. She glanced at Pete and noted with satisfaction that his color and good disposition seemed to have returned.

"I'll fix lunch, you must be starved!" Giving a call from the galley when lunch was ready, Janet waited for the men to come below. She had spread out the assortment of food that they had brought. "Nothing like salt air and sunshine to whet one's appetite," she said gaily, perching next to Pete. "Uhmm," she murmured ecstatically, obviously enjoying her fried chicken and buttered bread. "Heaven."

Pete watched her with amusement. "I don't understand how you can put away as much food as you do and stay so skinny. You damn well eat more than I do."

"High metabolic rate," Janet confessed between ravenous bites.

"Really?"

She nodded.

"No wonder. Well, anyway, I'm certainly glad I had you on my side down there," Pete grinned. "For damn sure I wouldn't have had a chance without you."

"What do you mean? I'm not nearly as vicious as that thing down there."

"Pound for pound, you did all right. Wouldn't trade you for anything," said Pete, steering Janet to the leeward side of the boat where they stretched out in the sun. As they talked they could hear Todd in the background fiddling with the short-wave receiver. Apparently more emotionally drained than she realized, Janet fell sound asleep. But sleep was out of the question for Pete. He was restless and keyed-up. Quietly slipping away from Janet he went aft to talk with Todd.

"How about finishing my history lesson? I like your island lore."

"Okay what do you want to know?"

"Well, what's the story with the medical school? How does it figure into things?"

"It doesn't, but thank God it's here. Without the money the American students spend the economy would have collapsed long ago. As it is, island people can barely hang on."

"What's the story about the Bianca C," Pete asked impulsively.

"The Bianca." Todd's eyes seemed to come alive as he remembered the events that took place more than twenty years ago. "The Bianca C was a 594' cruise ship that was headed back to Venezuela from Georgetown Harbor. As it was leaving there was a gigantic explosion in the boiler room killing one man. The crew helped all of the passengers off with no casualties but a fire raged unabated for three days. Everything possible was done to put out the blaze but it was impossible. It burned to the very end gutting the ship. When the fire was finally put out, what remained of the ship was a charred ruin. When it didn't sink they set about salvaging her until finally, stripped clean, she was sent to the bottom."

"Over the years there had been a lot of interest in diving the Bianca C, but make no mistake about it, it was serious business. She is settled in deep. Oh, I'd say one hundred and fifty feet down with a strong current—maybe two knots. You have to hold fast to the wreck or you'd be swept away. For safety sake, dives had to be a very controlled with experienced people. For a long time it was an attractive nuisance for diving buffs. With the lure of seeing big fish inhabiting the wreck everyone wanted to make the dive. Gossip had it that there was a four-hundred-pound grouper said to have taken up residence in the smoke stack.

"With dreams of excitement and the lure of salvage money a lot of people dove the Bianca C— a lot of people who had no business going. The main problem with Scuba equipment here on the island is that it's old and unreliable. On a dive, particularly on a deep dive like the Bianca, you had better have dependable equipment. A few of the young lads who went were inexperienced and got into serious trouble. They hadn't received proper training, don't you know, and through ignorance or bad judgment they misjudged their air supply, stayed down too long. When they did come up it was too fast, an almost fatal error. A couple of them were airlifted to

Barbados or Trinidad for recompression for the bends." Todd shook his head sadly. "Over the years, the wreck was stripped clean. Even though it was an attraction for experienced divers, it really wasn't worth the danger involved to go down. It's just as well that it's been covered over. It would only have lured more people to their deaths."

"Isn't there anything about this place that you don't know?" Janet asked, joining them.

"I've lived here a long time, girl," smiled Todd pointing to land. "That's Calivigny Island." He indicated a small island in the near distance. "It used to be part of my snorkeling agenda. You could wade in from the opposite side of the island and just drift with the current clear around to the other side all the while getting the scenic tour of the reef off shore. It was a nice take. There used to be a big swanky hotel and a gambling casino on the other side of the island."

"It looks deserted," said Pete, shielding his eyes from the sun in order to see more clearly.

"It is now. There was a fire. Everything was completely destroyed. Nothing left but a mass of rubble, broken glass, stones and burned-out timbers. The government's taken over the island as a military training station. It's strictly off-limits—forbidden." They fell silent as Pete contemplated his surroundings.

"We're coming up to Prickly Bay. I've found a little spot of my own that you may be interested in," said Todd with a mischievous grin. "Occasionally find a few lobsters. You like lobsters, don't you?"

Pete's face lit up with interest. "I sure do," he smiled. "But wait. Isn't that Hog Island?" Pete asked trying to orientate himself to the irregular coastline.

"Passed it, that's it over there," said Todd pointing. "It is deserted and very private."

"Jan and I went snorkeling in the cove."

"Todd laughed. "Waste of time, but you're on vacation so it doesn't matter."

"Turned up a surprise or two," smiled Pete.

"Or three," added Janet.

"Oh?" Two faces with smug expressions stared at Todd.

"We found some chests," Janet blurted out unable to contain her enthusiasm.

"Sea chests filled with gold?" Todd grinned patronizingly.

"Well, not exactly," Pete hedged, suddenly feeling rather foolish. "Actually we don't know what was inside. We didn't have a chance to open them." His voice sort of trailed off.

"Why not?"

"Well, they were sealed and we couldn't get them open."

"Where are they?"

"Hog Island," said Janet.

"And what did your friends think about your discovery?"

"Well, we haven't told anyone about it. You're the only one we've mentioned it to. We didn't want anyone else to know really. We were afraid they might get to them before we do." Janet hesitated. "They really look important, Todd. We're so near, couldn't we go there and see if we can get them now?" she wheedled.

"Can't get the boat up the narrows now, girl, low tide. Besides, they've probably washed out to sea."

"No, they're too heavy for that," Pete confirmed.

"Ah," scoffed Todd. "Every charter sailing along here scuttles their garbage. There are crates everywhere," he said impatiently.

Janet was disappointed and her face readily expressed those feelings. Although Janet did not say another word in argument, and although Janet could not explain her strong feelings, she was not sure that she believed Todd Murdock.

Chapter 21

HILLARY WAS AWAKENED by the sound of footsteps on the tile floor in the corridor outside her bedroom. She sat propped up in the king-sized four-poster bed with mosquito netting cascading down around her afraid to make a sound as she watched the bedroom door slowly opening.

"Jonathan, it's you. You frightened me to death."

Juggling a bucket of champagne and two crystal wine goblets he came into the room. Smiling roguishly he switched on the tape deck, loosened his tie and slipped out of his jacket.

"What are you doing here?" Hillary asked in astonishment, and not too pleased at that.

"Actually I was on my way home when I was overwhelmed by an irresistible impulse to see you."

"Do you frequently just pop into ladies' boudoirs in the middle of the night?"

"Only in necessary circumstances."

"And tell me," Hillary inquired shrewdly, "in anticipation of these rushes of compulsive spontaneity, how does champagne materialize as if by magic?"

"From the wine cellar downstairs," Jonathan whispered mischievously.

"Here?" she squealed in disbelief at his presumption.

"Here," he nodded guiltily.

"But how on earth did you get into it?"

Sheepishly he produced a key. "Property Management privileges," he said matter-of-factly.

"Reprehensible!" she scolded. "I am shocked at your audacity. What would you have done if I had called the police?" she asked sternly as she dangled her legs over the edge of the bed.

He walked to the telephone, picked it up and held it to her ear so that she could listen. There was nothing to hear. The line was dead. Putting her hands to her head Hillary groaned and fell backwards on the bed.

"Not again," she wailed.

"I've tried to ring you all day," he explained, but I couldn't get through so here I am." They looked at one another and reflecting upon the absurdity of the situation, they both broke out into laughter. Hillary shook her head in mild disapproval. "But in the middle of the night, Jonathan? You are wicked," she scolded.

"Hillary, ten o'clock is not the middle of the night. Besides, my meeting just this moment adjourned." Jonathan set up the champagne on a bamboo table between two comfortable chairs on the balcony. He couldn't help but to reflect upon the change that had taken place in Hillary since he had first met her more than two weeks ago.

Having been orphaned by the death of her mother, subsequently devastated by the unexpected death of her stepfather, and finally completely shattered when she was jilted by her fiancé, Hillary had been understandably despondent and reclusive when she had first arrived at Seaside Manor. With the passage of time in a holiday environment she was slowly working out of her depression, gradually recapturing her former spirit and fun-loving nature.

Since she met Jonathan, it had seemed perfectly natural for her to turn to him with her problems as Osgood had done with his. A gentle confidant and kind friend, Jonathan had been supportive yet non-pressuring. He was also very good company. Over the past weeks she had discovered that life could be worthwhile again.

The two of them, snatching happy hours together, swam, sailed, played tennis and took early morning rides along the beach. As she gradually got to know Jonathan better, Hillary's defenses and apprehensions seemed to melt away as she became more comfortable with him.

She accompanied him to various local functions and dinners and before his eyes, her confidence blossomed. Charming and graceful, she was a young woman, intelligent not only in knowledge but in restraint of opinion and information. She had that special facility for dealing with people who are sometimes impertinent in their inquisitiveness, even to the point of being obnoxious. Not surprisingly she was an asset to him and had surpassed every expectation he might have had.

Non-pressuring in his relationship with Hillary, Jonathan had done nothing to take advantage of her emotional vulnerability. He had been waiting for the right moment to express his innermost feelings. Tonight, uncertain of her response to him, Jonathan had come to see Hillary not only as friend and confidant, but also as a man very much in love with her.

He plucked a bougainvillea blossom from amongst the mass of vines overhanging the balcony. Absently he gazed into the starry night as if mesmerized by the opulent splendor of the moon reflecting its silver image upon the heliotrope surface of the sea. Faintly aware of tree frogs echoing in the distance and of waves crashing onto the beach below, he was also conscious of music softly playing in the background.

He turned and leaned against the railing. Thoughtfully he swirled the champagne around in his glass as he regarded Hillary sitting in the wicker chair opposite him. Although she was partially in shadow, from time to time moonlight caught the shimmer of her hair giving it the effect of fine, spun gold. Her slender hands with their carefully manicured fingertips were delicately folded in her lap.

"I'm sorry if I frightened you when I came in," Jonathan said earnestly. His seriousness yielded to laughter. "Did you think it was Willard coming back to get you?"

"It crossed my mind," Hillary said mirthfully.

Silence seemed to weigh heavily upon them. Finally, in a change of mood Jonathan asked, "Did you realize that tonight would have been the first night we didn't see one another since you came to the island?"

"Yes, but I thought, typical. A fickle fellow that Jonathan." Hillary smiled. She had a nice smile. In his quiet moments alone whenever he thought of her somehow he always imagined her with a smile. He sat down in the chair opposite her.

"I missed you," he said from the anonymity of the shadows. There seemed to be tension in his voice.

"I missed you too," she said lightly. She was suddenly awash with moonlight as wind tossed the overhanging tree limbs about. Her eyes had gone smoky gray.

"Did you?" Somehow he hadn't expected her to admit it. Hearing her say it made him hopeful. "Even though I was at a cabinet meeting it felt strange not to have you near. It made me realize how much I've enjoyed being with you these past weeks." He paused; hating to say the words, knowing the answer would be even more painful to hear. "When do you go back?"

She seemed to hesitate. Indecision? Reluctance to leave? He couldn't tell.

"Another week or so."

"What will you do?"

"Oh, I don't know. Try to get on with my life I suppose." She sighed. "It's helped, being here." She turned to face him. "You've helped, Jonathan." She looked into his eyes. Impulsively he took her hand in his.

"Would it confuse matters if I asked you not to leave?"

She seemed suddenly flustered, shy. "I don't really want to go." She paused, and then continued. "I've been having a lovely time actually, but then, I can't stay forever, can I?"

"You can stay longer," Jonathan said simply. "Stay. It would please me very much if you did."

Cupping her chin in his hand he tilted her head up so he could see her face more clearly. "Don't look so bewildered. You don't have to leave if you don't want to." He was losing her and panic crept into his voice. He watched her wondering what she was thinking. He spoke in a whisper.

"Don't you understand what I'm really saying?" His eyes were warm and tender. Jonathan stood up and taking her hand in his drew her up to him. She seemed distant, uncomprehending. He put his arms around her and held her lightly as he looked into her face.

"Hillary," he whispered softly, "I'm in love with you. I don't want you to go." He searched her face waiting for a response. Her eyes misted with tears and she tried to turn away so that he wouldn't see. But he did see and felt so pained at her hurt that he pulled her to him and wrapped his arms around her protectively.

She seemed so delicately fragile in his arms, so perishable. He thought he detected a slight tremble as she murmured, "Jonathan, I…. ".

"Shhhhh." He stilled her protest with a small gentle kiss. Regarding her expectantly, he smiled. "Do you know I've wanted to hold you from the first moment I saw you."

"I almost thought you didn't think of me in that way."

"Think of you…" he said in astonishment. "I've done nothing but think of you. A moment doesn't go by that I don't think of you." Clasping her hands in his he kissed her fingertips and looking at her again, he hugged her to him. He wanted her to feel the security of his arms, the love bursting inside his heart.

Her pained expression and tear stained cheeks disquieted him. He didn't know what to do. Impulsively he kissed her softly, chastely, as one kisses a child to console it. But when their lips touched in a kiss so sweetly tender and ever so gentle, their feelings for one another that had gone unrecognized ignited as though by spontaneous combustion.

Between kisses Jonathan whispered, "What do you feel, Hillary? Tell me."

"I feel love," she breathed. "Oh Jonathan," she murmured while kissing him, "I feel lots of things—surprise, happiness, contentment. And yet, in a way, I'm frightened. Everything's happened so quickly. It's as though I'm on the edge of a dangerous crevasse. Inside me, something is prodding me forward to jump across to you, to the other side, yet something is warning me to stop, telling me that if I try to leap to the other side I'll fail and I'll fall into the abyss. I'm unsure of myself. I don't know whether I can successfully make the leap. Inside I'm quite frightened. You see, I've just recently tried a leap and fallen off a cliff. I've just barely survived falling into the abyss." Jonathan tightened his grip around her, feeling uneasy at the thought of anything happening to her.

"Don't be frightened. I'm here to help you."

She tried to smile but her lips formed a tense grimace of resignation.

"Are you too frightened to try?"

"Well, if you'll be there to help me, I could try." She buried herself into him. "As long as you're holding me I feel very safe."

"Free yourself of the past, Hillary. You're here in the present with me."

"But what about tomorrow and the day after tomorrow? What of the future, Jonathan?"

I'll always be here for you to rely on. I'll always be here, Hillary. Believe that. Trust me."

Soft music flowed out of the stereo speakers. Recognizing her romantic favorite, Jonathan smiled. In a romantic gesture he danced with her and when the song ended he stopped.

"Don't stop just yet, please," she whispered as she wound her arms around his neck. He kissed her on the forehead and continued, moving to the music as if in a trance. He stroked her silky hair and smiled tenderly into her gentle face. He loved the feel of her against him, her scent, her. Suddenly he didn't ever want to let go of her and as he felt her snuggle into him he knew he was hooked.

He kissed her forehead, her cheeks, and her lips. Jonathan, who had inherited the hot sensuality of his island ancestry but had buried it beneath a mask of English reserve, was committing the unpardonable. He was feeling emotions, long stifled and dormant. Powerful emotions and the force of them alarmed him.

Jonathan Ward was a man accustomed to self-discipline. He was in control of his life, of his emotions, of himself. The realization that he was no longer in control unsettled him. His feelings for Hillary had made him vulnerable and for Jonathan, as with certain men, vulnerability is a sign of weakness. Her lips yielded. He kissed her again and when she returned his kisses they both knew they had made the leap into the unknown.

"If you only knew how much I desire you at this very moment." He breathed heavily as he searched her face for a clue to her feelings. He thought he detected a trace of apprehension. "I ache with wanting to make love to you." Kissing her passionately he held her to him. He was keenly aware of her softness, her warmth, his hardness. "But I'd rather lose you than do anything to hurt you." He kissed her several times more—small, brief kisses as though weaning himself away from her. His eyes glowed with the love he felt. "We must stop, I must go!"

It took all his willpower to stop kissing her. His decision was even more difficult since Hillary, as though in a trance with half-closed eyes, suddenly seemed reluctant to have him leave. Quickly, before he could change his mind he collected his jacket and tie and walked towards the door.

"Later," he whispered not trusting himself to even look at her.

Chapter 22

"JONATHAN!" THE DESPERATION in her voice impelled him to look back. She ran towards him flinging her arms around his neck. "Jonathan," she whispered unsteadily, overpowered by her own passion, "I love you too." With unrestrained enthusiasm she showered him with kisses. Totally thrown off balance by the force of her unexpected onslaught, Jonathan careened into a chair by the door with Hillary collapsing top of him.

"Now, you can't go. Don't you see? You care! You're decent and good and loving and kind and honest and you truly care."

Having assailed him with a torrent of words, Hillary looked fondly into his eyes and briefly hugging him to her, kissed him. He was momentarily startled into immobility. Yet, he still dared not respond. Gently Jonathan held her back.

"Hillary," he whispered, urgently trying to convey the gravity of the situation, "I must leave," he said grasping her hands with his hands while he pressed firmly emphatic, "while I can." He looked at her beseechingly.

All at once she seemed calm, lucid. She stared back into his blue eyes unflinchingly. Her eyes were smoky, sultry. Her lips were parted in anticipation. "Do you really want to go?"

"For your sake, I must."

She looked up at him, eyes smoldering, lips pouting. "What do you feel, Jonathan? You do love me, don't you?"

His eyes searched hers and the feeling of their shared intimacy blazed bright. "That is why I must leave."

A silent moment passed between them. They kissed with a poetic tenderness. Gently, as her lips touched his she whispered softly, "If you must do anything, make love to me."

Suddenly they were wildly kissing. Unbuttoning his shirt, she caressed him, softly running her hands across his back. He balked when she began to unfasten his belt to undo his linen trousers but as they dropped to the floor and she began stroking him, his resolution dissolved. He took off his under shorts and when he turned around she was standing before him naked in the moonlight, her blonde hair falling about her shoulders, a triangle of light hair just as luxurious, just as thick, at the join of her legs. If he had thought her beautiful before, he had slighted her. Seeing her naked for the first time standing in the moonlight, she was exquisite. She came to him and he groaned as he felt her breasts crush against him. The sweet ecstasy of their naked bodies warm against one another, finally touching, sparked an even more insatiable desire for one another.

She was completely without inhibition. His mouth over hers, they kissed exploring with their tongues, causing little shivers to run through them. He kissed her breasts, the softness of her stomach, the gentle curves of her hips and as he ran his hand down along her legs she whimpered and rose to meet his touch.

He delighted in the soft, smooth, caressing touch of her fingertips as she played against his skin luxuriously, finally touching him between his legs. As their mouths hungrily discovered one another they climbed to the emotional edge of their passion, poised as if surfers primed in anticipation, at the giant crest of a wave before beginning the exhilarating ride to shore.

In their prolonged contact she was aflame with excitement and wet with desire. Throbbing and moist from her wetness he slid into her and she gasped with the first feel of him, gripping him to her. She was hot inside, tantalizingly hot and he could feel her muscles rhythmically contracting around him. The pleasure was so intense that for a moment neither of them dared move. As he thrust into her she burst into a frenzy of undulations aggressively rising and swirling to meet his every penetrating thrust until in their final moments, she held her breath becoming so pale he thought she had fainted. Their heads bursting, physically and mentally drained, they collapsed and she lay clinging to him trembling in the aftermath.

"You are wonderful," she whispered, playfully nibbling his ear. Under her, still inside her, he hugged her to him, lazily stroking her with his fingertips as he smiled the smile of a man who had a special secret. Soon they were asleep in one another's arms.

He was mad about her, besotted. Reflecting on their past weeks together, Jonathan recalled the pride he had felt, was feeling, as Hillary charmed everyone who met her. Quiet, reserved, coolly elegant, she was an extraordinarily lovely woman with a subtle sensuality. Subtle, he thought with a smile. He smiled because he knew that underneath that proper façade a volcano raged.

They lay atop the bed quietly gazing at one another. Propped up on one elbow Jonathan gazed at Hillary intently as though committing her image to memory for the moments they would be apart. Regarding him, she dreamily traced his handsome features with her fingertips.

"Jonathan? Are you sorry?"

"Sorry." He pulled her to him and tumbled with her into a spiral across the sheets. "How could I ever be sorry?" He squeezed her, playfully kissing her nose. "My little engine," he teased. Suddenly sensitive to a motive for her inquiry, he looked at her questioningly. "Does that mean that you are feeling remorseful?"

"I guess I just wanted to know whether I please you."

"Please me? You are perfection," he uttered without hesitation. She still seemed perplexed. "Come on, Hillary, out with it. Please tell me what's bothering you." Leaning against the headboard, supporting his back with pillows, he pulled her across him and held her in his arms. Sitting next to him, with her knees drawn up she nestled comfortable against him. He puffed at a stray hair on her cheek and when it resisted he brushed it back from her face.

"It's just that I'll be leaving soon and...."

"Ah, so that's it. But I thought we'd already solved that little problem. You're going to stay right here with me." He squeezed her playfully. "Do you imagine I would ever let you go now that I've found you? It's too late for that. I could never give you up, now." His eyes scanned her face. He wore a very tender expression that resulted in a kiss. "You mean everything to me, don't you realize that?"

"Oh Jonathan, I can hardly believe it but I feel the same way too." Tears had crept into her eyes and she buried her face in his neck. "Would you like to share a secret?" she whispered.

"Of course I would, I love your secrets. I want to share everything about you."

"You said you knew everything about this house. I'll bet there is a part of it you don't know about. Would you like to see?" He nodded. "Come, it's outside."

She led him out into the darkness where they could see the lights twinkling across the island. Hand in hand they walked through the night air to the crest of the mountain to the Thinking Garden.

"Isn't the view wonderful?" Hillary breathed. "And look!" she exclaimed leading him toward the telescope. "You can see everywhere."

"At night? I've never heard of being able to see through a telescope at night."

"Neither had I, but with this one you can." Next, she led him to the tub. "And wait until you see this." She opened the tap and jets of warm water swirled into the lava pool as they waited at the side of the cliff silhouetted in the moonlight. Feeling the gentle cooling breezes through their hair and across their skin they could taste the salt air as they smelled its clean freshness.

Enjoying the newness of their intimacy they slipped into the warm waters of the lava pool. Jonathan stretched out on the top step, a ledge rimming the inside of the pool that doubled as seating. He lay in the partially filled lava pool looking up at the stars pointing out constellations to her. Hillary sat on the bottom of the tub next to him, her back to his feet, her fingertips lightly skirting over him as she looked skyward to the places where he was pointing. Soft music coming from somewhere off in the distance filtered up to them.

Jonathan's right hand was touching all of her that he could easily reach in the semi-darkness. Momentarily he was delighting in the soft curves of her breasts. He breathed a small sigh of contentment. As he did she rose up out of the water and kissed him on the lips. He crushed her to him feeling her breasts warm and wet against him. She slipped back into the heated water. The jets were gurgling in the background. Idly stroking her breasts with his right hand he took her right hand in his other hand and directed it downward toward himself. She fondled him and stroked him, then suddenly surprised him by leaning over to kiss him provoking a groan as she took him into her mouth. Under the stars as the waters of the pool surrounded them, they made love in the lava pool nature had, with its volcanic intensity, etched into existence.

Spent but happy, they crept back into the comfort of the giant antique bed seeing themselves reflected in the bank of mirrors opposite them. "Tomorrow, when I'm bathing in the Thinking Garden I will have special, secret thoughts of you," Hillary whispered to Jonathan dreamily.

"And I will think of you, my darling. For we each have a secret garden. Mine is a garden within a garden."

"Jonathan, this is my honeymoon." Hillary cried out impulsively. Jonathan tightened his grip around her delighting in what she might say next. "You know," she explained, "If I had married Adam, we would have been on our honeymoon and you and I would probably not have met. Does that mean this is now our honeymoon?" she giggled.

"By definition it's not a proper honeymoon unless the parties are married to one another first."

Hillary frowned. Putting her arms around him she lavished him with kisses again as she sighed, "Jonathan, you're so sweet." He basked in the abundance of her attention like a well-fed cat dozing in sleepy contentment beside a warm fire in winter. She cuddled up against him, soft and smooth, and irresistible.

She wriggled to get his attention. Her movements caused him to stir inside her. Aroused, he began to kiss her anew.

"Oh Jonathan," she said exuberantly, "Let's have a real honeymoon. Let's get married!"

With the pain of remembering his almost forgotten honeymoon of long ago, Jonathan shriveled.

"What's wrong?" Hillary pouted.

"I 'm going to tell you a story," began Jonathan. "And when I finish I want you to know from deep within your soul that there is nothing that will ever change the way I feel about you."

The time had come. Yes, regrettably the time had come for him to tell Hillary about his past. About his estranged wife, Esmee, and their son, Hamilton. He should have told her before, but he had been afraid, terrified of losing her and yet, he knew that he still might now.

Chapter 23

WITH EXPECTATION OF salvaging the sea chests they discovered near Hog Island, the McKenzies climbed into a motorboat and headed for Mosquito Bay on the other side of the peninsula. The sea was choppy out of the protection of Prickly Bay and waves and salt spray splashed over the bow of the boat dousing them as they battled the rough water. Once in the shelter of the cove protected by its offshore reefs, they made their way across smooth, calm seas towards the beach where they ran the whaler up onto the sand.

Climbing out of the boat they took a few minutes for a quick dip. Invigorated by a swim and once again refreshed after their bumpy noisy ride, they carried their belongings toward a large shade tree. "Don't' touch the tree, Jan, it's poisonous.

"The ficus?"

"It's a manchineel tree," Pete contradicted, "and its sap is like acid that can cause burns and blisters, even blindness if it gets into your eyes. As a matter of fact, just sitting under the tree when it is raining is hazardous because the raindrops falling through the leaves become toxic from having come into contact with the leaves."

"How do you know all this or are you making it up just to scare me?"

Pete laughed and shook his head. "There's a warning notice plastered to the bulletin board at the cottage as big as life. I just read it."

"Well," said Janet, "since I see nary a rain cloud, let's leave everything right where it is until we come back to collect it, okay?"

Pausing to chug-a-lug a drink of lemonade to quench the overpowering thirst he had acquired on the ride over, Pete dug through their totes for their snorkels, masks and fins. Spurred on by the titillating notion that they might find some sort of treasure, their enthusiasm and expectations were running very high. Following a grid pattern they diligently began combing the underwater area where they had last seen the three boxes.

"Hell," muttered Pete, "even if the boxes are filled with trash we'll at least have solved the mystery once and for all."

They searched for over an hour even in areas out of the scope of the grid in case tides or currents had moved the boxes. They found nothing. Disheartened and disillusioned they came to the disappointing conclusion that the boxes had been removed. The possibility of someone physically taking the boxes away prompted suppositions of an even greater mystery.

Reconsidering the theory that the chests had been trash and were swept out to sea, Pete analytically looked seaward at the rough surface chop. He continued his gaze across the coral reef and into the cove where the surface waters became calm.

"Damn!" he muttered, kicking a clump of sand. "Jan, those boxes couldn't have floated away. It would be impossible. Someone took them. I just know it."

"Do you think Todd had anything to do with their disappearance? He came on pretty strong about discouraging us."

Pete screwed up his face and reflected on Todd's negative attitude when they had discussed the boxes. He shrugged his shoulders. Grumbling he packed up for the ride back to Prickly Bay.

"I don't know, but Todd knows more than he's telling us. That's for sure."

Temporarily putting his disappointment aside, Pete set about finding the grotto and perhaps a lobster. As he rounded the headland coming into Prickly Bay he headed for the opposite shore along the peninsula. From sightings on the opposite cliff and a tree on the beach he had noted previously he tried to pinpoint the grotto location from the day before.

"Anything look familiar?"

"Vaguely, but I don't see the entrance if that's what you mean," said Janet.

"It should be right along here."

"I don't hear anything," said Janet as she listened for the sucking sound she heard yesterday as water flowed into the cave and was expelled.

"The tide is in. You may not hear it at all."

"Somehow it doesn't look right. It's different," said Janet.

Racking his brain to remember Pete suddenly brightened.

"You're right. There was some sort of vegetation."

Janet scowled as she looked at the blank rock face of the promontory.

"That's what the matter is. There was a cactus or something on the right side of the opening, remember?"

"Hey, that tree looks familiar," said Pete, as he moved closer. "Funny we didn't notice that formation before," he said pointing to an outcrop of lava.

"Probably too busy looking at the trees," giggled Janet. "Besides, you were hot on the trail of lobsters not cliffs."

"The grotto is to the left of that lava wall. That's rather an interesting formation in itself."

He studied it as if seeing it for the first time. A freestanding wall of lava rock in the foreground of the coastline created a natural screen standing apart from the headland. Guiding the boat to the end of it Pete could see that the sea flowed in and around it freely. Positioning the boat obliquely Pete could see a cave behind the baffle that totally obscured it. While he could not move the boat any closer without jeopardy of being drawn into the boulders by the wave action, Pete's interest was piqued. Grabbing his mask he slipped over the side of the gunnel after cautioning Janet not to get too close for fear she'd crash the boat on the rocks. Within moments of his foray to the other side of the wall he returned to the whaler.

"Take the boat away from here and pretend you're fishing or something. Come back for me in thirty minutes. I don't want you to be seen lingering here."

"What are you doing?"

"I'm going back. Hand me my bag of tools."

"What are you up to?"

"I'll explain later. Please, just do what I'm asking you and hurry." Taking his bag of tools, he submerged.

Pete carefully picked his way along the slippery algae-covered boulders approaching from leeward of the rock formation. Swirling water came up in frothy surges of heavy wave action rising up over the boulders and ebbing away in a rip tide effect leaving the rocks momentarily exposed. Timing the wave action he climbed through as the water ebbed leaving the rocks briefly visible. It took all his strength to hold his ground when the forward surge came and not to be pushed forward or dragged back on the ebb of the wave. Either way he'd be dashed against the boulders.

Once on the other side of the baffle he found a naturally formed shelf protected by the wall. With the force of the waves deflected, he was able to stand in front of the cave. To the left of him between the cave and the grotto, a cactus and a thornwood tree co-mingled in weather-beaten existence clinging side by side while serving to obscure the cave from the side traffic entering and exiting the mouth of the bay.

Storing his mask on his forehead to look around, he gave the cave a quick once over. Staring in stupefaction, he felt a bolt of lightening surge through him. Hidden behind a concealing screen of manchineel branches was a cache of boxes.

The cave was about fifteen feet wide and fairly deep. In front of it the immediate foreground was a result of rockslides and surface breakage with boulders extending out into the water to form a barrier. Approaching from the sea, a natural ledge on the right was under about a foot of water. Pete's mind, racing ahead, conceived it as a sort of loading area where a boat could come in right next to the area harboring the boxes. The boxes had been placed inside the cave and although some natural growth was present someone had taken extra care to camouflage them with boughs from a nearby manchineel tree.

Walking in front of the cactus growing at the edge of the cave Pete stepped down through the rocks into the water. Submerging he found the opening to the grotto and went up inside its shadowy interior. Surfacing within it he looked around him in the dimly lit cavern and seeing a patch of daylight beaming through the opening from the adjoining cave he went to the hole and put his face to it peering into the next chamber. He could see the piles of boxes clearly. He could also see beyond to the water.

Carrying the tool bag that weighed him down enough to sink easily, he started to exit the grotto when his heart almost stopped beating. A huge green moray eel almost seven feet long glided past him seemingly unconcerned as it slithered into its hole at the entrance of the grotto. Pete noted its home as he watched in fascination as the creature wound itself into the opening of its innocent-looking lair.

Returning to the cave behind the barrier of branches he contemplated opening the boxes. If he did, he had to do it in such a way that they would not appear to have been tampered with. Should he? He considered.

There were about a dozen chests of varying size, each stenciled with a number code and what appeared to be a color code as well. There were other identifying marks in Arabic. The chests looked identical to the ones he saw at Hog Island. There were 1A's, 2 B's, 3's, A's and B's. The writings in Arabic were particularly puzzling and his curiosity was getting the best of him.

Pete began unscrewing the hinges on one of the smaller boxes, a 1A. With the light from his underwater flashlight propped up against one of the boxes he pried the screws out of the hinges while he nervously listened for unexpected company.

The boxes in the cave were not resting in water but occasionally a surge of water swept up and around the edges of the shelf. He removed the hinges without too much difficulty. He came to the supreme moment—he was about to open the lid. He took a deep breath, one last cautious look around and then lifted the cover.

Dark blue plastic encased the contents. Pete pressed down on the plastic. The contents within felt solid, hard. He lifted the loose plastic material out of the box and found it was the excess on the top of a plastic bag. A metal clamp secured the contents. Prying the clamp apart he opened the bag. He was not at all prepared for what he saw and was momentarily stunned. Guns! The chest was filled with brand new handguns.

He guessed there were at least fifty Belgian-made nine-millimeter automatic Brownings. A goddamn arsenal he thought as his heart throbbed and his mind whirled. Puzzling over the ramifications he felt a chill of fear for the impending danger that the presence of such a vast stockpile of guns foretold.

The identifying number on the box was 1A. He replaced the metal clamp on the plastic bag, crimped it together, closed the box and began screwing the hinges back on. He was nervous and checked his watch. He had ten minutes before Janet was due back. He selected another box, a 2B. It was a larger box. Sliding it away from the other chests to allow more elbowroom he proceeded to open it.

Nervous and keyed-up he began to sweat. It was a cold sweat brought on by anxiety. Standing at the side of the baffle he could see a yacht leaving the bay and he had the ridiculous notion he was on display. In spite of his feelings of misgivings, his curiosity did not allow him to leave. He was driven to see the contents of the boxes for fear they too would disappear, as had the first three. He would not make the same mistake twice. And now, he had become more than idly curious to know the reason arms were being collected and secreted.

The contents of the second box were similarly packed in blue plastic coated with cosmolene, the lubricant used to protect weapons. Peeling the inner wrapping back with the same sense of dread he had experienced when confronted with the contents of the first box, he was not to be disappointed.

Individually packed as neatly as wine and lovingly cradled in a rack, were a dozen M16 American made rapid-fire assault rifles stacked in two tiers of six. Notably light-weight, approximately eight pounds with a full magazine, they were internationally recognized as deadly. Pete secured the plastic and resealed the box replacing it in its original position. Climbing up on a box he cautiously peered into the bay from behind the wall. There was no one in sight, not even Janet.

There was only one number three and he was almost afraid to look. He checked his watch noticing with some concern that his time was about up. He couldn't stop now—he had to know. Compelled to find out the worst, he drove himself, racing against time. The screws were coming out faster now that he had gotten the hang of it. Barely discernible in the distance he heard the whine of the boat motor as Janet approached. He hoped it was Janet. Horrible thought. He hurried with the last screw.

"Damn!" he mumbled as he dropped it. Clumsily he lifted off the cover and unclasped the band. Fumbling with the plastic he fairly tore it open. "Oh my God," he groaned, "HAND GRENADES."

Chapter 24

ETE'S TEMPLES WERE pounding, and his mouth was dry. He was pressed to move as quickly as he could. His mind whirled with unanswered questions as he labored to restore the boxes positioning them exactly where he had found them. He heard the noise of a motor growing louder as it approached.

Curiosity tugged at him as he glanced at the A's and B's unopened and unexplained. He was out of time. He had tarried here too long. To be conspicuously loitering at the opening of the cave would invite suspicion. Suddenly it hit him. He beamed. The A's and B's must be ammunition for the 1's and 2's. He hoped he was right because he wouldn't have time to find out

Hurriedly moving to the partially submerged 'loading' ledge he tumbled in over the side, submerged his tools and headed towards Janet in the boat. Reaching it he climbed in over the gunnel and lay on the bottom of the boat with what Janet called a 'stupid expression' on his face. He lay there quaking with exhilaration and apprehension.

"And yesterday you couldn't imagine why I had to come out because of the cold," chided Janet. "And now look at you. You look frozen." She was of course referring to yesterday when she had left the grotto chilled to the bone to return to the boat.

My God, he thought, she has no idea of what I've been doing. She probably thinks I've been exploring the grotto looking for lobster. His mind whirled. Should I tell her? No. He had to think it through alone first without any input from her. He had to work it out in his own mind. He was so charged up he couldn't think clearly let alone speak. Gratefully he felt a towel plop around his shoulders while he continued to sit in a state of bewilderment.

Deep in thought he didn't seem to hear Janet let alone respond to her as she tugged at his arm. She persisted, making him focus his attention overboard. There, swimming alongside the boat was a giant sea turtle heading out to sea. Curious, they followed it for as long as they could see it, but when it dove they lost it.

Grateful for the solitude, Pete did some heavy thinking with poor results as he pondered during the long stretch of silence. Suddenly finding the silence unnatural he checked Janet to see why she was being so quiet. Of course. He smiled. She was plugged into her Walkman listening to a tape.

Normally Janet and Pete had an understanding whereas on occasion if something was bothering either of them the other would tactfully wait until the troubled one was ready to discuss the matter. Although the arrangement had worked in the past, Pete felt that this was different. He could not remember ever having to struggle with a dilemma of the seriousness he was faced with at this very moment. He knew he had to tell Janet about his discovery but he couldn't bring himself to do it just yet.

He watched her as she headed back to the boatyard. She didn't seem to be taking his solitude as anything out of the ordinary, in fact, she was so preoccupied with her tape, she seemed oblivious to him and any problem he might be having. He was relieved because he knew what her reaction would be and he was not prepared to cope with her response. They returned to the cottage for a late lunch.

Later that afternoon when the fishermen arrived back on the beach the McKenzies walked over to examine their catch. Out of curiosity people always gathered around the incoming fishing boats to inspect, admire, or to buy. This time when Pete and Janet reached the fishing boat they were both completely taken off guard. Janet was absolutely stricken.

Amongst the catch of the day was a live Hawksbill sea turtle. Just as Janet was wondering whether it was 'their' turtle, one of the fishermen threw the giant amphibian to the sand on its back and swiftly and deftly slit its throat and hind legs. With its head elevated on the sand which sloped down to the water's edge, the turtle lay helpless and dying, its red blood spurting seaward as it dispersed into the water creating a frothy pink foam.

Rendered helpless, the huge bulk writhed in its final agonizing death throes while Janet tightening her grip on Pete's arm and in the fascination a horrible sight occasions, barely breathed as she watched.

"It's crying. I can see tears coming out of its eyes. Oh, how cruel." She shuddered and turned away very close to tears herself.

"You interested in bracelets, combs maybe, Mistress?" a fisherman inquired of Janet. "We polish and sell the shell whole or we can make nice jewelry?"

"No!" Janet exclaimed hotly, whirling around and glaring at the peddler. She was trembling and fairly shouted. "No!"

"The meat's a delicacy," another fisherman explained to Pete. "Only one third of the body weight is useable meat, the rest is waste."

Pete couldn't resist asking the obvious. "Where did you capture the turtle?"

One of the fishermen shrugged vacantly. Another responded. "Just beyond Prickly Bay."

Suddenly aware his arm had gone numb with Janet clinging to it, Pete took her hand and led her away from the dying creature. He was certain there would be nothing he would be able to say to Janet to convince her that this was not a bad omen.

Chapter 25

THE RED CRAB was a brightly illuminated oasis showing no effect of the power failure in L'ance aux Epines. As the McKenzies were seated at a candlelit table on the terrace, they could hear the piano tinkling gaily in the background. The familiar music made them feel instantly right at home. Griffon, acknowledged them from the bar and came over to join them carrying his drink. Greeting Janet with a cheery, "Hello beautiful," he reached out for Pete's hand, pumping it heartily. "Haven't seen you two in a while. What have you been up to?"

"Nothing much. Went to Hog Island today. Did a little snorkeling."

"From the looks of your tans I'd say you had a good time. Find anything good?"

Pete frowned and shrugged noncommittally.

"Nothing except sunburn, sore muscles, and a headache from overexposure," said Janet regarding Pete with sympathy. She decided not to mention his encounter with the moray.

"Sounds like a bummer," consoled Griffon. "You're supposed to be here having fun."

"We went out with Todd yesterday," said Pete.

"I hope he gets better reviews," Lester laughed as he waved goodbye to someone leaving. "Todd take you down?"

"No, Jan and I went alone. Todd doesn't dive, does he?" Pete asked almost as an afterthought.

"Doesn't dive? He used to be a frogman with the U. S. Navy. UDT." Noting Janet's puzzled expression Lester quickly added, "Underwater Demolition Team."

"I was beginning to wonder whether he could even swim," grumbled Pete in amazement.

"Well, well, well. Isn't he full of surprises? I wonder why he never told us," said Janet. "He told us everything else."

"I'm not surprised," said Lester. "It's typical of Todd though; he's a pretty private guy. Incidentally, I spoke with Doc Rutherford about the article on the medical school and he said it was okay with him if you want to do it."

Janet touched Pete's arm and sat poised, anxious to see his reaction.

"That's great," beamed Pete. "I appreciate the introduction, Lester. Thanks. For that bit of good news let me buy you a drink."

"I've got another tidbit for you." Lester smiled expansively. "They're having a party for the British Ambassador Saturday night. It's being held on one of the yachts. Don't be surprised to receive an invitation." Lester winked at Janet.

"For us?" She squealed in delight.

"Doc's doings. Figured if you wanted to write an article it wouldn't hurt to have a little background—meet some of the government people. The Prime Minister will undoubtedly be there too."

"Oh Lester, what fun! The Prime Minister and the ambassador!" With a typically female change of attitude she scowled conveying an expression of utter misery. "My God, whatever will I wear?"

"Women," said Pete, shaking his head mirthfully.

Janet stuck her tongue out at both of them in exasperation. Startled, the men broke into good-natured laughter.

"Don't worry about it, my dear," soothed Griffon. "Most of the people will be dressed rather casually. This is the tropics remember. The reason I'm telling you ahead of time is to give Pete a chance to do his homework. He'll want to be on top of the situation with a few facts here and there."

"Good thinking, Lester. I appreciate that."

"Before I get back to work I thought I might mention that I'm going into town early Saturday morning should you want a lift to the school. On the way back I can show you the airfield. You're welcome to come too, Janet."

"I think I'll spend a lazy day on the beach reading," said Janet smiling benignly at Lester while giving Pete a mischievous glance. Rolling her eyes heavenward and tilting her head coquettishly she added, "Or I may go shopping, or do my nails."

"Uh oh," said Lester. "You're in for it now, my boy."

"Oh my God," Pete sighed, "Shopping? Are you really? With all the clothes you brought?"

"Maybe," she said with a capricious toss of her head.

Just about then, Pete mimicking a feeble old man with no teeth saying, "Maybe…." he got caught at it by the waiter who gave him a strange look. Feeling totally foolish Pete cleared his throat and sat up in his chair to better hear the waiter recite the specials. Lester and Janet laughed loudly at his embarrassment.

"You ought to try the special," suggested Lester.

"Oh, what is it?" asked Pete.

"Turtle steak. Fresh today."

Janet groaned and shifted uncomfortably in her seat as Lester continued. "It has a good flavor, tastes rather like beef." Pete hesitated as Janet shot him a significant glance. "In years to come you won't see much of it," Lester continued, "so you should try it at least once."

"I suppose," said Pete. "What about you, Jan? What would you like?"

Janet struggling with the image of the slain turtle still fresh in her mind, glared at Pete reproachfully. She pointedly announced, "I'll have lobster." When Griffon left them Janet whirled on Pete. "How can you?"

He shrugged without replying. Suddenly he was 12 years old again.

"Well, say something!" Janet demanded.

"I was just curious," he offered lamely.

"Oh Pete. You were as upset as I was when you saw that turtle murdered on the beach and now you're going to eat it? For heaven's sake, how can you?"

"It's the same as if it were a cow or a pig or a lobster." He hoped she understood the point he was making.

She grimaced. "I suppose," she retorted grudgingly. "But it was heartbreaking to see."

"And I guess we don't usually get to see, do we?"

"I guess that's it," she sighed, letting the breath go completely out of her. "Personal involvement. I'm sorry honey, I wasn't trying to ruin your dinner," she said softly, "but giant turtles somehow seem…special. Maybe it's because of their antiquity. Oh, I don't know." Her voice trailed off. "Let's just forget it."

"If it's going to upset you that much I can still change my order. Want me to?"

"That's sweet. No, I'll be okay. But I appreciate you're offering to. Thanks." She reached over to pat his cheek.

During their dinner Pete couldn't help noticing two blacks sitting at the table next to them. An unusual pair, one of the men, his hair bleached to a reddish blond color and plaited into a multitude of thin braids all over his head, flashed a mouth full of teeth edged with gold. He wore a number of silver rings all over the fingers of both hands and Pete couldn't help noting that the index finger of the man's right hand was missing the first joint.

His companion, although less conspicuous was unusual as well, being distinguished by virtue of a scar across his right cheek proceeding across to his ear, apparently the result of a fight or accident. The lower part of his ear was missing where the scar would have continued. Ill-kempt and unsavory looking, the men had intrigued Pete because of their conversation.

From the fragments of patois Pete could decipher, the men were involved in carrying out some type of secret plan. Vehement about the correct approach, they expressed mild, if vocal, disagreement with one another. When they suddenly realized they had attracted Pete's interest they abruptly stopped talking and quickly moved away presumably to the bar inside to play darts. Their entertainment gone, the McKenszies enjoyed the remainder of their dinner without incident. They had a coconut ice for dessert and shortly afterwards they departed for their cottage.

Worn out from an exhausting day, the McKenzies returned home in relative silence. Since the power was still out in their cottage Pete and Janet strolled a little way along the beach, finally succumbing to the inviting comfort of the sun loungers bordering a pine grove. Settling into the chairs they stretched out to relax as they watched the anchored sailboats dance at their moorings.

All at once, from behind them in the darkness of the jungle fringing the beach, they overheard people talking. Immediately recognizing the voices Pete crept closer to listen. The voices were excited, agitated. It was the men from the Red Crab.

From what Pete could discern from the exchange, the men were arguing about something, a shipment of goods they were supposed to intercept. At a time to be specified later, they were to redistribute the contents of the shipment. They seemed to fear some sort of retribution if they were unsuccessful and there was a poignant urgency to their words. Taking into consideration the hour, the place and the circumstances, their behavior seemed definitely suspicious.

A couple came towards them along the water's edge. They were holding hands and the girl was laughing. Pete concealed himself against the trunk of a tree. The couple headed for the sun loungers but realizing Janet was lying there, they continued on. The two in the brush, hearing the pair on the beach stopped mid-phrase and when Pete scanned the brush where the shadowy figures had been standing, there was nothing. It was as though they had evaporated.

Pete and Janet went inside, undressed and went to bed. The electric power was still out and they tried to read by flashlight but it was futile. Janet fell asleep almost immediately, a victim of too much wine.

Pete was restless and wide-awake, thinking. He couldn't help but wonder about the conversation he had overheard at the Red Crab. He was sure it in some way tied in with his discovery of the arms, but how? The only real clue he had that could shed light on the mystery was Todd Murdock himself. Reviewing the events in his mind, he decided to do what he knew he must do all along; he would arrange to meet Todd Murdock alone. Finally he fell into a fitful sleep. When the power returned some time later, all the lights that had been left on suddenly blazed bright and the illumination from the lamp next to his bed shone across Pete's face like a beacon awakening him. Before turning it off, he looked at his watch—it was one fifteen.

Annoyed at being awakened, he padded to the bathroom, relieved himself and went back to bed. As he lay in the darkness settling down to sleep he heard a faint sound come through the still night air. There was no mistaking it. It was an airplane coming in for a landing.

Chapter 26

A T 9:30 ON Friday, the next morning, the taxi pulled up to the main office of the Victoria Island Yacht Service and Pete found his way to Todd's office. It was air-cooled, spacious and conveniently open to the marina. The office, doubling as an equipment holding area for parts ordered for yacht and boat owners, was cluttered with magazines, charts, advertisements and pieces of equipment with notes tacked on to them. The effect was disorderly and chaotic.

"How's it going?" Pete asked, shaking Todd's hand genially.

"Not bad," Todd responded smiling affably.

"I didn't know you were head man of the whole operation here," said Pete.

"The boatyard near you is my real pet. It's close to my home, but this is much more commercial. We handle everything here."

"Speaking of commerce, Jan and I are interested in an inter-island charter. Maybe you can help us plan it and arrange it?"

Casually glancing about, Pete continued speaking in a lower, barely audible confidential voice. "Todd, I've got to talk with you privately. It's important. Somewhere away from here where we'll be alone."

"Tonight?"

"Sorry, can't tonight," said Pete.

"Then why not come by the house Sunday night for a drink. We'll see if we can plan out a charter to your satisfaction." Someone had come into the office looking for an engine part. Todd scribbled out his address on a piece of paper and handed it to Pete.

"Bring Janet along. She'll particularly enjoy the sunset from the veranda at that time of evening. Around 5:30 okay?" Todd smiled his easy-going, crooked-toothed grin and shook Pete's hand as he saw him to the door.

Pete continued to be amazed at Todd's facility for seeming to take everything in stride as though every event no matter how unusual was treated as the most normal thing in the world. If Pete didn't know better he could easily be convinced that a serious thought never entered Todd's mind that would cause him the least concern let alone worry. And that would have been a big mistake.

Chapter 27

EARLY SATURDAY MORNING as planned, Pete McKenzie and Lester Griffon headed for Georgetown School of Medicine. It was market day and the ride to town was perilous as they avoided streams of pedestrians and farmers walking produce and livestock to the marketplace from all over the island. Just ahead of them a farmer led a shackled steer along behind him

"He'll slaughter it, drain it, cut it up and sell it on a first-come, first-serve basis right in the square itself. It'll be completely gone by noon," said Lester. Chuckling at Pete's reaction, Lester continued. "It doesn't seem sanitary but the people are clean and food is cooked and eaten long before it has an opportunity to become contaminated. Like the French, their way of life is built around day-to-day consumption. The women are particularly good cooks and accomplish wonders with the native spices."

"To that I can personally attest," acknowledged Pete with a knowing glance as he patted his stomach. "We've been eating foods I can't even pronounce."

Primed with talk of food they remembered they hadn't eaten breakfast and Griffon abruptly brought the car to a stop on the shoulder of the road. He returned from a bakery with a dozen fresh warm muffins. Handing Pete the bag, Griffon started up the engine and drove along toward their destination. The men continued their conversation as Pete passed out a muffin and took one himself.

"I'll drop you off and come back for you in a couple of hours. That should give you plenty of time," said Griffon. "Then we can pop over to the airstrip. It's on the way home." Pete nodded in agreement.

Rutherford's office was located on Grand Anse Beach. Griffon pulled up to the modest one-floor cement building and with Pete in tow, headed towards the doctor's office.

Dr. Herman Rutherford was a tall, soft-spoken man in his sixties with slightly long graying hair and a neat if somewhat disheveled appearance imbuing him with the comforting familiarity of a friendly country doctor. When he spoke he projected a decidedly informed professional image confirming, should there have been the slightest doubt, that he knew his business.

Their meeting was pleasantly cordial and while Rutherford veered away from idle conversation he listened attentively to Pete's proposal. Rutherford's decision to put the school's facilities at Pete's disposal was more than Pete could have hoped for. It was apparently Rutherford's logic that co-operation for the purpose of the article would foster a truer more accurate piece which would benefit both of them. Pete was therefore given the run of the school and a guide was to be provided whenever Pete should find one helpful.

"Pete, I ask only this," Rutherford was saying, "I'd like to see a final copy of your material before it's submitted to your editor. Not for censure, just for my own information." Pete readily agreed. "And, I'd appreciate your maintaining a low profile as to your project incurring minimal curiosity and interest from the students themselves so as to interfere as little as possible with the workings of the school and the studies of the students."

Pete found the requests more than reasonable and the men shook hands at the conclusion of their conversation. Pete felt he had made a friendly liaison with Rutherford should he run into difficulty. Little did he know...............

Chapter 28

Rick Benson, a second year medical student, started Pete's tour of the school in the basement giving Pete a general overview of normal operations. They passed through the receiving area, the refrigeration lockers, the laboratory and finally, the incineration room.

"We get twenty cadavers a term depending upon the size of the student body. Usually the corpses were indigents or were drawn from mental wards. The bodies come from the States or South American or even here in some cases. Cadavers are difficult to come by though and sometimes we are grateful for even an unorthodox acquisition. They're anxious to get rid of, we're anxious to receive."

"How do they arrive?"

"Most often by boat. They come in zippered heavy nylon-reinforced plastic bags. Sometimes they come in canvas body bags but that isn't as common. More expensive. The shipment is usually delayed for as long as six months before we receive the cadavers, but they're embalmed so that it doesn't matter very much if they're refrigerated." Rick made a face of disgust and held his nose. "They're kept under refrigeration here, just at freezing. Heat is the biggest factor in their deterioration. The fresher we can keep them, the easier it is for all of us."

"Where are they stored?"

"In these lockers," Rick explained, pulling out two drawers. "These units are refrigerated, but in case of a power failure, which is a frequent occurrence here, we have generators to assure a continuous thirty-two degrees. Actually, the cadavers are kept in surprisingly good condition."

To illustrate his point, Rick peeled back the protective green sheets which covered the bodies of the two corpses in the drawers. Seeing the bodies, Pete gasped involuntarily.

"My God!" he breathed. Stunned, he took hold of the edge of the drawer to steady himself.

"Mr. McKenzie, are you all right? Maybe you'd better sit down for a minute," said Rick with obvious concern. "you're white as a sheet." Pete took a deep breath to clear his head.

"It's ok, I'm all right," said Pete. "I just didn't expect...."

"Oh I'm sorry, we've become so hardened to it that I tend to forget that most people are unaccustomed to seeing cadavers. I have to remind myself of the terrible effect it has on people."

"I'm all right now," said Pete nervously shifting his weight from one foot to the other. "It was just the first shock of seeing them. I didn't expect..."

"Think nothing of it," sympathized Rick. "It happens all the time."

Still in shock and confusion Pete continued to study the faces of the deceased until, staring unseeing, he drifted into deep concentration. Gradually the faces before him blurred and swirled together. In his thoughts they became a tangle of reality and unreality, laced with impossibility. His shocked response was, of course, the result of recognition. There was no mistaking either of the dead men. Pete recognized both of them. They were unforgettable. Blacks, one with reddish plaited hair and silver rings on the fingers of both hands with a missing tip to a right index finger; the other, his face scarred, with an earlobe severed.

They were readily distinguishable, unfortunately for them, by everyone. Just hours ago they had been alive and drinking at the Red Crab and now, they were here, dead. For all intent and purpose they had been killed, disposed of, covered up. But by whom and why and with what connection at the school to so swiftly and efficiently absorb and conceal?

"Tell me, where did these two cadavers come from?"

"South America, I believe, but here, let me show you. We'll look it up. It'll give you a chance to see how 'Records' works. When a shipment of cadavers arrives a Bill of Lading accompanies it. We keep a permanent record of this logbook right here. See," said Rick. "They came from South America last week. See, the date's right there."

"Interesting," commented Pete, jutting out his chin, stroking it, concentrating. "May I see the book for a moment?"

Rich placed the logbook in front of Pete. He scanned the page. The log registered eight cadavers received. Under close scrutiny, however, the number eight gave telltale signs of having been altered, an error perhaps. He examined the Bill of Lading stapled to the page. It also confirmed eight cadavers of South American origin. The number eight on the Bill of Lading appeared to have been altered as well. Scanning the small hand-written entry at the side of the page though, Pete found what he was hoping for, a discrepancy. The deliveryman had made a notation when he had signed for the cadavers.

He had written a six with a circle around it contradicting the "corrected" eights written everywhere else.

"There seems to be a discrepancy here," said Pete casually.

Rick peered into the logbook. "Oh, that's Francis," said Rick as though that explained everything. "He transports the cadavers for us. He's extremely conscientious but I suspect he's illiterate. He's probably just got his numbers mixed up"

"You said earlier that the cadavers came from the States and South America. You also mentioned that you occasionally receive an odd one. What did you mean by that?" asked Pete seeming to be only mildly curious.

"It's strange you should ask about that. Actually there have been a few bodies that didn't seem to fit in. At least I didn't think so. Take these two for example. The other six cadavers are not in nearly as good condition as these two and yet, these two haven't even been embalmed. And they're usually blank—no jewelry, no clothes, nothing. I find these two stick out as out-of-the-norm of what we usually get, but as cadavers are extremely hard to come by, no one would ever complain. We're grateful for every one."

"I suppose," said Pete.

They took a walking tour of the classrooms, the library, and the laboratory and ending on a positive note, Rick brought Pete back to the main entrance. Lots of unanswered questions, thought Pete. And finding out as much as he had been learning in such a short time, came the sudden realization he and Janet might know too much.

The two new cadavers knew more than was good for them and look where they ended up.

As far as Pete was concerned, this latest development—his discovery of the two dead bodies—couldn't be swept under the table. A chance conversation overheard in the Red Crab, two blacks planning to carry out a political scheme, and now barely twelve hours after he first saw them, they turn up dead, murdered.

With all the unrest recently, the dead men wouldn't even be declared missing as their friends and families would probably only think they had left the island. And the paperwork cover-up? And the unfinished airstrip with planes landing and taking off? What did it all mean? And Todd. Pete had almost forgotten about him. A former U.D.T. man who kept trying to cover up Pete's findings and had tried to warn him away. There was quite a pot brewing here all right.

Chapter 29

A S PETE SAT on the school steps waiting, a Minimoke roared up, Bimini top fluttering in the breeze, Griffon at the wheel. "All set?" Lester inquired as Pete made his move toward the vehicle. "How did you make out with your interview?"

"I can do the article if I want," said Pete as he swung his lanky frame into the Moke.

"Good, and how did you get on with the old man?"

"Not bad. I certainly can't complain. He was very generous."

"He'll be at the shin-dig tonight. It's just as well you got a chance to meet one another. Got some good material for the article?"

"So far so good," Pete smiled noncommittally.

"It's still early," said Griffon looking at his watch. "Do you still want to see the airport? We've got time."

"Sure," said Pete with a groan as they slammed into a series of ruts.

The airport runway loomed ahead, 9,000 feet long and 150 feet wide not counting two twenty-five foot wide shoulders. The skeletal shell of the terminal building was already underway with its auxiliary aircraft parking, a private VIP hanger, and an area for the Prime Minister's private plane.

"Technicians representing English and Finnish companies are installing electrical, navigational and communications equipment," said Lester.

On the way they had passed some long buildings which Pete had silently observed were being guarded by trained attack dogs behind barbed wire fences. "Parts storage," had been Lester's only comment.

A mini city of long, tin-roofed huts barracking Cuban engineers, technicians and advisors, 500 in all, seemed quietly deserted in the heat of the morning while soft Spanish music gave a friendly atmosphere to the area.

Pete surveyed the project. It was a vast undertaking. Months of work had stretched into years, but the results were amazing. Mountains had been carved away and removed, salt marshes had been filled in, and valleys built up as the work force relentlessly worked to tame the jungle wilderness and unpredictable seas in order to make the land conform to the needs and architectural ideas of those in charge.

As they rode through the area Pete saw Russian made Kraz 10-ton, ten-wheel dump trucks and other Russian-made heavy-duty equipment. Seeing the trucks caused Pete to reflect on the gossip he had heard regarding the Russians themselves.

The Russian diplomats on the island, while driving Mercedes and living in luxury homes and buying only the best items at the supermarket, had the reputation of being very cheap with their dollars (US dollars, incidentally, no EC currency for them, even though they lost out in each currency exchange not carried out in the bank). They were outright stingy as they haggled with the beach vendors marketing simple wares at pitifully low prices to begin with.

The Russians lived very well indeed and that fact left them open to criticism because of it because it was contrary to the political philosophy they espoused. Under communism everyone was supposedly equal. They had not endeared themselves to the locals because of their miserly bargaining practices and contradictory living habits. Politics do indeed make for strange bedfellows, Pete reflected.

They came to the runway which was impressive, vast and incomplete. It was dotted with empty steel oil drums necessitating the Minimoke to veer around each one as if negotiating a course in a downhill ski run. Going from opening to opening they traversed the landing strip. The reason for the obstacles Pete was told was to keep unwanted planes away, to prevent them from landing. Pete reflected to himself, at least unauthorized planes.

Chapter 30

"HERE, NOW DO me," said Janet passing Pete the soap. He began to lather her up while she stood face raised to the showerhead, eyes closed, allowing the water to pour over her.

"Come out of the water a little," Pete directed, changing places with her and taking the force of the shower spray over him. He proceeded to lather Janet into a sudsy, whipped-cream state. Blithely she submitted to the sensations accompanying his scrub down. He was thorough and didn't seem to miss a spot.

"Hmm, that feels good," she sighed.

"You feel good." He pulled her all slithery and slippery against him and kissed her. They were under a deluge of water from the shower spray which washed over them carrying Janet's foaming white veil of suds down the drain. The intimate familiarity of bodily contact had stimulated them. "I love making love to you," he breathed into her ear as he worked his way to her mouth. He slid his open mouth across her face cool and wet from the droplets of the shower spray.

"I wish we didn't have to go just yet," she whispered nibbling his ear. "Maybe we could be a little late," she eyed him impishly.

"Hmmm," he groaned as he seemed to think about it. "Later," he said with finality.

"Oh piffle. I guess I know where I stand." She abruptly exited the shower leaving Pete standing there covered in soapsuds, her soapsuds. Looking back at him she suppressed a mischievous giggle.

While they were getting dressed for the ambassador's party their conversation turned serious. Having thought everything through, Pete was now ready to hear Janet's input before making his decision. He had confided in her and now he braced himself for her response.

Unmindful of her nakedness Janet leaned forward to dry her hair with a blow drier. Pete was sprawled across the bed waiting for her to speak. He could feel the chill wind of her disapproval approaching on the horizon. He knew from experience that when it hit it would be with the fury of a cyclone.

"Well, what are you going to do?" Janet began calmly, her lips pinched into a tight suggestion of irritation.

"I honestly don't know," Pete answered, closing his eyes as he lay back across the bed in a state of confusion.

"What are you out to prove anyway?" Janet asked, suddenly angry. "Can't you just mind your own business and stay out of it? Why are you involving yourself, us, as a matter of fact? This was supposed to be our delayed honeymoon. Frankly, this is not even my idea of a vacation anymore. Besides, from what you're telling me, we could be in mortal danger. Why do you insist on doing this anyway?"

"Jan, we're just discussing it." He sighed in exasperation. "I haven't done anything yet."

"Except keep secrets from me, for one." The look of hurt in her eyes was unmistakable. "Spending all your time with all these men instead of with me."

"Jan," he coaxed, "come on." He tried to soften her, make her understand, but in his heart he knew she understood him all too well. She knew better than anyone else what made him tick. For her to adjust to it was another matter. Pete had an undeniably inquisitive mind. It was inherent in his personality. While he didn't seek out adventure for adventure's sake, if in the course of events he was carried into one, he couldn't, wouldn't shun it. Janet's ability to accept this attitude was for her a bitter pill to swallow. Conservative, predictable, she was not one to take chances without a compelling reason. He admitted his actions would be difficult for most wives to accept although he hadn't really thought about it.

"I know how you operate, Pete," Janet lashed out at him, vehemently throwing her towel down on the bed. "And I know you're already involved more than you'd like to admit even to yourself."

Remaining silent, Pete scowled. She was right, damn it.

"Don't you realize what has been happening? First you're with Todd, and then you're with Lester, then Todd again. For a man supposedly on his honeymoon, I'm surprised you have time to be with me at all. Oh, and I forgot," she added sarcastically, "duty even calls you to this party. If it weren't for the people you expect to see at this party you wouldn't even be interested in going. You'd probably have begged off to stay home and screw. And that wouldn't be the first time. For you not to cut and run tells me you are in deep. Oh Pete......." She relented and put her hands on his arms and looked up at him. "Don't you understand? I love you and I'm worried. You're taking unnecessary chances with us, yes us, and with our lives. I don't want anything to happen to you or to us. Whatever is going on here isn't our problem. Besides, whatever it is can't be changed in a couple of days."

"Jan, you're getting all worked up for nothing. There's nothing to worry about." Her eyes focused on him shrewdly. She seemed to want his reassurance and the fact that he was offering none seemed to confirm her fears.

"You've discovered enough weapons to supply an army and you tell me there is nothing to worry about? I am not a fool Pete. Before you leave this room I want to know what you plan to do. Unfortunately, as your wife, your plans include me. I have a right to know what's going on. Be fair."

"Jan, I haven't got a plan." Suddenly he seemed totally deflated. "I'm going to talk to Todd on Sunday before I do anything. Give me till then." He looked very disheartened as he put his arms around her. Still preoccupied, he checked his watch for the time behind her back so that she didn't notice.

Clinging to him as though for refuge she moaned, "Oh Pete, what are we going to do? I can't seem to reach you."

Gently pulling himself away, he tapped her thighs in a gesture intended to hurry her along. "Tonight's a night for fun. But, we've got to get moving. Come on now, get beautiful and let's put a little hustle into it or we'll be late."

She didn't move. She just kept staring straight ahead.

He kissed her to reassure her. "Come on, don't worry, I'll be careful," he smiled. His face had an earnest quality, serious and idealistic, just like a Boy Scout. He was innocent and duty-bound. She bristled at his words and pursed her lips. She knew what his decision was going to be even if he didn't.

Chapter 31

THE MEKENZIES WERE ferried by motor launch from the boatyard pier to the gleaming yacht, Isabella, which was anchored in the center of Prickly Bay. Once aboard, they were greeted and taken personally by Dr. Rutherford to be properly presented to their hosts, the British ambassador and his wife, Margot.

The gathering included a distinguished company of cabinet ministers, diplomats, project heads, architects, UN representatives, bank officials and local professional people.

Circulating amongst the guests, immaculately uniformed stewards offered goblets of champagne from silver trays while at the same time they directed guests to a long table laid with spotless white napery on which was spread a sumptuous selection of imported hors d'œuvres. As the party progressed and as everyone began to get better acquainted, the cocktail chatter grew louder and more animated.

Just after six, as the sun was setting in a magnificent display of color, Sir Jonathan Ward, the Prime Minister, boarded causing a mild sensation of whispers and nudges and knowing glances all around as he entered with Hillary Warren on his arm. Perfunctorily greeting the ambassador and his wife and introducing Miss Warren, he went on through the ranks of ministers, diplomats, and honored guests finally coming to his father, Cecil Ward, a tall distinguished, elegant-looking gentleman in his own right.

From the moment of Jonathan Ward's arrival a transformation occurred on board the ship. It was unmistakable. As though a pilgrimage were in progress people flocked in his direction to speak with him, to touch him, hear him, see him, and for those too shy, to be near him perhaps 'accidentally' touching him. Yet, the man seemed to understand and comply, respectfully accommodating each person who wished a brief moment of contact with him.

To be truthful Pete was not impervious to the magnetism surrounding Jonathan Ward. He was strongly aware of it himself, sensing the electricity, the aura. Undeniably the man had charisma.

Quietly observing the proceedings from the sidelines, Pete made the rounds of cocktail chatter with Dr. Rutherford, a Cuban architect, a project coordinator for the airport and a United Nations advisor on Resource and Development. The guests, many of them international people, proved to be an interesting, heady assemblage of bright, talented people.

Watching these elite socializing and doing business, Pete couldn't help but be reminded that Victoria Island, in the painful throes of changing its destiny, was being charted by this very group. It was at that moment of realization that Pete knew that he too must make contact with Jonathan Ward, but for a reason none of the others would probably suspect. Pete felt compelled to warn the Prime Minister he was in danger of being murdered.

By warning Jonathan Ward, Pete would in effect be joining him, placing himself in grave danger as well. Lest he have any doubt as to the gravity of his decision, he had only to reflect upon the two dead men in the school morgue. Guiltily, he looked across the saloon at Janet. Had he subconsciously known his decision all along?

Oblivious to his attention Janet was caught up in conversation with Hillary Warren and Hamilton Ward, Jonathan's son. Hillary was quite a looker, thought Pete as he studied her. Softly elegant in silky white evening pajamas she exuded a classic simplicity and style. Judging from the way young Hamilton was looking at her, her appeal had not escaped his attention either. On very friendly terms, they obviously knew one another well. Actually Pete remembered hearing they had been at school together in England although at the time, neither of them knew one another well enough to realize they had a common link to the island. They were a striking couple. As Jonathan joined them, Pete was astonished by the remarkable father-son similarity of their appearance. In West Indian elite society, the man, often light-skinned to begin with, will wed a Caucasian woman, usually a natural blonde. On the basis of that premise, with their combined good looks, should Hillary and Jonathan wed, they would have beautiful fair children.

Chapter 32

JONATHAN WARD WAS born into a well-to-do family of landowners. Definitely of the ruling class, he had been schooled in England where he had been guided into politics out of a family philosophy of inherited responsibility. Father and son, both charming and charismatic, were very popular with the people and it was readily apparent why.

Pete glanced over at Janet and realized with some degree of pride that she could certainly hold her own in the looks department. She was bright too. Guiltily he remembered their passionate verbal exchange and reflected upon Janet's apprehension about his involving them. He also recalled he had told her he wouldn't make any decisions until tomorrow. He had begged more time and yet, here he was, about to make his move without even saying anything to Janet about it.

He would wait. There was still time. He would wait until Sunday. Janet was right. He shouldn't get involved. Certainly he had no right to put her at risk. And yet, emotionally, Pete knew he was involved deeper than he cared to admit.

Janet, pleading with him, had asked him how he could expose them both to the danger and the life-threatening forces of a revolution. But was he? And just how far did he have to extend himself?

Although Pete argued with himself using every logical rational he could think of, the stubborn seed of righteousness within him would not die. Finally, with his jaw set into the hardness of steel, he knew what he must do. He must save Victoria Island from communism.

Pete McKenzie was a risk-taker by nature. He was also idealistic and what he thought he perceived to be happening on Victoria Island would be history in the making. He felt privileged to recognize the events being laid out before him, to see them coming, recognize them, watch them unfold, be part of them and if he chose, to alter their outcome. He must take action.

Victoria Island's rapid development by questionable world powers spelled trouble. He recognized the same faltering steps taken by the United States hundreds of years ago. They were repeating themselves now, here. With a sense of nostalgia for the past, Pete viewed his involvement in Victoria' Island's future as an historical opportunity to be instrumental in the nation's development. It also gave him a chance to further a journalistic career that would get him out of a boring job and back into the active, exciting lifestyle he had thrived on and missed.

Pete recognized Lester Griffon across the room. He was in a discussion with the Prime Minister. In the course of their conversation they were facing in Pete's direction.

Pete signaled Lester hopeful that Griffon's inclination toward congeniality would earn him an invitation. Lester, as Pete had hoped he would, beckoned him toward them to formally introduce Pete to the Prime Minister. This was the opportunity Pete needed. He had to think fast to make the most of it. He was certain it would be his only chance.

Almost immediately after Lester had introduced them, Pete feigned an accident and spilled an entire drink down the front of Lester's shirt causing him to rush away to attend to himself. Properly contrite in the brief embarrassing moment that followed, Pete established eye contact with the Prime Minister and in an unhurried manner designed not to attract unwanted attention, he said, "Sir, I must speak with you privately. It's a matter of the utmost gravity. I know of a planned attack on you."

Jonathan Ward eyed Pete with curiosity, hesitated briefly in appraisal of his physical and mental rationale while he continued to smile pleasantly as a waiter passed between them with a platter of hors d'oeuvres. The men regarded one another in silence.

"So, Mr. McKenzie, you were saying your business is?"

"I'm a pilot and free-lance writer. Did you not hear me, Sir?" Pete's eyes searched Ward's face. Could he be hard of hearing, Pete wondered.

"Yes." Ward responded simply. "So, you're interested in antiques. That's a hobby of mine as well. I've acquired something quite extraordinary I'd like to show you. From one connoisseur to another. Come…"

Smooth, thought Pete, smooth as silk. He followed Ward down a companionway to the rear of the ship, below deck to the master stateroom. Once inside the spacious quarters the Prime Minister locked the door and turned on the stereo. Background music softly filtered through the room. Casually, Ward gestured toward a comfortable chair and smiled. "Mr. McKenzie, what's on your mind?"

"At great personal risk to my wife and myself, I've come to tell you that someone has assembled a cache of arms and ammunition for the purpose of overthrowing you and your government." He hesitated. "Unless you yourself have amassed the arms," he added as an afterthought, "I thought you should know."

The Prime Minister smiled benignly. "A plot has been suspected for some time. I haven't been able to uncover it. Please Mr. McKenzie, Pete, tell me what you know. You do me an invaluable service." Ward smiled affably.

Pete was impressed. Cool, he thought, and a true politician. Scared shitless and he's still smooth as silk. Ward took out a small pad and took notes as Pete recounted the bizarre chain of events. When Pete had finished giving the details of his information to the Prime Minister, Jonathan Ward sat in undisguised puzzlement.

"What do you propose to do?" asked Pete.

"I don't know. What do you suggest?"

"Me? Are you serious?"

"Of course I'm serious. You know more than I do at this point."

"I can't believe you didn't know."

"I'm a simple man, Mr. McKenzie. I confess that I lack sophistication in these matters. I certainly don't have your curiosity or the means of getting around in relative anonymity."

"You're asking for my help?"

"I have no right to ask for your help, technically, morally, or under any circumstances." He smiled and shrugged with a gesture of hopelessness. "But, if it should be offered…"

"I can't go into this blindly," said Pete. "This is serious business."

"I'll give you a brief rundown. A coup is being planned to depose me in favor of a new Prime Minister, a prominent local leader."

"Why?"

"It's apparently been decided that I'm an obstacle to the Island's aims. The new man's ideals are supposedly more in keeping with the Island's plans for the future. You understand politics, Pete. Power, greed, money? They want to arm the island militarily. That is completely opposed to my national objectives—to what I've been striving for all my life. They want to use Victoria Island because of its strategic position in the Caribbean. As you know we are less than 100 miles off the coast of Venezuela in a deep-water channel through which tankers carrying 56% of all U.S. imported oil enters the Caribbean. Soviet MIG-23's— of which three squadrons are based in Cuba— striking from Victoria Island could wreak havoc on nearby oil refineries, transshipment terminals, and tanker lanes. According to their thinking the new airfield would facilitate Cuban troop shuttles across the South Atlantic to Angola and Ethiopia. Soviet munitions could then be routed without detection directly to trouble spots. Moscow already has landing rights to Soviet TU-95 long-range reconnaissance aircraft. They also want to capitalize on Victoria Island's vote at the international organizations— the U.N., O.A.S., and the Non-Align Countries Organizations. They know exactly where I stand and have indulged me so far, but we've reached an impasse. As they view it, I've become an embarrassment inhibiting their progress."

"If we break this plot couldn't they simply repeat the attempt at a later time?"

"If I can get to the point where the airport is completed and tourists begin coming in full force, it would be too controversial for them to act against us militarily or otherwise."

"Will they go so far as to kill you?"

"Without question."

"It's the Cubans then?"

"They're merely the implements. In reality it's the power behind the throne."

"The Russians?" Ward nodded somberly.

"Who have they chosen to take your place?"

"Clarence Charles, one of my ministers."

"If.... something should go wrong? Who would you want as your successor?"

"Should I need one, it would be Cecil Ward, my father. He's been in government all his life, knows the people, the ideals of the country. He's retired but he would know what to do. I've kept him current. And then there is my son, Hamilton."

"Apparently they're moving towards a target date. To confiscate their arms and ammunition would only mean more would be brought in. There might even be another cache hidden somewhere else. To be successful, you've got to outmaneuver them," said Pete.

"They need arms for about 500 men."

"Could they get men here that quickly?"

"They're here. The airport workers are all trained military men."

"Jesus! They've covered everything." Pete began pacing. "If we could discover their plan. But, whether we do or not, we must wipe out their stockpile of arms. They should feel confident it's here but ..."

"We, Mr. McKenzie?"

Pete smiled. His mind in gear, his imagination fired, he had leaped into the air, caught the pass and suddenly he was running with the ball.

"What do you propose we do, blow up the ammunition?" asked the Prime Minister.

"On the contrary, let them see their stockpile, rely on it. But when they go to use it, let it be worthless."

"Worthless? You mean sabotage?"

"Sort of."

"Will you need help? Men?"

"I'll need one man. Frankly I don't know if I can trust your men. One loose word and it'd be curtains for all of us. Since it's my life that'll be hanging in the balance, I want someone I know I can trust." Seeing the look of disappointment in Ward's eyes, Pete added quickly. "It's nothing personal. I've already got someone in mind."

"Who?"

"He's the best in the business. The trouble is he doesn't know he's on the team yet."

Chapter 33

I N THE WEST Indies that time just around sunset is loveliest. The sun, retreating in a fiery ball of gold, hangs as if suspended against silver blue clouds and violet hills to radiate a myriad of luscious hues. As its glow sweeps heavenward it illuminates the sky with vibrant color reflecting luminous on the water's surface. Shimmering violets suffused with orange dapple the sea and stretch toward shore to glow pink on the wet sand beach. The air, pungent with the smell of salt, is cool and fresh, soft against hot suntanned skin. Sunset is the perfect time of day for quiet conversation, favorite drinks and plantain chips served on the veranda as a prelude to dinner.

Pete and Janet walked to the point of land at the end of the peninsula. The awesome sight of the waves crashing against the coastline was a spectacle they never seemed to tire of. In fact, they seemed fortified by it. They started back. It was getting late and Todd would be expecting them.

The great house was set high on a promontory with a commanding view of Prickly Bay. Once opulent, the mansion had fallen into disrepair. Overgrown with foliage and badly in need of paint, the great house still maintained an attitude of hauteur, which seemed to allude to the nostalgia of the past with its unspoken history whispering through the trees.

The McKenzies paused at the signpost, number forty-seven, the address Todd had written down for them. Walking along the drive they were held at bay by a barking dog that had darted out from beneath the porch. A door opened and, hearing the commotion, a male voice called out, first to subdue the dog, and then in welcome to them. It was Todd.

"Down boy, down…" Todd commanded and then, pleasantly, "Good evening." His relaxed manner served to neutralize the animal's aggressive behavior and it obediently retreated flopping under the shade of a large flamboyant tree.

"Sorry my wife's not here, she's in Trinidad visiting relatives," Todd apologized as the McKenzies trailed along behind him through the dreary high-ceilinged main room to the west veranda. A breathtaking view of the yachts moored in the bay below them captured their immediate attention and made the dreary surroundings fade into the background. On the very top of the hill the atmosphere was serenely quiet.

"What can I offer you?" asked Todd pointing to a makeshift bar set up on a side table of the veranda. Settling on a Carib and a shandy Pete and Janet made themselves comfortable on the settee. Todd took his favorite seat, a straight-backed chair, which he proceeded to tilt against the wall, balancing it on two legs. Sitting precariously with his head against the wall, he set his beer down on the floor.

"What can I do for you?" He smiled genially.

"You can help us," said Pete tersely.

"Sounds serious."

"It is."

"Okay, shoot."

Pete stared at Todd for a moment without speaking.

"Tell me what you know about the boxes we saw at Hog Island."

"The treasures?" said Todd definitely poking fun at Pete as he smiled his usual broad-toothed grin.

So, he was going to play cat and mouse.

"Murdock, please don't be cute. Something important is about to go down here and whether I like it or not, I'm being carried into it. I want to know what the hell is going on."

"Pete, I've tried to tell you before, the boxes aren't anything. They're probably trash. Happens all the time. Forget about them. For heaven's sake, don't ruin your vacation fretting over them."

"Did you know that the boxes we found at Hog Island are gone?"

"No, but it wouldn't surprise me."

"Well, they are. And, furthermore, they are not scuttled trash. And, more to the point, you knew that all along, didn't you?" Discerning no visible reaction from Todd, Pete continued. His expression was severe with a glint of steel in his eyes. "Get one thing straight Todd, I mean to find out what's going on here. It would make life a lot easier for both of us if you'd level with me, but if you won't," he shrugged, "I'll poke around on my own. The only problem with that is that in the process I may inadvertently make a mess out of something very important. Something I feel in some way is going to affect you."

"Why do you feel compelled to poke around at all?"

"One, there's a story here. Two, I'd like to break it. In addition, I have a personal reason. It has to do with history, patriotism, whatever. I feel there's a lot at stake here, and when the dust settles, I'd like to think I've been helpful to my country."

"And what about you?" Todd abruptly focused his attention upon Janet who was quietly sitting at the sidelines looking rather uncomfortable and apprehensive.

"Whatever Pete wants to do, I'll go along with."

"Okay. Tell me what you know and what you want to know."

"I know the boxes are gone from Hog Island. I also know where they are." Watching Todd's facial expression Pete thought he detected a glimmer of interest at this last bit of information. He continued.

"We were having dinner at the Red Crab on Friday night when we overheard two men talking. When they noticed my interest in their conversation, they suddenly seemed concerned about being overheard and they left."

"Later that evening we were sitting on the beach when we overheard them again. They were on the vacant lot near to us. I couldn't fully understand them, but it seemed to me they were working on some sort of plot to knock off the Prime Minister."

"When by chance a couple came walking along the beach the men got spooked and took off. The very next morning, Saturday, when I went into the medical school for an interview and to gather information for an article I was writing, guess what I found?"

Todd shrugged.

"The same two men I had overheard in the Red Crab and on the beach. They were dead, on a slab in the school morgue. They were being passed off as medical school pathology cadavers."

"Jesus!"

"My sentiments exactly," Pete chimed in.

"They aren't wasting any time," said Todd. He got up and began pacing the floor.

"Whoever moved the boxes from Hog Island may have done so because they knew that Jan and I saw them or they may have relocated them because they're ready to make their move."

"Do you know what's in the boxes?"

"I do now," said Pete. "What I don't know is why they're stashed where they are or who put them where they are."

Todd's expression was grave. "The boxes are a stockpile of arms and ammunition for a revolution—a coup against Jonathan Ward.

"By whom?"

"It's communist inspired."

"I thought Ward was a communist."

"Not really. He's been walking a fine line. Ward is not the government's number one man any more. With the airport about to be completed, Ward has outlived his usefulness. Up until the present he's projected the type of image they wanted the world to see while they worked to complete the airport. But now, they don't want him. He's too moderate. In military terms, he's become expendable."

"So they are planning a take-over?"

"Yes, but they don't want it to be obvious. While they want a man of their own choosing in power to run the island, they want the changeover to be done smoothly, subtlety. The island's business is to continue as usual while the Reds lay the groundwork for a military base. They would then be free to orchestrate subversive activities from behind the scenes."

"What's the United States government doing about all this?"

"Watching and waiting."

"And at this point you are the United States government?"

Todd grinned. "I'm a United States citizen, and as far as anyone is concerned I'm here as a private individual. The local government knows nothing other than that."

"What's going to happen now?"

"I don't know whether or not he realizes it, but the Prime Minister is in serious jeopardy. My concern is that the United States needs him right where he is. He's holding everything in check. For as long as he can do that, we're glad he's in power. But the Reds are getting ready to make their move. And, when they do, he's a dead man. And," continued Todd looking extremely grave, "if they even suspect that we're involved, we'll be marked men as well."

"How do you communicate with our people?"

"That's been a problem, particularly lately. Can't trust the telephone or the mail. I've been in touch mainly when I'm out of the country. In a real emergency I can fall back on my radio transmitter, it can reach anywhere in the world. At the moment though, everything is quiet, too quiet. I've been watching and waiting but my gut reaction is that the situation is rapidly becoming desperate. Confidentially, that's why my wife and family are in Trinidad. I sent them there."

"What are you supposed to do now?"

"Keep an eye on Ward."

"Doesn't he know what's happening?"

"I can't tell him anything. He's got his own grapevine."

Suddenly thoughtful Pete asked, "Who killed the two men I saw at the Red Crab?"

"Could be either side, but the PRB (People's Red Brigade) was probably responsible.

"Clarence Charles, Ward's replacement, had them killed?"

"It's hard to say. The PRB members are supposedly his own forces but in reality the Reds have infiltrated them. It's impossible to know who is loyal to him and who is not."

"I spoke with Ward the night of the party. He said he didn't know anything about their being killed. I believe him."

"From your description the men were inept. By calling attention to themselves and the project they showed themselves to be very unprofessional. The Soviets detest inefficiency. If for no other reason than to show their disapproval they would have eliminated them."

"The killer must have some connection with the school in order for the school to absorb the bodies overnight."

"He or they might even be working at the school."

"How bad does it have to get before you step in?"

"It's pretty close now. To be openly talking about eradicating Ward, to be discussing distribution of the arms..."

"There's one more thing."

Todd looked up expectantly. "Go on."

"Do you remember when you took us looking for lobsters at the mouth of Prickly Bay?"

"Yes."

"Well, there's a hidden cave there. I went in to get a closer look." Pete's face fairly glowed.

Todd grinned back. "And?"

Pete smiled with self-satisfaction. "There is a secret cache of chests stowed in a network of underground caves.

"Did you get inside this time?" Todd asked incredulously.

"Wasn't going to make the same mistake twice."

"And?"

"You were right. Arms and ammunition. Belgian-made nine millimeter automatic Browning hand-guns, American-made M-16 rapid-fire assault rifles, hand grenades and, although I didn't open them, boxes of ammunition for the rest."

"Well, I'll be damned!"

"You didn't know?"

"I knew something was coming off but I didn't know there was a stockpile."

"Now that you do know, what do you propose to do about it?"

"Obviously I can't tell you, can I?"

"You son of a bitch! I didn't have to tell you any of what I found out."

"No, you didn't. But you have, haven't you?" Gently Todd added, "Let us work with the information, Pete. Best you and Janet keep out of harm's way."

"Well then, I'll also tell you this. I'm throwing in with Ward. I had hoped you and I could work together."

"Are you crazy?"

"Maybe, maybe not. But the reality is that your objective is the same as mine. I would have thought your main interest would be to get the job done." Pete was putting the squeeze on Murdock and Murdock knew it.

"I don't think you realize what you're asking. As far as anyone else is concerned, whether we live or die is inconsequential. We are insignificant. But even more to the point, because of your lack of experience, you threaten the life of everyone connected with the project." Pete sat mute. He was unmoved by Todd's realistic assessment.

"You've put me in a position where I have to take you in. You'd be more dangerous to the operation left on your own. Another option is to kill you—a diving mishap, a car accident, it happens all the time. But, fortunately for you, I am short-handed. It's too late and too obvious to bring in someone new. I guess whether I like it or not, you're it. As for Janet, send her home, this is not a woman's business."

Janet was stunned at her off-handed dismissal. Furious, she was afraid of what Pete would answer. Before he could say anything, she defiantly announced, "I'm staying. Pete, if you try to make me leave, you'll have to come with me."

"Girl, why don't you just go home? You don't realize what you're getting yourself into."

"If Pete is doing this, then I'm staying too."

"Oh God, when she gets that look she never changes her mind"

"Shit," said Todd as he spat over the porch railing. "I hate working with women. They're a real pain in the ass."

"As long as we know where we stand with one another," Jan fired back.

"Terrific, we're fighting amongst ourselves already," said Pete sarcastically.

"There will be no time for that," said Todd sternly. "We'll either have to pull together or we'll all go down. And it won't be just us, you know. The whole project will fail. Remember that. And there's no assurance we won't go down anyway—America, this little island everyone is coveting, Ward—the whole shooting match.

"You are civilians. Up till now you've had no idea what to expect. I've tried to give you some idea and now I am now going to give you one last chance to back away, to finish your vacation and just go home."

"Janet?" Pete looked over at her. Her expression made it clear she was adamantly opposed to leaving alone. Pete had his jaw set in resignation. He could not let go of it. "Count us in," he answered.

"Okay McKenzies," said Todd with ambivalence. "Let's go over our plans."

"If the Reds remain confident that the arms are safely hidden, they will leave them where they are. That would be to our advantage. But should they get it into their heads to move the arms and we lose track of them, we're finished."

"If we succeed in thwarting this coup, what's to say they won't attempt another?"

"Time will be on our side. As soon as the airport becomes operational and the day-to-day economics of the island improve, the island's increased popularity as a tourist spot will reflect Jonathan Ward's leadership. For Cuba and the Soviets to risk a takeover at that point would send all the free countries on the run in support of Ward and the country. Nobody would want to risk that kind of confrontation."

"Last night at the ambassador's party I learned there are Russian diplomats here."

"There are. The Libyans have diplomats here as well. They don't seem to like one another though."

"Are any of the diplomats KGB agents?"

Todd laughed. "That would be too obvious. That's why I wouldn't rule it out. They probably are. There are also trained intelligence people here who have, shall we say, blended in. The most logical cover would be as a member of the staff at the school."

"Do you know their immediate plan?"

"They're moving for a coup, but should that not materialize they know they could knock out Ward at any time. He, himself, is very conscious of this possibility and has bodyguards around the clock. The irony is he feels threatened by the CIA and for months has feared a U.S. attack similar to that of the Bay of Pigs invasion on Cuba. His paranoia has subsided somewhat but people who live in the coastal areas say his men still regularly patrol the beaches between two and three in the morning. Fearing infiltration, the patrol has even asked that evening barbecues be stopped. I really don't know if Ward has considered the likelihood of a personal attack by the Soviets, Cubans or his opposition in government but I don't think he's ruled it out."

"I am amazed you didn't know about the arms cache."

"Unfortunately my resources are limited. That's been a real problem. When even a delay in transferred information can mean the success or failure of a project, or an individual's life for that matter, you learn the value of good people fast." Todd lit a cigarette. "Tell me where the cache is hidden."

"It's in a cave at the mouth of Prickly Bay behind a natural baffle."

"On the right side of the bay coming into it?"

"Yes."

"I know the place. The local boys used to play there in the grotto. A few years back a youngster got trapped in one of the caves. The tide came in too fast making escape impossible and he drowned. There was a lot of superstition connected with the incident and the place was totally abandoned. When the initial uproar died down the people seemed to have forgotten about its existence completely or viewed the site as taboo."

"Well somebody remembered it," said Pete. "Somebody who knows the island well."

"If the Cuban objective is to quietly bring in arms, that means they already have military personnel here waiting. There would most likely be a set target date for distribution and mobilization. One way to put down the coup would be to wait until the stockpile was complete and then destroy it. This information would be impossible to know without inside informants, so that is out."

"There is a second option." They came indoors and Todd spread a navigation chart across the top of a table. The three of them circled around the map staring at the region Todd indicated with a pencil. "This is the cave area," he began, "and this is Prickly Bay. Across the bay, at Mace Point there is a sheltered cove with a sand beach surrounded by a shallow coral bed. With only one avenue of entrance from the sea, there is nothing of interest there."

"I propose we empty the chests, substitute ballast, and reseal the chests, giving the outward impression they have remained intact. When the time is ripe for the Reds to make their move, they'd probably move the chests to a more convenient location so they could distribute the weapons. By the time they realize the weapons are gone, it would be too late. The perfect sting."

"How are we to take the arms out from under their noses without being seen?"

"That will be tricky, I admit. We'll have to work at night to dismantle the boxes. After taking the contents, we'll fill the boxes back up with sand. The trick is to be fast and thorough, before they realize what's happened."

"You really think we can pull it off?"

"I certainly hope so."

"What if we're found out?"

"Then it's a case of kill or be killed."

"When do we begin?"

"Right now." Suddenly serious, Todd lowered his voice and appeared stern. "There's still time to walk away. Nothing has changed for you up to this moment. It's you that dealt yourselves into the hand. You can just as easily drop out."

Janet was grateful for a last-ditch opportunity to persuade Pete to go home. Her eyes made contact with Pete's but when he briefly caught her glance, she knew she had lost. She could see his intent written on his face. His mouth seemed to go hard and his jaw was set in cold determination.

"I'm in," he proclaimed to Todd.

Chapter 34

THE McKENZIES WERE on foot headed for their cottage when they heard what sounded like firecrackers exploding followed by dogs barking and people shouting. They had just left Todd and didn't know whether to go back to the greathouse or to continue on toward their cottage. Nearer to their cottage they headed there.

As they darted along the beach they were stopped by a tall neatly dressed man with a flashlight who asked them who they were and where they were going.

"Who the hell are you?" demanded Pete.

"Night watchman, Sir."

"We live in one of the cottages on the beach and we're on our way home. What's happened?"

"Don't know. Sounds like trouble up the road."

"We were taking a stroll and heard a commotion. Is it a car accident?"

"No Mistress. I don't think so. Someone in a passing car say that something happened up the road at the Manor. Until I find out, you best go along home." He shined his flashlight across the remainder of beach in the direction of their cottage.

"The Manor?" Did they mean Seaside Manor?"

"I suppose so," said the watchman, "but that's all he say."

Pete fumbled with the lock on the cottage door and grumbled aloud. "The door must have been unlocked the whole time. I just locked it by mistake thinking I was unlocking it." Realizing his problem he tinkered with the lock and after a few moments he got the door open.

"What do you think happened?" Janet asked as they carefully made their way through the darkened rooms. "God," she mumbled, "what a time for a power failure." She felt along a shelf for the candles and matches she had set aside in case of emergency. Finding them she ignited a match but before she could light the candle, the match flame blew out.

"Don't light de candle," a gruff voice warned from the darkness. Janet screamed. Hearing her, Pete spun around and rushed toward her as though an electric shock had motivated him sending him stumbling into a chair in the darkness.

"What's wrong?" he called out to her.

"Somebody's here in the cottage," Janet whimpered.

"Janet, where are you? Give me your hand." Blindly she lurched toward the sound of Pete's voice. Finding her hand in the darkness Pete gripped it tightly and lunged toward the door. They reached it at the same time that the night-watchman reappeared.

"I heard a scream. What's happened?"

"There's a prowler inside our cottage."

"Come out here," the policeman commanded as he entered the bungalow. Beaming his flashlight about he passed from room to room to inspect the bedrooms, bath and kitchen. He paused; the kitchen door was slightly ajar.

"You can come back inside, he's gone. Did you see him at all?"

"No, it was dark. I was trying to light a candle when he blew out the match and warned me not to light the candle. That's when I screamed."

"Everything is all right now," said the watchman softly as he regarded Janet with kindness, "and doan worry, he's gone. It's safe to light de candle now." Uneasily Janet did as he directed.

Meanwhile, seeing that the candle yielded little illumination, Pete carried it into the kitchen where he hunted for a kerosene lantern he remembered seeing earlier in the cupboard. Lighting the lantern, he returned to find Janet bolting the door after the watchman who had gone outside to search the premises. In a few minutes the watchman returned to report that he could find no one.

"Oh Pete!" Janet whimpered. Frightened, with her nerves completely unstrung, she flung her arms around his neck for sympathy and comfort.

"It's all right, he's gone" he whispered as she dissolved into tears. He held her as she sobbed. Gradually he could feel the tension easing out of her until she was once again calm.

Time seemed to pass slowly as Pete paced about within the confines off the bungalow. The sound of men combing the tangle of vines, shrubs and overgrown foliage in the jungle surrounding the cottage was unsettling. It seemed a large-scale effort, certainly more than what he would have expected for a random prowler.

Pete wondered if Todd knew what had happened up the road. He tried to telephone him but he couldn't get through. His curiosity mounting, he thought about going over but he didn't have the heart to suggest it to Janet who was still on edge. So he waited, trying the telephone from time to time.

The electricity returned and the surge from the refrigerator going on reverberated through the quiet of the cottage. Pete dialed Todd again. This time the call rang through. When it became clear no one would answer at the other end, Pete hung up. He was puzzled but he couldn't help but wonder if anything had happened to Todd or to the PM up the road.

Chapter 35

WHEN TODD MURDOCK received a call to active service four years ago he had not been surprised, he had actually been expecting it. When he had first moved to Victoria Island he was glad he had chosen it because of its tranquil serenity. It was to have been a haven for his shattered nerves and fragile body and for a time it was. But, over the years he had been witness to a gradual if not subtle change in the island's leadership and politics transforming it from the garden paradise he had sought out to the international trouble spot it was now. Murdock at age fifty-three had been forced into early retirement because of physical injuries he had received in the line of duty. Leaving a life of duty and intrigue he had come to Victoria Island to begin anew.

Absorbed into a complacent lifestyle on the island, he enjoyed the brief changes of scenery and short hops to other locations, the conviviality of the people he met, his wife and family. Nevertheless, Murdock keenly missed the mental stimulation and challenge connected with his former job.

A trained professional in intelligence he had earned a great deal of respect and had been considered tops. Reflecting upon his past he genuinely missed the excitement, danger, and self-satisfaction connected with service well done.

Gunned down in a face-to-face encounter with a political terrorist, Murdock had been severely wounded. His prolonged battle for survival resulted in a lengthy hospital stay and painful recuperative period. For a man unaccustomed to failure that time of his life had been one of disappointment and bitterness. He had refused to succumb to the doctors' initial prognosis of permanent paralysis. Through determination and persistence he gradually mended through sheer willpower.

Felled while on the job, Murdock remained on the Central Intelligence Agency payroll listed, "Inactive–subject to recall." Serving the CIA as an observer in the Caribbean since he had moved to Victoria Island, Murdock had a gut feeling that sooner or later he would be called back to active duty. When he received word from headquarters informing him that his long-time friend, Henry Waterman, would be coming to see him, he knew that the moment he had been expecting had come.

That was four years ago. Reuniting in Barbados after eight years' separation from active duty together, Murdock and Waterman picked up exactly where they had left off. As they spoke with one another the years had melted away until suddenly they were current, back in harness together. When their conversation inevitably turned to the serious business at hand, very little needed to be spelled out.

The men had been partners for almost twenty years and they knew each other's ways very well. They had always been able to anticipate one another and even now without having discussed it in detail, they knew exactly what had to be done and how to go about it. Todd was already knowledgeable in local politics and government affairs having kept current right along. Military discipline and training had done that. In the course of formulating their plans, each man knew he'd get maximum professional support.

With so much happening on the island recently, it had become necessary for Murdock to step up his reports. Incidents of tampered mail, tapped telephone conversations and the execution of a dissident by firing squad were all noteworthy and reported along with the fact that arms and ammunition were being smuggled into the country for the purpose of a military coup. He had also learned that a Mafia organizer who had supplied and arranged for some of the guns had been murdered. The body, found in a swimming pool, had subsequently disappeared and the crime went unsolved. Most crimes went unsolved.

Not to leave anything to chance, Murdock had also submitted as part of his report, a request for information on the McKenzies, a security check.

Murdock's most recent instructions from headquarters, received via Barbados, called upon him to prevent a coup against Ward. It went without saying that he had free-reign to use his discretion in the employment and utilization of operatives. With this in mind he thought it would be a good idea to check out the McKenzies in case he was forced to throw in with Pete. With all the double-dealing going on around him he couldn't afford to be caught with his guard down. His request for a national security check and background investigation had come in.

Pete McKenzie and Janet McKenzie were "Cleared for Top Secret." Murdock breathed a sign of relief. The McKenzies were clean.

Chapter 36

Jonathan Ward was on his way to Seaside Manor to have dinner with Hillary. He was deeply troubled and his fine handsome features showed signs of fatigue. A coup was definitely in the making and for the first time he admitted to himself that he was in danger.

Gradually he had come to realize what he had refused to acknowledge all along. A rift had been developing within the People's Red Brigade, his own party. One of his ministers, Clarence Charles, had become very vocal openly challenging him at every opportunity and to make matters even worse, Charles had gained the support of some of the other ministers. Extreme left in his views and political stance, Charles had, almost without Ward's noticing it, emerged as the favorite amongst the Cuban and Soviet hard-line party members. Feeling threatened, Jonathan Ward recognized that his local PRB forces would be no match against the militarily trained Cuban 'airport workers' should a confrontation arise. To be truthful, he couldn't even be certain of full PRB support. It suddenly occurred to him that Charles had been more actively involved with the army recently.

Since Ward had returned from his recent visit to the United States, Clarence Charles had been pressuring Ward to share the leadership of the country with him. Obviously, Jonathan's visit to the United States had been interpreted as an attempt at reconciliation with the United States. Fearful of that possibility Ward's comrade had to take measures to safeguard the course they had been following. Ward could see no way out of it. A loss of control was imminent and he was powerless to stop it.

Murdock's discovery of the arms buildup had been devastating enough but the last blow had been delivered at the meeting today when Charles had asked Ward to either join him in joint leadership or step aside completely. Ward had been so stunned he couldn't reply. Visibly shaken he was given twenty-four hours in which to respond.

On the drive to Seaside Manor he considered every possible solution. Disbelieving the whole sequence of events he had become apprehensive about his own safety. He knew they would do anything to get at him now. With a jolt he realized Hillary would also be a prime target. She would have to leave the island immediately.

He considered moving her to Trinidad or Barbados but ruled it out because it was too close in proximity. She would have to go back home, to London. The thought of sending her away tore at him. She had come to mean a great deal to him. The thought of being separated at all was painful, but to be separated for an indeterminate length of time, perhaps years, was a bitter pill to swallow.

Perhaps he was overreacting, he thought, as he got out of the car and passed through the courtyard on his way to the west veranda where he knew Hillary would be waiting.

They had settled into an existence simulating married life. Although Jonathan didn't live at Seaside Manor he was there most of the time. They shared intimate dinners for two as well as quiet evenings together whenever his schedule permitted. They coveted their free time and could barely wait until they could be together. They had fallen in love.

Jonathan stepped onto the veranda and when Hillary saw him her face brightened with happiness. It pleased him to see her reaction. She hurried toward him. She always ran to kiss him when he first arrived and as if by conditioning he came to anticipate the feel of her in his arms.

Suddenly a shot rang out just as she reached him and came into his arms. Hillary moaned softly as she slumped against him. Before he could grasp what had happened, she had gone limp in his arms and it took all his mustering to keep her from slipping completely out of his grasp to the floor. An idyllic greeting had dramatically changed to one of insanity.

Jonathan's driver, recognizing gunfire, raced into the house to find the Prime Minister standing with Hillary in his arms bathed in blood. Shouting instructions to take cover he pushed the momentarily dumbstruck Prime Minister toward the shelter and relative safety of the house. Jolted into reality Jonathan staggered toward the house carrying Hillary to an alcove banquette. With the commotion of the first few minutes, chaos reigned.

Tiff, the gardener and houseman ran the length of the house closing and locking the louvered storm doors along the rear of the house. Jonathan's aide was on the wireless calling for help in the form of armed militiamen. Carrie came running and upon seeing Hillary blood-soaked and white as a sheet from shock ran wailing incoherently to fetch blankets and towels to comfort and aid her mistress.

Hillary lay pale and lifeless with Jonathan at her side holding and comforting her. Obviously in shock himself, Jonathan's eyes were glassy and his face was white. There was a trail of crimson blood from the terrace to the sofa appearing all the more ghastly contrasted against the white sofa fabric.

Carrie, wailing with tears streaming down her cheeks, tried to wash the blood from Hillary's legs before covering her with a blanket. Almost shyly she asked Jonathan whether they should try to get Hillary's clothes off to determine the extent of her wounds.

This innocent inquiry seemed to pull Jonathan out of his immobility and lethargy. He couldn't just stand there and let Hillary bleed to death. He had to do something. Suddenly motivated, he began to respond and take charge. Willing himself to take command of the situation, Jonathan ordered his aide with the wireless to commandeer a helicopter from the Ambassador's yacht.

While Ward's driver was radioing instructions over the wireless for PRB soldiers to be dispatched immediately to hunt for the assassin, a noted surgeon visiting the medical school was sworn to secrecy and brought in to examine Hillary. He confirmed what they already suspected. She had been shot through the back with the bullet exiting her left side. Recommending that she be hospitalized immediately, the doctor gave her a shot of adrenalin and stemmed the flow of blood until permanent surgical repair could be made at the hospital.

Jonathan paced the floor impatiently as Hillary alternated between coherence and incoherence. Time seemed to be slipping through his fingers and Hillary with it. In spite of everyone's protests, Jonathan did not leave Hillary's side and insisted upon accompanying her to Barbados. His decision to leave made everyone conscious of the risk not only to the country's political stability but to Ward himself and foremost in everyone's mind was the fear of a coup similar to the one Jonathan made against Eric Knight while Knight had been out of the country.

"The helicopter is here," someone whispered.

They made their way to the helicopter which had been cordoned off by a circle of armed soldiers. Jonathan, usually impeccably immaculate, was covered with blood. Oblivious to that fact he carried Hillary onto the transport. Not trusting anyone else to touch her, he traveled the bumpy stretch with her held protectively in his arms.

Before departing, Ward's final instructions were to conceal his absence at all costs and to have his father, Cecil Ward, brought to Seaside Manor. The soldiers were to continue to search for the sniper and his father was to notify Pete McKenzie to come at once.

Flight time to Barbados was approximately forty minutes by plane. Jonathan had considered going directly by helicopter but knew it would take twice as long and would be less comfortable than his private plane. In the meantime, the hospital had been alerted to have a doctor and an ambulance waiting on the landing strip in Barbados.

Word of the assassination attempt spread like wild fire. A special task force set up headquarters at Seaside Manor. For reasons of security they could not send information out over the phone or wireless for fear of being intercepted so they gave instructions verbally. Saddened by the crisis that had happened; the men followed their orders to the letter. They knew that any new information would be filtered down to them as soon as it came. Apprehensive and fearful, everyone seemed to sense something terrifying in the air, as wild animals know instinctively when danger is near.

Cecil Ward arrived inconspicuously by private car. He slipped into Seaside Manor almost unnoticed. With no advance warning and little information the elderly statesman was filled with dread when he saw the cleanup going on. Instantly fearing for his son's well being, he was shocked to learn it was Hillary who had been shot. The elderly gentleman, ashen with concern timorously sank down into the sofa cushions and unashamedly wept. He had grown very fond of Hillary, had revered her as a daughter. The thought of such an act of violence to her shocked and grieved him beyond comprehension.

Servants scurried about expressionless scrubbing, polishing, and disinfecting. Their cleanup effort was being performed in an uncommon frenzy of nervous energy. Frightened and traumatized, they were all suppressing great anxiety.

Carrie and Tiff had just finishing mopping up. Keep them busy, Cecil thought to himself as he asked them to prepare something to eat and drink for those who would be working there for the long hours to come. He also suggested that the louver doors be opened to allow the breeze to clear the staleness from the area. From the balcony he could see soldiers searching the grounds and the waterfront. They were scouring the neighborhood for the would-be assassin.

Cecil understood why Jonathan had sent for him. His mere presence would have a calming effect on the people in the house and lend stability to the situation. It was his function to demonstrate courage and to be an inspiration to those around him. He hoped he could be an inspiration for he certainly was not feeling the part. But it was important at this critical time and he truly hoped they would not be able to detect that the confidence he was portraying was not genuine.

As he examined the note Jonathan had left for him in a sealed envelope Cecil's expression became severe. The importance of secrecy connected with Jonathan's absence from Victoria was not to be underestimated. Cecil Ward didn't know that he agreed with Jonathan's reason to leave the island, but under the circumstances he could certainly understand his son's action. Cecil knew Hillary meant everything to Jonathan. Powerless to do anything but pray, Cecil did just that as he settled down to wait for word from Jonathan about Hillary.

Sitting, thinking, Cecil pondered the message regarding Pete McKenzie. Vaguely the old man remembered seeing him at the shipboard cocktail party. Fortunately his son had told him about their conversation. Yes, Cecil would set the plan in motion immediately.

"Find Pete McKenzie," he directed an aide. "Ask him to come to Seaside Manor immediately. Tell him it's of vital importance." As Carrie passed out food to the staff, Cecil Ward smiled philosophically. What was it about food that nourished the soul as well as the body?"

Chapter 37

AN ARMED PEOPLE'S Red Brigade soldier appeared at the door to summon Pete, by name, to Seaside Manor.

"My God!" Janet whispered, "What do they want with you? You can't be under suspicion for whatever happened, can you? They did find us wandering around. Are you under arrest?"

"My wife, I don't want to leave her alone." He wasn't sure whether it was safer to leave her behind or to take her with him. "Can one of your men stand guard? We've just had a prowler in the cottage and she's frightened."

"Yes, Comrade, a soldier will stand guard." the soldier replied tersely.

"Oh lord," moaned Janet at the salutation, 'Comrade'.

"What do they want with me?" asked Pete.

"I don't know, Comrade. But I was told to bring you directly."

"Oh Pete, do you have to go?"

"I won't be long, I promise. And don't worry. If I can, I'll call you." As a soldier was taking his place outside the door of Janet's cottage, Pete kissed her on the forehead, gave her a hug, brusquely disengaged himself and left.

Arriving at Seaside Manor Pete was ushered to the main reception area where Cecil Ward was pacing the floor with a walkie-talkie in his hands. He was apparently in touch with the patrol searching for the prowler. It seemed amazing to Pete that the PRB would have organized such a massive response. For a moment Cecil was unaware that Pete had entered the room.

"Sir?" said Pete expectantly.

"Ah, Mr. McKenzie," said Cecil Knight extending his hand. After the men shook hands Cecil indicated that Pete should be seated. "My son has told me of his meeting with you, of your arrangement." The elderly gentleman appeared grave as he scrutinized Pete's face. "This is no time to mince words. There's been an assassination attempt."

"How bad?" Pete impulsively strained forward to the edge of his seat.

"The bullet missed Jonathan." Cecil looked pained. "It hit Miss Warren. We don't know how serious yet. She's been taken to a hospital in Barbados, unconscious."

"Oh my God!" Pete uttered in astonishment.

"She apparently moved in the way just as a shot was fired at Jonathan. From the direction he was facing I believe that had the bullet hit him, it would have been fatal. As far as Hillary is concerned, we don't know yet. A Stateside doctor who examined her before she left thinks the bullet may have bypassed her vital organs on its way through. We just pray to God that she'll be all right." The old man was deeply moved and his lips quivered as he struggled for self-control.

"Having failed in the assassination attempt, the opposition will put their other plan into action right away. Jonathan left word to give you the go-ahead. He wants you to begin tonight."

"Tonight? I don't know if we can move that quickly. We need equipment, supplies. I don't know if the tanks are even filled." Pete groped for words as his mind tried to work out the details.

"Tell me exactly what you need," said Cecil Knight in his unruffled manner. "I'll have it delivered to you immediately."

"Can I call my partner?"

"Absolutely not!" The phone is certainly tapped. Who is your partner anyway?"

"Todd Murdock."

"Oh yes," said Cecil with faint recognition.

"Perhaps I should mention, sir," said Pete, "that Todd's helping the United States. He does not want it known that he's helping me. I'm afraid that's a condition, sir."

"I see," said Cecil. "And what is his interest in this project?"

"Your government's stability."

Cecil Ward looked embarrassed. "I guess we've had you fellows wrong," he said sheepishly.

"The image our government gives publicly is not always accurate. I must have your word that our support is to be kept strictly top secret."

"You have my word, Mr. McKenzie."

"What do you want us to do with the arms we recover?"

"Use your own discretion. I'm sure you both know secrets are a rare commodity here."

McKenzie looked at his watch. "I'll give a supply list to your man as soon as I check with Todd. After I pick up my wife we'll get ready to leave."

"Your wife?" Ward questioned.

"Need all the help I can get, Sir."

"Of course it's your decision Mr. McKenzie," said Cecil smoothly. "You know the danger involved." Danger. Was Ward's remark intended to rankle Pete? It did, but he didn't have more than a fleeting moment to consider it.

Pete hurried to the great house and getting out of the car he was instantly held at bay by the Todd's dog until Todd came out to call it off. They spoke briefly and went into the house where Pete filled Todd in on news of the assassination attempt, Hillary Warren, and Pete's meeting with Cecil Ward. Todd agreed they had to move the arms immediately.

Quickly mulling over in his mind what he needed to do to be ready, Todd decided he was in pretty good shape. He had been getting his gear together right along.

Jotting down a couple of items he handed the list to Pete who went outside to the waiting car and pressed the paper into the driver's hand with a few verbal instructions. To save time, Pete rode down the road with the driver, getting out at the cottages. The driver continued on. Janet, who had been anxiously awaiting Pete, rushed up to him.

Briefly he filled her in on what had happened to Hillary and about the plan.

"Poor woman," Janet kept repeating, shaking her head sadly as the full realization of the horror came through to her.

They sneaked out of the cottage by the kitchen door leaving the sentry at the main entrance to create the impression that they were still inside. Within minutes they would be at the great house with Todd leading them over a back path to the marina where a boat would be waiting.

Chapter 38

IN RESPONSE TO his request for an immediate reply Todd Murdock had received coded instructions from headquarters, which had sent him into a fury.

"Isn't that the damnest thing?" Todd marveled aloud. "They just snap their fingers from across the world and I'm supposed to quell a revolution." He slammed a log book down on the desk upsetting his bourbon and water in the process. Cursing under his breath he hastily mopped up as he muttered. "I'll never understand those people. They seem to have absolutely no idea of what's going on."

"Well, if this is my baby, they'd better not complain about how I get the job done. It's my ass, and things are going to be done my way."

He scowled and scratched his head as he lapsed into serious thinking. He was formulating a plan. The cache of arms had to be removed and fast. That had urgent priority especially in view of the assassination attempt. He stroked his chin. Jonathan Ward had to be saved. From himself if not from the enemy and from the sound of it he's barely here by the grace of God already.

He made a mental note to assign security to Hillary and Jonathan in Barbados. That was sure a damn foolish move leaving the country. Todd shook his head incredulously. "Love," he grumbled cynically. "Clouds a man's judgment. It gets in the way every time."

He smirked maliciously. If only I knew the Cubans' plans. There's just not enough time. Think, Murdock, think.

Who could be at the school? Some of the professors are foreign teaching fellows and doctors come in from all over the world. The opportunity for infiltration is wide open. They'd have access to the morgue, the record books. Pete's hunch that the Reds ordered the two men from the Red Crab murdered had merit. Finding their bodies at the medical school certainly strengthened his case that a KGB agent is under cover at the school. Boris Ogarkov, the Russian diplomat is probably his contact.

Boy, he'd sure like to see the look on their faces when they open the boxes and find sand. Gleeful for a moment, his mood fell flat. Self-doubt gnawed at his guts. Had he lost his nerve? His touch? Had the years taken their toll? Had too many years gone by? He had to pull this off. Out of action for so many years, Todd was experiencing a severe loss of confidence.

He heard the dog. Someone was on the premises. He looked out the window. It was McKenzie. Christ, I don't believe it. He's even got his wife with him. Nervously he ran the palm of his hand over his face. Wiping the perspiration off his brow with the sleeve of his forearm he sighed heavily. I just can't seem to get a break. Do they think this is some kind of fishing derby we're going to? If the Reds decide to come after the arms tonight, and it's more than likely that they might, I would, it'll be a miracle if we're all not killed.

Chapter 39

THE MEN STOOD on the pier and hastily discussed the weather conditions, which at the moment were not favorable. The tide was coming in and there was a slight surface chop. Intermittent cloud-cover and a full moon provided the mixed blessing of excellent visibility.

They quickly climbed aboard the boat and cast off. Silently slipping away from their mooring they glided out into the channel and headed out of the marina toward the mouth of the Bay.

"This is the plan," said Todd, setting the tone as he assumed command. "We'll open the boxes, substitute ballast for the arms and ammo, and then reseal the boxes. With any luck they won't detect the switch until it's too late. Boy, what I wouldn't give to see the look on their faces."

"We'll start loosening the screws on the boxes; take them about half way out, working about four boxes at a time. Finish them up two boxes at a time. That way, if we're interrupted before we're done, we won't have everything dismantled. The half completed boxes should hold together so it won't be suspected they've been tampered with. Anything open, we'll push in over the side."

"Open the 2B's first. They hold the most important weapons, the automatic M16 rifles. When we've finished, we'll stack the boxes we've finished with in front so if someone comes for them they'll take those first. If something should happen and we can't empty all of the boxes or if we run short of time, we'll pitch the unopened boxes into the water or take them with us and try to make a run for it."

"Empty the boxes with the ammunition last." Todd said tersely. "If worse comes to worse we may need to use the ammo to blow everything. I'll set a charge, just in case. They can't be allowed to get those weapons. We'll have to play some of this by ear."

Todd continued. "As we collect the weapons, Janet, that's where you come in. We're counting on you to back the boat in so we can load up and get out. You can't stand idling near the cave; it'd be too conspicuous. Do you think you can do it?" Without waiting for an answer, he continued. "It has to be done without a hitch. If you're not familiar with the boat, go around the bend and practice maneuvering while you're waiting for us."

"Is he joking?" Janet whispered to Pete. Pete raised an eyebrow and shook his head as he mouthed an emphatic "NO."

"Be back here in fifteen minutes," said Todd matter-of-factly. Synchronize your watches. It's ten fifteen." He raised his head as if expecting a question. "Got it?"

"Got it," said Janet. Her voice held a note of asperity.

The men climbed out onto the ledge with tools to dismantle the boxes and a couple of underwater lamps which they were counting on to provide illumination. In the darkness, Pete, grateful for his wet suit, climbed back into the water and submerged with the Scuba tanks. He put them in the grotto as a safety precaution—a little ace in the hole in case of trouble.

"Hey, Todd you ought to know there's a giant green moray eel at the entrance to the grotto. A real monster! He lives in the saucer-shaped coral formation just to the right outside the opening of the grotto as you go in. His house is right in the way so take care. He's nocturnal. If you come across him in the dark, you'll be in for real trouble especially if he latches on to you. I just had a run-in with a small viper moray. Hate to think what it'd be like with the giant green moray."

"With any luck we won't be going swimming tonight," said Todd brusquely. "All right, let's go. We've got to have at least four of these babies ready for Janet when she gets back here."

But they didn't. They only had time to remove three plastic bags of arms from the boxes. Todd moved the emptied boxes to the front of the cave while Pete continued to work on the hinges of the fourth box. They heard Janet approaching.

Grateful for the moonlight, she backed up to the ledge, maneuvering against the wind and waves. Unfamiliar with the boat, she throttled down too much; the engine sputtered and almost stalled. Quickly she gave the engine more gas. Satisfied, the engine recovered and resumed purring as though nothing had happened. Pete smiled to himself as he stole a glance at Todd who seemed to be glowering. Setting his jaw in a painfully tolerant expression, Murdock remained silent.

Janet managed to come in on target. Waves slapped at the hull while the surface current tried to push the boat away. She was having difficulty; the boat was big and awkward to handle. Pete had to give her credit. She was managing. If she was unnerved, she wasn't showing it. Knowing her, he knew she wouldn't give Todd the satisfaction of seeing her lose her composure.

Todd seemed to be scrutinizing Janet's performance but she totally ignored him. Apparently that was her way of coping with him. Pete suppressed a chuckle. If Todd had imagined that Janet was a pushover, he was in for a rude awakening.

While Todd hefted three bags of arms aboard the boat Pete got the fourth box open and empty just in time to send the contents off with Janet. Todd checked his watch. It was ten forty.

"Okay girl, good job. But it's taking us too long." He complained. "Come back at eleven sharp."

Janet smoldered. She wondered how long it would be taking if she wasn't there to run the boat.

Chapter 40

"SHALL I STAY and help?" she asked. "It will speed things up."

"Too risky. If someone should come along all three of us would be caught red-handed," said Todd.

"Well, I'm certainly a sitting duck out there. If anyone takes it into his head to board the boat, the most I could hope for would be to jump overboard. Any other suggestions?"

"Yep. Here, take this," Todd said dryly as he handed her a rifle. He ignored the surprised look on her face. Shoving a cartridge into the gun he handed it to her loaded and ready for business. Giving her a few instructions in its use he commented, "Now, let's just hope you won't have to use it. But remember, if you do, make it worth the effort."

Slowly exhaling, Janet solemnly considered his meaning. Meeting Todd's gaze, she obediently took the boat away from the cave and out of sight. She was running scared, very scared.

The men worked feverishly to empty as many boxes as they could. The next four opened without difficulty and they were feeling somewhat pleased with their progress when their confidence suffered a jolt. They heard a boat approaching. From the sound, they knew it was not Janet.

They immediately checked their watches and looked at one another. It wasn't Janet. She wasn't due until eleven. It was ten fifty five. Todd motioned Pete to speed up. Adrenalin pumped through them as they raced against time stacking the plundered boxes at the front of the cave. Pete madly screwed down the hinges fudging on a few screws here and there while Todd scuttled the guns in the blue plastic bags over the side in the direction of the grotto.

Just as the pair caught sight of the open fishing boat and its three male occupants bearing down on them heading for the landing, Pete and Todd submerged into the water bubbles away from being detected. The pair retreated into the grotto and from within its sanctuary they were able to see and hear as the Cubans began loading the boxes into their fishing boat. The soldiers were in good humor and joked amongst themselves as they passed around a bottle of rum.

Todd assessed the size of the Cuban boat and expelled a small sigh as he realized they'd have to make a second trip or send another boat. Watching from the eerie calm of the grotto, Pete and Todd bided their time until the Cubans finished loading their boat. As Todd anticipated, they were taking the boxes nearest to the water, the ones Pete had already emptied. The soldiers were almost finished. Suddenly Pete gasped. He had hoped they wouldn't have room for that one. That was the one he had not finished bolting together and he was afraid it wouldn't hold. If it didn't it would ruin everything and the Cubans would know immediately that something was wrong.

The Cubans picked up the box. Pete held his breath. A long suspenseful moment hung in the air and passed. The box was holding. Pete exhaled softly in relief.

Suddenly the box seemed to slip out of their hands and the men nearly dropped it into the water. Pete was sure the screws gave way where they weren't all the way into the hinges but he couldn't be certain. He clenched and unclenched his fists while he muttered under his breath in silent frustration. His eyes were glued to the soldiers' faces trying to read their reaction.

The problem caused an immediate response and considerable speculation as one Cuban examined the box. Feeling screw heads protruding out of the hinges he became suspicious. Showing the other two men the problem he voiced his concern. But his objections were good-naturedly overruled by his companions who said they merely stumbled. Carefully they continued to load the box into the boat. The other two seemed to be more concerned by the fact that the boat was now overloaded. Downplaying their comrade's objections they finished off the last of the rum and turned their efforts toward departing without capsizing the boat.

As soon as the Cubans were out of sight Todd and Pete swam out of the grotto and raced back to the cave with the same thought on their minds, what had happened to Janet? Had the Cubans seen her? Captured her? They listened. There was no sound other than that of the departing Cuban motor launch receding into the distance. The night air, still except for the waves lapping the rocks, calmed their fears.

Jolting Pete into reality Murdock warned, "They'll be back. We've got to finish emptying the rest of these boxes. Hurry."

Feverishly they emptied the boxes and resealed them without taking the time to refill them with ballast. By the time they heard the sound of a boat approaching they were almost finished. Pete stood poised at the edge of the shelf ready to tumble the bags in over the side. If their visitors turned out to be Cubans they'd scuttle the ammo and retrieve it later. The water wouldn't damage it. Todd climbed on top of one of the boxes to see who was coming. He was relieved to recognize the silhouette of his own boat.

"It's Janet," he whispered.

As soon as she pulled along side the ledge they bombarded her with questions as they loaded the bags of weapons and ammunition on board.

"Obviously you saw the Cuban fishing boat?"

"Yes, so I didn't come near."

Murdock scowled. "Did they see you?"

"I think they did, but they didn't seem to be suspicious. There were other boats out there too."

"We still have time," said Todd pointing towards the grotto.

Cautiously inching himself into the pitch black water, Pete submerged, gradually descending to the bottom in search of the bags Todd had scuttled over the side. He flicked on the underwater torch. The bags were right where Todd had dropped them. One by one Pete handed them up to Todd. As he pulled the last one up out of the water, Todd impatiently signaled Pete to get into the boat.

"Let's get the hell out of here," he whispered as he put the engine in gear.

"We're in good shape," agreed Pete with relief. "It'll take them a little while to off-load and depending on how far they have to go, we've got time to spare. They may not even open them tonight."

"Congratulations McKenzies," breathed Todd as he grinned at them, stupidly euphoric.

"We did it!" proclaimed Pete, shaking hands with Todd. Todd looked at Janet sheepishly. He took her hand and placed it between Pete's and his own.

"We did."

Janet gasped involuntarily. "The Scuba tanks! What about the Scuba tanks?"

"Shit!" Todd groaned, hitting the boat with his fist. "I completely forgot them."

"Can't we just leave them?"

Furious, Todd pulled at his hair. "No, we can't. By tomorrow they'll be searching that place with a fine tooth comb."

"So what?"

"What do you mean, so what? How many people do you know on the island with Scuba tanks? It's very recognizable equipment."

"Okay, let's just get it over with," said Pete plopping his heavy frame on the edge of the gunnel. "Come on, get your ass in over the side, Murdock, and bring a torch or we'll be here forever."

The men dropped in over the side while Janet idled a safe distance away. Nervously fretting over their absence, she compulsively camouflaged the plastic bags with beach towels. Scanning the water's surface and listening very hard, she anxiously waited for the men to return.

Chapter 41

J ANET HADN'T HEARD a sound. The Cuban boat seemed to have materialized out of nowhere riding the incoming current toward her while she faced the cave mesmerized by the shadows dancing across the water's rippling surface. Its engines cut, the boat approached stealthily, concealed by temporary cloud cover. Striking with the lightening speed of a marauding nocturnal carnivore stalking its unsuspecting prey, a Cuban soldier leapt into Janet's boat and seizing her bodily, commanded, "Don't make a sound!"

He was upon her before she knew what was happening, his hand roughly clamped over her mouth to muffle a scream as his .45 went to her head. Her chest heaving and her face pale with fright, she was forced to stare with intimate proximity into the stern uncompromising eyes of her captor. Remaining perfectly still, wide-eyed with terror, she shrank away from the gun pointed at her.

"Do exactly as I say," the Cuban soldier ordered menacingly. She nodded and gradually he loosened his grip on her, allowing her to go free as he watched her intently for the slightest hint of insurrection. She dared not but obey. Looking down the barrel of the pistol leveled at her she imagined he was a crack shot the way he handled his weapon and, she considered soberly, as close as he was to her, he didn't have to be a crack shot.

"Start the engine and back into the cave," he ordered roughly with a Spanish accent.

My god, they know! They must have been watching the whole time. Undisguised defeat flooded Janet's face. As she guided the boat into place the Cuban soldier concealed himself in the shadows. It was a trap! Pete and Todd would recognize the boat and wouldn't even be suspicious. But they would. She wasn't supposed to bring the boat in. Oh, she grieved; Todd would probably just think she had done something dumb. Think Todd, think! Don't be taken in.

She looked at the Cuban boat tied up along side her boat. Two of the men were putting on Scuba gear. Fear rose up in the back of her throat like bile and she felt nauseous. They even had spear guns.

This is it. We're all going to be killed because we forgot the air tanks. Tears came to her eyes and she bit her lips while she struggled for self-control. She had to do something. What? What?

Suddenly she remembered the automatic rifle she had hidden under the bench seat on top of the anchor line. Frantically she tried to mull over in her mind the instructions Todd had given her. She wished now that she had paid more attention. Somehow she had to get her hands on that gun. And, when she did, she'd have to be quick, decisive. Her moves would have to be forceful, unhesitating. But could she? Did she have the nerve? Could she pull the trigger? Kill someone? Oh God, she couldn't. She thought of Pete. Todd. It would be self-defense, wouldn't it? She knew she had to do whatever she had to.

She regarded her enemies. Their attitude was one of impersonal detachment. She wasn't dealing with convicts or rapists or even an insane madman. These men were professional soldiers, trained killers, whose job it was to carry out orders. And, just like Todd, they wouldn't hesitate.

Janet considered her fate. The Cubans couldn't let them go even if they wanted to. That would be contrary to their training as soldiers.

The Cubans were professional all right. They were detached, unemotional. Yet, looking into the face of her captor she couldn't help but wonder whether he felt the same regret she was feeling. She chided herself for her foolishness. He wouldn't allow himself sentiment. It had been trained out of him. That bit of insight brought her back to reality. Determined to harden herself she knew she couldn't be soft either. She couldn't afford to be weak. Not now when there was so much at stake, their very lives for heaven's sake! She had to psyche herself up so that when an opportunity for action presented itself whether in a split second or in an hour, she had to think and react with the same degree of detachment that they would. Her life, Pete's, Todd's were depending upon her.

Self-doubt nagged at her. She wasn't a professional and didn't know if she had what it took to deliver like one. Damn him. She lashed out angrily. Why hadn't Pete listened to her? They wouldn't be in this mess right now if he had. And when he wouldn't listen, what was the matter with her? Why did she have to get involved? How could she be so stupid as to let herself get into this mess? Helping the CIA— untrained, unprepared. Dumb, Janet, dumb. And now, all of their lives were depending upon what she would or might be able to do. A shiver ran through her.

No matter how she tried to avoid facing it, the same disturbing fact confronted her. She was the only one who had the slightest chance to bail them all out of their dilemma. Whether she liked it or not the next move was up to her and adjusting to this reality was extremely difficult for her. In coming to terms with her inabilities, she realized that beyond her immediate problem, she was being called upon to help her country, to give her best.

Analytically assessing the situation at hand, she watched as the two men in Scuba gear went over the side of their boat and to the ledge. Climbing out of the water they went into the cave. The soldier from her boat joined them after giving her a stern warning. Although he continued to direct his pistol at her from time to time, he was not giving her his full attention. She supposed she appeared so immobilized with fright it was no wonder he viewed her as incapable of anything serious. While the men engaged in animated conversation, a fourth soldier joined the others on the ledge, passing across Janet's boat to get to the shore. He went to the cave where he began loading boxes onto the Cuban boat.

Janet was waiting until the men were all within firing range at the same time. She felt it would be soon. It had to be soon, before the divers went into the water. Realizing they were almost ready to enter the water, she was extremely nervous and began to perspire from tension. She couldn't let the Scuba divers go into the water. If they did, Pete and Todd would be taken by complete surprise.

Where were Pete and Todd anyway? Carefully she sneaked a look at her watch. She was shocked. Hardly any time had elapsed. It was as if everything were happening in slow motion.

Time seemed to be standing still. The situation was so bizarre she felt as if she had a part in a play, a bad play at that.

Why couldn't, why wouldn't her mind accept that this was really happening? Because in her world this couldn't be happening, that's why. Not to her. She wasn't a crusader or a spy for heaven's sake. But, she reminded herself; she was not in her world at the moment. Reflecting upon Pete's words she realized she was not even in her own country. Anything that happened to them here would be, because of the political implications, conveniently attributed to a freak accident—a mysterious disappearance at sea or some other innocuous explanation to the United States government.

And who would know anything different? She had stepped over the edge of reality like Alice through the looking glass into a world unlike any she had ever known or experienced before. She had entered a foreign country where risks were commonplace and the stakes high. Not a gambler, or a spy, Janet was definitely out of her element.

She thought of Pete and in her mental turmoil she cursed him bitterly as one accuses a loved one who has died prematurely and is blamed for dying. Well he wasn't dead yet, she thought furiously, and he won't be if I have anything to say about it.

In the moments that followed Janet readied emotionally for what lay ahead. Biding her time until the men came into position, she affected a pose of meek passivity hoping the soldiers would be lulled into letting their guard down. As soon as the moment was right, she'd open fire. She considered nothing but their total annihilation fearing they'd outmaneuver or overpower her if she showed any mercy at all. Trained soldiers gave no mercy; they were trained to be ruthless. She couldn't afford to lose on a technicality. She was convinced that their lives were at stake. Surely her gunfire would alert Pete and Todd and they'd come back.

"Oh God, I pray I can do it. Oh Pete, where are you?"

Suddenly silence hung heavily in the air around her. Its significance immediately came through to her causing her to turn pale with fear and loss of courage. The soldiers were clustered together. The opportunity Janet had been anticipating was at hand.

Stealthily she lowered the side of the storage bin and in the shadows the cloud cover afforded, she groped for the M16 automatic rifle. It seemed to slide out toward her of its own accord. Suddenly there was a lull in the conversation. She strained to see what was happening. Did they see her? Were they even watching her?

The divers were standing at the edge of the rock formation putting on facemasks. The Cuban soldier with the pistol perfunctorily glanced in her direction. He noted that she was slumped against the cushions where he had left her. He put his gun down and turning toward his partner, he helped him pick up one of the chests to move it.

Boldly Janet stood up dramatically brandishing the M16 automatic rifle. Completely caught off guard the soldier's first response was one of amazement quickly followed by the unmistakable look of blood-curdling anger. Their startled expressions registered the gravity of the situation, hitting home. Suddenly she had become the tail wagging the dog yet, in her brief moment of triumph, she knew defeat. She could not gun them down in cold blood.

"Stay where you are!" she called out.

In the next instant, all hell broke loose. Either sensing her lack of bravado or reacting with professional instinct, the divers jumped into the protection of the water. The Cuban who had held her at bay lunged for his gun while the unarmed soldier who had been loading the boxes scrambled behind them for cover.

As the divers disappeared into the water, Janet unleashed a spray of bullets catching the soldier reaching for his gun. He fell wounded into the water trailing a stream of blood while the man behind the boxes surrendered with his hands held high over his head

"Oh God, I've botched it," Janet muttered to herself as she sprayed a burst of gunfire into the water where the divers had entered. If nothing more, the commotion would serve as a warning to Pete and Todd below. Keeping an eye on the Cuban who had surrendered, Janet waited expectantly for something more to happen. The lonely quiet that followed covered her like a blanket, warm and oppressive, suffocating her senses. She felt claustrophobic, fearful, as she watched the water for a telltale bubble, a ripple, or movement, some activity, but there was nothing.

Her emotions were charged with energy. Why didn't someone surface? Oh Pete, come up. Come up. Suddenly it occurred to her that she was in grave danger naively bobbing on the water's surface like a shiny lure, fair game for all. The Cuban divers could surface anywhere, to surprise and overcome her, or they could go for help and return with reinforcements. What should she do now? Think, Janet, think.

She couldn't put her gun down. She couldn't leave. About all she could do was keep out of sight, stay alert and keep her gun trained on the benign looking unfortunate soldier who as she was, caught in the wrong place at the wrong time. As the evening progressed, time weighed heavily upon her and in her state of mind her imagination was running wild.

Of one thing she was certain—sometime within the next hour something had to give because they would all be out of air.

Chapter 42

J ONATHAN WARD SAT in the room adjoining Hillary's at
the hospital in Barbados. Guards stood outside the door
and a plain clothes detective was outside the window.
Dazed and disheveled Jonathan was a tragic figure as he sat
with his head in his hands giving the appearance of a derelict
amnesia victim.

The connecting door to Hillary's room was ajar. Jonathan
glanced into the room and his eyes came to rest on her empty
hospital bed. A chill of foreboding touched his heart.

"God in heaven, please let her live." He made the
pronouncement with such force it was as if he were willing it.
He stared into space as he echoed the same plea in his mind
over and over again. A guard entered the room and addressed
him

"Dr. Ellis is here, sir. He'd like a word with you."

Jonathan rose to his feet. His expression was solemn.
The guard shook his head slightly. Their eyes met briefly as
Jonathan acknowledged the message. For a moment Jonathan

couldn't be certain whether the guard was withholding bad news or whether he was simply responding sympathetically.

"Please have him come in," Jonathan said abruptly, unable to conceal his impatience. Clearly agitated and dreading the worst he nervously ran his fingers through his hair and tried to compose himself.

The surgeon, a grey-haired man of about fifty, strode into the room expressionless. Smocked in surgical green he had not taken the time to remove his mask and it hung loosely around his neck. Jonathan perceived a weariness he himself readily identified with.

"How is she?" Jonathan asked anxiously.

"She's in intensive care being closely monitored. The bullet passed clean through missing her vital organs. She's very lucky in that respect."

"Is she out of danger?"

"Barring an unforeseen complication, I'm optimistic. She's young and healthy." He smiled genially trying to dissolve some of Jonathan's anxiety. "Allow me to be frank, Mr. Ward; the danger to her has not passed. She's in even greater danger now."

Jonathan looked at David Ellis in puzzlement. Ellis met his eyes steadily holding them without speaking a word as if waiting for his meaning to register. His eyes were penetrating and grave.

"Mr. Ward, you're dealing with an assassin, a terrorist. His primary objective is you. Having failed in his attempt he will most likely try again. He will do anything to get you or to get at you," Ellis said pointedly. "That does not rule out kidnapping and in Miss Warren's condition that could be disastrous if not fatal."

Jonathan remained rigid, pensive. Deep in thought he sighed involuntarily as he assimilated what Ellis was saying. Finally, Jonathan realized that Ellis was right.

"They wouldn't harm her here, would they?" Jonathan asked suddenly considering that possibility.

"I've seen it happen before. Take care, Mr. Ward. A sniping incident or a terrorist bombing the hospital would be horrible disasters."

"I appreciate your concern. If Hillary is strong enough to travel, I'll arrange for her to be moved to London immediately. May I see her?"

"Of course."

Jonathan stood quietly at the side of Hillary's hospital bed and as he looked at her he was inconsolable. Involuntarily tears came to his eyes. The sight of Hillary lying there so deathly pale, almost comatose, frightened him beyond belief. She seemed unfamiliar, remote, a waxen figure, not at all like the warm, vibrant joyous Hillary he knew and loved.

In his imagination, he could hear her speaking to him as if from a dream. In one of her depressed moments she had termed herself a loser. That was when he had first met her. He had tried to comfort her at the time and it pained him to recall the incident now.

"Oh my darling, no," he whispered as he reached out and took her hand in his. It was cool and limp and so slight, almost child-like. She didn't move. She was sound asleep, no doubt heavily sedated. Poor darling, she didn't even know he was here.

A frown crossed his brow and he was suddenly afraid. Had she slipped into a coma? Or was she unconscious? In panic he called her name several times as he squeezed her hand trying to rouse her. She stirred slightly. Relieved to see a response he was calmed and reassured. Encouraged he stroked her hair as he watched her steady breathing.

He would arrange with Dr. Ellis to have her moved to a London hospital as soon as she was well enough to go. He would get her away from here for her own safety as well as for his own peace of mind. He could deal with his problems as long as he knew she was safe.

Torn between loyalties he planned to return to Victoria Island today. He would reclaim his government; let his people see that he was at the helm, leading the country strong and unafraid. Assured of the support of the people he wondered if that would be enough.

Tenderly he leaned across Hillary and softly touched her lips with his own. When she gave not the slightest trace of recognition or movement, he was completely crestfallen. Quietly, he wept.

Finally, he pulled himself away. He'd return later when the anesthesia had worn off. In the meantime, he needed time alone to think through his problems, time to formulate a course of action.

He had to stop Clarence Charles.

Chapter 43

P ETE AND TODD were collecting the equipment they had stored in the grotto when they heard two boats pull up overhead. Immediately suspicious Todd raced to the peephole in the grotto and climbing out of the water onto the shelf, he went to the opening in the wall connecting the grotto with the cave to see who had come. Cuban soldiers. It was serious; they were holding Janet at gunpoint. Two Cuban divers were suited up and on their way down and a fourth man was loading the boxes into their boat confirming to Todd that the Cubans didn't know the boxes had been stripped of their contents. Should they realize that the boxes were empty, the whole project would be blown sky high.

To save the situation Todd had to get out of there with the arms. The fact that the Cubans had found them there changed everything. To protect the project's secrecy the Cubans had to be prevented from reporting their findings to their superiors. They had to be silenced.

Christ, thought Todd. His sole advantage over the Cubans at this very moment was that he knew what was going on topside. Other than that slim advantage the Cubans were holding all the cards. In an underwater confrontation they'd be dealing one on one and with a little luck they might pull it off. He remained optimistic. Meanwhile, the soldiers' topside wouldn't know what had happened in the water until after it was all over. If Pete and Todd survived the first round in the water, they'd have at least an even chance the second time around with the men topside. It could be done.

Suddenly there was a commotion in the cave. Machine gun bursts crackled through the still night followed by a scream. Todd recalled he had seen a Cuban with a pistol aimed at Janet, but no rifle. He was extremely worried for her. He didn't know what was happening but he would bet the divers were on their way down.

Somehow more mysterious, more frightening at night with their torch extinguished, the blackened sea closed in around them. They virtually disappeared into the liquid darkness to wait in familiar surroundings near to the entrance of the grotto.

All of a sudden the relatively tranquil waters were transformed into a teaming froth of confusion engulfing them in a violent turbulence that hurtled them spiraling and churning into a white-water maelstrom. In a desperate effort to find out the cause, Todd flicked on his underwater lantern.

The reason for the turmoil became chillingly apparent. Sharks surrounded them. Hungry feeding sharks primed into frenzy, surged through the water, thrashing and circling. The sharks were obviously excited by the scent of blood spreading through the water. Their prey was instantly recognizable, a Cuban soldier, either mortally wounded or dead. Fully clothed, the soldier's body was being dismantled by the unruly mob of feeders. Shaking and tearing at his body with their massive jaws, the sharks efficiently dismembered what remained of the soldier. His shredded fatigues were torn free and floated suspended, gyrating in ghostly silence like sea grass in a tidal current.

Perilously close to the ravenous savages, Pete and Todd retreated. They were thankful for the lantern light that had prevented them from straying into the middle of the foray to be attacked and eaten alive. As they backed away, one of the sleek, torpedo-shaped dynamos surged past them looking them full in the face with its enormous eyes. Built for tremendous speed and power the giant animal swung around to make another pass, coming even closer.

Off to their left, as if materializing out of nowhere, the monster moray eel made an unscheduled appearance. The giant, thick, leathery-skinned moray slowly uncoiled itself from out of its home in the coral. Apparently curious, it came out of its nest to witness the commotion, perhaps enticed by the smell of food by this time scattered everywhere. Nonchalantly it skirted the area of the bloodbath searching for particles of stray flesh that dangled suspended before slowly sinking to the bottom.

Providentially the eight-foot-long eel had a deterring effect on the sharks. Sometimes poisonous to eat, the green moray was a bluish slate-colored creature covered with a film of yellow mucus blending its hue to green. It was apparently viewed as unappetizing and not worth the effort of a confrontation. As the eel silently propelled itself past the men it seemed to set up a subtle barrier that caused the shark to suddenly back off. Whether from a territorial awareness or out of respect for a formidable adversary, the sharks withdrew and distanced themselves from the eel. Retreating, the sharks continued to swim nearby waiting to see what else would be churned up from the darkness of the ocean depths.

Pete and Todd had become so engrossed in basic survival they had almost forgotten the Cuban divers converging upon them. Boldly advancing towards them in the dim light, the Cubans unwittingly swam directly into the path of the moray eel. Further agitated by the tumult in the water and seeing a form being thrust at it, the creature, feeling threatened, lashed out viciously.

The moray lunged for the unprotected soft spot of the Cuban diver's neck snapping at him with knife-like teeth. Powerful yawning jaws took hold in a vice-like grip as the eel wrapped itself around its wet-suit-laminated foe. Squeezed into helplessness as the creature sunk its teeth deep into his flesh, the Cuban flailed about helplessly as he tried to free himself but to no avail.

The other Cuban, witnessing the horrifying spectacle of his partner's attack by the mammoth creature, was frozen into immobility.

Taking advantage of his opportunity Todd extinguished his torch and raced over to the Cuban. Reaching him in the darkness he grabbed for his air hose severing it, while at the same moment he forcefully tore off the Cuban's facemask leaving him to sputter convulsively as he clamored to the surface to breathe. Todd made his way to the boat, visibly trembling. Pete followed. A shark fin tipped the water's surface down current from where the Cuban had been killed by the eel, waiting.....

Someone had bolted to the surface. "Pete? Todd?" No response, only strenuous coughing as the figure gasped for breath trying to clear his lungs of sea water. Within moments two more people bobbed up.

"Pete? Todd?" again no response. Finally one of the men waved acknowledgement.

"Hurry!" Janet called out. "I see shark fins out there!" God, what more could happen to them?

The Cuban had been slowly drifting away either by accident or design but when he heard Janet's warning he started swimming back towards the boats.

Pete and Todd climbed aboard and shucked off their Scuba gear. They had barely collapsed into the boat when Janet thrust her rifle into Todd's hands. Jerking the throttle into gear she pulled away from the cave. Passing the Cuban diver in the water, Todd aimed the rifle at him but didn't fire.

"What's wrong?"

"Can't!"

"Cold feet?"

"No."

"What then?"

"Can't shoot them here. Can't leave a trail of dead bodies with bullets in them at the cave site."

"Its a little late to be particular, isn't it?"

"You've got to understand the nature of the beast, my boy."

"What's he mean?" whispered Janet.

"I don't know. Let's just get the hell out of here!"

With its engines fully accelerated, the big old boat reared up from the sudden forward surge leaving a frothy turbulence in its wake causing the Cuban in the water to bob up and down like a cork in a windstorm. Leveling off they headed out of the bay into open ocean. The old vessel was not built for speed but it was long on endurance as it lumbered along heavily taking the force of the waves. Salt spray intermittently blew back over them as they rounded the headland. They were in the clear.

When the first bullet whizzed through the boat just missing them they realized it wasn't over yet. They were in for trouble. The Cuban boat was giving chase.

Todd took the helm, keeping the throttle at full speed. Clouds drifted away from the moon allowing them to see the Cuban boat more clearly. As it pursued them the soldiers rained bullets in a shower around them

Janet took the controls while the men armed themselves with a couple of pistols, another rifle and some ammo. Pete opened the bag with the hand grenades.

"This ought to slow them down a bit," he said as he released the pin, counted and hurled the grenade from the stern of the boat. The explosion illuminated the sky as a fountain of water erupted. The Cuban boat slowed to pass through the heavy chop but kept coming.

They couldn't risk being caught with the evidence or, even worse, to let it be confiscated. They'd have to jettison the weapons. They'd do it when they were over deeper water where the current ran strong. There, no one would be able to retrieve it.

The Cubans opened fire again. To make them back down Pete and Todd began pelting them with hand grenades.

"They're madder than hell," said Pete grinning.

When they came to unobstructed open water the Cubans opened fire again. They were getting close. A bullet found its mark grazing Todd's temple. Blood trickled down into his eyes from his forehead. He cursed and fired off a new barrage of gun bursts from the M16 repeater.

"The time has come," said Pete. "We've toyed with them long enough. If they should suddenly decide to turn tail and run we'll really be in trouble. We'd never be able to catch them and we can't let them get away. If we blow them up out here nobody will find a trace of anything."

"You're catching on," said Todd.

"Jan, hold steady on this course and don't do anything sudden."

Todd was bleeding profusely. He was a grizzly sight as he mopped up with his shirtsleeves. The Cubans were beginning to overtake them.

Pete angrily pulled the pin releasing the timed firing mechanism on the grenade. "Baastards!" he screamed at the Cubans. Suddenly he seemed to freeze. Standing at the stern of the boat about to hurl the hand grenade he felt the hard, dull impact of steel cut into him. Feeling the hot sting of it tear into his flesh, he knew he'd been hit, but he felt no real pain. It was more like a paralysis and he couldn't move. Looking down he could see his blood flowing down over the hand holding the grenade. His arm felt wooden, lifeless.

Janet shouted his name and let go of the wheel causing the boat to lurch wildly. Jumping back to the wheel she brought the boat back under control while Todd simultaneously made a grab for the grenade. He fumbled when he was thrown off balance as the boat lurched. He couldn't direct it. Barely able to catch hold of it he knew he didn't have time to wind up and throw it before it would explode so he continued the forward motion of his catch and swung it out of the boat in a lob, tossing it overboard into the oncoming Cuban boat.

Witnessing the confusion on board Todd's boat the Cubans attributed it to their having wounded the men. Moving in for the kill they took point-blank aim on the trio as they called out something in Spanish. At precisely that moment the grenade detonated.

The explosion was terrifying. The clumsy old wooden boat shuddered as it lifted out of the water by the force of the concussion while the Cuban boat having received a direct hit completely disintegrated, scattering its occupants into the sea, so much flotsam. What remained of the debris seemed to sink in moments.

Todd took the helm while Janet, shell-shocked and spattered with blood, blindly tore strips from the towels to bind up the men's wounds. They continued along the uninhabited coastline in darkness. Todd had extinguished all running lights.

Chapter 44

THE CHEYENNE PIPER Apache turbo prop transporting Jonathan Ward from Barbados to Victoria Island landed late afternoon at the new airfield. Jonathan couldn't help but reflect upon the irony of his opposition to the communists while at the same time flying around in a $2M plane personally presented to the island's PM by Fidel Castro. There were many inconsistencies in his life these days.

His private jet rolled to a stop on the tarmac in the area especially set aside for the Prime Minister's plane, his plane. Jonathan was escorted to an armored amphibian personnel carrier, another gift from Fidel. It pained him to see such a display of security was necessary to protect him in his own country. Jonathan went directly to the Manor House where his father greeted him with warmth and enthusiasm. Cecil was obviously very glad to see for himself that his son had not been injured in the assassination attempt.

Chatting over tea father and son brought one another up to date. There was much to discuss. Using Seaside Manor as a headquarters and meeting place until tighter security could be implemented at Government House, Cecil had arranged for a secret top-level meeting later that evening to tap the brain-power of Victoria Island's intellectual elite—cabinet ministers, old-guard leaders, friends, professionals, and the so-called young blood of the nation.

The island leaders were gathering to assess the crisis that was facing their nation, the threat of a communist take-over. Jonathan, to get financial support for the construction of an international airport on Victoria Island, had aligned his government with those countries who promised to give their support. Most of the countries had been communist countries. In return for the seemingly cheap price tag of mimicking the communist votes and political stance, the communist countries aided Victoria Island financially as well as technologically.

With the new airport almost completed however, Jonathan had it in mind to gradually break away from its dependence upon these countries. Having outlived their financial and technological usefulness, the communists were to be phased out allowing Victoria Island to go back to its own way of self-government. It was at that point that Jonathan realized the communist block had invested their time and monies for a purpose other than philanthropy and they would not let go of their ties to the island. Jonathan found himself in a very dangerous situation as a person and as a government head. Having compromised the country's position politically he had alienated virtually the entire Western world and, in trying to break with the communists, he would now alienate both factions. There was no one he could turn to.

To have subsequently discovered that his "friends and allies," with a support group 500 strong on the island in the form of Cuban technicians and airport personnel, had attempted to kill

him and overthrow his government in favor of a puppet of
their own choosing, Clarence Charles, a hard-line communist
party member and cabinet minister under Ward, was a bitter
blow to Jonathan Ward.

Victoria Island was being used as a political football. Should
the Reds gain control of the nation and the fringe benefits
that went along with it, namely access to the shipping lanes
and strategic command of the new airport viewed by the West
as an airbase in the western hemisphere, there would be no
turning back.

Paradoxically, while Jonathan's death would barely make
newspaper headlines abroad, Clarence Charles would as a
matter of course move up to take his place subtly moving into
the Prime Minister's seat to govern Victoria Island. As a local
islander in politics many years, what would seem out of the
ordinary? It would seem a natural course of events.

The change from a free government to a communist-
backed government would be complete, creating little if any
immediate impact on the world scene. But, it would be like
setting a time bomb. The future impact would be catastrophic.
Jonathan pondered. Time and circumstances were against him.
Politically friendless in the Western world, he was caught in
the middle of a no-man's land.

As he saw it, there was only one way out. He had to go
public. He had to show evidence of the assassination attempt
and prove an arms build-up for the purpose of a revolution.
To gain the support of the free world Jonathan would have
to publicly expose the communists' objectives and convince
the western world that the success of the revolutionary forces
would detrimentally affect everyone. He would document his
allegations, produce detailed data of the arms stockpile and
show proof of the assassination attempt. And to win their

unconditional support he must stun them with the alarming fact that the Russian diplomat stationed in Victoria Island, Boris Ogarkov, had been detained and was being questioned as a KGB agent discovered in acts of espionage and intelligence gathering.

Jonathan's only hope was that the West would be so outraged that they would come to Victoria Island's defense. Recognizing that the CIA was already covertly involved, Jonathan hoped the United States would openly back him if they were given the opportunity to do so under the proper auspices. Politics being politics he also knew it had to "look right". That was why he had to publicly order the Cubans out of Victoria Island immediately.

With this plan in mind, Jonathan would return to Barbados to see Hillary safely off to England to recuperate. While he was there he'd hold a press conference to break the news worldwide.

He would announce that a move to overthrow Victoria Island by forces outside the local government had failed and that as Prime Minister he was taking steps to oust the communist faction responsible. Going further he would explain that the Cubans under the direction of the Russian Communist party were covertly preparing the Cuban airport workers (trained military personnel) to carry out a revolution. Jonathan would put the world on notice to observe what was happening. Meanwhile, the nearly completed airport project would continue with local workers until it officially opened on the first anniversary of the People's Revolution, March 17.

That evening the cabinet ministers who were not communists assembled at Seaside Manor. It was a consensus of opinion that once the airport began generating tourist business, the climate for the Red takeover would be changed. The real strength of the communists lay in keeping the people of Victoria Island poor and under control. Once tourist dollars and Western attitudes began pouring in Victoria Island's identification with and economic dependence upon the free world would make it almost impossible to return to its former attitudes and lifestyles, particularly for the youth of the society.

In a surprise move the ministers recommended the reinstatement of Cecil Ward to office. It was felt that by dividing the power line, Victoria Island put the communists in the position of having to do away with both men—father and son. Since this would be too conspicuous to accomplish under the scrutiny of a watching world, Victoria Island would strengthen its leadership and control.

With the airport being constructed to woo tourism it would be impossible for the country to suddenly reject tourism in favor of communism. And, with the people's hopes for financial gain, long denied, finally coming into focus and about to become a reality, the country couldn't suddenly take a step backward. The people wouldn't stand for it.

Jonathan was very much aware of the risk involved in leaving the country, especially at this critical time but he had no choice. He remembered all too well it had been precisely when the former Prime Minister, Eric Knight, had left the island that he himself had led a coup ousting Knight almost five years ago. It had been a bloodless coup, he noted with pride.

To minimize the danger to himself, he planned to leave in secret. Perhaps he could arrange for what's his name, McKenzie, the American pilot here on vacation, to take him. He'd' speak with Todd Murdock about arranging it.

What would a few nighttime hours mean to McKenzie? Jonathan would make it financially worthwhile to McKenzie.

Ward smiled as he envisioned McKenzie on the beach soaking up the sun in typical tourist fashion. His eyes twinkled benevolently. McKenzie was probably bored and in need of a little excitement by this time anyway.

Chapter 45

I T WAS WELL after midnight when Todd pulled up along side the pier of VYS, Victoria Yacht Service. Cutting the engine he secured the old craft and took a long hard look around. The marina was deserted. He shouldn't have been surprised. The pulse of an island is reflected in its marina. With the first sign of any trouble the yachts move on and the tourist population nose-dives.

Word of the assassination attempt had inevitably spread like wild fire. With gossip ranking high as a pastime, everyone knows everything about everyone else sooner or later.

Holding Janet and Todd for support Pete made his way through Todd's office to the bathroom where he was helped into a chair. Carefully Todd peeled off Pete's wetsuit that was frayed where the bullet had ripped through it. Pete had lost quite a bit of blood and looked ashen. His right arm and the side of his chest under his arm were roughly abraded where a slug had grazed his flesh. Luckily his wetsuit had absorbed most of the damage. Even so, he was scraped raw. The bullet had grazed him, passing between his arm and his side. His biggest setback was from loss of blood.

Sitting him on a chair in the shower Janet helped Pete get washed. The warmth of the water seemed to help his circulation, counteracting the effects of shock. Dried off and in fresh clothes with a stiff drink from the bar Pete began to feel a lot better as he lay on the couch in the office.

While Janet took a turn in the shower Todd hosed down the boat. He brought their weapons inside and locked them in his private storage locker. He looked around him when he came back outside. In silent contemplation he sadly shook his head. It was the worst he had ever remembered. The marina was totally quiet and empty. There wasn't another soul to be found anywhere.

"It sure doesn't look good!" he said under is breath. The three of them confined themselves to the privacy of the back room After they had all showered, Janet administered antibiotics to the men's wounds and Todd poured them all another drink. Todd expressed relief at not needing to call in a medical doctor. That would certainly have thrown up a red flag and invited suspicion. It was a bad time to stir up anything more.

Todd put the car in gear and headed for the cottages. Although the local people had been cautioned to remain indoors for their own safety there was no official ban on travel so they easily passed along the roads. It was late and there were no cars on the street. Most of the people were abiding by the voluntary curfew pending capture of the gunman. Shy and frightening easily the local people were almost superstitious in times of crisis. Todd knew from experience that their mood of apprehension was pervasive and that an attitude of fear and gloom would prevail until the sniper had been captured.

The McKenzies got out in front of their cottage and Todd continued on home. Dead tired Pete and Janet undressed and crawled into bed. Exhausted and in shock from the trauma they had endured, they slept soundly until dawn when Pete awoke with the first rays of the sun. He looked out the window.

The tide was out and almost all of the yachts had left with it. Pete got up and went to the bathroom. Returning, he went to bed and tried to go back to sleep. Wretchedly uncomfortable because of his wounded side, he tossed and turned until finally falling into an uncomfortable sleep.

It was the maid's day off and Pete and Jan got up late. They felt as if all their strength had oozed out of them. Emotionally and physically depleted they spent the morning recovering on the beach, dozing in the shade under a sea grape tree within sight of Prickly Bay. Trying to keep cool as they snacked from a bowl of fruit, they half-heartedly attempted to read, but they couldn't stay awake, drifting between wakefulness and slumber. Succumbing to exhaustion they catnapped.

The day passed uneventfully with Pete throbbing in painful discomfort, grateful to be alive at all. Just after their early evening shower there came a knock on the door. On answering it, Pete was handed a sealed envelope. It was a note from Cecil Ward requesting a favor of him.

Chapter 46

ESMEE TAYLOR WARD, Jonathan's estranged wife and the mother of his twenty-two-year-old son, Hamilton, lived in the same attractive Mediterranean villa near Government House that she used to share with Jonathan.

Passionately smitten with Esmee in his youth, Jonathan cavalierly ventured into a loveless marriage after he discovered Esmee was carrying his child. Marrying to give the child legitimacy, the couple legally separated some time after the child was born.

Sensitive and personable, Hamilton, known as Ham to his family, was a brilliant student and capable athlete. Extraordinarily good looking, he was the image of his father when Jonathan was the same age. Jonathan couldn't help but feel great pride in his son, and once he learned that Hamilton had intentions of following in his father's and grandfather's footsteps by studying for the bar, Jonathan's pleasure was boundless.

It was no wonder that when Cecil Ward received word his daughter-in-law and grandson had received a telephone threat on their lives he immediately dispatched personal bodyguards to collect them. Especially alarmed because of what had happened to Hillary, Cecil made immediate arrangements to have Esmee and Hamilton safely escorted out of the country. Not willing to trust anyone local because of the recent political unrest within the PRB, Cecil Ward sent word to Pete McKenzie appealing to him to personally fly Esmee and Hamilton to Barbados in secret. And, Cecil considered shrewdly, since Jonathan would have to return to Barbados for a press conference, it would be logical as well as prudent for Jonathan to accompany Esmee and Hamilton. With Jonathan's pilot conspicuously off duty, it would not be apparent that Jonathan was planning to leave the island. With any luck at all, maybe he might not be missed until his appearance on television the next morning pinpointing him in Barbados.

Cecil Ward sat on the veranda thoughtfully sipping his tea as he waited for Esmee and Hamilton to come down to breakfast. Jonathan, freshly showered and changed, joined him. Both men were bone weary and they sincerely looked forward to the family get together that evening without the stress of business or politics.

Their unexpected reunion provided the background for pleasant dinner conversation and an intimate family discussion, which at any other time would easily have been taken for granted. Tonight, their time together would be savored by all of them, particularly Hamilton who had made known his plans for the following year abroad. They were, for the time being at least, a family again. Singly, it was as if each in his own way was preparing his inner resources for the challenge of the evening's meeting and perhaps the unpleasant days that were to follow. In any event, Cecil Ward was feeling special pleasure and pride in having his family together and safely around him.

Much later that night, a short time after the last cabinet minister had departed the meeting, Pete arrived at seaside Manor to take Jonathan, Esmee and Hamilton to the airport. Arriving in a rather ordinary looking car so as to not attract attention, Pete proceeded to the airport, traveling along the main road, empty because of the late hour. They made rapid progress, as the airport was only a short distance away. As they turned into the access road for the airport they could hear the chugging of the asphalt plant up the hill. The airport workers were working around the clock in shifts.

Continuing along the desolate stretch in pitch darkness, they didn't see a soul. Suddenly a huge hulk loomed up in front of them blocking their path. Pete slammed on his brakes. A cow! Its tether snagged in the brush, the creature cowered in fear, mooing, its eyes bulging in the glare of the headlights of the car.

Hamilton got out of the car to untangle the rope. Just as it was freed, the animal lurched and moved off disappearing into the brush at the side of the road. Hamilton got back into the car after he fastidiously dusted of his trousers. When he made a joke of the cow encounter they all laughed. Pete drove on.

It was after eleven o'clock when the Wards boarded the aircraft that was to take them to Barbados. The black, unmarked plane used by the Georgetown School of Medicine seemed sinister as it blended enigmatically into the shadows. Used to make inter-island transfers of medical supplies and personnel between Victoria Island and St. Vincent, it had been commandeered to fly to Barbados instead of its scheduled early morning 1:10am run to St. Vincent. Pete had been

amused to learn he would be flying the mystery plane that had
been haunting his imagination night after night.

Stowing the luggage in the tail section, Pete perfunctorily
checked the plane's tires, flaps and landing gear with a hand
torch before boarding the twin engine Cessna. Lumbering
aboard he collapsed into his seat. Even after having rested all
day his side was raw and his arm hurt like hell. He tried not to
call attention to his physical discomfort but Pete knew it had
not escaped the Prime Minister's notice although he made no
mention of it.

Hesitant about speaking freely in front of the Prime
Minister's wife and son, Pete held to casual subjects, chatting
about the plane and the forthcoming trip. If Ward wanted
to discuss last night's incident at the cave Pete felt he would.
Actually, Pete was beginning to wonder whether Jonathan
Ward knew anything about last night's incident. Disquieted,
Pete fell silent as he reviewed the instrument panel and his
map and approach lanes into Barbados.

Suddenly Hamilton Ward leaned forward in his seat.

"Mr. McKenzie, are you all right? You look as if something
might be wrong. Are you well, sir?"

Esmee shot Pete a concerned glance. Her large doe eyes
were inquisitive, concerned.

"Pulled a muscle, that's all Mr. Ward," said Pete as he turned
to face Hamilton.

"Call me Hamilton, please. What a nuisance," Ham
sympathized.

"Sure is," said Pete glumly, nodding in Hamilton's direction.
He's nice enough thought Pete as he eyed young Hamilton.
Funny, by American standards Hamilton would be thought
of as a kid, yet Pete didn't view him as a kid. Hamilton
commanded a certain respect. He radiated maturity and

presence. He was obviously comfortable with people. This facility probably came from being an only child raised with adults and from being on his own away at boarding schools most of his life. Pete had learned from Todd that the family had instilled within Hamilton a family expectation of national service and responsibility. Noblesse oblige by definition means that with wealth, power and prestige come responsibilities, the training of royalty.

"Got into a bit of trouble on my last dive. Almost didn't make it back!" Pete had everyone's attention now, Jonathan's as well as Esmee's who smiled benignly as she carefully folded a headscarf in her lap.

"What happened?" encouraged Hamilton.

Recalling his encounter with the viper eel, Pete described how he had unwittingly plunged his hand into the opening in the reef.

"It was fortunate you weren't alone," said Hamilton.

"And wearing gloves," Pete added continuing. "Eels are not aggressive if you aren't foolish enough to antagonize them."

"I've never seen one at close range," said Hamilton with interest.

Esmee looked at Hamilton, pulled a face, and shuddered in revulsion.

Glancing from Esmee to Hamilton, Jonathan smiled, obviously amused by their reactions.

Esmee smiled at Jonathan. She knew he would side with Ham. They were cut from the same cloth, those two, she reflected to herself.

"We're about to take off, sir," Pete announced. The Prime Minister nodded. Pete turned toward Hamilton. "Would you like to sit up front in the co-pilot's seat?"

Hamilton grinned at the prospect and moved forward to the cockpit. "I've been telling my parents I ought to learn to fly. Living on an island, I find it would be a real advantage.

"Oh, Ham, it's too dangerous," interjected Esmee, looking at Jonathan for support in backing her up. "Besides, you haven't time."

Jonathan, his eyes twinkling, regarded Hamilton and then Esmee. Father and son were definitely in accord but Jonathan knew he had to placate Esmee. The ultimate test of diplomacy is reflected in family relations.

"Life is fraught with danger. One should be prudent. Yet, to be effective, one can't run scared.

"Are you ever frightened of anything, Father?"

"Of course. Only a fool is never frightened. But, taking chances solely for thrills is stupidity. Real gains are never achieved unless someone has the courage to risk, whether in business, politics, life, even love." Jonathan regarded Esmee pointedly as his eyes shifted back to Hamilton. "And should you ever risk the ultimate, your life, make the moment count."

Overhead, lights blazed across the runway. A network of underwater lights continued out into the sea illuminating the hidden recesses of the coral reef to extend beyond the runway transforming the black, forbidding water into a dazzling aqua pool.

Pete put on his headphones and scanned the instrument panel. Suddenly feeling conspicuously foolish he grimaced and removed his headset letting it hang loose around his neck. There was no control tower and no control advice. Consequently, there was no need of headphones. And, speaking of risk, this promised to be some solo. Suddenly Amelia Earhart popped into his mind. Successful in her 1935 solo flight from Hawaii to California she disappeared in 1937, lost at sea. They would be flying to Barbados blind, solely by instruments.

Keenly aware of the importance of the flight and his ability to deliver everyone safely, including himself, Pete felt uncommonly nervous. So much could go wrong. Mechanical failure instantly came to mind. Caribbean craftsmanship and maintenance is not synonymous with excellence. Best not to dwell on that, it wouldn't do any good. It was too late for that.

Luckily Pete had prior experience with the type of plane he was using and the electronic equipment was more than adequate. The nagging ache in his body and his throbbing temples did little to help settle him into the situation. Pete taxied to the end of the runway. Without control advice he would be depending totally upon navigational settings listed in his flight book. These he had already punched into the equipment. Once he was within range of Barbados Control, they would help bring him in.

Pete glanced back at the Prime Minister and his wife. They were in quiet conversation and seemed comfortable. Pete caught Hamilton's eye. Hamilton was studying Pete's every move, every facial expression as Pete preoccupied himself with what he was doing— adjusting the instruments and controls, checking them.

"Prepare for takeoff. Please fasten your seat belts." Pete's voice was authoritative, reassuring, and professional. Used to the big ones, commercial passenger planes, Pete likened flying the smaller plane to comparing a doctor working in an operating theater in a controlled situation with a large supporting staff and ready equipment and supplies taken for granted and an ambulance paramedic working under stressful emergency conditions with only the bare minimum in equipment and help. Pete had been out of the "Terry and the Pirates" comic strip character mode of flying for a number of years.

A helicopter pilot with the U. S. Army for five years before being trained as a commercial pilot Pete found himself back in the wellspring of action and adventure. He sure as hell hoped he would have total recall should anything go wrong.

The light plane picked up speed as it rolled down the runway. Lifting off part way down the strip, Pete banked into the wind, circled and came about passing over the beginning of the runway heading out to sea. The water preceding the landing strip was ablaze with a network of underwater lights illuminating the sea. The dramatic spectacle reminded Pete of the lighted underwater approach to the airstrip in the Seychelle Islands off the coast of east Africa in the middle of the Indian Ocean. They were very similar. The Seychelle Islands he reminisced with a wry scowl. They'd gone Red too.

Suddenly the airport lights were extinguished and the plane was plunged into total darkness except for the faint glow of the instrument panel. The landing gear fully retracted. Pete quickly reviewed the navigational settings. Thrusting the throttle forward to give the engine more power, he slowly pulled back on the wheel. The plane began to climb. When he reached an altitude of 3,500 feet Pete leveled off and maintained his heading. He turned on the radio receiver, settled back into his seat and looked out the window.

The night was clear with a few clouds. One had just blotted out the moon causing the gray iridescent water below to glisten surrealistically. Almost absently Pete regarded Hamilton who immediately returned his glance.

"Once we're within range of the control tower in Barbados, they'll see us on their radar screen and they'll automatically come in on the radio frequency we're set up for to bring the plane in.

Hamilton nodded. "How long?" he asked.

"We'll be hearing from them in about twenty minutes," said Pete. This comment set off a wave of conversation and exclamations about the weather and the view. Typical, thought Pete, but it helped to pass the time.

Ten minutes out of Barbados, a controller's voice crackled over the radio receiver. Pete grinned at Hamilton who seemed very interested in the procedure. Given the new headings, Pete punched the information into the instrument panel. Within minutes the airstrip seemed to appear out of nowhere to spread out before them, a carpet of lights inviting them in from out of the darkness.

Moments later they were climbing out of the light plane and stepping into the balmy night air. Collecting their belongings from out of the plane, they walked into the terminal building where they cleared customs and immigration immediately because of the late hour. They went outside to find a taxi.

Pete routed a sleeping cab driver out of his slumber and engaged him for the short drive to their destination, the private Oceanside home of the Taylor family which bordered the hotel property of the Sandy Lane Hotel on St. James beach in Barbados.

Chapter 47

J ONATHAN HAD SCHEDULED a press conference for ten o'clock in the morning at the Sandy Lane Hotel. By eight o'clock he was on his way to visit Hillary at the hospital.

Pretty as a picture, Hillary was sitting up in bed looking well scrubbed and cheery. The sight of her looking normal and well evoked a sigh of relief from him as he leaned in to greet her with a kiss and a bouquet of fresh flowers from the hotel florist. Exclaiming with delight at Jonathan's unexpected visit, Hillary spontaneously put her arms around his neck pulling him toward her, but before she could kiss him she involuntarily grimaced with pain and her breath caught with a sharp, stabbing intake of air.

"Oh," she breathed as she stiffened, collapsing back into the pillows.

"Oh Darling, I am sorry. It's painful, isn't it? Is there something I can do for you?"

"Something just caught," she whispered. "I just need to be still for a moment." Speaking with difficulty Hillary reached for Jonathan's hand and pulled him close. He held her hand and stroked her hair as they waited for the pain to subside.

"I'm so sorry for all of this. I feel it's my fault. Can you ever forgive me?"

"Jonathan, dear, no. I'll be all right, really. When I think about it I can't help but feel that if I hadn't been there, you wouldn't be alive now and on your way to deliver your speech. Darling, don't you see? In my own way I'm helping you to do what you've wanted to do most of all, to help Victoria Island. And, if you weren't here to do it now, the country would be lost."

"But to see you wounded like this, it breaks my heart." He smiled at her wanly and squeezed her hand.

"To see you at all means the world to me." She looked up into his face with the eyes of a woman completely in love. Her smile totally disarmed him. All too soon he was on his feet and getting ready to leave for his press conference.

"Hillary, darling, please try to understand what I'm about to say to you." He searched her eyes in anticipation of her response. "Forgive me darling, but for safety's sake I must send you away." The misery in her eyes was immediately apparent. "Please darling, understand why you must go." Jonathan spoke softly as if to ease the pain for both of them. "It'll only be for a little while, until the danger has passed."

Hillary forced a smile to ease Jonathan's feelings of guilt. "Poor Jonathan, so many problems." She shook her head sadly. "But then, you knew when you first met me that I'd be trouble, didn't you?"

"Everything worthwhile can be trouble," he said with a small attempt at humor.

"Trouble? You're agreeing with me?" she challenged. Her laughter was brittle with false gaiety. "It'll give me great comfort to know you'll be better off without me," she said, pretending to pout.

Recognizing the brave front she was putting up before him for what it was, exactly that, a front, Jonathan pulled her into his arms. His expression was tender yet grave.

"Don't say that, don't ever say that, not even in fun," he said solemnly. "You're the best thing that ever happened to me."

Her courage seemed to evaporate and she was suddenly in tears. "Oh Jonathan," she sobbed, "will it ever end?"

"My angel," he whispered clasping her to him. "The most important thing to remember is that I love you."

Momentarily content, Hillary nestled into his arms sweetly fragile with the scent of wild flowers about her. Kissing her, Jonathan tasted the salt of her wet tears against her cheeks, bittersweet on his lips. As she gave herself up to him trustingly, the impact of her response conveyed a sense of sadness, a despair bordering on desperation.

Savoring this private moment together knowing not what the future held for them, they let themselves become enveloped in the passion of their time together. For the time being everything worldly ceased to exist. Kissing her tenderly, longingly, Jonathan revealed to her his panic at the thought of life without her there beside him.

"I'm a bad penny, the cause of everything bad that has happened," he said morosely.

"Come away with me, Jonathan," Hillary said brightly. "Let's make a fresh start in England together. Be my shiny good-luck penny."

"I would give my soul to be able to, you know that. My heart, my soul, they're yours. But, as Prime Minister, I am bound by my responsibilities here. With a revolution imminent I can't just walk out on my people and my country. Don't you realize what that would mean? What kind of person would I be to neglect my duties? I'd be giving my country over to communism. I can't be so selfish as to satisfy myself at the expense of all of the others."

"It seems hopeless."

"Darling, life should not be hopeless." He squeezed her hand and kissed her on the nose.

"How long do you think it'll take to resolve everything?"

He pursed his lips in contemplation. "I honestly don't know. But every day will seem like an eternity to me." Looking into her soft green eyes he saw her despondency.

"For me as well," she sighed. Hungrily she lavished him with kisses and clung to him. She paused and smiled at him tenderly. Seemingly resigned to the situation, a frown creased her brow.

"The bad penny?" he whispered.

"When will I see you again?" she asked gloomily.

He shrugged. "You know it'll be just as soon as I can."

"Oh Jonathan," sniffed Hillary trying to hold back her grief. "Why do I feel this is goodbye?"

He sighed heavily. "I don't know my darling. I just don't know."

Chapter 48

J ONATHAN ARRIVED AT the Sandy Land Hotel a few
minutes before ten o'clock, the time of his press
conference that was to be carried live on the local
television and radio stations. The conference room was
bustling with journalists and cameramen jockeying for
positions as they eagerly anticipated a story. Jonathan came to
the bank of microphones tentatively, almost timidly, but when
he began to speak his voice was clear, steady. The area set
aside for his announcement was filled to capacity and perfectly
quiet.

The Prime Minister began by describing the plight of
Victoria Island. Winding up he made an impassioned plea to
the free world for help. He cited the assassination attempt
of the previous day resulting in the critical injury and near
death of an innocent bystander. Smoothly, convincingly,
he revealed everything: the threats to his family, the Cuban
military presence, the behind the scene involvement of the
KGB agent responsible for two known murders of Victoria

Island nationals, and lastly, the stockpile of weapons amassed for a Soviet-backed revolution.

This last information caused a sensation. With flash bulbs popping and voices shouting questions, all decorum was lost. As video news cameras silently continued to record the Prime Minister's shocking accounting of what had been taking place on Victoria Island, dignity and professional courtesy vanished as reporters competitively vied for even more information than they had been able to assimilate and digest already.

Those present, mostly international journalists and foreign correspondents trained in world politics, immediately grasped the importance of what they were hearing. Well aware of the underlying significance and far-reaching importance of the news on the world at large, they instantly recognized the value of the story as a hot property and they jumped on it aggressively bombarding the Prime Minister with a torrent of questions. Soon, completely overwhelmed, the Prime Minister was rescued by an aide and the question and answer period was brought to a close.

Jonathan left the building emotionally drained but relieved. It was all out in the open now. His nerves were raw as he walked along the fringe of beach toward the Taylor home at the far end of the hotel grounds to join Esmee and Hamilton who had been watching him on television. He felt as if a great weight had been lifted from his shoulders.

Meanwhile, in a fishing boat just off shore, three men with binoculars were keeping the Ward family under surveillance. Having pinpointed Esmee they also sighted and observed a male figure in white standing near to the breakfast table. Intermittently, another male figure came into view and receded, being partially obscured from view by the pillared architecture of the room.

The men beached their boat and came ashore. The pale stretch of palm-fringed beach in front of the house was deserted except for a male figure jogging along the beach.

Suddenly the ground shuddered and there was a terrific explosion from within the house. The figure on the beach was thrown to the ground. Staggering to his feet the runner sprinted across the manicured grounds toward the lush foliage beyond and disappeared. Almost immediately fire erupted from within the structure as help came running to the house from all directions.

The first person at the scene of the holocaust was Hamilton Ward. Miraculously he had escaped the bomb blast by having just moments before stepped outside to meet with the tennis pro. Racing back to the house when he heard the explosion, Hamilton came upon the terrifying scene and realized instantly what had happened.

"Mother! Father! Oh my God, No! No!" Falling to the ground on his knees he screamed as though he had gone mad and in a sense he had as he wildly pounded at the sand with his fists. And then, suddenly leaping to his feet he frantically charged towards the burning building as if to go inside but because of the searing wall of heat he was forced back.

The men from the boat hit the beach and reacting immediately, took Jonathan gently but forcibly away from the flaming inferno into protective custody on the boat almost before anyone who had arrived at the scene knew what was happening.

In the confusion that followed, awestruck bystanders milled about in an almost religious silence, as they seemed to contemplate the enormity of the devastation before them. The groundskeepers, manning ordinary garden hoses, worked futilely trying to contain the blaze until the fire department arrived.

It was some time before anyone was able to enter the once sumptuous Taylor home. The building, in flames, raged out of control for hours. Finally, when the fire had been put out and allowed to cool, a recovery team entered the tangle of debris and searching the ruins, they recovered the charred bodies of a man and a woman amongst the embers. The remains were subsequently identified as the Prime Minister and his wife, Esmee.

Chapter 49

PETE DREADED THE return flight to Victoria Island. What in God's name would he ever say to Hamilton Ward? What in God's name could he say? What could anyone say?

It had been arranged with Todd through Central Intelligence that Pete would return with Hamilton in the early evening while it was still daylight. He would carry the remains of Jonathan and Esmee Ward on board the plane with them. Playing it close to the vest he had chartered a private plane.

The somber trip to Victoria Island contrasted bitterly with the happy mood of the flight to Barbados. Stealing a glance at Hamilton in the co-pilot's seat beside him Pete felt a wave of sincere sympathy.

Ever since the death of his parents Hamilton had not let Pete out of his sight. Whether out of identification, security, a need of companionship, or simply fear that Pete might also befall a tragedy, Hamilton trailed about after Pete like a lost child. Pete doubted that Hamilton was even aware that he was behaving as he was. In any case, Pete was concerned.

Trying to interest the Prime Minister's son in the instructions coming from the control tower in Barbados on the headset, Pete saw that Hamilton did not seem to hear or care. His expression was completely blank. When they were beyond the range of radio communication with Barbados, Pete made an attempt at conversation.

"What will you do?"

Hamilton shrugged. "Help grandfather so that everything my father worked for won't be lost."

"Hamilton, if I can help in any way I hope you know you can count on me as a friend." Pete had felt compelled to offer his support. Look at what he had just been through for God's sake.

Hamilton regarded Pete warmly. This was the man his father and grandfather had grown to trust. "Thank you. That means a lot to me." Appreciation glowed in his blue eyes but the boyish innocence Pete had seen only the day before was gone, suddenly replaced with harsh realism.

When Pete touched down at 5:45 p.m. there was a faint tropical haze around the mountaintops in the distance. The air had gentled and the hot, dry oppressiveness of midday had given way to a soothing, balmy freshness. It was the time of day everyone usually looked forward to with pleasure.

The men deplaned. The new airstrip was empty except for Todd Murdock who was waiting for them. Pete walked over to him to discretely inquire about the body bags in the cargo area of the plane with the remains of Jonathan and Esmee Ward.

"Leave 'em. Somebody'll be by later to pick 'em up," Todd said unemotionally as he stubbed out a cigarette. "How's it going?"

"Rough. The kid hasn't eaten or slept since it happened."

Todd shook his head as Hamilton joined them, getting into the car.

Hamilton's depression seemed to lighten as he got closer to his destination. In familiar surroundings he relaxed into small talk and ended up inviting Pete and Todd for lunch on the following day. Pete felt encouraged.

As they pulled up to the entrance of the Manor House, Pete was the first one to get out of the car. His optimism about Hamilton's well being was short lived. He reached out for Hamilton just as the kid focused on the two black wreaths that had been placed on the entrance doors of the house.

Seeing them, Hamilton went white and passed out.

Chapter 50

THE FUNERAL PROCESSION was dignified in the British tradition of pomp and pageantry. Military personnel were smartly turned out in white dress uniforms adorned with shiny brass buttons, gold braid and spit-polished shoes. They ceremoniously shouldered the twin caskets of the Prime Minister and his wife through the streets. Following along behind the family and notables, neatly attired school children regimented by parish colors, trouped the processional route with solemn austerity as spectators flocked from the cities and countryside to take part in the farewell ceremonies.

The mood of the people was dark. In mourning since first learning of the assassination, the populace of the tiny island had not set aside their grief. And, it would be some time before they would be able to do so.

Jonathan Ward had been a popular leader who was regarded with genuine affection. Respected by the people of Victoria Island, he had been their salvation and their hope and they had loved him. And now, he was gone.

Seated dead center in the hastily built grandstand, Cecil Ward and his grandson, Hamilton, were about to address the crowd that had gathered in the hot afternoon sun. Two caskets were grim reminders of the Wards' personal loss. They rested nakedly to either side of them. A pleasant breeze floated across the waters of the Careenage to relieve the midday buildup of searing tropical heat that had accumulated on the pavement and buildings. As the sun fell lower in the sky, the stifling temperature began to drop encouraging more people to turn out to hear Cecil Ward's memorial address.

Flanked by flags and the coffins of the martyred Prime Minister and his estranged wife, Esmee, Cecil Ward rose from his seat to address the expectant crowd.

Brothers, Sisters, I come to you today to convey my sympathy. You have lost a brilliant leader, a dedicated worker, and a loyal friend." His voice cracked when he heard a sob from the audience. "And I… have lost a son."

"I come to you in your time of grief to offer you an opportunity to right a wrong. We cannot bring Jonathan Ward back, but we can see that his plan for the new airport goes forward. His work should not have been in vain. Now, more than ever before it is imperative that we double our efforts to finish the airport project. That was Jonathan Ward's goal and it should be your goal. Make it a reality."

"In order to bring financial stability and employment to Victoria Island the airport must be completed. By encouraging free enterprise here, our people will not find it economically necessary to leave our shores to seek employment elsewhere because opportunities are not available here."

"I have invited the United States, Britain and Canada to help us during this time of crisis. We have been unwittingly used as a pawn in a scheme beyond our comprehension. Lives have been sacrificed yet many more might have been lost had it not been for Jonathan Ward's bravery in confronting his opposition."

"By his final act of bravery in Barbados when he made all the facts known to the world, Jonathan Ward gave you his legacy of freedom, of independence, of prosperity for you and your children after you. He has given up his life for you; don't let his death be in vain. Go! Be guided by the course his hand has set. Live by the example he set for you by giving of your time, talent and energies. And work. Complete the project by our target date. Achieve for our children the dream of economic freedom and prosperity that we have held these many years. Our goals can only be accomplished through your strength and unity of purpose. We must all help build for the future so that we might all share in the riches of our nation. Ours is a small nation, small in size but large in spirit and in life. Make it bigger than life."

Cecil Ward held his arms overhead in a victory gesture and thunderous applause and cheers rang out around him.

"And now, I present Jonathan Ward's son, my grandson, Hamilton. You know of him already. He is our living symbol of the future, flesh and blood proof that youth, vitality and dedication cannot, will not, be destroyed."

Hamilton stood up. The crowd showed its pleasure with more applause. Tall and handsome, Hamilton had inherited the same charismatic appeal of his father. Immaculately elegant in tropical white, Hamilton, bearing an uncanny resemblance to his father, came forward to speak.

He addressed the gathering. From the moment he began to speak a hush fell over the crowd. His likeness to his father in speech, appearance and mannerism was eerie.

Speaking softly and clearly in well-modulated tones, Hamilton referred to his affection for his father. He spoke of his father's goals for the future and repeating his grandfather's theme that the country's aim should not be diverted; he called for unity and dedication among the young. He made an appeal for the support of all the people, instantly capturing their loyalty and their hearts by asking them for their help humbly admitting he was new to the job and had "big shoes to fill."

While Hamilton was speaking, a slip of paper was put into Cecil's hand. Looking quietly pleased he discretely passed the note to Hamilton who glanced at the message. The missing boatload of Cuban arms had been seized and destroyed. Hamilton nodded an acknowledgement to his grandfather and continued his speech.

In making reference to his mother, Hamilton hit home without realizing it. Recognizing Hamilton had lost both parents in the disaster, the crowd was well aware of the devastating effect on the young leader's personal life and they seemed particularly touched by his humility and candor. To signify their support and agreement with him, they cheered him loudly and enthusiastically when he finished. It had become clear that Hamilton had the peoples' mandate for leadership of the country. But then again, reflected Cecil Ward, so had Jonathan.

The funeral had evoked a turnout 30,000 to 40,000 strong, more than anything Cecil and Hamilton might have ever imagined. It was certainly more overwhelming than anything Clarence Charles would have expected. When he realized the magnitude of support and acceptance Hamilton and Cecil Knight had achieved, Clarence Charles was frightened. It became clear he had to move in, and quickly.

Throughout the funeral service Clarence Charles had adopted an attitude of quiet repose as he respectfully mourned the loss of his friend and colleague, the late Prime Minister. Playing to the crowd he was magnificent.

Crystallizing his thoughts Clarence Charles saw his opportunity to get the support of the cabinet ministers enabling him to assume power immediately. If he acted while the Wards were still off balance from Jonathan's death, still grief stricken, they would be easier to deal with.

Frightened into acting rapidly to consolidate power, he could not allow the Wards to establish control over the situation. And it was happening already, the people were moving their loyalties from the dead son, Jonathan, to his father, Cecil Ward and Jonathan's son Hamilton. Clarence Charles had to nip the trend in the bud before Hamilton and Cecil Knight established a base of their own.

In the Wards' speeches, Clarence Charles had noticed there had been no mention of his own involvement with Jonathan Ward's death. Clarence Charles took that to mean that they didn't know about his involvement in the assassination. They had passed off Jonathan's death as an act of terrorism, disassociating him from it completely. But soon, when the time was right, Clarence Charles would show the Wards how they would be dealt with. But first, he would try a soft approach.

However, Cecil and Hamilton Ward had known of Clarence Charles' involvement. They hadn't mentioned it at the funeral because they feared that by throwing the gauntlet down they would only serve to widen the rift causing even more bloodshed. If Jonathan's supporters knew of Clarence Charles' deed they would take the law into their own hands to move against Charles and Cecil feared a bloodbath. By giving the impression the country was temporarily without leadership it was believed the opposition would show its true colors.

With the speeches concluded, the procession wended its way along the narrow streets to the cemetery high on a hill overlooking Georgetown Harbor.

From another sunny hilltop far across the sea on the isle of Capri off the southern coast of Italy, Hillary Warren sat reading the day's old newspaper account of Victoria Island's last tribute to the martyred hero, Jonathan Ward. Her tears spotted the newsprint staining it black as she read the tribute. While a country paid homage to its slain leader, Hillary mourned the loss of her beloved.

Chapter 51

PRIOR TO THE Prime Minister's press conference in Barbados, Todd Murdock had, without Jonathan Ward's knowledge, arranged for protective security for Hillary Warren as well as for the Prime Minister. Unaware he was under surveillance from the moment he had arrived in Barbados, Jonathan traveled about freely, from the Taylor mansion, to the hotel, to the hospital, and finally back to the Sandy Lane Hotel where he had scheduled a press conference.

Automatically going about his business, Jonathan was oblivious to those positioning themselves around him. His protectors, unobserved but ever vigilant, monitored Ward's movements. They discretely blended into the Prime Minister's landscape of activities and situated themselves wherever he was and in anticipation of where he was expected to be. Jonathan was being guarded from an attempt on his life.

Meanwhile, off shore, three men posing as tourists on a pleasure boat were also observing Jonathan Ward. Listening on the shipboard radio as the Prime Minister was concluding his speech, the men in the speedboat moved closer toward the beach.

In the question and answer period following his speech Jonathan was deluged with inquiries. He tried his best to answer everyone but the reporters, becoming overly enthusiastic and unruly, overwhelmed him. Realizing that the situation was getting out of control, an aide came forward to conclude the question and answer period. Relieved, a visibly rattled Jonathan ducked out a side door of the Sandy Lane Hotel and headed back to the Taylor mansion adjacent to the hotel property on the beach.

Grateful to have the ordeal of the press conference over with, Jonathan walked along the beach on his way home, stopping to engage in conversation with some friendly fishermen accidentally crossing his path as they came from off their boat. Welcoming the diversion Jonathan paused to talk with the men for a few minutes. It never occurred to him that he was deliberately being delayed.

The bomb blast erupted with such force the ground trembled beneath him and knocked him to the ground. It took all his effort to retain his equilibrium. Ahead of him, directly in his line of vision, he watched in horror as the Taylor family home crumbled, collapsed and was engulfed in an inferno of flames.

Staring in disbelief Jonathan ran shouting toward the house where he had only that morning left his family. Responding instantly, the fishermen caught hold of him and restrained him. They held him forcibly while they quickly identified themselves explaining that he must do as they directed for his own best interests. Convincing Jonathan to get into their boat, they led him, confused and dazed, into the speedboat as he watched in horror at the tragedy being played out on the beach.

As the speeding boat put distance between them and the shore a feeling of hopelessness swept over Jonathan as he thought of his wife and son and of what Hillary had said only that morning. She had been right. Would it never end?

Hours later, groggy but not remembering how he had arrived where he was, or where he was, Jonathan found himself aboard a Boeing 727. Although comforted in his observation that the plane's interior was marked with an identifying British Airways' logo, he was unsettled to also note that the plane bore no other similarity to a commercial airliner. In fact, as Jonathan became more coherent he was further disquieted as he began to wonder whether he had had been rescued or kidnapped.

As Jonathan drifted deeper into his imaginings the all-too-familiar "fishermen/tourists" who had without a doubt saved his life, sat down across the table from him. As the men talked with him over coffee, Jonathan was to learn the reality of what had taken place on the beach in Barbados. Without a doubt, the bomb blast had been meant for him. Three people had been killed, his wife and two males. It was believed that the two males were Jonathan and Hamilton. Nothing was done to contradict that conclusion.

As far as the entire world knew, Sir Jonathan Ward, Prime Minister of Victoria Island was dead, the victim of a terrorist bomb blast in Barbados. In order to support that erroneous impression and to play it straight, Jonathan Ward had to disappear until the killers could be found, identified, and dealt with. In order for the subterfuge to be successful, the assassins must believe that they had been successful. Jonathan would have to 'disappear' until those responsible were located and dealt with.

Jonathan had but one question. "Of the two males, was it known for certain whether one of them was Hamilton?"

"It was believed that the men were hotel employees. We have it on good authority that your son was not among them. I am happy to report to you, Sir, that your son is alive and well."

Feeling the pressure of tremendous emotion, Jonathan was torn between feelings of sadness and guilt for Esmee while at the same time, great joy for the news that Hamilton was alive. Hamilton is alive!

Meanwhile in his mind Hillary's voice and words continued to haunt him.

"Will it never end? Oh Jonathan, will it ever End?"

Chapter 52

AT THREE O'CLOCK in the morning someone banging on the front door roused Cecil Ward out of a sound slumber. Sleepily he stumbled to the door. Cracking it open he peered out to see who was there. Three armed Peoples Red Brigade soldiers pushed past him into the house brandishing loaded weapons.

"Get dressed!" one of the men commanded as he looked around searching the house to make sure Cecil was alone.

The elderly statesman quickly put on his clothes and tossed a few things into an overnight bag. Under cover of darkness he was brought to an army camp at Point Saline where he was detained in one of the barracks. Point Saline, Cecil knew, was a Peoples Red Brigade stronghold of Clarence Charles' supporters. Armed with weapons and ammunition in underground magazines, Point Saline, because of its coastal location and superlative fortification, was considered the best of the PRB encampments.

This was the work of Clarence Charles, Cecil thought to himself. Thinking back he remembered Clarence Charles, Jonathan's one-time friend, at the funeral and rally. He had outdone himself as he played to the crowd's sympathy to gain support for himself. Confident of the strength he felt he had gained within the party, Clarence Charles had even tried to secure Cecil's approval of his takeover of the post left vacant by Jonathan.

Outraged by his audacity, Cecil had said so in no uncertain terms bringing their opposition to one another out into the open. Furious with Cecil, Charles obviously in a retaliatory show of strength, was already making plans to permanently take control of the country.

Yes, Cecil Ward knew he would be held incommunicado until Clarence Charles was permanently installed as the new Prime Minister. Prevented from leading opposition forces by being held in captivity, Cecil Ward lay on a folding cot, unable to communicate with the outside world. Wearing simple cotton underwear, afraid to eat or drink for fear of being poisoned, Cecil was unaware of what had been happening outside his prison walls. Cecil feared for Hamilton's safety because he knew that Hamilton had to be held captive as well for the plan to be effective. Forced into cooperating by signing falsified papers to do with national events and meetings, Cecil did this all the while suspecting that Hamilton was being kept prisoner, which of course, he was.

Recognizing one of the guards as a former supporter in his own time of government service, Cecil prevailed upon the man's former loyalty to him to deliver a message to Pete McKenzie. In desperation, he reasoned that if someone at least knew where he was perhaps something could be done to change the course of events.

Conscience-bound by past allegiance to Cecil, the guard delivered the message. The result was more than Cecil could have hoped for. The information that reached Todd Murdock by way of Pete McKenzie was subsequently smuggled out of the country and into friendly hands.

The CIA knew from the outset that they couldn't allow Clarence Charles to assume power. They set their wheels in motion instantly. In order to prevent Charles' ascendancy, the CIA arranged for a special commando group of the Special Forces to be secretly readied to invade the fort at Georgetown Harbor, isolate it, free Cecil and Hamilton Ward and withdraw. Trained for infiltration and recovery in trouble spots around the world within a forty-eight hour strike-force capacity, the task force was set to neutralize the camp at Point Saline. Successfully accomplishing their mission, it was hoped that once freed, grandfather and grandson would be able to assume leadership. However, this plan was to be put into effect only as a last resort as military intervention of any kind was the least desirable way to see to Jonathan Ward's reinstatement. It was hoped the tiny nation could rectify its internal problems on its own, from within.

During this highly troubled and dangerous period, the underground of the island community's intelligentsia went into operation smuggling information out of the country in an effort to get help for Cecil and Hamilton who were being held captive. Mindful of telephone taps and informants, the people, working under great secrecy and stress, pleaded for an intervention by the Western world.

The weapons already stockpiled at the fortress were enough to supply a regular army of people and even more were being accumulated. Although a cache had been seized and destroyed by instruction of Jonathan Ward, the military hardware available to the PRB at Point Saline and Calivigny was massive.

Meanwhile, confident of his position, Clarence Charles in a radio announcement to the country pleaded a definite soft-sell posture. Having persuaded the ministers to join forces with him he was now looking for popular support. In his bid for leadership, Clarence Charles, in the course of his message, spoke of Jonathan Ward in flattering terms and by doing so attempted to endear himself to the populace. He made every effort to further his cause.

"But," explained Clarence Charles, "one-manism, the heredity of power descending from father to son was not the policy of the island's government. Since Cecil Ward and Hamilton Ward are not directly involved with politics, it followed that they should not be able to assume leadership in a heredity system of one-manism. The party, government and people should determine its leadership."

As has happened throughout history, in times of confusion people seem to want and need direction. Any steadying influence will be grasped as a drowning man grasps anything that might support him. It was during this period of crisis that Clarence Charles had made substantial inroads in his campaign for power.

Chapter 53

FOLLOWING THE BOMB blast in Barbados, concern for Hillary's safety intensified prompting an immediate shift into high gear in an effort to get her out of the country before nightfall. Leaving late Sunday night she touched down in London the next morning before being rerouted on to Naples, Italy with her destination Capri.

It had been arranged that she stay at the secluded resort home of Jonathan's long-time friends, Jack and Margot Lord, who were currently vacationing on a yacht in the Grenadines. The small but luxurious villa in Capri boasted a splendid view of the Mediterranean while at the same time afforded Hillary anonymity insulating her from the prying eyes of the paparazzi who would surely be trying to track her down as the romantic interest in the sensationalism surrounding Jonathan's death.

Sedated and under the custodial care of a nurse-companion until she arrived at the Lord home where staff was in residence, Hillary arrived in Capri late Monday, physically exhausted and emotionally drained. Listlessly sinking into despair following the news broadcast televising word of Jonathan's death, Hillary desperately craved solitude. As in the past, whenever disaster struck she turned inward. Aching with emptiness all too familiar to her, Hillary wept within the confines of her bedroom. Meanwhile, unseen by her and just outside her shuttered windows, the village of Capri seemed joyfully sunny and serene, its crisp atmosphere rarefied by the altitude. Its pedestrian traffic was waning to a minimum.

Absorbed into the activity of a steady stream of tourists exploring the island, Jonathan passed through the cobblestone streets of Capri unnoticed, well aware that local residents customarily remained at home when tourists were out in force. Bypassing familiar village shops and thronged open-air cafes he wended his way up to the more residential, private section of Capri.

Nearing his destination he paused before continuing along the steep, winding coastal path toward the main house which he had come to regard as a home away from home. Birds chirped noisily in the background as they fluttered from branch to branch in the treetops and within the lush shrubbery nervously aware of his presence. While he paused to catch his breath, he took in the brilliance of the sea sparkling in a 360 degree panorama around him. Breathing deeply he was suddenly conscious of the intoxicating aroma of baking bread heavily fragrant in the air. Recognizing the intrinsic simplicity of the place, of his own fundamentally basic origins, he pondered the complexity of his life. He resumed walking.

When Jonathan had suggested Capri as a place of recuperation for Hillary there had not been even the remotest possibility that he would have been able to join her. Quickly reflecting upon his two recent brushes with death, he resolutely tightened his lips. He was lucky to be here at all.

From a political point of view, Jonathan's safety was of paramount importance necessitating a network of operatives discretely positioned in key points not only on the premises but throughout the island. Jonathan, armed with the flimsy protection of a counterfeit passport verifying his identity as a British businessman, went underground.

As the world waited to see the outcome of the political insurrection taking place in Victoria Island, Jonathan awaited word from a higher source than himself as to what course to follow.

In the meantime, Jonathan mused as he hurried along the country road; he had a very precious commodity at his disposal—time.

Chapter 54

J ONATHAN LET HIMSELF into the house through the French doors at the side terrace as he normally did. Theresa, the housekeeper, was so thoroughly engrossed in mopping the kitchen floor that she didn't hear him. He was suddenly there, behind her, from out of nowhere. Completely startled, she screamed and then recognizing him, she threw her arms in the air and began fanning herself to disguise her fright all the while broadly smiling. Happy to see him she greeted him with loud exclamations, enthusiastic gestures and offers of food and drink.

Thanking her and declining any food, Jonathan smiled broadly as he put a finger to his lips and whispered, "Shhh. Where is la Signorina? I want to surprise her."

"Ah," she exclaimed smiling knowingly and nodding her head, "la Signorina is upstairs in the main boudoir, the one facing the sea."

Jonathan gestured with a hand in the air that she should wait, and walking to the desk he removed an envelope from the drawer. Turning to face Theresa, he handed her the envelope after hastily sealing it.

"Give this to la Signorina," he whispered conspiratorially, again signaling secrecy with a finger to his lips.

Theresa hurried upstairs and gently awakening her new mistress, she handed the envelope to Hillary and waited for her to open it. When she opened the envelope, Hillary sat staring at its contents. Obviously perplexed, she frowned and fidgeted in visible discomfort.

"A cruel joke and certainly one in very bad taste to say the least," she said scowling. "Who gave this to you?" Hillary croaked shakily as her eyes narrowed with suspicion.

Theresa merely shrugged her shoulders noncommittally while Hillary continued to clasp the contents of the envelope to her bosom. Her heart beat wildly when she saw the contents of the envelope, a copper penny.

"A gentleman, Signorina," continued Theresa as she shyly averted her eyes from Hillary's penetrating inspection.

"What did he look like?"

Before Theresa could reply, the door slowly swung open behind her. Hanging back out of Hillary's view, Jonathan beckoned the housekeeper to leave. Hastily exiting, Theresa brushed past Jonathan whispering that she would return shortly with the evening meal.

Jonathan strode into the room. Hillary was dumbstruck. Within seconds she was in his arms whispering his name over and over, kissing him, caressing him, holding him, all the while gazing at his face as though he were a dream. Numb with emotion she was barely able to see his face through the blur of tears streaming down her cheeks.

Unseen by either of them, Theresa discretely left dinner for two set up in front of the tiny fireplace while the reunited pair idled outside on the balcony overlooking the blue Mediterranean. The sky was ablaze with color and so lovely it inspired within them renewed optimism for the future.

Far removed from governments and subterfuge, the stuff their world seemed to be comprised of, they were for the time being at least, at peace and lovers once more.

Chapter 55

HILLARY'S SCREAMS CAUSED lights to blink on throughout the house and within moments Theresa was banging on the bedroom door. Awakened out of a deep sleep, Hillary bolted upright in her bed, the sound of her own voice foreign and terrifying. Disorientated and in a cold sweat she clutched at Jonathan nervously, her eyes frightened and wild with the look of a hunted animal.

"Thank God," she groaned thickly, coming awake, the words sticking in her throat. "I was dreaming. I thought that I had just dreamed that you were here."

"Shhhh," he soothed. "I'm here, right beside you." Kissing her forehead Jonathan noted it was hot and moist, almost feverish. "Shhhh," he whispered as he stroked her hair. "It isn't good for you to get yourself worked up."

"Signora, everything is fine," said Theresa. "See for yourself. Signore is right here." The housekeeper regarded Jonathan uncertainly. "Some tea, perhaps, Signore?"

"Tea darling?" asked Jonathan. Hillary shook her head no. "She's all right now, Theresa. Thank you."

Taking leave, Theresa muttered something inaudibly consoling as she slowly left the room.

"Jonathan, just hold me," Hillary whispered. "And, Jonathan, please leave the lights on. I just want to look at you, to see that you really are here."

Sleep was out of the question. Her nerves shattered, Hillary lay cradled in Jonathan's arms, her heart pounding, and her breathing rapid. Staring out of the bedroom window she felt as though she was being absorbed into the darkness outside, slowly diminishing into insignificance as one by one, the lights in the rest of the house were extinguished creating a black void, an empty nothingness which seemed to be enveloping her. Her only salvation seemed to be the solitary light from the bedside lantern which warded off total darkness and a loss of self.

Peace restored, the household settled down to sleep while Jonathan's newly appointed bodyguards matter-of-factly reported the false alarm into their walkie-talkies. Trying to shake herself free of the black mood which had settled over her, Hillary fell upon Jonathan protesting bitterly about the risks he had been taking, reminding him that while he had been lucky before, he was in graver danger now. Complaining loudly and with passionate vehemence she was satisfied only when Jonathan promised never to leave her again. It was only after she had extracted his solemn pledge that she was able to drift off into a fitful sleep.

While Hillary lived in terror that Jonathan was slated for assassination, Jonathan's attitude had been more cavalier. Having delivered his now famous speech in Barbados in which he had laid bare all of Victoria Island's internal problems, Jonathan, because everything was out in the open and because he had subsequently been declared dead, somehow felt invincible. By virtue of his last act as a leader, he had preserved forever his good name and reputation by crossing over the line away from the very Marxist philosophy he supposedly espoused. Publicly exposing Soviet plans to use the international airport under construction in Victoria Island as a military installation and openly acknowledging communist involvement within the Island's internal and governmental machinery, information the Cubans desperately wanted kept secret, Jonathan had committed political suicide within the party.

It had been inevitable. Jonathan knew from the very beginning that he was playing with fire. Inheriting a history of graft from the previous administration Jonathan was cut off from "proper" channels of financial aid. Desperate for airport project funds to redeem the national economy, he had tried to solicit aid from whomever he thought might contribute. When Cuba came forward offering technical and financial support Jonathan jumped at the opportunity.

Three years into the project, courting favor by parroting leftist party-line rhetoric, Jonathan watched and waited as the airport project ground to painstaking completion. It was at about that time that Jonathan began to realize he was being edged out. Walking a tightrope of political mimicry as he played for time, Jonathan had hoped to ease the Cubans out. What he hadn't figured on was that backed by the Soviets and the Libyans holding the purse strings, the Cubans had become too powerful and wouldn't let go.

Hoping to find a solution with the help of the very same cabinet minister he himself had installed, Jonathan took Clarence Charles into his confidence as he had done so many other times in the past. But, shrugging, Clarence Charles had little to suggest to his stymied friend.

The truth of the matter was that Clarence Charles saw an opportunity to further himself by doing some politicking of his own. Ingratiating himself to the same high-level Soviets expressing disagreement with Jonathan, Clarence Charles had begun to pave the way for is own political aspirations.

As the Soviets observed Clarence Charles's shift in loyalty away from Jonathan Ward they realized that with a little patience on their part there would be no need for them to oust Jonathan Ward. They immediately implemented a cunning deception to promote Clarence Charles. By offering to send Charles to the Soviet Union to see first-hand, the inner workings of the USSR, it was hoped Clarence Charles would become even more aggressive about taking over the leadership in Victoria Island. As Jonathan had already visited the Kremlin he saw nothing unusual about Clarence's visit.

The prestige Clarence gained by being singled out for the honor of going to Russia seemed to attract many supporters who had been undecided while at the same time reinforcing those who had already made a commitment to him. While Clarence Charles was growing in strength, Jonathan was desperately trying to ease away from the hard-line leftist stance he had so vocally proclaimed. In order to maintain the country's independence Jonathan realized he had to disengage himself from the communist format, and very soon. He also realized he could not do it alone, he needed help.

In an effort to cleanse Victoria Island's tainted-by-association reputation, Jonathan went to the United States in order to effect reconciliation with the West. With the airport almost completed, it was time to get back into the good graces of the free world. But the President of the United States would not see him and shunted him onto a lesser official. A man of pride, Jonathan was humiliated by the perfunctory treatment of being kept waiting and being accorded a curt audience. His attempt at solidarity was not even given serious consideration. As he walked out of 1600 Pennsylvania Avenue, the most famous address in the world, he felt let down, his cry for help unanswered.

The Soviets, suspecting Jonathan was attempting reconciliation with the West, accelerated their plan to elevate Clarence Charles. From that moment on Jonathan was viewed as a traitor. Distrusted by both sides—the United States as well as the USSR, Jonathan became persona non grata.

Ever since childhood Jonathan was raised in a climate of political activity. He had been completely adsorbed by politics. Primed to serve his country with complete dedication, work became his total existence. Unaccustomed to living a so-called normal life, his social life suffered.

Suddenly absolved of all governmental responsibility he was inexplicably content to leave it all behind him. Basically a loner, Jonathan, the man, was extremely shy. Conservative in his association with women, his relationship with Hillary had come about innocently, almost without his realizing it. As they grew closer and his interest in her developed, he was forced to admit that by his own choosing she had become inextricably woven into his life. He had become very attached to her.

In the days ahead, Jonathan and Hillary lived in Capri simply. Whether taking an evening stroll and supping at a nearby bistro or sampling pastry at one of the local patisseries, Jonathan was like any man in love, attentive and loving. Never more than an embrace away Jonathan felt closer to Hillary than ever before, and as if in response to his gentle love, Hillary blossomed, recovering from her wounded state swiftly and miraculously.

One particularly fine day they took a picnic lunch to the summit of Ana Capri. There, stretched out on a blanket under the shade of a large cypress tree, they reclined just of out of sight of the public observation area feeling happy and light-headed from the wine.

"You seem especially radiant today," smiled Jonathan.

"That's because you are here. You have a marvelous effect on me," said Hillary with a toss of her head sending her hair billowing in the balmy breeze.

"You have quite an impact on me as well," Jonathan countered pulling her across to him. And I want it to be that way forever."

"Forever," she sighed dreamily. "Can happiness so glorious really last forever?" She snuggled in his arms.

"When anyone is this happy, forever isn't long enough." Jonathan paused and for a moment he held his breath before continuing. He seemed to choose his words carefully. "I passed a little shop this morning and found something that may please you."

Hillary sat up and disengaged herself. "Oh, a surprise?" said Hillary primed for a present.

He smiled, watching the little-girl anticipation in her expression.

"Come on now, don't tease. Show me what it is."

"Not so fast," he said, deliberately procrastinating.

"Am I to find it on my own, is that?" She ran her hands over his pockets feeling them for a hidden package.

"Hey, stop that! That kind of behavior can get a girl into big trouble."

"Umm," she inflected. "In trouble with you, consider that?" She hugged herself mischievously. "I'd risk getting into trouble with you," she giggled.

Protecting himself from her mild foraging, he fended off her probing gestures.

"You can't imagine what I went through," he complained deliberately attempting to pique her interest. "The tourists this time of year are absolutely vicious."

"Jonathan, you're such a tease. Come on, show me what it is."

He took her hands firmly in his own to prevent any further examination of his pockets.

"First, a toast." Handing her a goblet and filling it with champagne, he was suddenly serious as he raised his champagne glass to hers. "To us!"

Hillary touched her glass to his, and clinked them together. He watched her face as they sipped from their glasses. Suddenly Hillary gave a squeal of delight, her facial expression lighting up with surprise.

"Oh no, Jonathan, you didn't!"

He smiled, obviously pleased with her reaction.

"Oh yes, you did! Oh, Jonathan."

Nestled at the bottom of her glass a huge diamond engagement ring sparkled brilliant through the bubbles of her champagne.

Chapter 56

THEY PLANNED TO wed in a simple ceremony at the village church the following week. Legally separated but not formally divorced from Esmee, Jonathan was now suddenly free to marry because of Esmee's tragic death. He would be able to marry Hillary without complication.

Their lives seemed to take on a new dimension as they reveled in a joie de vivre brought on by the close calls they had had with death. Modest pleasures they had formerly taken for granted were savored. Feeling very much in love, they coveted their second chance at life, rushing headlong into the bounty of their expression, disregarding form, convention and propriety as they joyfully shared mind, body and spirit.

There was, however, one serious flaw of omission. Jonathan didn't think it important enough for him to worry Hillary so he simply didn't tell her. Each morning before she awoke, Jonathan walked to the village for a newspaper. His real reason for going had been to meet with Luigi, a local merchant working as an undercover agent with the CIA. Luigi was Jonathan's contact in Capri.

According to information smuggled out of Victoria Island, the situation had worsened. Cecil and Hamilton Ward had been put under house arrest and Clarence Charles, responsible for the revolutionary upheaval which was taking place, had assumed leadership of the government. The Cubans had completely taken control of the airport project, putting aside any attempt at camouflaging their part in the takeover of a sovereign government, and three political prisoners had been shot by a firing squad.

Fearing for his family as well as his country, Jonathan was greatly troubled. It would only be a matter time before the government of Victoria Island would shift to the far left.

He emerged from out of the gray drizzle to slip back into bed before Hillary awakened. A feeling of personal hopelessness disheartened him. As if sensing his presence Hillary migrated to him, cuddling close. He remained still for some time thinking. After much soul-searching he knew what he must do. He sighed in resignation.

Suddenly conscious of the scent of Hillary's cologne subtly invading his nostrils, Jonathan was more aware than usual of her softness pressed against him. As he lay in the quiet of early morning, his desire for her increased. What began as sweet, chaste kisses grew into fierce passion....passion stemming from his need to possess her for all time.

Chapter 57

THE NEXT MORNING Hillary awakened later than usual. Her first thought was that Jonathan had not yet returned from the village, but when she saw the envelope resting on his pillow the sight of it caused a sudden rush of panic within her. It was as if she knew, had secretly known all along, that one day it would be there instead of him. Hadn't she felt all along that it had been too good to be true. Had he left her yet again?

Her first reaction of cold, numbing, paralyzing fear was quickly followed by gut-level emptiness. She read the note with misted eyes while involuntary sobs followed echoing within the solitude of her heart. Early morning clouds dissipated and gave way to a bright new day. What did it matter? Jonathan was gone.

Jonathan's words came alive in her thoughts as she heard his voice, saw him before her eyes.

"I will love you forever...."

"Forever," she repeated morosely.

She regretted she had not told him of her fears. And now, it was too late. If only she had talked with him, perhaps he wouldn't have gone. All the familiar feelings of the past—the long ago hurts, the disappointments with Adam, and now Jonathan—everything surfaced to rekindle her memories and inflict more pain. How could he have done this?

"Forever," she repeated, spitting out the words vehemently. If only she had told him, perhaps he would have considered her, them. Maybe he wouldn't have left.

He would be in grave danger in Victoria Island. They were set on killing him. Why didn't he seem to realize? Or care? Was he really that courageous? She got up and walked to the window. Perhaps she could reach him before he left the country. For a moment her eyes brightened with hope, and then dimmed. She knew that would be impossible. He was probably already on a government plane.

Governments! She hated politics. What did governments care about people? Sadly she reminded herself that whatever Jonathan was to her, he was first and foremost a leader to his people.

She would have to wait and see....another few days and he'd be back. By then she'd know for certain. She was only two weeks late. It shouldn't matter all that much. They'd be married within a week's time.

Chapter 58
October 19, 1983

A S JONATHAN WARD'S plane touched down on the runway at Victoria International Airport, huge crowds had already begun to flow into Fort Frederick for a massive political demonstration. The event promised to be super-charged, brimming with joyful enthusiasm and good will as the people of Victoria Island gathered in support of their returning leader.

Excitement was electric in the air as the townspeople bustled about with an almost nervous energy, hastily attending to last-minute chores before linking up with family and friends for the sociable walk up the hill to the fort. All paths seemed to converge toward a single destination, Fort Frederick's main square, a giant open arena at the very top of the ancient fortress. Starkly naked, silhouetted against the hot, sunny sky, the citadel majestically rose up from out of the glistening azure sea to crown the capital of Georgetown.

They came en masse from all over the island, a pilgrimage through tree-lined streets and gaily painted houses over-shadowing mature shrubs and hedges. Sunlight shining on the foliage rendered it a transparent lime green where it was touched by the brightest rays, and where it wasn't, in the shade, the foliage was a deep, cool, forest green.

Strongly French in architecture, the buildings were quaintly charming, the scene picturesque, coming alive with local school children eagerly anticipating a family outing as they tried to catch a street-wise chicken hopefully pecking between the crevasses of the cobblestones.

When Jonathan emerged from the airplane, the crowd went wild, clamoring forward, surging around him until, suddenly surrounding him, the well-wishers clasped his hands and patted him on the back to congratulate him. The steel band was trilling melodiously in the background as Jonathan circulated among his people pressing the flesh and basking in glory. It was a day to be long remembered in history books around the world. Jonathan Ward had returned a national hero.

Hurried along by his aides to keep to his time schedule, Jonathan set out to join the others at Fort Frederick. But first, the motorcade detoured to the military installation at Point Saline.

Shocked at seeing the Prime Minister, the PRB soldiers guarding Cecil and Hamilton Ward offered hardly any resistance, putting aside their weapons altogether when they recognized him. Freely passing about the complex in search of his father and son, Jonathan located them with the help of the soldiers. Surprised and grateful for their sudden opportunity for release, Cecil and Hamilton quickly dressed and collecting their meager belongings, they spent a few private moments with Jonathan before continuing on to the fort together.

People lined the car route from the airport. They had turned out in great numbers. As the motorcade whizzed through the tiny hamlets toward its destination, Jonathan was overwhelmed by the show of popular support. His flagging confidence bolstered by the encouragement of the people reminded him of his national commitment and as he basked in the exhilaration of the hypnotic chants and forceful slogans of the crowds clamoring for his attention, he felt invigorated. A surge of adrenalin rushed through him and his thoughts suddenly focused on the here and now. Lost in the glory of adoration, Jonathan felt his obsessive dedication to duty taking hold of him until suddenly, it was so strong nothing else seemed to matter or exist. His carriage erect, head held high, he seemed godlike, invincible, and omnipotent. Jonathan sat in the transport proud, reveling in the aphrodisiac of power.

Arriving at the fort Jonathan was greeted with a tumultuous roar of welcome before being immediately lifted aloft onto the shoulders of those first reaching him. The people were expressing such joy at seeing him. It was as if he had been resurrected. At that moment he felt truly immortal!

Chapter 59

WHEN CLARENCE CHARLES had first learned that Jonathan Ward was alive, his first reaction of amazement and disbelief was quickly replaced by fury. Having worked long and hard to solidify national support for himself he was not about to let it slip through his fingers. Almost helplessly Charles watched public opinion immediately begin to shift away from himself back to Jonathan Ward. He felt hopeless, beaten. But he couldn't give up, wouldn't give up, not now while he was so close. His dream of power was burning too bright to be snuffed out.

Politicking his way to the grandstand, Jonathan spoke to everyone he came into contact with—friends, well-wishers, supporters, and relatives. Happily reaping glory, pressing the flesh in the midst of the hubbub, he seemed unaware of the noise growing louder in the background.

Military personnel carriers authorized by Clarence Charles were slowly grinding their way along the widest approach up the mountainside toward the fort. Slowly pulling into the courtyard, one by one, they assumed a parade formation.

Jonathan and a group of people he had been speaking with had moved out of the center of the square into the shade where they continued in animated conversation. The people had come out 25,000 to 30,000 strong in a grand show of support for him. In his easy-going, affable manner Jonathan was expressing his gratitude to the crowd while across the courtyard Hamilton and Cecil were being fed and brought up to date by family and friends very happy to see them out from under arrest.

Suddenly machine gun bursts filled the air. The school children thronging together smiled. A treat! A display! The soldiers were firing a salute. It was only when they saw their friends falling at their feet around them that they realized that the bullets were real.

As bodies began crumpling to the ground bloody and mutilated, the screaming began. Stunned, the crowd froze into immobility as the shrill, earsplitting cries of the dying reverberated within the amphitheater. The more agile of mind and fleet of foot, recovering first, began a swift evacuation as marksmen from the armed personnel carriers opened fire upon the crowd again. It was a massacre.

The most obvious and expedient escape route was over the fortress walls into the tangle of trees and vines and scrub growth twenty to seventy-five feet below.

"Jump!" the frantic mob yelled at the front-runners stalled at the brink of the precipice blocking the way. Goaded into action by the shrieked command, those who had hesitated hurled themselves off the wall, plummeting toward almost certain destruction as they scattered to the ground like strewn debris. They hit the trees with such force that many of them were impaled on the branches while others, having been struck by machine gun fire before jumping, crashed off balance, breaking their necks or damaging themselves in other injuries. Those surviving the leap ran headlong down the steep hill through the narrow streets running as fast and as far as they could toward the safety of the wooded countryside.

Those in the center of the courtyard were trapped, immediate targets for the madness that was to follow. Confused and obviously lost in the commotion, two small schoolboys accidentally collided with an agitated PRB soldier. Tearfully the boys asked the soldier what to do, where to run. Responding in a shockingly brutal act of cruelty, the soldier, primed for action, gunned down one of the children. The other one, fleeing for his life, was stopped in his tracks, shot dead, as he tried to get away. The sight of this atrocity evoked such wrath on the part of a nearby woman, a mother herself that she whirled on the uniformed brute in outrage, coming face to face with her own son.

Meanwhile, below the fortress in the sea, a nurse dragged herself up from out of the rocky coastal waters. Spent with exhaustion from having swum around the point she climbed to the sanctuary of the hospital. She had survived her leap from the fortress wall and had escaped. But her agony was not over. Within minutes of changing into a clean uniform she would be reminded anew of her own brush with death as the wounded and dying began to trickle into the understaffed facilities of the hospital for treatment.

Outside the walls of the fortress, at its main entrance, a woman passed the time of day pleasantly. She was in no hurry, the day had been declared a holiday. She sipped a soft drink while relaxing on a park bench, dimly aware of the noises growing louder around her. Smiling, she seemed pleased. Her grandson was one of the soldiers inside. Suddenly people were rushing past her from out of the enclosure. Curious, she stood up to see what was happening. Soldiers standing on the wall above her seemed to be firing. Cowering in fear the woman murmured aloud.

"My God, they're shooting." A bullet struck her and she groaned, slumping to the ground unnoticed, her soft drink still clutched in her hand.

Yes, soldiers were firing. Shooting sporadically into the crowd they brought down scores of people, felling them as though they were objects of a target practice. Within moments the quaint passageways leading up through the whitewashed buildings were littered with the mangled bodies of the dead and dying.

In the days to follow, news of the massacre circulated like a forest fire in spite of every effort to conceal that it had happened at all. But what had happened? No one really seemed to know. As townspeople tried to reconstruct the facts leading up to the tragedy they remained mystified. It all seemed meaningless. While the nation had been divided in its politics, now the people were bound together by the bond of tragedy which had without their wanting it to, involved them all. Of one thing they were certain, although momentarily dormant; a perverse insanity had taken hold of the country.

Chapter 60

ALMOST IMMEDIATELY CECIL and Hamilton Ward were pushed into the bullet-proof personnel carrier of a defecting PRB supporter. Weak from their previous ordeal, their emotions were once again assaulted by this newest atrocity. Glancing toward the place where Jonathan had been standing Cecil could see nothing; Jonathan had disappeared in the scramble. Having just been reunited with his supposedly dead son, Cecil feared anew that Jonathan had been slain. Traumatized and near collapse, Cecil was almost dragged into the departing vehicle.

The personnel carrier moved down the road unchallenged. Further on ahead another carrier was stopped by the side of the road, its crew on the ground beside it apparently relaxing, the aroma of the weed heavily pungent in the air. They were childishly gleeful over their part in what they apparently considered a war game. Passing freely in the military transport Cecil and Hamilton made it away from the fort desperately concerned for Jonathan's well being.

As they headed for the outskirts they listened to the radio sending instructions to the general population. A forty-eight hour, "shoot-to-kill" order had been immediately put into effect obviously intended to prevent opposition forces from congregating to implement a retaliatory plan of any kind. There had to be a cooling down period, time to reassess, to clean up and to cover up.

Standing in the center of the sun-drenched drill field inside the fortress, Jonathan was caught in a sweep of machine gun bursts. Hit, he spun around on impact, clutching his chest. His expression contorted, vivid with agony and shock, he clumsily slipped to the ground, his eyes straining to see where his father and son had been standing only moments before in the unfocused last image he had of them. His vision dimming as consciousness ebbed away, his final thoughts were of Hillary and even now, she brought him comfort. The coup was successful, Jonathan Ward was dead.

In the aftermath, PRB soldiers combed the island in search of Cecil and Hamilton Ward. Fanatically purposeful, Clarence Charles would not rest as long as his opposition was alive. Soldiers stopped fleeing citizens recognized as pro-Ward supporters and questioned them. Detained and harassed citizens learned of several indiscriminate executions and more brutality. Hard times were upon them and a climate of foreboding persisted.

Mentally swamped with bloody images of their slain loved ones and their own uncertainties for the future, townspeople were under great strain. Suffering hysteria and uncontrollable weeping, no one envisioned either a clear course of action or salvation.

In the days that followed, a shoot-to-kill order remained in effect while a massive clean-up began. Sworn to secrecy, drivers for the fishery trucks were enlisted to collect and dispose of the dead, mostly by sea. Any man who refused was threatened until coerced into submission. After having carried out their grizzly task, the drivers who could be found were killed in an effort to conceal their part in the cover-up.

When the curfew was finally lifted for four hours so that provisions could be gathered, the people were once more openly in touch with one another. Cautiously, friends and relatives searched out loved ones in an attempt to ascertain those missing.

Enforcing the curfew once more, soldiers patrolled the roads with loudspeakers warning everyone to remain indoors. With telephone communications out, radio bulletins geared at unification tried to rally everyone in support of their new leader, Clarence Charles.

Chapter 61

HILLARY SAT IN the crowded waiting room, her thoughts a jumble of confusion. As a dozen patients awaited examinations or the results of tests already administered, she studied them from behind her magazine. On the surface these strangers seemed so uncomplicated and predictable. Were they really? She couldn't help but wonder how their lives compared with hers. As Italians, did they view life differently? They seemed so natural, so happy. She couldn't help envying them.

The women sat quietly, occasionally making a comment aloud to relieve their boredom. Plain but neatly dressed, they seemed to possess an earthy spirit of vitality, an unspoiled goodness.

Pretending to read, Hillary leafed through an outdated Italian magazine. As she felt the women's eyes curiously inspecting her, she withdrew into herself. Conspicuously different from the others in attitude and appearance she felt the focus of their attention. The room had grown warmer. Idly returning their glances she dabbed at her temples with a linen handkerchief. She looked at the wall clock over the door. Time was passing slowly and she was feeling uncomfortably warm. To pass the time she fell to daydreaming.

Jonathan. Had it only been a week ago that they had been discussing wedding plans? How she missed him. Just as she had begun to trust the stability of their relationship, it was over before it had even begun. Jonathan was dead. Before the room full of strangers could see, Hillary caught a tear before it materialized.

When Hillary had originally thought she might be pregnant she had been thrown into a tailspin. Girlishly romantic, she had anticipated courtship and a wedding before settling down with a family. A premature pregnancy flawed her concept of convention. Now, suddenly, even that didn't seem to matter. But, she pondered anxiously, being a single woman with a child is an awesome responsibility. There would be a stigma attached to her and to the child, regardless of the circumstances. What did it matter? Nothing seemed to matter any more. At least if she were pregnant she'd have a tangible result of their relationship. She'd have a baby of her own to take care of. A child. And no one could take it from her.

But what if it proved to be a false alarm? That possibility upset her, for in her own mind she had already accepted the idea that she was pregnant. Knowing she was seemed to give her a sense of purpose, a reason to go on. What if it weren't true...oh, but it had to be true.

Having found happiness with Jonathan, Hillary had realized her ideal. She saw now, in retrospect, that she had not known happiness with Adam. Adam did not have the qualities that she had so admired in Jonathan. In fact, she had not realized anyone as fine as Jonathan could exist and she doubted that there could ever be anyone who could take Jonathan's place, ever. Convention no longer seemed important. Hillary wanted desperately to bear Jonathan's child.

The nurse called out Hillary's name. "The doctor is ready to see you. You may go right in."

Hillary rose to her feet putting down the magazine she had been absent-mindedly scanning. Gathering courage, she smoothed the wrinkles out of her skirt and walked toward the door. She crossed the threshold into the doctor's private office. He was sitting behind a huge polished desk. Rising to his feet he extended his hand in a friendly professional manner and smiled.

"I have good news for you, Mrs. Warren. I believe congratulations are in order." Her emotions strained, Hillary fainted dead away.

Chapter 62

THOUGH CIA OPERATIVES were already meshed into the local society and were keeping abreast of current events, information was hard to come by. As intrigue mounted, intelligence people infiltrated as journalists, reporters and photographers. On the island itself, an underground network of nationals worked diligently to leak information out of the country. Tightening up secrecy, Clarence Charles ordered all vocal Jonathan Ward sympathizers jailed.

Eye witness accounts of the atrocity swept the island spreading growing feelings of unrest. Rumors of an invasion circulated leaving the inhabitants frightened and jittery. Those who could leave the island left. Locals with maritime contacts packed up their families. Relying on instinct they escaped by whatever means they could, fleeing on private yachts, commercial vessels, or as stowaways. The last commercial plane to leave the island carried vacationers, students and businessmen. But, for the majority of the island's poor, there was no opportunity for escape.

In an effort to prevent a mass exodus of medical students, the school chancellor, fearing lost tuition revenues, announced he had spoken with government officials in charge and that they had assured him of the safety and protection of the students. He was also told that the airport would be open the following Monday and at that time everyone would be free to come and go.

News leaks smuggled out of the country were handled very amateurishly by a free world unaccustomed to the ways of the iron curtain. The lives of those supplying the information were seriously jeopardized by reporters not recognizing the importance of confidentiality. Those receiving information did not seem to grasp the seriousness of the situation or understand the peril to those being held captive or to those under surveillance, where on an island so small, telephone operators could easily recognize and identify the voices of those giving information and placing the calls. Despite the danger, one message was heard loud and clear. HELP! SITUATION DESPERATE. WE ARE BEING HELD CAPTIVE. PLEAD INTERVENTION.

Friday afternoon the curfew was lifted for four hours to allow people to buy food. In an obvious attempt to show the world that the island had returned to normal, local radio news broadcasted that tourists were seen swimming in the sea, which indeed people were. With the airport closed, however, the island was buttoned up. Those who did not get off were stuck there. As the curfew resumed, quiet returned. But it was too quiet. Something was about to burst.

That same evening Todd Murdock went night fishing. Taking to the sea alone in his boat he was an accustomed sight performing a familiar ritual. And fishing he was.

Linking up off a desolate stretch of rocky coastline with a confederate from the CIA, Todd learned what he had already surmised. An invasion was eminent. Given new instructions, Todd's first priority was to arrange for Hamilton Ward's evacuation to Barbados. In addition, he was to submit maps and intelligence information pinpointing targets such as the radio station, gun emplacements, military campsites, as well as troop concentrations. Working his internal intelligence sources he was to locate the whereabouts of Cecil Ward. With a task force on its way preparing to infiltrate, any information Murdock could supply would be crucial. Indeed, without it the project would fail.

Murdock's flinty eyes narrowed with determination. He would do what was required. He nodded in assent.

"Take care, Todd." His friend cautioned. "The situation is out of control. There's no telling what might happen. It could go either way….and, well, I needn't tell you the danger of that."

Chapter 63

CECIL AND HAMILTON Ward had become hunted men. Hiding in the private home of a confederate in a residential area in the hills, they were scheduled to be moved, disappearing into the protection of the island's underground.

From their cottage on the beach the McKenzies heard only sketchy news but when Todd Murdock arrived he personally brought them a full accounting of the mass murder. They soaked up the details eagerly.

"They'll be watching everyone like a hawk from now on. Any suspicious behavior will be dealt with quickly, you can be sure of that. They've got their backs to the wall."

"They wouldn't kill you?"

"This is all out war, girl. I'm fair game."

"What about us?"

"You must get off the island immediately. Things are going to get even hotter than they are already."

"How? The last plane has left. The airport is shut down."

"You, my boy, are going to fly out of here."

"You're crazy," said Pete raising his eyebrows.

"How?" asked Janet.

"In the Prime Minister's private plane. Tonight."

"How can we get to it? Have you forgotten the shoot-to-kill curfew?"

"I'll take you to the new airstrip by boat. There's a desolate stretch of beach not far from the hangar."

"Here we go again!" Janet groaned. "It's like a bad dream that never ends."

"There's one hitch."

Nervously Janet rolled her eyes heavenward and began pacing the floor and shaking her head. "Only one?"

"What?" Pete asked.

"There will be one extra passenger."

"You're coming?"

"No. I've got work to do here. Particularly now."

Pete hesitated briefly before pronouncing the words. "Hamilton Ward."

"Yep," Todd put in quickly. "We've got to get him out of here. The future of Victoria Island depends on it."

"Do you know where he is or where to find him?"

"Leave that to me." The silence was heavy with tension as they stared at one another.

"I'll get a few things together," Janet announced about to burst with nervous energy. She headed for the bedroom, grateful for something to do. The men moved toward the door speaking in low, inaudible tones.

"What about you?"

"I'm needed here. And, I'm counting on you to carry an important packet of information out of the country with you. Give it to your contact in Barbados. Your part in this is critical."

"Promise me one thing?" asked Pete.

"Fire away."

"After I deliver Hamilton safely to Barbados I want to come back into Victoria to cover the story here. I'll need your help.

Todd studied Pete for a moment, thinking.

"I'll make arrangements with the Captain of the Gliding Star out of Trinidad to pick you up in Barbados. He puts in here regularly to pick up and deliver supplies. Once Hamilton touches down in Barbados your responsibility for him will be ended. Our guys will pick him up as soon as you land. From then on he'll be under U.S. government protection until its safe for him to come back here." Todd made a notation on a slip of paper and handed it to Pete. "Here's the name of a friend of mine Janet can stay with in Barbados."

"Where do we meet you tonight?"

"I'll leave a dinghy on the beach in the next cove. Row out to me beyond Prickly Bay. From there we'll go along the coast to Black Bay on the southern tip of Point Saline. You'll be near enough to make your way from there."

"Let's go over it once more in detail."

"Okay," said Todd, lowering his voice. "This is the plan...."

Chapter 64

FRIGHTENED BY THE lawlessness taking place in their own back yard, a bloody massacre and a radical political shift to the far left, the leaders of Caricom, the Caribbean Integrated Community, met with one another in Trinidad to decide what to do about Victoria Island. The Prime Ministers of Trinidad, Jamaica, and Barbados called for a complete boycott and discussed the possibility of an armed intervention.

Initially dissenting, Belize (British Honduras in Central America), the Bahamas, Trinidad, Guyana, and Montserrat disapproved of a proposed military intervention citing it would be interference in the affairs of a sovereign government. As the situation on Victoria Island deteriorated further however, Caricom was forced to do something. They decided to intercede. Collectively calling upon Victoria Island's logical protectorate, England, for help, they were both surprised as well as disappointed when England declined.

As frenzied ham radio operators risked their lives to transmit pleas for assistance to anyone who could hear them, Caricom next pleaded with the President of the United States for his support. Meeting with the Secretary of State and the Joint Chiefs of Staff to discuss the situation, the President agreed to support the slender military might of the Caribbean multinational forces of Caricom which were to include St. Vincent, Antigua, St. Lucia, Barbados, Dominica and Jamaica. After carefully weighing the danger to the American medical students and other United States' citizens on the island, and in consideration of the ramifications connected with the island's recent political stance which was seen as a military threat to the western hemisphere, they agreed that they had no other choice but to help.

Annoyed with Caricom's decision to intervene, it was the "Kabaca" of Guyana himself who first leaked the invasion plans to the Revolutionary Military Council of Victory Island. No lover of the United States in the first place, Guyana's President then offered political asylum to Clarence Charles.

Exercising diplomatic protocol, the State Department forewarned a neutral Cuba just hours before the invasion that the strike was imminent assuring Castro that it was not directed at his workers. This tip-off infuriated the Pentagon. Given the opportunity to alert his technical work force on Victoria Island, Fidel Castro told them not to fight unless attacked, but if they were, to defend themselves. While he did not send reinforcements he did send in an army Colonel, Jose Hernandez, to organize and coordinate the defense of the airport and the island. Meanwhile, Russian spy satellites had been tracking U.S. fleet movements all week.

By notifying Cuba of the imminent invasion, the United States hoped that the Cubans, realizing the hopelessness of the situation, would lay down their arms without attempting to fight a force they knew they couldn't defeat. Instead, however, because they were forewarned, the Cubans readied themselves for combat under the direction of the new man who had just been flown in. Had they been ordinary airport workers they would have been unarmed and unprepared for combat and there would have been no military conflict with them. This was not the case however. The Cubans had all been trained militarily. They were a crack, professional force.

Victoria Island's political instability was well noted in the world by this time. With the around-the-clock shoot-to-kill curfew in effect following the massacre, everyone on Victoria Island was in a state of jeopardy, literally held hostage while the new government, fearing a counter-revolution because of their part in the massacre, tried to keep a lid on the situation.

The United States, long concerned about the communist take-over of Victoria Island and its development for purposes other than tourism, now feared for its medical students who quite conceivably could be used as hostages much the same way United States' citizens were held hostage in Iran. Learning through a network of sources that the American students were confined to their quarters because of the curfew and that their classes had been suspended, parents and officials back home in the States worried. A situation so volatile was bound to be unpredictable as well. Under pressure from all directions, the United States government prepared to take action.

Using the safety of its citizens as a pretext to mount a full scale military landing the President charged 61-year-old Chairman of the Joint Chiefs of Staff, a U.S. Army General, to organize the intervention. Personally unassuming but well respected for professional competence, "Fighting General Jack" forged the Army, Navy Air Force and Marine units into one hard assault force within a few days' time, rerouting ships carrying Marines to Beirut for Victoria as a precautionary measure in the event the Americans were endangered.

After the massacre on Wednesday, October 19, 1983, rumors of an invasion began circulating that Friday, substantiated by a mass deployment of United States forces toward Victoria Island. Meanwhile, confined to their homes and places of business with food and water in short supply, the people of the island fearfully waited and prayed.

As the Caribbean multinational forces joined by the United States were being hyped up in preparation for the invasion, Pete worked on the text of his story from Victoria Island. He planned to call it in to his news affiliation from Barbados before he infiltrated back into Victoria Island to cover the war first hand.

"On Wednesday, October 19, 1983, the Prime Minister of Victoria Island, Jonathan Ward, was slain by a mutinous band of politically radical leftist PRB soldiers firing into a crowd of his supporters killing more than one hundred of them. The political situation desperate, other prominent leaders are in hiding while the new government has enforced a round-the-clock shoot-to-kill curfew. As rumors spread and tension mounts, Victoria Island is braced for a military invasion."

Chapter 65

WEARING DARK CLOTHING to blend into the night, Pete and Janet sneaked out of their cottage and ran for cover hiding in the shadows of the trees fringing the beach. Darting along the shore to the peninsula, they picked their way along the rocky coastline to the next inlet. It was deserted. The rubber dinghy Todd had provided for them was in plain sight, from all appearances it seemed to have washed ashore. They paused to listen. There was no sound except the gentle wash of water rhythmically lapping the shore. They climbed into the dinghy and began rowing out to the mouth of Prickly Bay hugging the coastline to remain as unobtrusive as possible. As planned, they proceeded to row toward Murdock's sailboat which was anchored out of sight around the point and within minutes they were climbing aboard, ready to set sail for the beach at Black Bay off Point Saline and the airstrip. Hamilton Ward was already aboard.

The weather conditions were ideal and they made good time. Before being ferried ashore they conferred with Todd for last-minute instructions and then, the three of them disembarked onto the sand beach, silently creeping up to the runway. Once there, they got their bearing and looked for the Prime Minister's private plane. It was on the other side of the runway. Crouched at the side of the airstrip they took a few unruffled minutes to set their plans. They were aware of soft music coming from the Cuban barracks. It was late, the men were asleep. There were no sentries; they were stationed at the checkpoint at the entrance to the airport. Arriving by water, they had circumvented the sentries. Security seemed non-existent on the strip itself.

In planning their move, Todd and Pete had tried to synchronize their departure with the time the school plane normally came in for a landing. By adhering to a familiar pattern, perhaps their leaving wouldn't seem so out of the ordinary to the Cubans who were accustomed to hearing a plane for the medical school come and go at that hour. If the Cubans could be taken off guard, even momentarily, that would give Pete the edge he needed to get off the ground and airborne.

He trio darted across the field, moving some of the empty oil drums dotting the runway out of the way, creating an open space in which to taxi. This accomplished, they pushed the light plane onto the field into position for takeoff. Before boarding, they took one long last look around. The night was still, peaceful.

"So far, so good," said Pete, glancing at his watch. It was 1:10 am, their target time. Pausing to embrace, they boarded the plane.

The plane roared to life shattering the stillness of the night as well as any notion they might have had about escaping undetected. The noise was incredible. Moonlight and the head lamps of the plane were their only source of illumination taking the edge off total darkness. They began moving down the runway through a maze of oil drums, silently grateful for the full fuel tank clearly visible on the gas gauge.

The plane chugged forward making a terrible racket as it coasted down the air strip. Bouncing along the tarmac, they gathered speed until suddenly they pulled away from the ground. They were in the air.

Heady with exhilaration they watched as a small band of Cubans, still in their underwear, came running out onto the field, automatic machine guns blazing. Hopping up and down on the strip, shouting obscenities in Spanish, the outraged Cubans fired on them as the airborne trio, stunned by the suddenness of their appearance, in total disarray, roared with laughter, completely cracking up in spite of the danger. Suddenly a spray of bullets ripped through the wing of the plane reminding them of the seriousness of the situation.

As the plane climbed higher, their last view of the enormous airstrip was condensed into a small lighted halo ringed around the spot where the Cubans had launched their last stand.

Exhilarated by their daring escape the fleeing trio concentrated on Barbados, less than an hour away. Pete's attention was drawn to the control panel. His pulse quickened as he felt a sudden twinge of anxiety. The fuel indicator was dipping.

"Didn't the fuel gauge read full when we took off?" he asked out loud.

"Yes," Janet and Hamilton answered in unison as their eyes immediately focused on the dial.

"Then something is wrong."

"What do you mean?" gasped Janet.

"Either the gauge is fouled or we've been hit. The fuel gauge shows our consumption at a faster rate than we're able to use it. Fuel is dropping pretty fast. We've sprung a leak."

"How serious is it?"

"I don't know, but it looks bad. It's dropping pretty fast."

"Oh God, after all we've been through, don't tell me we're going to end up crashing into the ocean, in the dark? Oh God, with sharks and everything out there."

"Stop it!" said Hamilton. "We're going to be all right. It seems to be slowing down."

"It's probably almost empty, that's why," Janet moaned.

"It has slowed down a little," observed Pete. "With a little luck…."

"What do you mean?"

"It's all going to depend on where the bullet entered the tank or fuel line. If it pierced the tank in the top half, we should have enough fuel to make it."

"And what if it didn't?"

"We'll just have to keep our fingers crossed. It looks like it's going to be pretty close. Just in case, pull out the life vests, will you Ham? Help each other put them on." Pete conveyed a glance of seriousness in Hamilton's direction while his voice maintained a casual tone so as to not panic Janet any more than she was.

"By the way," said Pete, changing the subject. "Todd meant for me to tell you Hillary Warren left Capri and is in London. Todd wanted me to give you her address and telephone number." Securing Janet snugly into her life vest, Hamilton folded the slip of paper and put it into his pocket.

"I'll give her a call when we reach Barbados."

Chapter 66

THE SMALL PLANE was given immediate clearance to land in Barbados. Its exterior riddled with bullets and its fuel gauge on 'empty,' it touched down and quit just as it reached the apron of the tarmac. Gradually three occupants emerged into the semi-darkness of the lighted airfield. Disheveled and emotionally spent they crept out of the disabled craft, briefly clinging to it for support until they collected themselves. Shocked by the degree of damage the plane had undergone, they maintained an almost reverent silence as they surveyed the destruction the light plane had withstood under fire. They had cheated the grim reaper, all right, but not by much. Pete produced a flask from out of the cockpit.

"Where was that when we needed it?" Hamilton said grinning.

"That's all we would have needed," Pete gasped in horror at the idea of being anything less than clear-headed while fighting for their lives. "Let's drink to continued good health."

Before they could finish their toast a stranger came up to them and identified himself. It was Hamilton's contact. Asked to wait, the government man, presumably a CIA agent tactfully positioned himself a discreet distance away as Hamilton said goodbye to Pete and Janet.

It was an awkward moment charged with unspoken emotion. As the finality of separation hit him, Hamilton realized that in all likelihood he would not see the McKenzies again. He felt a great sense of indebtedness, particularly to Pete who had been close to him during the most traumatic period of his life. Lingering to express those sentiments of appreciation and gratitude he was almost at a loss for words.

Pete pressed his business card into young Hamilton's hand. Ham smiled, relief easing the tension in his face. The gesture of bonding was simple but direct. Satisfied, Hamilton resignedly turned away. Tall and erect, with the carriage of a leader, he walked toward the unmarked plane alongside his assigned escort where together they evaporated into the predawn mist.

Coming off their adrenalin high of exhilaration the McKenzies filed through customs feeling suddenly exhausted. Taking a taxi to the nearest hotel they unwound under the soothing magic of a hot shower with a stiff drink to calm their nerves. Setting the alarm clock they fell into bed bone weary. Cuddled close, they slept, too exhausted to worry about Pete leaving in a few hours on a very serious undertaking. The 'fool's errand," as Janet called it, would take Pete over the threshold back into the war zone.

Chapter 67

HAMILTON WARD WAS flown directly to Caracas, Venezuela to secretly meet with United States government officials there. After a preliminary briefing he was to continue on to Washington to meet with high-level State Department officials for the purpose of organizing a government in exile.

Hamilton Ward was needed alive to form the nucleus for a temporary government that would be able to stabilize his country until a duly formed democratic government could be elected. As a familiar national figure he could easily assume command of Victoria Island. Pro West, he was to help form a coalition government representing the factions within the population combining right and left to represent a moderate political viewpoint.

Hamilton flew to Washington where he met with the Pentagon people. There, in an exchange of ideas, they formulated a plan of action to be put into effect after the situation on Victoria Island cooled down. In the meantime, it was decided that Hamilton be kept on ice until the time was ripe for him to surface. They agreed London was as good a place as any for him to wait it out. Eager for the opportunity to settle family matters, Hamilton immediately left for England to see Hillary Warren.

Hamilton arrived in London earlier than Hillary had expected. She was in the garden as he walked toward her. It was as if for a moment her mind was playing a trick on her. He looked so much like Jonathan she was reminded of another reunion in Capri when she had thought Jonathan was dead and he had come back to her. Was it Jonathan now? Her heart skipped a beat. Maybe, yes....maybe....

She rushed toward him from the iron settee where she had been sitting and just as she reached him she collapsed, sobbing into his arms, her hopes dashed by reality. Mutually devastated by their emotional encounter they comforted one another.

Tenderly holding Hillary in his arms Hamilton could feel her despair, her heartbreak, as the intensity of her grief poured out of her, leaving her racked with convulsive sobs. He understood her misery all too well. Although he did not outwardly demonstrate it, his own grief had the same magnitude of emptiness.

After a time they came inside to have tea. Their conversation was general and for a while they engaged in polite pleasantries and then, suddenly, erratically, the conversation shifted. Frustrated and in need of a confidant who would understand, Hillary abruptly confided that she was pregnant with Jonathan's child. While appearing to take this news in stride, Hamilton was shocked. As Hillary continued to unburden her heart she tearfully fondled a photograph Hamilton had brought with him to show to her. It was a snapshot of Jonathan with Hamilton when he was a small boy.

"I was almost illegitimate. Did father ever tell you that?" Startled by the bluntness of his remark Hillary shook her head. "It's true," he smiled. "I wouldn't lie about a thing like that." He paused and shrugged. "The more I think about it, I'm not surprised he didn't tell you though. Father was very much the romantic. Honor, duty, that sort of thing. But it is true. Nevertheless, my parents were quite young when my mother found herself....... in the same situation as yourself. She was a Catholic so the course for her was quite clear. She wanted to have the child, me. And as for Father, there was no question either. He was against abortion."

"I think that my mother had always loved my father. It was just that he never felt exactly the same way about her. Even then though, he put the country first. But he didn't let her down. While there doesn't seem to be a stigma for illegitimate births in the islands, in the upper classes it is considered déclassé. It just isn't done. Coming from a prominent family, Mother would have been scandalized. They both knew that. Father made the only choice he could. He did the honorable thing. He married her."

"I don't believe anyone else knew their secret except Grandfather." Hamilton smiled in amusement. "Grandfather seems to know everything." Sensing his humor was making Hillary uncomfortable, that she was in some way interpreting it as censure of her, Hamilton took her hand in his and held it to reassure her. He held her eyes with a penetrating stare. "I'm telling you all this for a reason."

"Your father and I were to be married this week," Hillary muttered almost incoherently. "He never knew." Tears silently cascaded down her cheeks. Frozen as though in a trance she spoke as though she hadn't even heard a word he was saying.

He put his arms around her and held her while she wept. "Look, I know how worried and upset you must be."

"I want to have the baby," Hillary said stubbornly.

"Are you sure?"

"Very sure," she said with determination.

"Then there's only one thing left for you to do."

"What?"

"Get married."

Hillary laughed nervously. "Get married? To whom? My track record for marriage hasn't been too good."

"You can marry me," Hamilton said quietly.

Hillary shrank from him as though the very idea repelled her.

"I know," he said gently. "It's not what you had planned or wanted. But think about it. It would solve a lot of problems for you, for both of us right now."

"For you?" she said in surprise.

"Certainly. You'd be doing me a favor."

Unconvinced, Hillary laughed in spite of herself.

"Oh Ham. What a wonderful gesture on your part, so decent and generous. You'd have made your father even more proud of you than he was already." She bit her lip as she thought about Jonathan. "I'm so proud of you I could cry."

"Come on Hillary, please don't." He tightened his grip on her arms.

She chose her words carefully, not wanting to offend him. "I appreciate your thoughtfulness more than I can say, but I couldn't, really. I'll manage on my own. I will"

"I'm proposing a legal ceremony, nothing more. I'll stay around if you need me until the baby comes. I think Father would have approved. He'd understand what I'm trying to do."

Hillary was genuinely moved by the honesty of Hamilton's gesture. As she got all misty-eyed again, he instinctively reached out for her drawing her into his arms.

"I'm so sorry for being such bad company. This is terrible to put anyone through," she wailed.

"Don't worry about it. I understand."

He couldn't tell whether she was relieved or appalled. He had not meant to offend her; he just wanted to do the right thing. Somehow he had to reach her, to help her make the right decision. In her frame of mind he wasn't sure what she might do.

"You can see why it would be best, can't you?" he coaxed. He tilted her head up so that he could see her eyes. She tried to look away. He persisted.

"If you marry me the child will have a name, a father, and ties to a family."

She shrugged meekly.

"We're both without parents. At least the child will belong. It will bear the family name, Jonathan's name."

Soothed by the warmth of Hamilton's embrace, Hillary took comfort in his strength. He seemed so certain. He was so convincing. It would be for the child after all.

Feeling her frail, childlike frame against him, racked by the sobs of her grief, he became painfully aware of her youth and lack of sophistication. With her vulnerability at its lowest ebb, he knew he had to be the one to give her direction. If she should turn to anyone else, someone unscrupulous, who knew what might happen?

In identifying with Hillary, Hamilton had, for the first time in his life confronted his own aloneness. There was only Cecil, his grandfather left now. The duties of government and state seemed to rest solely with him. A crystallization of this realization unnerved him. He wondered whether he was capable of taking up the reins of his father. Self-doubt nagged at him. He couldn't expect Cecil to stand up under the new responsibilities—he was too old and not in particularly good health. He had to do it. It was up to him to carry on the family name.

By marrying Hillary he'd safeguard his father's reputation. At the same time he'd perpetuate the blood line of his family. And if his father's child was a son, there would be another heir. All his life he had been raised to uphold the values of honor and principle.

He remembered what his father had once said. "If you do something, do something worthwhile, and make the moment count."

Chapter 68

ILLARY SAT ON a park bench in the London cemetery where Jonathan's family had a section set aside for them. It was a peaceful place, grassy with large trees and plantings set out over a rolling hilltop. Sunlight streamed through the leaves to dapple the ground with dancing shadows as a light breeze sent lithe tree limbs and branches into motion.

It was a warm, sunny day and Hillary had impulsively begged to go along with Hamilton while he arranged for a memorial to commemorate his father. Waiting for him, she sat thinking. Although leaves were falling from the trees it was like a perfect summer's day, warm and wonderful. Contemplating the patterns of human behavior she sat watching the other mourners roaming the grounds. She had had more than her share of death to last for the rest of her life. But, she supposed, sooner or later everyone takes a turn to remember, to hurt, to cry.

When the idea of marrying Hillary had first come to Hamilton, he had to admit it had seemed mad at first, but the more he had thought about it, the more logical it had become. If only he could persuade her to go along with him. It would certainly tie up all the loose ends for all of them. He decided to bring it up again, later.

Back in her flat as he prepared drinks for them, Hamilton grew jittery. He was not sure how Hillary would react and he wanted things to go smoothly. A lot was riding on how he broached the subject. There was absolutely no telling what her response was going to be.

"Remember the story I told you? About my mother and father?"

Hillary stiffened. "Yes."

"Well, I think ....we should do the same thing."

"Thank you, no. I'm already pregnant," she said sarcastically.

"I'm referring to our getting married," he said, a bit irritated.

"Again? You're going to bring this subject up again?"

"We've got to talk about it."

"I've thought about it and decided it's a ridiculous idea. Good grief, don't you realize how embarrassing it would be? And what would Cecil think? It would look so...so, tacky! Going around with Jonathan and marrying you. Don't you realize what you're asking? You, who value respectability and propriety."

"Well, it'll look a damn sight worse when you start wheeling a pram around without a husband. Think what Cecil will feel about having a bastard for a grandchild? With a son who's dishonored the family name? Will that go down easier?

Imagine, my brother a bastard! And where will that leave you?"

"Are you worried about the baby, me or YOU?"

"Hillary, what's the matter? This isn't like you." Hamilton softened and came over toward her. "Come on, let's sit down and talk about it without being angry. There's no reason to quarrel. I'm only trying to help. Surely you know that."

"What woman wants to get married because she has to?"

"So, that's it."

"Partly. By marrying you I don't get a husband, I get a whole goddamn country. Maybe I don't want a country. That's how I lost Jonathan in the first place. He left me to go back to his country. Next thing I know you'll be going back, and then the baby will be expected to go back when he's grown, if it turns out to be a boy. If I'm going to wear black from here on out, I might as well end it here and now. What's the point?"

"After the baby is born you can do as you like, live as you please. This is just a formality. It's just to make the birth legal. Will you promise to at least think about it?"

Visibly upset, she sat swirling a glass of wine in her hand.

"All right. I'll think about it."

Hillary did warm to the idea of Hamilton's marriage proposal. The more she thought about it the more she felt his plan had real merit. At least she had to admit to his logic. Regarding her pregnancy, no one knew she was pregnant except for the doctor in Capri and as far as he would be concerned she was just another faceless tourist. Even if he did put two and two together to know who she was, how could he know whose child she was carrying?

By marrying Hamilton, the family secret would be kept. Jonathan's honor would be preserved and the Wards would have an heir. Best of all, she would have Jonathan's baby. If she accepted Hamilton's proposal it would be a marriage of convenience, with no strings attached. Everyone would be bailed out. Except for her, everyone would be satisfied.

She would think it through.

Chapter 69

HILLARY AND HAMILTON were married in a simple civil ceremony in London. Retaining Hillary's rented two-bedroom flat in the Knightsbridge section of London, off Hyde Park; they were as inconspicuous as possible, blending into the neighborhood like any other newly wedded couple. But they weren't any other couple. They were the future Prime Minister of Victoria Island and his wife.

Together constantly out of necessity, they got to know one another quite well. An unexpected bonus to their arrangement was that they were uncommonly compatible. Familiarizing themselves with the area they went on long walks talking about anything and nothing frequently ending in heated debates. Evenings they went to the cinema or out to dinner although sometimes they ate in the flat, jointly cooking up a simple meal more often than not laughing over their failures at haute cuisine. Vocal, spirited, opinionated, they acted as many married couples might have, yet neither of them forgot for a moment the purpose of their unusual living arrangement.

Primarily however, Hamilton followed the news pertaining to Victoria Island fanatically. Fearing for his grandfather he read every bit of news he could lay his hands on while eagerly absorbing everything broadcast over the radio or television. What he didn't learn through public channels was covertly supplied to him by his liaison in London. Meeting with his contact on a regular basis Hamilton was kept abreast of all events pertinent to Victoria Island as sophisticated plans were being formulated to overthrow Clarence Charles and, as a by-product, the communists who had taken over the island. As a national figure with the ability to assume control of the island, Hamilton was being briefed and readied for the counter-revolutionary movement.

But, as time went on Hamilton grew restless, impatient. Agonizing over underground reports of a possible invasion he continued to worry about his grandfather and the destruction warfare would bring to his already besieged people. Waiting, worrying, unable to act on his own, he was helpless to do anything until he was called upon. But when that moment came, he would be ready.

Although he suspected Hillary knew how upset he was, Hamilton tried to keep his anxieties to himself as much as possible in order to shield her from any reference to the past. They had become quite good friends. What began as a mutually convenient co-existence had developed into a very satisfying relationship. He didn't want to do anything to jeopardize that relationship.

One evening, after a particularly pleasant dinner out, as they were on their way up to their flat chatting enthusiastically about a variety of subjects, Hillary suddenly delighted in remembering an incident she had almost forgotten.

"Did I tell you who I saw yesterday?"

"No, who?" Hamilton responded with exaggerated animation.

"Adam. I saw him in the grocery store."

"That son of a bitch. What did he want?" Ham pushed open the apartment door with such force it slammed back against the wall.

"Nothing much," said Hillary suddenly losing her enthusiasm. Put off by Hamilton's unexpected reaction she continued warily. "He hadn't heard I was back and was rather surprised to see me."

Hamilton threw his keys onto the kitchen table and glowered.

Hillary continued uncertainly. "He invited us out for a drink. Can you imagine? He wants to meet you."

"I'll bet," Ham responded sarcastically. "He's got a hell of a nerve. You told him about me?" Hillary smiled mischievously. "What did you tell him?"

She was openly toying with him now. "That you were cute!"

He tickled her, forgetting his irritation. "Come on, out with it. Tell me all of it."

"I told him we were married."

"What did he have to say about that?"

"What could he say? That's when he invited us for drinks." She burst into laughter.

"That's all? That isn't all, is it?"

"It is."

"Is he married?"

"Not any more. It didn't work out. In fact he apologized to me. He admitted he had been a beast. Of course, I had already figured that out for myself."

"So all is forgiven?"

Hillary shrugged noncommittally.

"And when is the big day?"

"Oh, I told him I'd check with you first."

"You did what? Are you mad? Why didn't you tell him no straight out?"

"I didn't say we'd go."

"That you would even think about doing anything with him after what he's done to you absolutely amazes me. How could you even consider seeing him again?"

"Why are you shouting? We don't have to go. If you'd rather not, we won't. It doesn't matter. I don't understand why we're quarreling over something so ridiculous and unimportant."

"I'm not quarreling and I'm not meeting him for any goddamn drink. And furthermore, neither are you!"

"Ham, this is so silly. I just wanted him to see how...."

"There are no buts about it Hillary."

She was standing by the kitchen sink confused, forlorn and seeming as if she were about to cry. Suddenly the expression on Hamilton's face softened. He paused and breathed a long breath.

"Hill, I'm sorry. I didn't mean to shout at you. I don't know what came over me. If you want to go, go. I'll even take you." Stammering, he apologized again. He looked at his watch and then, just as suddenly as his mood had come and gone he whirled around on his heels toward the door.

"Hillary, I almost forgot, I have something important to take care of. Don't wait up for me. I'm sorry, I'll explain later."

Before Hillary had time to protest Hamilton was gone.

Chapter 70

HAMILTON RETURNED AFTER midnight, well after Hillary had gone to bed. Rummaging through the refrigerator for a beer he opened a bottle and sat down at the kitchen table. He glanced at his watch. It was almost 12:30. He had just learned the invasion was to take place that morning and he had been alerted to stand by for further instructions.

He had been sharing the flat with Hillary for almost two weeks, yet so much had happened between them. The time span seemed much longer. Soon her fears would be realized. In a few days, possibly a week from now, he would be leaving. Strange, but up until he had heard about the forthcoming invasion he had almost looked forward to going. Suddenly he wasn't so sure. He felt very tired and confused. He had always thought he knew himself fairly well but at this moment, given his present circumstances, it was as if he were a stranger even to himself.

Hamilton had been clandestinely meeting with an operative of the CIA keeping abreast of happenings on Victoria Island so that at a moment's notice he would be fully briefed and ready to return when the time was right. Bound by confidentiality not to tell anyone, he had not told his wife. His wife. That was ludicrous. Hillary was and continued to be his father's wife. And with her constant demonstration of love for his father what chance would any man ever have up against her tenacious loyalty to him.

His father was gone yet his presence remained very real and unassailable. Although Hamilton felt a sense of guilt about his relationship with Hillary he also realized that it wasn't his doing that circumstances had joined them together. In fact, the situation had become a real headache for him.

If Hillary hadn't been pregnant he would never have gotten involved with her. In the past he hadn't paid much attention to her, hadn't even noticed her. Well, that was a lie. Hillary was the kind of girl everyone noticed. Pretty, fun to be with, she was different from anyone he had ever met. But, she had been his father's woman and that had clearly meant "hands off" to everyone.

Hamilton had dated a lot of girls while he was away at school, but most of the ones he'd been physically attracted to were either stuck on themselves— snobs, or empty-headed and uninteresting. Lacking a serious romantic interest he buried himself in his studies. Studious and ambitious he excelled, as his father had before him.

But, he recalled wistfully, there had been a girl once. Her name was Carolyn. He had thought he had been in love with her. Blonde, blue-eyed, slender, she was a California girl and a real live-wire full of personality and wholesome good looks. Somehow though, he had known from the beginning that they weren't right for one another. Even so, he had found her irresistible and incredibly bright and entertaining. She had captured his heart and his fancy.

She had come to the islands expressly to see him, he recalled with some embarrassment. Island hopping on a chartered yacht they went to carnival in Trinidad spending an idyllic couple of weeks together. They had had a wonderful time and although it seemed they never stopped laughing there was something forbidding in her personality, something that unsettled him. Carolyn was given to unpredictable moods and lapses into depression. She often seemed distant and remote. At one point he wondered whether she was taking drugs her personality had such mood swings. In any case, he couldn't seem to get close to her.

She had let him sleep with her, but that was the point, she had let him as though it had been a duty. Even in their lovemaking she had been cool, as if there was an invisible barrier between them. They had been intimate, yet Hamilton had never felt close. While he had enjoyed making love to her, more precisely to the idea of making love to her, he couldn't seem to break through her reserved constraint. He remembered, even now, how frustrated he had felt at the time. It had been maddening how she could be at once friendly, yet at the same time aloof.

When it was time for her to leave to go back to the States, they both knew their relationship wouldn't have worked, yet neither of them addressed the issue or wanted to openly admit their inability to communicate. As Carolyn boarded the plane to leave they both realized they'd never see one another again. Whatever they had had was over.

Chapter 71

HILLARY WAS DIFFERENT. They had been together constantly yet Hamilton didn't tire of being with her. She too was witty, charming, fun to be with, but in addition she also had a genuine quality, and for Hamilton that was important. Pangs of guilt gnawed at him. He felt like a real heel. After giving her his word he'd stay by her, here he was, about to leave. It wouldn't even be a month.

They would have more time together, he reasoned, perhaps another week before he would have to leave. He'd try to make it up to her, make her understand. It wouldn't be for long. But whatever he might reason he knew in his heart that to a woman in her circumstances there could be little he could say to soften the blow of his seeming abandonment. However he dealt with the issue, he wouldn't go about it in the same way his father had. While he couldn't very well admit it to Hillary, his opinion of what his father had done bordered on contempt. After seeing the effect it had had upon her he certainly couldn't repeat the same behavior. No, he'd meet the issue head on. He'd tell her.

Why was he making so much out of it? He'd probably only be gone a week and she could join him if she wanted to. Had he gone off the deep end? It shouldn't be such an issue. He just didn't want to hurt her. He was supposed to be her friend. He was her friend, goddamn it! He just didn't want it to appear to her that he was taking advantage of her. Why should she think that?

Why did he care what she thought about what he was doing? He didn't. He'd just tell her he was going and that would be that. It was business, his duty. He had an obligation to settle matters at home. He felt uneasy and guilty again. Why was he feeling so unsettled? He wasn't sure what he felt anymore.

He knocked on the door to Hillary's room before he entered. There was a light coming from beneath her door.

"Hello," he called out to test the climate of her reception to him.

"Come in." She was in bed, reading.

He walked to the bed rather sheepishly and hesitated. "I just wanted to apologize for what happened earlier this evening. I'm sorry. I didn't mean to shout at you."

She smiled up at him and then her expression became serious.

"What came over you? Is something wrong?"

"Adam, for one thing."

"You don't even know him."

"I know, but I do know you and I don't want him ever to have the opportunity of being unkind to you again."

She smiled sweetly and when she did, something about her clicked in his head. She had been lying in bed with a book propped up across her stomach but the moment she saw him she put it aside, immediately sitting up. Feeling he had used bad judgment in intruding upon her unexpectedly, he suddenly felt uncomfortable and inhibited. Their conversation was typically friendly, but as they spoke he was more aware of her than usual. Perhaps it was because of the intimacy of their surroundings or maybe it was because he was feeling considerably loose having put away a few beers over the course of the evening. In any event, as he took her in he seemed to be seeing her in a new light.

She was really quite appealing. Softly feminine in satin and lace without a trace of makeup, she had the shiny, scrubbed radiance of a peaches-and-cream complexion. Her blonde hair was casually swirled on top of her head and secured with a pink satin ribbon while short tendrils still damp from her bath dangled carelessly as they clung to the nape of her neck and framed the sides of her face.

She was really quite beautiful, he thought to himself. His sudden awareness of her as a desirable woman seemed to both surprise and unnerve him.

"I can't understand for the life of me why you'd want to see Adam again. I guess that really bothers me."

"Well," she replied coyly, "it's silly really, but…I guess I just wanted to show you off." She spoke shyly and with embarrassment.

"Show me off?" he repeated dully.

"Yes," she admitted self-consciously. "Put yourself in my position. Adam had just told me his marriage was finished. Just like that!" She snapped her fingers for emphasis. "This, mind you after he jilted me for that woman! Well, here I am newly married to the brightest, best-looking guy who just happens to be extremely successful and…" she groped uncertainly, "obviously wonderful. Well, I guess I just wanted to rub his nose in it a little. He was probably assuming that he could just walk back into my life and take up with me again with just a crook of his little finger. Well, I thought to myself, let him just realize the big mistake he's made!"

"You were making him jealous?"

"Not jealous, just showing him I can get along on my own without him. I wanted him to see I haven't been pining away waiting for him to come back." Suddenly she slammed her book shut and seemed sad. "It was all show, but he didn't know that." She faltered. "Part of me was afraid." She was hesitant and tense.

"Afraid?" Hamilton asked in shocked surprise. "He wouldn't do anything to hurt you, would he?"

"I wanted him to know you were around so that he wouldn't start calling me. I didn't want to have to deal with that. The thought of it made me nervous."

"That part about me, did you make that up too?"

"No, it was true. Everything was true except for the real reason you married me," she answered despondently. "I couldn't very well tell him I was pregnant, could I?"

She began to fidget with the edge of the counterpane. "He would have loved that! Obviously he doesn't know I am pregnant. I would prefer that he didn't know, at least not just yet." Putting her fears into words exposed her, hurt her, and her eyes began to tear.

"Do you still love him?" Hamilton asked gently.

"I thought I did once, but that was a long time ago," she said dreamily. "A very long time ago," she added with defiant finality. "Say, what are you talking about? Did you forget? I'm a married lady now!" She smiled gamely but looked as though she was about to cry.

"That's right, you're my girl now and don't forget it," he said with forced cheer. "Isn't that right?" He patted her reassuringly.

"That's right," she agreed with a weak smile.

"Hillary, I hope you're going to understand what I have to tell you. I feel like a heel to bring it up now, but I feel I must."

"Sounds serious."

"It is, and it's to be kept just between us, promise?"

"Promise." She waited expectantly.

Hamilton hesitated and then began, his gaze leveled on her. "I'm on stand-by alert to go back to Victoria Island."

She closed her eyes tightly and collapsed back into the pillows. "Oh no!" she groaned.

"It'll only be for a short time," he added quickly. "Until things clear up and then you can come back too. By then it'll be perfectly safe."

A dreamy, far away look came over her. "That's what your father said. He left in the middle of the night without even saying goodbye. That was the last time I saw him. We didn't even have a chance to say goodbye." She mourned anew.

"I won't do that."

She looked at him and seemed undecided as to whether or not she should believe him. Sensing her distrust, he reflexively pulled her to him as she tearfully collapsed into his arms.

"I won't do that, I promise," he whispered again.

Eager for reassurance, she looked up at him her face red, tear-stained and troubled. Deeply moved he was at a loss as to what to do. She was inconsolable.

"Believe me, this is different. I've got the backing of the U. S. Government. Come on, Hillary, it won't be the same as when Father went. The island will be under Martial Law. I won't be allowed to go until its safe."

"I don't believe you," she wailed throwing her hands up in the air in despair. "What if I asked you not to go, to give it all up?"

"I can't do that!"

"You could if you wanted to."

He seemed to consider it. "I wish I could. I'd much rather be here with you," he smiled engagingly.

"Cecil's already there, why can't he do whatever is supposed to be done?"

"He could, I suppose, but it wouldn't be fair. Grandfather is getting too old to take on so great a responsibility."

"Then let me come with you when you go," she coaxed.

Leaning forward he kissed her on the nose. "I think it would be best, young lady, if you stayed right here."

"If it's safe, why can't I go?"

"Living conditions are bound to be terrible. It'll be like camping out. You'd be miserable. Besides, I'll be working around the clock organizing a new government. I'll be totally immersed in work."

"Duty calls," she said sarcastically. "Again!"

His voice softened and he spoke gently. "My personal feelings are separate from my national responsibility. It's not as if I were abandoning you, you know, is that what you think?" He regarded her quizzically, then smiled and stroked her shoulder. "I'm not abandoning you," he said simply. "Hey, I've gotten used to having you around," he grinned.

"Me too," she blurted out. "Ham, what will I do while you're gone?" She paused and her face flushed pink. "I'll miss you," she sniffed. "If something were to happen to you too, I just couldn't bear it." Overcome with emotion she threw her arms around him and burst into tears, burying her face into his chest. "Ham, I don't want you to go," she pleaded. "I'm afraid for you."

He had to cheer her up. He felt responsible for knocking the pins out from under her. Trying to change the subject he noticed a glass of wine on the stand next to the bed and picked it up.

"Come on, drink your wine, it'll make you feel better."

"I've had too much already," she said, making the excuse of the baby. But she took a sip anyway. He laughed and shook his head in amusement.

"We've got the makings of a real crying jag, haven't we? Well, come on, it's not going to be all that bad. Cheer up. Let's see if there's some music on the radio."

"That's how it all started," she said gloomily. "Moonlight, wine, and music on the radio."

"Well, we are not by the sea. In fact it's damned cold outside," he sighed. "I'm not used to cold weather anymore, either. And as for the wine, it seems we're way ahead in that department." He found a station playing an up-beat song. "There," he announced with satisfaction, "that's at least lively."

She was suddenly miles away. This mood of despondency both worried and upset him.

"Hillary, my father is dead, gone. I don't like the idea any better than you do, but we've got to face it. And you have got to stop this obsession about him once and for all. Pick up the threads of your life. Go forward!"

"Everybody I've ever loved has been taken from me," she said morosely. "My parents, Adam, Jonathan. It's me, isn't it? What's wrong with me?"

"Stop talking nonsense. Of course it isn't you."

"I have nothing, no one," she raved maniacally.

"Yes, you have" he offered cheerfully. "You've got me."

She looked at him scornfully. He was beginning to wonder whether she had heard a word he had said, let alone know who he was. As though in shock, she put her arms around him and remaining almost motionless, she stared into space.

"It'll be all right," he whispered. Apparently she had more to drink than he had thought. "You'll see, everything will be all right."

Chapter 72

H E DIDN'T KNOW why their emotions had spilled out of control, it had felt so natural. All he knew was he was kissing her, holding her, and she was responding with unbridled desire. She was tantalizing and desirable and his mind blurred in the heady intimacy of the tender moment. With their desire increasing, he didn't stop—she didn't want him to. Feelings, long denied, overwhelmed him—overwhelmed them both.

"You taste so good, feel so wonderful….."

"I know," she whispered. "It's been so long. I've missed you, missed you so much…"

He was delirious with rapture, overcome with joy.

"Jonathan, oh Jonathan……."

When the significance of her words registered in his brain, when he realized what he had heard, it was as if he had had a bucket of cold water rained upon him. She didn't seem to realize what she had said and continued to kiss him passionately. Feeling humiliated, he gradually pulled himself away until finally he pulled her away from him roughly.

"Look at me! Look at me!" He demanded sharply as he shook her to reality.

"What's wrong?" she said thickly.

"I can't compete with my father," he muttered.

"Whatever do you mean?"

"Christ, you can't even keep our names straight!"

"That's cruel."

"You can't very well deny it. Kissing me like there was no tomorrow and calling me Jonathan. Come off it, Hillary. You thought I was my father."

"You're despicable," she shrieked.

"Well, you won't have to put up with me much longer." He leapt to his feet and bolted to the window, snapping open the Venetian blind.

"Time for greener pastures, is that it? Well. If you're rescinding our arrangement, I understand. That's about par for the course. I should have expected it. You were probably looking for an easy out."

"That's not it and you know it," Hamilton shot back sullenly, pacing the floor in a fury.

"Then I don't understand. Could it be you are reminded of death and are suddenly afraid to go?"

"No! Whatever I am, I am not a coward." He snapped the blind shut with a jerk, almost pulling it off the wall.

"I couldn't blame you," she taunted. "You'll be in danger. We both know that. Do you take me for a fool? That's why I thought you didn't want me to go. I thought for one brief moment that you might have been worried about me. Obviously you're just tired of playing house." Compulsively she placed her book on the nightstand. The empty wine glass almost fell over but she caught it.

"God, you're exasperating! I was worried. And I wasn't just playing house. I was hoping that you could separate me from my father, just once. Obviously, I was wrong."

He threw himself into a chair. She came over and started to massage his shoulders from behind.

"Such an ego," she soothed. "I didn't mean to hurt your feelings. I'm sorry, really."

"I don't need your pity," he said jumping up from his chair.

"I don't pity you."

"What do you feel, then, can you tell me that? Do you know yourself? I think you do but you probably won't want to admit it."

"What do you mean?"

"You know exactly what I mean. Something has happened between us. I feel it and I know you feel it too. Why don't you stop fighting it and let whatever it is happen."

She turned away and flung herself across the bed. "Don't you see, I can't!" she cried almost hysterically. "It wouldn't be right."

Suddenly he was standing by her side compelling her to face him.

"After all that's been happening around us you speak of what's right? Stop fighting it Hillary, let go of the past."

"Don't you understand? I'm carrying his child. I repeat, it isn't right."

Obstinately he pulled her to him and kissed her. "Then we'll make it right."

"Ham….." she whimpered, "please, don't…"

He lay back and stared at the ceiling. "Well, it's a beginning anyway." He said sullenly. "At least you've got my name right."

Chapter 73

BY MONDAY MORNING U.S. warships lay off Georgetown Harbor and could be seen from shore with a naked eye. Nursing emotions still raw from the trauma connected with the massacre just days before on Bloody Wednesday, the people suffered dizzying pangs of foreboding. They wanted to run, to hide, but they couldn't. They were trapped, forced to endure whatever it was that was to take place. As conjecture heightened their uneasiness they prepared for the worst. Most of them stockpiled provisions while those with the opportunity to do so sent their families to relatives living in the countryside. As an expectant quiet fell over the island like a shroud of doom, they waited.

The invasion began ominously as two groups of U.S. Navy Seals, commando-type specialists trained in seaborne operations, silently slipped ashore under cover of darkness. Their faces blackened, weapons in hand, they picked their way up the rocky coastline to infiltrate into enemy territory.

The first team was to locate and rescue Cecil Ward who was being held captive in the governor general's residence at the top of the hill overlooking the bay. Under house arrest, Cecil Ward, the Queen of England's representative, was considered by the free world to be the principal civilian authority on the island. He was needed by the intervening forces to help organize the new leadership of the island in the chaos that was certain to follow. His presence was sure to lend a stabilizing influence at a time of grave crisis.

The second team of Seals was to take command of the radio station, the symbolic power center of the island. Synchronized to strike after the invasion had commenced, they were not to let their presence be known before then.

The group heading to the summit laboriously picked their way up the steep cliffside. Enveloped in the atmosphere of the quaint 18th century city sprawling in a panorama around them as the city's lights twinkled benignly in the background, they knew it was but a matter of time before the tranquility of the island would be transformed into gun bursts and artillery flares as the city succumbed to the immobilization of electrical and communications power failures.

Seasoned combat veterans equipped with nighttime battery-powered starlight sniper scopes on their automatic rifles, the men proceeded up the rugged terrain in stealthy silence. As they reached the crest of the mountain their target came into view. Pausing just long enough to get their bearings, they moved in closer. Suddenly dogs were barking revealing their presence. They had been discovered. Driven back by gunfire from house guards, they had no choice. It was a do or die situation. They attacked and rushed the guards. Appearing as if out of nowhere, three Cuban-manned BTR-60 armored personnel carriers fired at them. They returned fire but they knew it was hopeless. Without the cumbersome weapons they usually carried to counter such attacks, disposable Laws anti-tank rockets, the Seals were rendered virtually defenseless. There was a lull in the shooting. Taking advantage of the unexpected opportunity they burst forward toward the house. They were to remain holed up with their charge for the next twenty-one hours. By the time reinforcements would arrive ten of their eleven would be wounded in the tug of war over Cecil Ward.

In the silver gray illumination of moonlight two warships silently made their way to off-shore positions at either end of Victoria Island in proximity to the airports as a task force of eleven support ships carrying men and machinery stood by ready to off-load their cargos of manpower and war toys. Using Barbados as a staging area, Jet Hawks and C-130 troop transport planes waited; ready to supplement the Army Rangers being dropped over Victoria International Airport's landing strip. The Marines were being airlifted onto the old airport runway at Pearl's. Ironically, that Monday evening soldiers had been told they were going on a late-night drill and were not given real bullets until 7 am Tuesday morning when live ammunition was handed out on aboard the C-130s. Right up until the moment of actual combat, every effort had been made to quash rumors of the invasion.

Initiating the assault in two main strikes, Vice-Admiral Leroy Montgomery, military strategist and operations officer of the project code named, 'Operation Tropic Fury,' launched the campaign from the communications center of the aircraft carrier Independence off shore from Georgetown Harbor.

Just before dawn on Tuesday, on the southeast coast of the island, choppers laden with 400 Marines from the helicopter carrier Guam, began their airlift of troops over rough seas and shoals to land onto Pearl's runway. With resistance from the rag-tag force on guard duty virtually non-existent, the airport succumbed quickly as its defenders threw down their arms. The Guam, having successfully completing its mission, was rerouted north around the island to join the rest of the task force to the northwest side of the island.

Meanwhile, off of Georgetown Harbor at 5:35 am, just as the sky began to brighten, the Independence began launching Navy C-130s toward the almost completed 9,000 foot airfield at Victoria International Airport. At precisely 5:37am five hundred U.S. Army Rangers from the 82d Airborne Division of the U.S. Army's elite Special Forces began to drop over the airstrip bordering the medical school facilities. When the first planeload of paratroopers bailed out they were met with immediate ground fire; the Cubans were ready for them.

Succeeding planes flying into a maelstrom of anti-aircraft and machine gun fire were told to abort. Fearing heavy casualties the command post ordered them to turn back. Responding instantly, the next two planes peeled off, their instructions, to circle back, coming in lower with cover from accompanying AC-130 gunships. Completing the second pass they made their drop from an altitude of five hundred feet, a maneuver not employed since World War II. As they released their cargo of paratroopers, the planes were protected by their escorts, the awesome AC-130 gunships—Spectre. The sky was filled with the activity of billowing chutes and a kaleidoscope of gun bursts.

A paratrooper is most vulnerable, in fact defenseless, when he is hanging from his harness in descent. By shortening his airborne time to nineteen seconds, he reduces his chances of being hit by sniper fire. However, should the parachute foul or snag even momentarily, there would be no time for it to open. His risk is greatest in the air.

From the moment the Rangers hit the air, Soviet-made AK-47 and machine gun fire pelted them, ripping through their parachutes. Helpless to do anything but look around, the parachutists drifted aloft while the Cubans tried to shoot them out of the sky. In their rapid descent, the Rangers assessed their individual strategies in relation to enemy positions while the Cubans continued to fire on them. Armored personnel carriers filled with Cuban troops and ammunition suddenly appeared within four hundred yards of the Ranger landing sites to aim mortars at the invaders. Taking cover immediately upon hitting the ground, the Rangers returned small arms fire as U.S. gunships protectively sprayed the resisting forces. As Cobra gunships whizzed overhead covering them from above, the Rangers moved to secure the airfield, clearing it of heavy construction equipment, barbed wire, empty oil drums, trucks and cars in preparation for helicopters landing more troops and equipment of their own. Dodging bullets and returning fire as they drove or towed obstructions off the runway they completed their objective smoothly. Suddenly it was as if a chain reaction was set into motion. The air was alive with U.S. Black Hawks airlifting men and machinery onto the field.

By 6:15 a.m. equipment and personnel began landing with all the thunder of rapid-fire U.S. Navy Cobras and Air Force AC-130 gunships, Air Force C-5As and C-130 troop transports and the supersonic boom of jet fighters. With an awesome display of air-to-ground activity jeeps, amphibious vehicles, personnel carriers and tanks poured forth from cargo bays as the battle raged between the Cubans and the invading Rangers. The skirmish continued in earnest as foot soldiers branched out toward the Cuban barracks.

As Victoria Island's radio station transmitted instructions to the people across the island in an effort to rally them to block the roads and join their militia squadrons to defend the island against the "enemy," the command center of communication control was receiving word that the Seals had secured the radio station. Calling in the exact coordinates of the radio station to the off-shore command center the Seals distanced themselves and waited. Within moments, a shell directed from an off-shore gun ship made a direct hit on the radio station destroying it.

Chapter 74

TODD MURDOCK AWAKENED early to begin his vigil. Looking in the direction of the Victoria International Airport for some sign of activity he scanned the runway, the control tower and the terminal buildings through his binoculars. There was no movement, no sound. As the quiet of morning gave way to the distant hum of aircraft, the sky was suddenly filled with billowing parachutes cascading toward the runway. U.S. Army Rangers landing in a torrent of bullets was the first news to be announced over the radio.

With the invasion under way, Murdock took it as his patriotic duty to maintain radio communications with the command center of the Independence, reporting all military activities taking place within his sphere of observation from the vantage point of his cliffside home overlooking Prickly Bay on the southern coast of the island.

Early on in the fighting, a Cobra helicopter gunship was hit as it passed over the peninsula opposite him. Bursting into flames the disabled aircraft crashed and exploded. In retaliation, a U.S. Spectre gunship circled the hills, its Gatling guns pumping several thousand rounds a minute into the underbrush knocking out the offending ant-aircraft gun emplacement responsible.

Meanwhile, in a ground confrontation, cross-firing field troops inadvertently shelled a civilian residence just moments after its occupants, American medical students, had vacated it to head for safer accommodations up the road. Observing activity on the peninsula through field glasses, Murdock saw movement passing through the dense vegetation. As foliage swayed in the breezeless morning, it was a dead give-away that infantry was on the move to position themselves in more strategic locations in the hills.

Without warning an explosion detonated at very close range. Reverberating from the blast, the foundation of the old great house shuddered as its ceilings spewed plaster dust while the chandeliers swayed. The dog, terrified by the sudden commotion, cowered, and losing control, wet the floor.

"That was almost a direct hit!" Murdock yelled into the microphone. "What the hell are you doing? You nearly took me out up here. Have you gone crazy?"

"Take it easy. It was an error. A rocket misfired."

"Misfired? Misfired? Tell the trigger-happy son-of-a-bitch to watch it. Do I need to strike the flag to show which side I'm on for chrissake?"

"Come on Murdock, it was an accident. Nobody's hurt. There's no damage."

"No damage? No damage? You should see the size of the crater out there! I'd be safer at the fuckin' Russian Embassy. Why don't you misfire over there? Drop one on them."

"Relax, Murdock."

"Relax my ass," shouted Todd gruffly. "Let's see how relaxed you'd be if they start shelling the ship."

As Murdock paced up and down, the dog looked at him soulfully. Murdock paused to give his loyal friend a reassuring pat on the head.

Chapter 75

A CTIVELY TRANSMITTING INFORMATION to the Independence, Murdock began to pick up transmissions from other parts of the island. Eager to participate, locals came forward to supply information, giving ammunitions storage locations, artillery positions, PRB hiding places. Lacking however, was news of Cecil Ward or information regarding the whereabouts of Clarence Charles who had gone into hiding, virtually disappearing altogether. Murdock couldn't help but wonder about Pete McKenzie, laughing as he thought about him. The guy sure picked a hell of a way to spend his vacation. Correct that, his honeymoon.

With Victoria International Airport secured, there was a lull in the fighting as ground forces spread out. Murdock walked along the veranda taking time out for a beer. He was bursting with hyperkinetic energy. Suddenly he had to take a leak. Whenever he felt unduly nervous he had to pee. He went inside to the toilet. Coming back outside, he lit a cigarette.

Murdock had a lot on his mind and he was struggling with the weight of it.

He had been sitting on information so explosive he was not sure who to trust with it. He had been afraid to tell anyone for fear the news would be mishandled, bungled or worse, suppressed. By a simple error in judgment he could be responsible for a nuclear war. He felt the time was ripe now. It would certainly get no better. Confronted with his information, the military would have to act. The way he'd present it, they'd have no choice. Once out in the open, Intelligence couldn't hide it, and the bureaucrats wouldn't be able to cover it up or ignore its existence, there wouldn't be time. Once they knew, everyone would be anxious to just get rid of it. He sure as hell would.

Leaving his self-assigned post Murdock drove up the road to the Redfern estate. Using a pass key given personally to him by Jonathan Ward in case of just such a circumstance, need, Murdock went directly to the Thinking Garden and old man, Osgood's most prized possession, his telescope with its specially ground lenses and night scope.

High on the hilltop with its panoramic view of the island Murdock swiveled the telescope to the south and out to sea. Scanning the area just off shore he sighted Glover Island. He calibrated the headings to the spot where Glover Island led across the inlets to Lighthouse Point on Victoria Island proper.

Murdock wrote down the compass headings charting the exact coordinates of the area which located precisely the secret deep-water Soviet submarine enclave at the Glover inlet.

Chapter 76

THE RANGERS RAN into more heavy-shelling as their choppers approached Victoria International Airport. Anti-aircraft guns secreted in the foothills vigorously pounded away at them until they were knocked out by U.S. Spectre gunships, the terror machines which were equipped with rapid-fire Gatling guns. The noise from the encounter was fierce as detonations rumbled and reverberated shaking the ground in thunderous spasms. Much of the flack was coming from the barracks area where Cuban workers building the airstrip were housed.

Fearing for the safety of the American medical students, the arriving Rangers landed and fanned out toward the medical school campus, a compound of five barracks-style dormitories, a lecture hall, a cafeteria and a basketball court which would later be used as a helicopter landing pad to evacuate the wounded. Dodging through withering AK-47 and machine gun fire, the Rangers advanced. The barrage came from Cubans dug in a defensive arc north of the airstrip. By midmorning, the Rangers knew they were up against heavier resistance than they had expected. Cubans, known to be on the island, were not just airport construction workers but well-trained military men and they were much tougher than anticipated. The Pentagon had expected to find about 500 Cubans on the island, including 350 workers and a small military advisory group. Instead, the landing troops faced more than 600 well-armed, professionally-trained soldiers.

At the first noises of low-flying aircraft and ensuing gunfire, the students at the Georgetown Medical School awakened. As explosions and detonations rumbled and reverberated around them the students did not know who was shooting at whom. Even worst, they did not know where the planes were coming from.

Students on the campus adjacent to the fighting couldn't believe what was happening and hid under their beds or in the safety of their metal and porcelain bathtubs as tracer bullets hammered through their open windows. The students, not realizing who the fighting forces were, were terrified and confused.

Feeling suddenly betrayed, one student groaned, "Please, let it be our guys. Please, don't let it be some tin-pot nation hoping to land and take over with fifty men."

Alone in his room Bob Fisher awakened to the rumble of aircraft passing overhead. He lay still for a moment to let the significance of what he heard sink in. Gunfire, artillery, anti-aircraft shells. He felt the ground shudder. His first impulse was to get out of the building to see what was happening. He couldn't suppress it. He ran outside to assess the situation

He could see smoke billowing in the air as the sounds of conflict intensified into the proportions of a large-scale battle.

He raced back into his room diving for cover as a passing plane swooped low over the building as it returned fire on a nearby anti-aircraft gun emplacement. As sleepy students were jolted awake they ran stumbling about the corridors in a daze of confusion. Fisher heard tracer shots rattling through the building.

"Get down! Get down!"

They heard an explosion and then silence. By then everyone was awake and checking with friends for news. As if unwitting participants in a West World scenario students clamored to the windows or ran outside to see for themselves what was happening. Rushing back to their rooms, they hurriedly tried to get dressed before the next barrage came. Intermittently they hit the floor or dove into their bathtubs until the attacks subsided. Gradually they were to learn what was happening as fellow students pieced together fragments of information gathered from ham radio communications. Scurrying about they nervously snacked on junk food to allay anxieties, while in the shelling phases they hid under beds and behind barricades. Their initial joy aside, their next fear was wondering whether or not the Cubans would try to take them hostage. That was another story. The United States military had hoped it would be routine to take control of the entire island in the first day. They were wrong.

The United States and Caribbean multi-national forces were fighting against very highly armed people with armored personnel carriers that were jammed full of ammunition. Although a number of them did put down their weapons from the beginning, many did not. Heavily armed and in uniform, those resisting offered a surprisingly strong Cuban effort facilitated by the leak from the 'unidentified' Caribbean country. Since Cuba had been tipped off to U. S. plans to invade at least twenty-four hours in advance, the Cubans were well prepared. While Castro did not send in reinforcements he did send an Army Colonel to advise the Cubans on the island. After a successful U. S. intervention the officer was subsequently demoted to a rank of private.

By 10 a.m. the Rangers had cleared the runway for the arrival of 750 additional troops from the 82d Airborne Division of Fort Bragg, North Carolina. But, as the reinforcements deplaned, Cuban armored personnel carriers moved into position on the edge of the runway and opened fire. From a Cuban barracks on the outskirts of the airfield came more machine gun fire. Two Americans, one airborne company commander and one squad leader slumped onto the runway, dead.

Off shore air power was called for from the U. S. aircraft carrier, Independence, off the southwest tip of the island, A-6 Intruders and A-7 Corsair fighters raced in to strafe the Cuban position. It took five hours to subdue the defenders and secure the airport. During the battle, a Cobra gunship was shot down. The southern part of Operation Tropic Fury cost eleven American lives. As the Americans mopped up at the airport, it became clear that the Cubans had turned the area into their private nerve center. Locals had been removed from the beach houses above the airfield and anti-aircraft emplacements were mounted along a ridge north of the runway.

Once the U. S. forces felt the Airfield was under control, they started sweeping through the Cuban complex of barracks and warehouses. They ran into resistance in three areas—the Cuban workers' shelter, a supply dump and a structure that turned out to be a major military headquarters. Combing the area they found six corrugated metal Quonset huts further up the road, in which they found a large cache of Cuban and Soviet weapons.

Terminating the ferocious attack dogs guarding the barbed wire enclosed premises they carefully made their way into the complex fearing the compound might be booby-trapped. Inside, boxes crammed with AK-47s, rifles, handguns, 120mm mortars, machine guns, anti-aircraft weapons, rocket launchers and hand-grenades were found stacked to the ceilings.

Much of the arms had clearly been disguised as ordinary Cuban imports when brought into the island. "Cuban Economic Office" was clearly imprinted on many of the crates along with coded identification numbers. There was an entire section of black boxes presumably set aside for covert shipment to contra rebels active in revolutionary activities.

Victoria Island, because of its recent political leanings and its strategic location geographically, had become key in the undercover transshipments of arms and ammunitions from communist block countries funneling their instruments of revolution to terrorists within the hot spots of the western hemisphere.

While fighting continued to the north, Rangers stationed at the Georgetown Medical School campus enlisted the students to set up a makeshift field hospital inside a lecture hall. A second casualty unit was put up inside a school library. Students tore up bed sheets for bandages and rearranged library tables to receive patients. Through the next day, dozens of soldiers limped in, mostly with relatively minor wounds. Once the Rangers cleared a landing area by pulling down the backboards of the basketball court, helicopters came in to evacuate the more serious cases to the American ships off shore. The school's meager supply of morphine was running low and wounded Cubans were also treated in the floating hospital facilities of the support ships.

One patient, an old militiaman with one arm shot off was brought to the school emergency facilities for treatment. He had killed two U. S. Rangers. "The big psychological problem for me was treating a militiaman who had killed two of our young men," said the medical student volunteer. "It was rough."

Other students trapped in their dorm rooms or cut off waited for help and tried to stay calm. As the conflict diminished into isolated spots of fighting or irregular sniper activity, the students tried to restore some sense of sanity to relieve the tension. They tried to have a party. The school provided the rum and the students cooked fried chicken sharing their food with the Rangers giving them cigarettes and thanks.

Chapter 77

FTER THE CURFEW went into effect Lester Griffon reluctantly closed down the Red Crab. Literally envisioning himself going bankrupt from loss of business revenue to meet his financial commitments, he tried to stay calm and to remember his blood pressure. But, with the restaurant mortgaged to the hilt, Griffon knew he couldn't afford to be closed.

Seemingly happy-go-lucky by nature, Lester projected the vibrant personality of a bon vivant. In reality, however, he was a worrier and a workaholic, a pessimist to the core. It seemed ironic that having always been conscientious about his own personal business dealings he was thrust into dire straights through no fault of is own, a victim of circumstances. To fail without contributing to one's own failure is a terrible thing. He tried to think; there seemed to be no course of action. He'd just have to go along and hope for the best.

His first problem was how to handle the power cuts during the curfew. Under normal circumstances he would rely on one

of his generators to provide electrical current as a back-up to
the frequent losses of power. He had two in case one of them
broke down. With the curfew in effect he didn't know what to
expect. All he did know was that with the restaurant freezers
filled to capacity he couldn't afford a power failure especially
if he couldn't get down to the pub to turn on the generator.
If the freezers had no electric power he'd lose everything. He
had no choice. He'd have to defy the curfew.

Griffon had spent much time and effort acquiring his food
supplies. They were trademarks of his restaurant—the draw.
Much of the foodstuff was imported and was impossible
to get on the island. When he thought of the months of
sharp buying, the months spent developing an assortment of
contacts to get into the good supply position he was in, not
to mention the outlay of cash, he felt sick. All his work, his
inventory, would go down the drain if he couldn't protect his
investment.

A successful restaurateur gives his customers what feels
and tastes good. In keeping with that basic philosophy Lester
Griffon offered a level of quality not expected on the island.
Offering a congenial atmosphere and an interesting menu of
basic food prepared with the little niceties associated with
a general willingness to please, Griffon, in providing extra
touches like imported butter, beef and cheeses; delicacies such
as lobster, turtle steaks and lambie, hand-made pastas, and an
assortment of imported beers, liquors and cigarettes, had build
a solid business. Under the threat of financial ruin, he realized
he had to be especially careful. His livelihood would depend
upon his ingenuity over the next few weeks.

In addition to the threat of power failure there was also the
fear of out and out pilferage, looting. Griffon suddenly felt
relieved that only last month he had installed a metal security

lock-up. That should prevent looting unless the place was actually shelled. Small chance of that. Hah!

Griffon secretly went back and forth between his house and the pub in deliberate violation of the shoot-to-kill curfew. He was not a particularly brave man nor was he foolhardy, but he was desperate. Driven to extreme by the threat of financial ruin, he furtively sneaked to his establishment a mile and a half away to check on his refrigeration equipment, making the pilgrimage to the pub every day, in order to activate his generator whenever the electric power went out. On the third day, returning to shut off the generator after the power had come back on, he discovered a new cause for worry. Fuel for the generator was running low. Even by conserving gasoline by shutting down the generator as soon as the electric power returned, he doubted he'd have enough fuel for more than two more days at the most.

Continuing his risky activities without complaint, he began to think it very curious that he never saw anyone else on the roads. Cows and goats were tethered in a variety of places where there was allowed grazing. Someone had to tend the animals on a daily basis. Why had he not seen anyone? Then again, no one had seen him. His luck seemed to be holding particularly well.

Occasionally he heard stray gunfire. He attributed it to snipers in the foothills firing nearby. Or, he considered, his drinking buddies with the PRB were just trying to scare the hell out of him. If they were, they were doing a fine job of it. Meanwhile, his apprehension grew with every trip.

Griffon began to wonder whether the PRB were turning a blind eye to his unlawful creeping about. If he had to permanently close the Red Crab they'd be "out-of-business" too, deprived of their hang-out. Politics aside, they were all friendly with one another. Or were they protecting a common interest?

Suddenly an incident that he hadn't given much thought to popped into his mind. On the very first night the curfew went into effect, when conditions were particularly dangerous, it would have been madness to go to the pub. Finally with the power out for a number of hours, he was forced to go. Arriving at the Crab, however, he found the generator on. He didn't know how or why but was extremely grateful and chalked the good deed up to a neighbor.

Lester Griffon smiled good-naturedly. Yea, live and let live. That was what it amounted to, war or no war. I guess some things will always be sacred. Apparently the Crab was.

Surviving the curfew intact, Lester had a new set of woes. Since the war blew in, his problems seemed to multiply.... along with his business. But somehow, his new problems were more to his liking.

Chapter 78

DOC RUTHERFORD, LIVING in a rented hillside home in L'anse aux Epines, had maintained communications with the revolutionary junta up until Monday morning when the curfew was rescinded signifying a return to normalcy. With the Intervention under way, however, he was not sure what the ruling junta's position would be regarding the safety of the students. Clearly cornered there was no telling how the new government would respond.

Having come out in defense of the ruling party's good intensions regarding the safety of the students, Rutherford felt betrayed now that it appeared the students were in danger. In fact, he was beginning to worry about his own safety. With the government out of control there was no telling what might happen. They could destroy the school and its equipment causing him to lose everything he had invested there. With no insurance for such a disaster he would never be able to recover. He was in a tight spot. In lining up with the big boys he had thought he had insured himself against anything like this happening.

Chapter 79

WITH FIGHTING CONTINUING around him Pete McKenzie took cover in the tall grass along side the cricket field. A group of armed Marines in camouflage fatigues, their faces painted green, passed him as they headed for some nearby buildings. They were on patrol, roaming the alleys and back roads looking for snipers. Pete had been taking still photographs of the action as he worked his way toward Todd Murdock's place on Prickly Bay.

The island, closed to the press, was very newsworthy and for the moment at least, Pete had a monopoly on its coverage. He wanted to make the most of what was sure to be an exclusive report. Having sent in a story on the revolution, he was now in a position to scoop everyone on the war. It was an opportunity of a lifetime and his big chance to make it as a journalist.

He had come back into the island by boat but not in the way he had planned. The inter-island schooner had not been allowed to put into port because of the curfew. For this reason he had to make a few unscheduled ports of call before the ship headed back to Trinidad, its point of origin. On his way past Victoria Island, however, the schooner captain arranged for a rendezvous with a fishing boat which brought him ashore during the night. With his face blackened to minimize his chances of being recognized, he disembarked near the marina by the Careenage. Arrangements had been made for him to be put up with one of the students he knew.

As bullets whizzed past his head, Pete kept down. He'd better be careful, he reminded himself, hang back a little. Pete's enthusiasm for capturing high-level action photographs had clouded his judgment regarding his own safety. Moving about in combat, he was at high risk, unarmed, unprotected.

Walking along a road he was stopped by a Marine who asked for his ID. He produced his passport and a press card. The soldiers clearly regarded his presence as a nuisance. When he asked for permission to tag along with the small patrol as they canvassed the area for snipers, they had mixed feelings. While they respected the work he was doing, they also realized the danger it would represent to all of them. Pete tried to convince the squad leader that it'd be safer all around if he joined them rather than wander on his own risking being shot by one of them in a tight situation that would demand instant reflex. Reluctantly they agreed. They were accustomed to correspondents on the front lines of combat. Journalists understood they were at their own risk and had responsibility for themselves.

Crossing the cricket field they found themselves the target of some sniper activity.

"Get down!" one of the soldiers warned. "They're up there on that ridge."

A helicopter, seeing the ground fire, came in near them and fired into the hills. The chopper returned and landed as if on some prearranged sign. The Marine ran out onto the field, gesturing the group to advance. Crouching low in the downdraft of the whirring propellers, the men obediently followed with Pete trailing behind, staying close to them.

"How would you like to go for a little ride?" asked the squad leader of Pete.

"Sure thing," Pete answered without hesitation.

"Good, come with me, we're taking you out of the action."

"Shit!" Pete muttered in irritation. They obviously found out he wasn't supposed to be there, that no press coverage was being allowed on the island.

Pete and the squad leader boarded. Just as they were about to take off a bullet crackled through the fuselage. The pilot gasped almost inaudibly as he slumped forward in his seat. As the squad leader straightened him up they could both see a dark stain appearing on the pilot's shirt front.

"Christ!" the squad leader yelled furiously, "The fuckin' bastards! I'll kill every one of the rotten reds with my bare hands!" Enraged, he fired off several rounds of ammo into the hillside.

"Let's get him to a medic," Pete offered lamely.

"By the time we find one the poor bastard will be a goner. We've got to get him to the ship's hospital. I'll get him there if I have to fly this crate myself."

"Lenny, none of us can take the chopper up."

"Well I say it's going up. Get out of my way."

Pete put a hand on the controls. "Take it easy. Move him over and get in. Show me where you want to bring him."

"You?"

"Me," Pete said with finality. "You want to sit here talking or get a move on?"

Lenny was silent, almost sullen as he moved his wounded friend out of the way. Easing behind the controls Pete lifted off with all the expertise and cool of Terry and the Pirates reincarnate.

"Hot damn," said the astonished squad leader with a low whistle as they were airborne.

Chapter 80

CARRIE WAS LONG overdue in visiting her family. She was worried about them. With the telephone out of order and having been prevented from leaving the Redfern estate during the curfew, she had not been in touch with them for days. She wanted to go home. She asked Tiff to take her to her sister's house. Going to the center for supplies anyway, Tiff dropped her off on the way to town.

On his way back to Seaside Manor, Tiff stopped for gas. Almost out of petrol completely, he patiently endured a long line before filling his tanks and getting kerosene for the lamps at home. Back on the road, he recognized the vehicle of a friend ahead of him. The driver, Andy Wilson, worked on a nearby estate in Westerhall, a private complex of large, spacious expensive resort homes. Andy was a friendly sort, beeping his horn whenever they passed along the road, usually stopping to pass the time or news of the day. On this occasion, however, Andy did not acknowledge Tiff at all. Perhaps it was because he had three male passengers in the car with him. Tiff didn't think this would have made any difference in Andy's friendly tendencies toward him, so he thought the incident strange. Suspiciously Tiff closed the distance between the cars. Andy's eyes registered momentarily in the rear view mirror but there was no hint of acknowledgement. As Tiff assessed his friend's behavior toward him there was no gesture of recognition from Andy. Something was clearly wrong.

At the fork in the road just ahead, Andy took the one leading to Westerhall. He veered off so quickly that Tiff couldn't tell the identity of the other people in the car. But something familiar about one of them kept nagging his memory, jarring his powers of recall. Was his friend in some kind of trouble? Or was he just imagining things. Well, it was Andy and Andy had purposely ignored acknowledging him. Why? He was tempted to forget about it and mind his own business but considering the violence taking place on the island recently; Tiff just couldn't ignore the situation. His friend might be in serious trouble. If he was wrong, he'd look foolish. So what? But if he wasn't wrong, he had to be careful. The implications could be very dangerous.

What would Mr. Jonathan have advised him to do? He was a smart man. Turning his thoughts around in his mind, he weighed them thoroughly as he sped up the center of the road. Suddenly he saw a name sign that prompted an instant reflex and decision. Swerving, he detoured into the driveway of the great house, Murdock's residence.

Chapter 81

WHILE THE SEALS at the governor general's residence hung on waiting for help to arrive, the Guam was being rerouted around the northern tip of the island and down the western shore. Twelve hours later, about a mile north of Georgetown, 250 Marines from the Guam hit the beaches along with fifteen amphibious vehicles carrying five tanks. They headed for the governor general's residence with their MA-60 tanks. The skirmish was brief as the Marines ambushed and captured the Cuban armored personnel carriers.

Bursting into the residence they were not at all sure of what they would find. They saw Cecil Ward almost immediately. The elderly statesman was happy and relieved, as he displayed a welcome banner. Seeing the men were wounded, the rescuing soldiers radioed the ship calling for a chopper to air-lift the former Prime Minister and the wounded Seals to the Guam.

The Cubans and militiamen continued to rattle the Rangers with sniper and mortar fire. They roamed the back streets, pounded on doors and melted into the hills seeking either new hiding places or sniper sites. Familiar with the island, the PRB and the Cubans continued to control the capital's small harbor area.

As rocket fire from off-shore ships returned fire from the buildings giving fire, shelling them, U.S. and Caribbean multinational forces rolled through the streets in jeeps blaring instructions over loud-speakers to the population to stay indoors. Happy for the intervention, the people willingly complied.

The evacuation order came at 9:45 the next morning. Snatching up all the luggage they could carry—duffle bags, back-packs, tennis racquets, guitars, and tape-decks— the students climbed from the adjacent campus to the Victoria International runway where a C-141 was waiting as Rangers solemnly kept watch on the surrounding hills in the distance. Aware of the danger, students could still hear the crackle of gunfire. The women were guided into the plane first. Before they boarded, however, they showed their appreciation to the Army men from the 82d Airborne Division who had risked their lives. They kissed them farewell.

Evacuation of the campus adjacent to the airfield was easy in comparison to the operation at the main campus on the beach, four miles to the north. There, two hundred students were holed up, surrounded by enemy forces and they were almost out of food. Having secured Point Saline and Frequente, the Rangers inched toward the campus on the beach at Grand Anse. Prey to small-arms ambushes from the hills beyond, the men were also being attacked by Cubans with rocket-propelled grenades and fire from armored personnel carriers. Fierce fighting continued around the campus, yet there was no sign of anyone. Keeping under cover, students stayed huddled in their steaming hot rooms behind mattresses propped up against sliding doors and windows. Twelve of them took refuge in the safest room in the dorm, the bathroom. The Cubans ringed the school in a defense stance knowing full well the U.S. would not use heavy fire power with the students so close.

At 4:40 p.m. Bob Fisher looked out over the bay and saw something right out of Apocalypse Now. A line of six helicopters were racing toward the beach. Simultaneously A-6 and A-7 fighters and AC-130 Spectre gunships moved in to strafe emplacements around the campus for a devastating barrage lasting fifteen minutes. During the fray, a burly black serviceman in a mottled green and brown uniform kicked in the door and leaped into view.

"U.S. soldier, freeze! Friend or foe?"

"Friend," the students called out.

"Fine, stay down," the soldier responded. Ascertaining they were all students, the soldier collected them and herded them in groups of forty toward the beach. Another soldier dropped a yellow smoke bomb on the span of beach to mark their exact location for the choppers coming in for the students.

Their faces blackened and weapons at the ready, armed soldiers stood six feet apart on each side of the students forming a protective gauntlet as they scrambled to the safety of waiting choppers. As shots whizzed around them, they slipped on the rocks in the water and stumbled as they were caught in the wave action. In the wild scramble to evacuate, one young woman fainted on the beach. Helping her, others were forced to hit the dirt under gunfire, as they crawled to the waiting choppers. Ferried to Point Saline the students were given orange juice and K rations captured from the Cubans before a C-141 carried them to Barbados.

Their primary objective accomplished, the evacuation of the American students, the military focused its attention on finishing what they had set out to do—eliminate the Cuban influence and restore law and order to the island.

While a team of 82d Airborne paratroopers staked out an elegant stucco house at Westerhall Point, three black men inside dressed in casual slacks and sport shirts sat around a table over coffee. They were armed, their guns in plain sight on the table. Suddenly, an American shouted at them to come out with their hands up. For a moment the men hesitated. Realizing it was futile to resist, they threw down their weapons, raised their hands and shuffled out into the sunlight. The paratroopers had captured Clarence Charles, leader of the rebel military junta whose takeover had prompted U.S. intervention. Their whereabouts pinpointed, aided by the information Tiff had given to Todd.

Slapping handcuffs on Charles and his two cohorts, the soldiers dispatched them to the U.S. helicopter carrier, Guam, off the coast for safekeeping.

Other sweeps continued across the island. Swooping low over Calivigny on the southern coast, soldiers speaking Spanish and English called upon Cubans and PRB soldiers and snipers to surrender and cooperate with the peacekeeping forces. Gradually peace was restored.

With the Intervention successful, the chairman of the Joint Chiefs of Staff was lauded for having organized the invasion. He had forged the diverse Army, Navy, Air Force and Marine units into one hard assault force. When he created a ruckus by barring reporters from the first wave it only enhanced his tough-brass credentials. With the island slowly being cleaned up, the next item on the agenda came up for consideration.

As strategists continued to orchestrate, the CIA offered its opinion.

"I think it's time to send in young Hamilton Ward. It shouldn't be too dangerous long about now, do you think?"

Chapter 82

TAKING ADVANTAGE OF an unusually fine day, Hillary and Hamilton Ward packed a lunch and drove to Richmond Park. Succumbing to the unexpected respite from cold weather, they stretched out on a blanket in the sunshine giving themselves over to total inertia as they listened to the radio softly playing in the background. Suddenly the normal programming was interrupted with news of the invasion. War in Victoria Island had become a reality.

Offering only sketchy information about the invasion because of the news black-out, the broadcast focused upon the events which had led up to the military intervention. It chronicled the island's revolutionary history, the communist presence, the bloody massacre, U.S. fears the American medical students would be in danger of being held hostage and the untimely death of Victoria Island's brilliant, charismatic Prime Minister, Jonathan Ward, who had led his people with intelligence and sheer force of personality.

Hearing the unsolicited play-back of an all-too-familiar story had a devastating effect on both of them as mental images of their slain loved-ones surfaced to torture their imagination anew. Enduring the detailed report in order to learn current information, they were disappointed to hear nothing about their primary concern, Cecil Ward.

Distanced by time and space from the tragic events which had emotionally brought them to their knees, they had escaped into a private world all their own as they nursed their wounds. Originally joining together out of a common need and purpose, they had ended by being a comfort to one another as they protected themselves from the outside world which had hurt them so badly. It had taken the war to remind them there was another world outside the one they had made for themselves. It was a world Hillary was not sure she was ready to face. And, she reflected soberly, no matter what Hamilton had told her, she knew he would be in danger as long as he was involved with the CIA and the politics of Victoria Island. How strange, she thought. She had been conditioned to expect his going all along, but now that he was, she was no better prepared to accept it than if it had been a complete surprise.

As Hamilton relentlessly switched from station to station trying to hear some word about his grandfather, Hillary fussed with the foodstuff wrapping and unwrapping it as she compulsively nibbled first olives and then crackers and then grapes. Thwarted by the lack of new information available from ham radio communications out of Victoria Island, Hamilton was sick at heart.

During the time period when no news was being broadcast over the radio, Hillary and Hamilton tried to put their thoughts of the war out of their minds but it was almost impossible.

Attempting small talk as they picked at their food, they communicated little but their own anxieties.

Unexpectedly, definite word came that Cecil Ward was safe. Flooded with relief, they embraced, scarcely daring to believe the good news they had just heard. As happiness dispelled gloom, their appetites returned and they attacked their lunch in earnest as they settled in for a real picnic celebration.

Within minutes there was another bulletin. Spellbound, they listened as the story announcing Clarence Charles' capture unfolded. Clarence Charles, the man responsible for Jonathan Ward's death, was found and taken prisoner to be questioned and kept aboard the Guam for safekeeping. Unabashedly vengeful, the pair leapt about like children, whooping and hollering and tumbling about causing passersby to smile in amusement as they strolled past them. Suddenly remembering Hillary's condition, Hamilton abruptly stopped, fearing he had been too rough and might hurt her. Exhilarated by the wonderful news, Hillary dismissed his fears as nonsense. His grandfather was safe, that was what was important.

Capping her own enthusiasm Hillary settled down next to Hamilton to listen to the remainder of the special news report. As Hamilton concentrated on the news broadcast, Hillary absently began to draw the profile of his face with her fingertips. How like his father Hamilton was in so many ways she reflected. Yet, in some ways he was completely different.

"You know, right now, at this moment, I feel as though everything is just about perfect," she proclaimed.

Hamilton couldn't have agreed with her more. He was feeling the best he had felt in a long time. But, in observing her, he couldn't help but smile. Her speech was slightly slurred. She had had a bit too much to drink. Noticing it herself, she wrinkled her nose at him and giggled mischievously as he remembered she used to do in the university library whenever she did some outlandish prank or mimicry and he would come forward to own up to being the cause of the disruption taking the blame for her.

"Come on," she said tugging at Hamilton's sleeve. "Let's go home. It's getting cold."

Moving quickly they discarded their trash and began collecting their belongings as they packed up. In her preoccupation with organizing the equipment Hillary tripped over the picnic basket and collided with Hamilton who was retrieving some fly-away paper napkins. As they both began to fall Hamilton instinctively tried to cushion Hillary's landing. Sprawling on the ground in a tangle of arms and legs they landed unhurt, bursting into laughter. They were a ridiculous spectacle crawling about on all fours. Watching the impish expression on Hamilton's face Hillary was forced to remark on his gallant if clumsy performance.

"You know, I've never known anyone quite like you. You're extremely thoughtful and considerate."

He shrugged off her observation.

"I want to thank you for being so good to me. No one has ever taken the time or interest to be so thoughtful of me before. No one." Suddenly embarrassed with her speech she hurried to finish. "Oh, I know you've been particularly kind because of your father and the child, nevertheless, I do appreciate your consideration of me. You couldn't be nicer or more thoughtful."

Staring at her, taking her in, he barely seemed to hear her. "I've always heard that pregnancy becomes a woman. In your case it's especially true."

"Such flattery, Mr. Ward."

"It's not flattery, I'm being quite truthful."

"My goodness," she flushed nervously.

"Actually, you're quite a remarkable girl. Although I've lived alone for quite a while and I enjoy a certain amount of privacy, I must say I feel very comfortable around you. I've gotten quite accustomed to having you around. I'm going to miss you, you know."

"Miss me?" she reflected, fidgeting. She didn't even want to think about it.

"Uhm Hmm," he uttered with a touch of sadness. He knew she knew exactly what he meant.

Her face visibly paled and her expression seemed pinched as if she were experiencing an invisible, inner pain. Her pride deserting her she flung herself into his arms.

"Oh Ham, don't go! I've been so worried about you. Besides, you shouldn't be leaving me, not now."

The intimacy of her nearness to him had an unsettling effect. She was close against him, her scent enveloping him. In a curious way, with all her zest for life, she reminded him of a robust young doe with all of its animal vitality. A young doe, clear-eyed, cold-nosed, and full of animation as it raced away from danger to hide in the woods. Nervous, frightened, she seemed so vulnerable and in need of his strength. Her upturned face was tear-stained as she barely formed the word, "please."

There was no question that he was deeply moved but he simply could not do what she asked of him. Not for her, not for him, not for anyone. If there had been the slightest possibility, he would have done anything for her.

She had evoked a gut response in him so visceral that his reaction was one of complete spontaneity. He chastely kissed her, a gesture meant to convey his strength, his support, and his feelings of affection for her, to let her know she was not alone, that he'd be there to bolster her flagging confidence.

"I won't be long. I'll be back before you know it. I promise." The words were said softly but lightly as he smiled at her.

These were not the words she had hoped to hear but, his words of reassurance were what she very much needed to hear. Hearing them she gripped Hamilton tighter, closer.

Disappointed, without any show of emotion, she resigned herself to the fact that he would go. Pressed to her he could feel the tremor of her nervous system, her beating heart. He would have given everything to have spared her this moment. He wanted nothing more but to lift her from her grief, yet he didn't know how. Her pain seemed so intense he wanted to share it, endure it, and lessen it for her.

Rocking her as if she were a child, he felt her relax. Comforted, she nestled even closer. To soften the blow of his departure he reminded her it would only be a matter of a few weeks or even days before he would return. Quietly she resigned herself to his decision

"It'll be soon then," she said, wiping away her tears and composing herself.

This was the response he was hoping for yet she sounded suddenly cool, aloof. It made him feel strangely lonely.

"I'll miss you Hill."

"I know," she responded, kissing his cheek in a parting gesture. "I'll be fine, you needn't worry."

She sounded suddenly different, aloof. And, all of a sudden he felt shut out. He felt a tingle he could not explain. He couldn't leave things this way. She was like a sister to him, yet he wanted more from her—but what?

His thoughts were suddenly in chaos—what the hell was going on?

Chapter 83

LL HE KNEW was that she was in his arms, clinging to him, smelling so sweet, feeling so delicious he didn't want to ever let her go. She seemed to belong there, be part of him. He hoped the wonderful feeling would never leave him. He kissed her, kept kissing her, and when she returned his kisses with a fiery intensity of her own, he knew he couldn't fight it any longer. He was hooked and he knew it. He put everything out of his mind but the feel of her in his arms. All he could think of was how much he desired her as a woman. Maybe he had always desired her.

As shame for his feelings of guilt, betrayal, and anguish welled up inside him, the pain of his stifled feelings sprang up within him until he could contain them no longer.

"Oh God, Hillary…." He murmured thickly, "I want you."

"Please don't leave me. Stay with me. Please don't go."

"I'm not leaving you. I'll never leave you. I'm just going for a little while. I've got to finish what I promised to do. I owe grandfather, father at least that much."

Half hearing him she insisted. "But I don't want you to go. Not ever again. Jonathan, please don't leave me."

As the terrible impact of her words came crushing home to his consciousness, he was shattered. Literally pulling himself away from her he suffered total disillusionment. It was as if she had gone out of her head, was experiencing some sort of delirium. She didn't seem to understand what had happened or why. She was reliving her last moments with his father. She couldn't forget. Perhaps she never would. Feeling as he did for her now, he couldn't cope with her confusion about him.

Quickly picking up their belongings he threw them into the car. "Come on, it's getting late."

They rode home in silence. They were both miserable but for different reasons. While Hamilton battled an inner frustration he could barely stand, Hillary didn't seem to realize what she had said or done to cause him to be so abrupt and angry with her. Suddenly he slammed his foot on the brakes and jumped out of the car and raced around to the passenger side. Pulling open the car door he rather forcefully shouted at her.

"Get out, quick!"

"What's wrong? We're in the middle of the street. In traffic." They were on the bridge.

"I know that. Please come out, it's important."

She got out. As she stood up in the road, cars whizzed by them traveling in both directions, their horns blaring as drivers and passengers shouted at them from out of their open windows.

"Who am I?"

"Hamilton, have you lost your senses?"

"No, I have not. But I will tell you this. I don't want to ever hear you call me 'Jonathan' again."

"Oh, Ham, have I done it again? I am sorry." She seemed clear-minded once more.

"Why do you do it?"

"I suppose it's become a habit. Not a very good one, I'm afraid. But I do know who you are, really."

"Are you certain?"

"Of course."

"Do you trust me?"

"You know I do."

"Then I want you to do just as I say, right here and now, promise?"

"Can't we move out of traffic first?"

"No! Will you do it?"

"Yes."

"Kiss me. Me, being Hamilton Ward as opposed to…"

"Ham, be serious. Get into the car." She seemed angry and out of patience.

"Hillary! I am serious." There was urgency to his tone that made her stop to reconsider. "I want you to kiss me here and now and then tell me you know the difference between us."

"I don't need to kiss you to know the difference. I know the difference perfectly well," she retorted hotly.

"Are you sure about that?"

"Yes. Now stop being ridiculous and get into the car."

"Well, there is one thing you don't know." He began to climb the struts of the bridge.

"Ham, come down from there!"

"Will you kiss me now?"

"What's come over you? I don't understand why you're doing this." He climbed higher and seemed to be dangerously clinging to the metal stays.

"Hamilton, dear, please come down. I promise I'll kiss you." Her voice had a slight inflection indicating fear. Her eyes were anxious. Her gaze was riveted on him.

"Do I need to jump to make you realize?"

"You're Hamilton."

"Are you worried?"

"Yes, yes. Now come down here!" she commanded angrily.

He drifted lower. "Will you kiss me if I do?" The bridge was jammed. As sympathetic bystanders hoping to avert a tragedy tried to calm the impatient horn blowers, others maintained a sense of humor.

"Kiss him, lady," a taxi driver yelled.

"Yes, as soon as you come down."

"Are you worried?"

"Yes, of course."

"Why?"

"I don't want you to hurt yourself."

"Would you care?"

"Certainly I'd care." She burst into tears. "Hamilton, come down here this minute," she sobbed.

He picked his way along the struts and as he neared the bottom he slipped, falling to the pavement. Bordering on hysteria, Hillary screamed, running to him. Hovering over him, panic in her face, she wrapped her arms around him. Seeing his mischievous blue eyes staring up into hers, she knew he was safe. Crazy but safe.

"That's what I wanted to show you. I just sort of wanted to speed up your realization of it. Time will be precious these last few days we have together. I want them to count."

"I can see I'm going to have to watch you very closely," she said. "You're pretty tricky."

"Come on, let's get out of here before the bobbies get here." Getting up, Hamilton paused to kiss her. As the bystanders cheered Big Ben clanged in the distance.

"I don't believe it," Hillary said in amazement when she heard it.

"You're sure hard to convince."

"Oh Ham, she whispered, "It's just that I'm afraid to be disappointed all over again. I can't endure any more. I really can't."

"You won't have to," he said holding her close. "Trust me."

"Oh, where have I heard that before?"

Chapter 84

HAMILTON WAS ON an Air Force jet bound for Barbados by the following Friday. They had agreed that within the week Hillary was to hear from him and was to decide whether or not to meet him in Victoria Island.

Having just seen Hamilton off, Hillary returned from the airport barely making it back to her flat. Doubled up in agony she went into the bathroom. She would have liked a cup of hot tea but she felt so ill she couldn't complete the simple task of preparing it. She took some sleeping pills and went to bed. She tried to sleep but she couldn't. She felt so terrible she thought she would die. As she felt worse, she wished she would die to end the torture. The pain was so excruciating she twisted the bed sheets to keep from screaming. She didn't understand what was wrong with her. All she knew was she wished Hamilton were there to take care of her and to comfort her. "Ham, oh Ham."

By morning when she came to consciousness after a fitful night of restless sleep, she felt better but she was bone weary, exhausted. Shivering from the cold, she got up to get a robe. In getting to her feet she felt light-headed and when she stood up by the side of the bed she swooned into a faint as she collapsed back onto the bed. When she saw herself, saw the bedclothes, she experienced a bone-chilling fear. It was as if all of the blood had drained out of her body to be spread out before her on the bed. She sickened at the sight of it, all crimson and wet over everything.

At first she was paralyzed with fear. Had she gone mad and tried to kill herself. She seemed clear of visible wounds. And then she knew. She had lost the baby.

Chapter 85

I N HAVING LOST her unborn child, Hillary had also lost
Hamilton Ward, whose only reason for marrying her in
the first place, had been to legitimize his father's child
and heir. Since she was no longer carrying the child, there
wasn't any reason to continue their marriage arrangement.
The relationship was finished.

The chain of events had all happened so quickly she was
at a loss as to what to do. She had become used to having
Hamilton around. In truth, she enjoyed his company and had
grown closer to him than she could have believed possible,
principally because it had been a time in her life when she had
needed stability and emotional support and he had been there
to provide it. There had never been any doubt in her mind
about his motive for any kindnesses to her. She knew full well
that while he was a good person and thoughtful by nature,
his behavior toward her was out of a family concern for the
original objective, Jonathan's child. Whatever had gone on
between them she viewed as separate and apart from his own

feelings. She had little doubt that he was motivated primarily from a business attitude.

As this harsh truth with all its subtle implications sunk in, she felt a genuine regret for she realized she had been living a lie. Overwhelmed by sudden loneliness she felt depleted emotionally as well as physically as she realized she no longer had anyone to turn to.

Succumbing to depression she numbly stared into space as her emotions built up within her. Suddenly overwhelmed, she felt she would burst. She couldn't hold back any longer. Screaming hysterically, she threw herself across the bed flailing about in a frenzied torrent as she struck out pounding the bed pillows furiously as she relieved the pent-up emotions of her pain and disappointment.

In losing the child she had lost everything she valued. First it was Jonathan, then the baby, and now Hamilton. It was happening to her again, all the old problems were returning. This time she wouldn't allow it. She wouldn't be made a fool of. She would make the break with Hamilton instead of waiting for him to do it. At least she'd preserve a small measure of dignity.

Writing through her tears of hysteria she drafted a letter to Hamilton Ward. She would make it easy for him to disengage himself from her. She would relieve him of his responsibility to her and make it clear his obligation was discharged. She would not use trickery, although she could to gain time, nor would she keep him with her out of pity for her. She'd simply tell him what had happened and explain that she would file for an annulment. By so doing, he'd be free to do whatever he wanted to do in government, in politics and in his personal life. She completed the letter and gave it to the mailman before she had time to reconsider her decision. Coming back into the flat she felt even weaker than she had before. She had to lie down. When the telephone rang she was right next to it.

"Hillary, I heard about the war in Victoria Island. I hope everything is going well for you. I see Hamilton has just returned there. I've just this morning seen him on television as he got off the plane. He's already talking long-range projects, reconstruction programs. You must be proud of him."

"Yes," she answered dully.

"I expect you'll be going there soon."

"That isn't possible right now. I'll probably remain here until Hamilton returns. It's still pretty unsettled there."

"He seems pretty dedicated to that country of his. I imagine you're eager to join him as soon as possible."

"As soon as it's safe," she said with a hint of tension in her voice.

"Well, listen Hillary, if there's anything I can do to help while Hamilton's away, please give me a call."

"Thank you."

"Say, listen. I have an idea. Why don't we get together for dinner?"

"Perhaps soon," she said politely formal.

"We've got a lot to catch up on."

"Yes, I'm sure a lot has happened to both of us."

"Do I detect a note of sadness? I think a bit of cheering up might be in order. Why don't we get together tonight?"

"No, I really couldn't. I'm not feeling all that well."

"Nonsense, you'll feel better if you get out of the house. It's settled. I'll come for you around seven."

Before she could protest the caller had hung up.

"Ádam? Adam! Oh God, no!"

Chapter 86

A DAM ARRIVED PROMPTLY at 7 p.m. He rang the bell several times but when no one answered the door he used his key for the first time in many months. He sensed something was wrong. It was too quiet, too dark. Except for a sliver of light coming from beneath the bedroom door, the flat was in darkness. Hillary had said she wasn't feeling well; perhaps she was resting, asleep. He walked toward the bedroom calling her name as he walked. Gently he opened the door. She was in bed. As he approached he stopped to shut off the alarm clock which had been ringing. How could she sleep with that thing ringing like that?

He found her asleep, under the comforter. She was ill. She was very pale. Something was very strange. He felt very uneasy. He scanned the room. Clothes strewn about, there was an unaccustomed clutter which he noticed immediately. What alarmed him the instant he saw it however, was the empty bottle of sleeping pills next to the bed. He immediately tried to rouse her. He couldn't.

"Jesus!" he muttered half to himself.

She was completely limp. Shaking her brusquely he got a brief flicker of response as her eyelids fluttered. He pulled back the covers to get her up. His first reaction to the blood stained sheets struck terror in his heart. My God, what has she done to herself?

He reached for the bedside telephone to call for an ambulance but thinking better of it, he moved in quickly, lifting her comforter and all, he went to the car. By the time they reached the hospital he was a wreck. They had pumped out her stomach immediately upon arriving. Thank heaven she was all right but he was at a loss as to what had happened. He promised to stay with her through the night and took her back to his own apartment. As they settled in to talk over warm tea and toast, the telephone in Hillary's flat rang incessantly, but there was no one there to answer it.

Adam lit a fire and helped her get comfortable. She seemed relaxed. More likely she was exhausted. He sat near to her.

"Why, Hillary?"

She shrugged.

"Was it because of the baby?"

She began to weep. He gave her his handkerchief and paused till she composed herself.

"Don't tell me you haven't told Hamilton. Doesn't he know?"

"No," she moaned.

"Why haven't you told him?"

She shrugged listlessly.

"Wouldn't he have wanted the child?"

She looked surprised. "Oh, that wasn't it."

"What then?"

She remained silent.

"Hillary, are you saying you don't love him?"

She seemed shocked at his question and felt very uncomfortable thinking about it. She didn't know what she felt.

"Whether you have the baby or not won't matter if he loves you. It's how he feels about you that is important."

"You don't understand," she said shaking her head.

"I guess not. Didn't he want the baby?"

"Yes."

"Do you think he'll blame you for losing it, is that it?"

"No."

"Then I guess I don't understand." He took a different tack. "Does he have someone else, is that it?"

"It's over with Hamilton and me," she said emphatically.

"Poor Hillary. What have you gotten yourself into this time? You've got to tell him, you know."

"I will. But when he knows, it will be finished between us."

"I don't understand how you can be so certain."

Her eyes flared, smoldered as she faced his almost defiantly. "I won't be hurt again. I won't be rejected, nor pitied ever again."

"You're referring to me, aren't you?"

"Partly," she said almost contemptuously.

"What happened between us was a terrible mistake on my part. I admit it. If you'd let me make it up to you, I'd like to."

"It's too late. Things are not the same as they were. I've grown up."

"Maybe I have too."

"For how long? Until there's another girl? And another?"

He seemed frustrated by her attitude toward him but he was too weary to quarrel.

Suddenly she sensed his defeat and softened, putting her hand over his. She had not meant to be cruel. "But I do appreciate your kind words of apology. Really."

He smiled. "What are you going to do now?"

"I'm going to do what I have been neglecting to do for some time. Take an active interest in the Redfern tobacco industry. It's about time I put my talents to work in the family business. Incidentally, I did not OD on sleeping pills, if that's what everyone thought."

"I know. The doctor said there wasn't enough in your system to do any harm. But, from the look of you when I brought you in, he couldn't have afforded to misjudge the situation."

"I guess I must have looked a pretty sight?"

"You had lost a great deal of blood. Apart from that, you were barely conscious from having taken the sleeping pills. I guess in your weak condition, they really knocked you out."

"My life's blood," she said, looking very sad.

"Tell you what. Stay here tonight. I'll send the maid over to your place in the morning to straighten things. Will you let me do that for you?"

She nodded and smiled weakly. She had grown tired. Leaning back into the pillows, she bordered on wakefulness as her eyelids began to droop.

"Rest. I'll bring you some more tea."

Hillary didn't seem to hear. Her eyes had closed. Adam tiptoed from the room and gently closed the door behind him. He sighed wearily. There was only one thing left to do.

While Hillary slept Adam placed an overseas call to Hamilton Ward leaving his own telephone number for the call-back.

Chapter 87

B Y SATURDAY THE armed resistance was finished. Road blocks continued as the military searched vehicles and checked occupants looking for stolen cars and PRB soldiers. During a week of mopping up after the intervention, the island underwent a complete change of character as leftist billboard rhetoric and slogans were torn down or white-washed and communist graffiti was eradicated leaving crisp, neatly painted walls in its place. The effort to sweep everything clean was contagious.

People in the streets and market square banded together in tight little groups, talking non-stop, bursting with hyperkinetic energy as they savored their new-found freedom. Wearing tee-shirts with slogans praising America for its part in the intervention, the people were unabashedly joyful and brimming with enthusiasm.

From the moment the plane landed at the new Victoria International Airport, Hamilton could almost feel the change. As he looked out of the window he could see a welcome-home banner strung across the front of the partially erected terminal building. A group of friends were lined up in front of it to form a welcome committee. Stepping out into the sunlight, he was greeted with the happy sound of people cheering as he walked from the plane onto the platform of the portable stairway. He could hear a steel band trilling melodiously in the background.

Getting into his car Hamilton asked to be taken home so that he could change his clothes and make a few telephone calls before meeting with local officials. On the way to Victoria Island he had been briefed and brought up to date on the events taking place. There was a big push on for elections. In a sense, he felt as if he had not been away. At that moment Hillary was a million miles away.

When he arrived at the house his grandfather was waiting for him. Hamilton was surprised. He had not expected to find him there. As they embraced, it was an emotion-packed reunion.

"Grandfather!" Hamilton choked out. "Thank God! I was so worried about you."

"I'm just a tough old stick," Cecil said grinning. "I made it through. Glad to see you my boy."

Hamilton glanced at his watch apologetically. He was running late.

"Go on. Don't let me interrupt whatever you were going to do."

"I'm just going to change my clothes and make a few telephone calls."

"Go ahead. While you're doing that, I'll fix you something cold to drink."

Hamilton placed a call to Hillary in London. There was no answer. Since they had parted, he felt an inner nagging troubling him. It was a feeling so real he could not set it aside.

"Have you heard anything about Pete McKenzie?" Hamilton called out from the shower.

"I understand he got here just before the action started. With the media blitz in effect, he was one of the few news people who had been able to infiltrate."

"He's okay?" Hamilton asked coming out of the bathroom with a towel wrapped around his middle.

"Not only okay, he's established a beachhead over there with Lester Griffon at the Red Crab. He's staying at a beach cottage right in the thick of it and seems to be having a hell of a time. Since the so-called 'occupation', the Crab's become 'the' place to meet. Wait till you see it. Military men, intelligence people, strutting around the bar wearing cut-off jeans and sneakers while packing hand-guns in their shoulder holsters and walkie-talkies dangling from their hips, It's like watching the cast for Gunsmoke, Back to Bataan, and Hawaii 50 with the lot of them turned loose all at the same time."

Hamilton grinned. "Lester must be in his glory."

"Glory be damned! He's got more business than he knows what to do with. And how's this for irony? The Army captured two huge Russian generators. To keep the Crab operating at full tilt they donated the generators to Lester to make certain that in case there are more power outages, the Crab can function without missing a beat."

"What about Todd Murdock?"

"Todd's earned my eternal gratitude. He performed an invaluable service feeding information to the fleet off shore. His house was shelled twice. The first attack left a crater in an adjacent field. The second shell struck the promontory and landed under the house. The shell didn't go off, the lucky bastard. He feels things are going well now. His wife and family are coming back."

"Is it perfectly safe?"

"Pretty safe."

"Safe enough for Hillary to come back? Which reminds me, you haven't asked about Hillary, Grandfather."

"Safe enough for you to come back. You seem to have taken a special interest in Hillary."

'She's been having a very difficult time of it."

"It pleases me to see you're looking after her. With your father gone she's like a duck out of water. You'd do well to find a nice young woman like Hillary."

"I have, Grandfather."

"Well now. You're certainly not one to let any grass grow under your feet."

"I hope you'll approve."

"From that smug expression on your face, I see you're up to something. Something's going on."

"Oh, before I forget, an Adam West called you. He left word for you to call him right away. He said it was urgent."

Chapter 88

EARING THAT ADAM West had called, Hamilton bristled uneasily. Adam? What the hell does he want? His immediate reaction was to ignore the message altogether, but as his curiosity overcame him; he thought better of his initial impulse and suppressed it. What the hell, he thought as he placed the call with the overseas operator. Waiting for the call to ring through, he heard a male voice come on the line.

"Adam West here."

"Adam, Hamilton Ward."

"It's good of you to call. Something has happened that you should know about. It concerns Hillary."

"Hillary? Is she all right?"

"She's here with me."

"What the hell is that supposed to mean?"

"Oh no, nothing like that," Adam added defensively. "But there is a problem. She's just had her stomach pumped out. Sleeping pills."

"Sleeping pills! Good heavens! But why? She was all right when I left her. What's happened?"

"She's just had a miscarriage."

"Oh, my God, no!"

"I'm afraid she's taking it very badly."

"She would. She wanted the child desperately."

"Now she's worried that with the baby gone, your feelings for her will be changed. I guess she feels responsible. That in some way she's failed you."

"That's ridiculous. Is she all right physically? There's no danger?"

"She's tired and needs rest, but otherwise there are no physical complications."

"Did she tell you what happened?"

"She said she took the pills after the miscarriage because of the pain. I got there after she was sound asleep and took her to the emergency room of the hospital when I couldn't wake her. Since we've come home she's been remote and distraught. Frankly, I'm worried about her."

"Let me speak to her."

"That won't do much good right now. She's fast asleep. Even if I tried to wake her, I'm not sure how coherent she'd be. I think it would be better if you call her in the morning after she's spent a peaceful night. But, when you do speak to her, don't be mislead by what she may tell you. It's my feeling she may try to cover up. She has this notion that you want your freedom and that she's in your way. I doubt very much that she'd want you to know about the sleeping pills. She hasn't even faced the fact that she's done it, the sleeping pills, I mean."

"In truth, she didn't take a fatal dose. I don't know if it's because she didn't have more pills to take, or if she just took a regular dose to stem the pain so she could go to sleep. At any rate, let's be glad she's all right now."

"I've been such a fool," Hamilton reproached himself. "There was so much left unsaid before I left her."

"Good Lord man, you mustn't blame yourself! There was nothing you could have done to prevent the miscarriage. It just happened."

Suddenly angry because Adam was with Hillary when he felt he should have been, Hamilton shot back, "What's your part in all of this?"

Understanding Hamilton's feelings of jealousy, Adam faltered and blurted out, "I guess I still love her. But seeing her when she speaks of you, I know she loves you. We've had our problems in the past, Hillary and I, but if I can make it up to her now, in some small way, I'd like to try. I'm afraid I've hurt her very badly. I'd hate to see her get off on the wrong foot again."

Hamilton was relieved but he also felt ashamed. What had he done? He had treated Hillary as his father's property, the custodian of his father's child. Out of what he had perceived as a family loyalty, a duty, he had put her off-limits to himself, denying his own feelings. While he had married her to legitimize her unborn child, instead of bringing them closer, the pregnancy had driven them further apart. No wonder Hillary felt let down. No longer pregnant, she had lost what she had treasured most, her child, Jonathan's child and her reason for being. And then, after he had left her, as his father had, she was alone, cut off again.

How could he make it up to her? Freed from what he had considered his duty, he was now in a position to make his feelings known to her. He wondered how she would react.

"I'll call her in the morning."

"Tell her you rang her flat and that the maid gave you this number. That'll keep me out of it."

"Do me one more favor, will you?" Hamilton asked.

"Of course."

"Make a plane reservation for her on the next available flight and see to it that she's on the plane. I want her to come home where she belongs."

"I'll do what I can."

Chapter 89

PETE McKENZIE SAT talking with two Marine buddies in Rudolf's on the Careenage. Taking refuge from the steamy heat of midday they sat in the cool, dark-paneled dining room downing a couple of beers as they listened to a harmonica player performing a solo rendition in the open doorway. Occasionally looking outside through blue gingham curtains they watched with interest as two girls strolled past the building before ducking inside to pass the time and rest their feet.

Pete paid the check and they got up to leave. The girls, locals, demurely eyed the soldiers with curiosity. Distracted by the unexpected attention, one of the Marines bumped into a chair causing it to scrape against the floor noisily. When the girls tittered over the incident the Marine got red in the face. Taking in the little scene two local men sitting at the bar made a comment meant to call down the girls for flirting with the soldiers. The young women became furious. Accustomed to being all but ignored by local men when foreign women were around, the girls seemed to be turning the tables and relishing it, driving home their point with a very heavy hand.

Sensing a possible brawl, Pete quickly headed for the door begging a ride home. They drove along the coast in relative silence before coming to a stop at the top of the hill. Pete climbed out of the jeep at the head of Murdock's drive where, as usual, the dog howled at his approach. Ignoring the dog, he proceeded up the steps to the kitchen door.

"Just in time for a cup of coffee," announced Todd coming out onto the veranda. They sat down. Todd put his feet up on the porch railing and faced the bay. It was clear, sunny and warm with the ocean breeze balmy against their skin relieving the tropical heat. The maid brought coffee and sweet rolls and set them down on a wicker table.

"Beatrice is coming back today," said Todd, referring to his wife. It occurred to Pete that he had never met her.

"I spoke with Connie in Barbados where Janet is staying, and it looks like Janet may be on the same flight with her."

"I talked with Janet a little while ago and she's on a later flight. Man, is she excited about coming back. She says the news from the States has it that the government is really glad the military came in down here. What with all the weapons and ammunition, not to mention the communist documents and agreements they found, all their suspicions about Victoria Island being used as a military base was right. What capped everything off was finding the submarine basin. How did you know about that, anyway?

"Off the record?"

"Of course, off the record. We CIA guys have to stick together," Pete needled.

"It was not generally known, but Osgood Redfern was an agent with British Intelligence. He had long suspected something covert was going on around Glover Island regarding a submarine facility. To get to the bottom of his suspicions he had a night-scope installed at the top of his property for the purpose of surveillance. The submarine basin turned out to be a rumor. There was no submarine installation. All the suspicious talk was designed for intimidation and fear."

"When Redfern satisfied himself he had conclusive evidence as regards Soviet/Cuban intentions however, he tried to warn his very dear friend, Jonathan Ward, about his part in the scheme of things. Ward didn't buy it and thought the idea preposterous. Apparently Ward was naïve about a lot of things going on around him. He was used to governing a small country like a business and he seemed to have little sophistication regarding international intrigue."

"In checking out the other cabinet ministers, Redfern hoped to find an ally in Jonathan Ward's good friend at the time, Clarence Charles. Instead he found Charles could not be trusted. While he was very bright and very efficient, he was also very greedy and lined up in opposition to Jonathan. Investigating him further, Redfern discovered that Clarence Charles had been smuggling large amounts of money out of the country and depositing funds in his personal accounts in Jamaica and in the Cayman Islands. Using his office of finance minister and his friendship with Jonathan Ward to protect him, Clarence Charles began operating on a grander scale of corruption. Although he couldn't prove it conclusively, Redfern also believed Clarence Charles was connected with the Mafia and dealing drugs through Miami."

"While the Soviets knew about Clarence Charles' personal abuses and would have used this knowledge against him to coerce him into doing whatever they wanted him to do, there was no need. Clarence Charles willingly did whatever was asked of him, dedicating himself to the communist objective."

"But, when Clarence Charles learned that Osgood Redfern knew about his financial indiscretions he feared Redfern would tell Jonathan Ward. As moral as Jonathan Ward was, Clarence Charles felt sure he'd be stripped of his office or be put in jail. In order to prevent Osgood Redfern from telling Jonathan Ward, Clarence Charles had Redfern murdered with the airplane mishap made to look like an accident."

"Ironically, Osgood Redfern had already told Jonathan Ward about Clarence Charles. But as Clarence Charles was an old school chum of Ward's, Jonathan refused to believe any wrong-doing. Finally, as the evidence became irrefutable, Jonathan confronted his long-time friend. Denying any guilt, Clarence Charles convincingly played the wronged man while all the time, incensed at having been brought to task, he arranged for two hired thugs to murder Jonathan Ward. Before they could carry out the murder, the men themselves were murdered and their bodies disappeared, showing up at the school morgue. I don't know if Jonathan had them killed or whether the Cubans arranged it because they weren't willing to risk exposing their intentions in such an obvious way. In any event, from that moment on, the two men were at a stand-off. Apparently warned by the Soviets to back off, Clarence Charles went underground and appeared to play ball with Jonathan Ward."

"Who covered up in the school?" Pete asked.

"Rutherford was in charge of the school and although he accepted favors from the government for the school in the form of tax rebates and land grants, he did not know about the murders or the extra bodies being funneled through the school's inventory of cadavers."

"I do know one of Clarence Charles' relatives worked on the receiving staff of the school. It's my guess that Clarence Charles had him do his dirty work for him. It was only after Clarence Charles began to get flagrant in his confrontations with Jonathan Ward that things started to pop. When terrorists tried to murder Ward in Barbados killing Esmee and a waiter instead of him, the CIA finally took a more active role. The CIA had received a tip something was about to happen, but they did not suspect or hear about anything as radical as what actually happened."

"As Clarence Charles got more power-hungry and nervous, he overplayed his hand. I don't think he intended for the massacre to happen. That was probably the spontaneous reaction of a trigger-happy soldier. Clarence Charles had planned an elaborate scheme to have Jonathan poisoned, blaming the CIA. After the massacre, the whole Soviet/Cuban project fell like a pack of cards. The rest is history."

"Clarence Charles is being held for trial. He's very much hated. In fact, if he were to get loose, the people would kill him themselves for all the evil he's done."

"The image the war department is trying to put out is that the Intervention was principally to evacuate the students. That's not entirely true. The government was after something much bigger, for example the presence of a submarine base. But, if the U.S. military had gone in and didn't find what they were after, the whole project would have been another Bay of Pigs. Using the students as their trump card, the military went in with a logical excuse and without press coverage. If they didn't find anything important, they would have accomplished their objective, saving the students. Finding everything they had believed to be there and more, they came out heroes proving to the world that they were right."

The telephone rang. Todd took it in the kitchen. It was Lester Griffon. The men spoke a few minutes and then Todd hung up and came back outside.

"Lester's got some lobsters he's willing to contribute if we want to have lunch on the boat or go out to one of the islands tomorrow. The girls will be back by then. It'll be a nice treat. What do you say?"

"You know how I feel about lobster," smiled Pete. "Sounds great!"

Chapter 90

THE PLANE LANDED late afternoon and the incoming passengers went through customs and left the sparse terminal building of the new airport without much fanfare. Hamilton had sent a car and driver for Hillary and as she collected her belongings, making sure her bags were all there, she recognized Janet and invited her to share the ride home. Catching each other up on general news, the women promised to see one another for lunch sometime soon.

Almost as an afterthought, Hillary spontaneously invited Janet and Pete for cocktails and dinner that evening—a sort of celebration. Having heard so much about them from Hamilton, Hillary realized how heroic their efforts had been in the past with the behind-the-scenes protection of all of them. She thought it would be as good an opportunity to celebrate as any. Suddenly it was important to her to have the house full and lively. She'd call Cecil and the Murdocks too. So much sadness had shadowed her life at Seaside Manor recently. She wanted to have something joyful happening there to dispel the gloomy memories she had been accumulating. Fearing the evening would be particularly unbearable alone, she rushed headlong into plans for a dinner party.

She came into the house to find fresh flowers everywhere. Carrie and Tiff were on hand to welcome her and when she told them of her plans for dinner they began preparations.

Hamilton arrived within a half hour after she did. She came out of the shower just as Carrie brought a tray of tea and cakes. Tea time.

From the moment Hillary and Hamilton saw one another there was tension in the air. It was an awkward meeting. At first they danced around their discomfort with greetings and polite small talk. Then Hamilton dived in. Not one to mince words, he was the first to speak.

"I'm sorry, Hill. I know how much the baby meant to you."

"I guess it just wasn't meant to be," she said simply.

"I was worried about you. Are you feeling okay?"

"I'm tired, but other than that, I'm all right."

"Come sit over here on the bed where you'll be more comfortable." He sat next to her and took her hand in his. "You know, all this has made me realize a lot of things I didn't know before."

"Oh? What?"

"Remember when I threatened to throw myself off the bridge to prove to you that you cared just a little for me? Well, when I heard what happened to you, it made me realize I cared a lot about you." Hillary smiled wanly. "I love you, Hill."

She collapsed into his arms. She'd been waiting so long to hear these words.

"Hey, don't get all misty on me again. This is supposed to be a happy time in a girl's life. A romantic time." He kissed her on the forehead. "I've been thinking about it all day and I've got something to give you." He handed her a white lace linen handkerchief tied in a knot. "This was my grandmother's. Open it. It's for you."

Hillary untied the fabric. Wrapped inside was a diamond wedding band.

"I want you to put it on, to wear it. I'm asking you again. Will you marry me?"

Hillary giggled, "We're already married."

"This time I'm asking you because I want you to marry me out of my free choice."

"You're not just doing this because you feel sorry for me, are you?"

"What do I have to do to make you take me seriously?"

"Maybe that's the problem. I take you too seriously."

"If you're telling me it's too soon, I can understand that. We can take it slow and easy."

"Hamilton, I have a terrible confession to make."

"Come on, tell me. It can't be all that bad," he coaxed soothingly.

"It's horrible." She twisted her handkerchief anxiously.

"Are you sure you want to tell me? You don't need to if you don't want to."

"I think I should," she said bravely. "Maybe you won't be able to understand what I'm about to say. I'm not sure I understand all that well myself. If you think I'm a terrible person, maybe you'll feel differently about giving me this."

She held up the ring. She hadn't put it on. Hamilton took it and slipped it on her finger. "I can't imagine your telling me anything so terrible that it would change my mind."

'We'll see," she breathed to herself miserably.

"You're such a worry-wart." He put his arms around her, as she began to talk.

"Remember how happy I was about the baby? Jonathan's baby? You knew how much it meant to me. How I felt about having Jonathan's child."

"Yes, I know, and I'm sorry. I wish there was something I could do to have prevented its happening."

"Oh Ham, it was awful. There was blood everywhere. When I realized what had happened I couldn't stop crying, screaming. You can't imagine." Her voice cracked. Suddenly a haunted, terrifying expression came over her face. "But then, when I realized it was over….."

"Go on…."

"I was….glad."

"Glad?"

"Glad."

"You were obviously terribly upset."

She was shrill, almost hysterical. "I'm telling you I was glad, glad I lost the baby. It suddenly felt dishonest having Jonathan's baby with you pretending to be the father. The more I thought about it, the more I realized it would make a mess of everything. I didn't do anything to make it happen, I wouldn't have done that, but why did I feel glad? I was actually relieved. Don't you understand what I'm telling you? What kind of a person am I? Why would a mother want to see her unborn child dead?" She began to sob

"Poor darling," consoled Hamilton gently. "You've been through so much grief and torment. So many shocks to your system. The miscarriage was a result of nature. Something you had absolutely no control over. You aren't glad, what you are really feeling is relief. The burden and pressure of pretense is no longer necessary. You just wanted something to come out right for once in your life. Something without complication. And, you're right, raising the child would have been messy. Sure, we'd have lived with it, handled it, but Christ, Hillary, let's make our own babies." Hamilton cupped his hands around her face and kissed her. She seemed numb to his touch.

He seemed suddenly rejected. "It's over before it's started with us, is that what you're saying?"

"No. It's just that I've felt so cheap and dishonest for such a long time. Carrying the baby and having feelings for you."

"Feelings? What feelings?"

"Hamilton, don't you realize? I've fallen in love with you. We've been so happy together. And you, you've been so patient and understanding." She reached up and put her arms around his neck and kissed him.

"Are you sure, Hill?"

"Very sure, and it feels so wonderful to know that you feel the same way."

"This is wonderful," he whispered. "With perseverance I finally got my girl. Now we really have cause for a celebration. Hey," he whispered, "any chance of postponing this party tonight?"

"Not on your life. We have a wedding announcement to make!"

"However," Hillary added suggestively, "there is nothing to say we can't start our celebration right now!"

Chapter 91

THE NEXT DAY Hillary and Hamilton Ward, Cecil, Lester Griffon, the Murdocks and the McKenzies gathered on board Todd's boat for a post-war celebration. Food and drinks, courtesy of Lester, were in abundance as everyone sat around rehashing their war experiences which in retrospect seemed amusing in the telling. Under blue skies with the promise of fair weather, the revelers headed for Dragon Bay. Reaching their destination they put down anchor. The clear turquoise waters were inviting in the heat of the day and everyone was looking forward to snorkeling along the coastline. As tired members of the snorkeling group began to trickle back on board for lunch, Janet lagged behind. Suddenly she called out, urgency clear in her voice.

"Pete! Come see what I've found."

He was at her side in moments. Reaching her, he plucked off her face mask and snorkel and as she flailed about in the water coughing and protesting, he pulled her away steering her back toward the boat.

"The last time I heard those words we were almost part of World War III. Now go on. Get up there. Get into the boat."

"Wait," she protested, "you don't understand….." But it was no use. He continued to prod her up the ladder.

"You're going to regret this, Pete McKenzie," Janet shrieked, glancing at Todd conspiratorially. "You really are."

"Another treasure, I suppose," Pete grumbled.

"You might say so," Janet taunted, shaking her hair free of water as she blotted herself dry.

Curious, Pete relented. "Okay, what was it?"

In an attitude of "I told you so!" Janet put her nose to his, her brown eyes flashing, as she stared into Pete's eyes.

"Lobsters! I just saw the biggest lobster." She hesitated allowing the crushing impact of her words to register. "I tried to tell you."

Pete whimpered as he stared bleakly into the water. Suddenly, in a violent eruption, the shimmering surface came alive as Todd surfaced triumphantly holding the granddaddy of all lobsters high overhead.

With a wide grin across his face Todd called out, "Lobster anyone?"

The End

Reading Group Questions and Topics for Discussion

1. Although on her honeymoon, Janet was the one who suggested that her husband, Pete, interview the head of the Medical school for a feature article. In helping him pursue his dream of being a journalist do you think she realized the dedication and perseverance journalism takes? Have you ever been in a relationship where you put someone else's happiness before your own?

2. Once Pete was involved with the interview and in the mystery taking place, do you think Janet had regrets about having encouraged Pete to actively pursue the story especially realizing the time and danger involved?

3. How do you feel about a spouse or friend involved in a field of work which would be time consuming and dangerous?

4. Would you try to prevent their doing so? Would this be selfish on your part or selfish on their part pursuing it?

5. Did you identify with Janet's bravery at the cave when all would depend upon you?

6. Would you have remained with Pete or would you have gone home as Todd wanted you to?

7. Do you think Hillary will like being a First Lady on Victoria Island?

8. Glamour aside, would you like this role and the responsibility it entails in addition to being married with children?

9. Would Hillary ever consider going back to Adam, her former fiancé? He seems to have turned over a new leaf and her life would certainly be less stressful and less dangerous.

10. Do you believe Adam has matured? He certainly acted responsibly when Hillary needed help.

11. Will Hillary ever be able to stop comparing the qualities between Hamilton and Jonathan?

12. Do you think Hamilton will ever forget or forgive Hillary for comparing him with his father? Does Hamilton believe Hillary loved Jonathan more than she does him?

13. Have you ever had occasion to experience this kind of jealousy with a spouse or a friend?

14. While Hillary originally felt she was in competition with Adam's girlfriend, she ironically ended up striving for attention from Jonathan and Hamilton whose duty and loyalty to their country always seemed more important in their lives than she was. On all three occasions she seems to come in second. Should she resign herself to being second?

15. Would you be satisfied with someone who always put you second? Second to their parents, second to their children, second to their job?

16. With your partner, are they first or second in your affection? Do they know where they stand? How does it affect them?

17. How will this story affect your future vacations?